ROAN

The Louisiana Gentleman Series by Jennifer Blake

KANE
LUKE
ROAN
CLAY
WADE

ROAN

Jennifer Blake

This first world hardcover edition published 2012
in Great Britain and in the USA by
SEVERN HOUSE PUBLISHERS LTD of
9–15 High Street, Sutton, Surrey, England, SM1 1DF,
by arrangement with Harlequin Books.
First published 2000 in the USA in mass market format only.

British Library Cataloguing in Publication Data

Blake, Jennifer, 1942-
    Roan.
    1. Sheriffs--Louisiana--Fiction. 2. Love stories.
    I. Title
    813.5'4-dc23

ISBN-13: 978-0-7278-8124-3   (cased)

All Severn House titles are printed on acid-free paper.

MIX
Paper from
responsible sources
FSC® C018575

Printed and bound in Great Britain by
MPG Books Ltd., Bodmin, Cornwall.

For my daughter, Lindy,
with loving appreciation
for her generous gifts of insight and inspiration.

1

The chance Victoria Molina-Vandergraff was waiting for came on the third night. She was ready, primed with rage, disgust, and a tentative plan. Still, she almost missed it.

One minute, she was trussed up on the floor of the stolen panel van as it careened around a curve on the dark dirt road, silently cursing the two jerks in the front bucket seats and cheering the cop who was hot on their tail. The next, she was tumbling over the gritty carpeting as they slid on rain-wet gravel. The vehicle left the roadway and bounced across what felt like a shallow ditch. For a breathless instant it was airborne. Then it slammed into a tree.

The screeching crunch of folding metal filled the air. Safety glass rained with a musical tinkling. Tory slid helplessly, scraping dirt from the carpet with her cheekbone before she hit a side panel. The van jolted back, shuddering. The engine died.

Headlights stabbed the darkness as the police car rounded the bend behind them. Brakes screamed and gravel flew as it slued to a halt. Seconds later, the officer's amplified voice, deep and edged with anger, blared from the unit's loudspeaker.

"Out of the vehicle! Hands in plain sight. Move!"

"Holy shit! What we s'pose to do now?"

The kidnapper that she'd dubbed Zits long miles back along the road from Florida growled the question as he glared at his pal behind the wheel. Big Ears whined an excuse as usual, even as he started the van and slammed it into reverse, spinning its wheels in the mud.

Zits let fly a string of curses as uninspired as they were virulent. Craning his neck to see out the window, he said, "Christ, if it ain't the sheriff of that hick town back there. Says so on his car hood."

"All I see is his big-ass gun," Big Ears moaned. He gunned the van hard, hunching in his seat at the same time as if he could make the vehicle move with his body. "We gonna die. I told you ripping off that convenience store was a dumb idea. 'Nah,' you said. 'They're backward as hell in a little old place like Turn-Coupe, Louisiana. Won't be no security camera,' you said, 'No alarm, no cops this time of night…'"

"How the hell was I to know?"

"You're the brains, ain't you? Now we're screwed. Backcountry sheriff like that don't give a shit who he shoots."

"It ain't gonna be me!"

Zits hit the glove compartment latch with his fist and reached inside for his pistol. Then he heaved from under the mangled dashboard and crawled between the seats into the cargo area.

"Where you going?" Big Ears demanded, even as he gunned the van again, gaining a few inches.

"To fix us a way out."

"And how the hell you gonna manage that?"

Zits, going to one knee beside Tory on the canted floor of the van, didn't answer.

She could see his teeth glinting in the glare from the

police cruiser's headlights. She pressed back against the side panel as he shoved the pistol into his waistband and pulled a knife from his boot. Before she could draw breath to scream, he slashed the duct tape around her ankles. Jerking her upright, he cut the tape at her wrists, then ripped it off along with several centimeters of skin.

"There now," he drawled in vicious sarcasm. "Looks like it's your lucky day."

"What are you going to—"

Zits didn't let her finish. He hauled her around and gave her a hard shove toward the rear cargo doors, even as he pulled his pistol free again with his other hand.

In that instant, Big Ears shifted the van into drive and stomped the accelerator. It roared and bucked forward into the tree again. Tory plunged toward the back door. Zits crashed into her. His shoulder hit her head, smacking her into the door glass. Her brain jarred in her skull. She was blind for a second as a red haze appeared before her eyes and pain surged in her head. Still, somewhere in her mind was the memory of the hollow thud made by Zit's pistol as it fell to the floorboard.

Zits cursed. Shoving away from Tory, he scrambled for the lost gun.

"Out of the vehicle! Now!"

"Damn lawman's coming after us," Big Ears gabbled in panic. "We got to rock this heap free, get her moving."

Suddenly, everything was surreal to Tory. The deep, vibrant voice of the sheriff coming out of the night was like that of some hero in an action movie. She dragged herself upright in slow motion. Through the back door glass, she could see the sheriff as a dark silhouette against the glare of the patrol car's headlamps. He stepped forward, and his shadow stretched across the road as tall and wide as that of some legendary giant. Behind her, Big Ears rammed the van's engine into reverse again, spinning the wheels until the stench of burning rubber filled the air and double sprays of mud spewed from the ditch to plop across the gravel road like small explosions.

"Yeah, we'll get out, but our gorgeous rich bitch is going first." Zits reached past her to shove open the rear door.

He meant to use her for a shield. It worked in the movies, using the victim to gain safe conduct, but Tory wasn't so sure the hick sheriff out there would cooperate. He had no idea she'd been kidnapped, didn't know her from Adam's Eve.

"Wait a minute!" Big Ears yelled as the van plunged forward again, rocking in its ruts. "We moved, feel it? We're 'bout outta here!"

She wasn't going with them.

Tory surged to her feet as Zits turned his head to measure their chance of escape, but the lurch of the van sent her sprawling. Her elbow came down on the missing pistol. Instantly, she shifted position, scooped it up.

Zits swung around. She saw the flash of the knife in his hand.

"Stop!" Tory leveled the pistol, tightened her finger on the trigger. She could use the weapon, thanks to private lessons in self-defense before she went off to college. And she would if it was her only choice.

Zits wrenched to a halt. They hovered in a stand off.

"I got it, Chris!" Big Ears yelled. "We're gone!"

The van was moving. She had to get out. There was no time to think, no time to plan. Lunging away from Zits, she scrambled for the open back door. She grabbed the frame and staggered upright, wavering an instant to gain balance. Then she jumped.

It was sheer instinct, what happened next; the results of years of adolescent gymnastic lessons and demonstrations from a skydiving team captain on how to hit the ground without breaking your neck. Tory rolled with her forward momentum, letting it carry her toward the sheriff, away from her kidnappers. At the maneuver's peak, she found her feet and came erect with wobbly grace and the heavy pistol still in her hand. She faced the sheriff, threw the heavy ponytail of her hair behind her back to clear her vision as she searched his dark features for some sign, any sign, of safety.

Then Tory knew. She felt it coming even before she saw the tall man in front of her steady his weapon, before she saw red-orange fire streak from its bore.

The single shot exploded like a cannon's roar. It punched her backward like a hard blow to the upper chest and shoulder. Her ponytail whipped over her shoulder and across her face. The pistol flew out of her hand. The gravel roadbed rose up and slammed into her. She lay too stunned to breathe, staring into the night sky while at the periphery of her vision the dark stain of blood spread across the dirty silk of her once-white jogging suit top like some night-blooming flower.

She heard the van's engine revving in the distance, felt the jolt in the roadbed beneath her as the vehicle spun free in a hail of mud and gravel. The lawman shouted an order, fired again. She flinched at the sound, a muscular reaction without meaning. But the van with Zits and Big Ears inside didn't stop. It hurtled forward with a clash of gears and the screech of dragging metal. Then it roared away into the night.

The pain hit Tory in a silent eruption. It tore at her shoulder and chest, a living thing clawing under her collarbone. She wanted to cry out, needed to fight it or get away from it. She couldn't. Her lips parted in a gasp of silent agony.

Tears gathered at the corners of her eyes and ran in hot tracks into her hair.

The crunch of gravel came as footsteps neared. A shadow loomed across her, then the sheriff crouched at her side. He hesitated, then stretched out his hand and felt the side of her neck where the blood throbbed under her skin. That touch was warm, impersonal yet expert. After a second, he released its exploratory pressure, trailed his fingertips across the gentle rise of her breasts under their silk covering. He whispered a soft curse and sat back on his heels.

She blinked to clear her vision, then fastened her gaze on the face of the man above her. His features were stern in the yellow-gold of the police car's headlights, though handsome in a rugged fashion. The silver glint of a star-shaped badge pinned to his shirt pocket was both the symbol of his supreme authority and a threat. The pressed, unsullied perfection of his uniform struck her as obscene compared to her muddy and blood-splattered grunge. She despised him on sight.

"You shot me." Amazement threaded her whispered accusation.

"What the hell did you expect when you came at me with this?"

He hefted the pistol he'd been holding against his bent knee, the one she'd dropped as she was hit. Apparently, he'd stopped to pick it up before he approached her. It was what he was trained to do, she supposed, the logical and safe reaction, but that cautious lack of haste about discovering whether she was alive or dead added to her sense of ill usage.

"I didn't," she said, biting off the words before her voice could betray her by wobbling.

If he heard, he paid no attention. He tilted his head and

spoke into what appeared to be a minimicrophone attached to his shirtsleeve. "Dispatch? Request ambulance for downed suspect. Gunshot wound. Location, Gunter's Road, two miles south of the intersection with Highway 34."

"On its way, Sheriff." That response came in the gruff tones of an older woman.

It seemed he had some small amount of consideration, after all. She tried again to make her position clear. "I'm not…not a suspect."

His gaze flickered over her face, but his expression didn't change. He angled the pistol, a handkerchief wrapped around it to preserve fingerprints, toward the light to inspect the chamber, then ejected the shells into his hand. He pocketed them before he glanced down at her again. Voice deliberate, he said, "Hold on. I'll be back."

Unreasoning panic swept over her. "Where…where are you going?"

"After the emergency kit from the unit. As I said, I'll be back."

A man of few words, or so it seemed. He hadn't bothered to ask how she felt, who she was, or what she was doing in the van. Certainly, there'd been no remorse for shooting her, not even a simple, "Sorry, ma'am," in that deep, molasses rich drawl.

Tory watched him walk away. His movements held assurance and rangy grace; they covered ground without making it appear as if he were in any hurry. His tall frame seemed to waver and blend with the shadows until he disappeared around the end of the patrol car and she was left to wonder if he'd been there at all.

By degrees, the stabbing pain in her shoulder began miraculously to ease though she could still feel the warm slide of blood under her armpit. A feeling of lightness drifted over her. She was so tired. She allowed her eyelids to close.

She was passing out. She knew it and didn't care. Oblivion beckoned with such sweet promise of escape from everything that had gone wrong that she didn't even want to resist.

Pain brought her back. The sheriff loomed above her once more, his hands on her shoulder as he applied firm pressure. She shuddered under his grasp, and was surprised by a wave of nausea. Immediately, she froze into stillness and lifted her uninjured arm to clap her hand to her mouth.

"Stay with me, honey," he commanded in the inelastic tone of those used to immediate obedience. "You're not getting out of this that easy."

"Out of what?" She forced the question through set teeth as her nausea eased

"Robbing a convenience store, for a start."

"I…didn't." There was so little firmness in the words that she wasn't surprise when he appeared less than impressed.

"Betsy doesn't lie. Neither does her surveillance camera."

The implication was that she did, had, and he wasn't surprised. She frowned as she thought that over. Her brain felt as if it were too big for her skull and was pounding against the bone above her eye in order to make more room. With careful fingers, she reached higher to explore the bump on her forehead.

He reached to catch her hand and lift it away while he studied the head injury. Deciding, apparently, that it could wait, he placed her hand at her side and began to tear open a couple of packages that must have come from his emergency supplies. She watched through her lashes as he moved with easy competence, placing the items taken from them on the only spot available that was both out of the dirt and free of the wetness of blood, her abdomen. It seemed he'd tended gunshot wounds before. She wondered in light-headed cynicism if he'd been the cause of them as well.

Tory was still exploring that idea when he picked up a pair of sterile scissors and began to cut away her silk top from the wound, exposing her shoulder to the cool night air. She parted her lips, breathing in strained gasps until she could find the strength to form words. "Don't," she managed finally. "Don't touch..."

He gave her a tight glance. "I won't ram the scissors into you if I can help it."

"I didn't mean..."

"Didn't you?"

He saw a great deal more than it appeared, she thought as she focused on his set features. There was intelligence in his eyes behind the shields of his long, dark lashes.

He dropped a compress bandage onto her shoulder then leaned over her once more, using his weight to hold it in place. She jerked, inhaling on a whistling moan, then clutched at him with a desperate grip of her free hand. Her nails sank into the muscles of his shoulder.

"Don't fight me," he said in strained patience and not even a glance at her clawlike grasp. "You're bleeding to death. The only way I have to prevent it until the ambulance gets here is to apply pressure."

"Hurts..." she managed.

"Can't help it. I have to be certain."

That might be so, but it made it no easier. He was so close, too close. She could feel the heat of him, catch the scents of clean uniform, soap, leather and warm male that mingled with the more immediate smells of mud and blood. His touch was firm, inescapable, but carried no hint of vindictiveness. A muscle stood out in his square jaw, and the skin around his mouth was pale, as if he might not be as unmoved as he pretended. He wasn't enjoying what he was doing, or so it appeared. It was some consolation.

She wasn't exactly having a ball, either. She closed her eyes again as the darkness threatened once more.

"Cousin Betsy will want to see you in jail for robbing her store. It's the second time she's been hit since she bought the place."

He was talking to keep her with him, Tory realized in vague appreciation. She wanted to deny what he said but had no breath left for it. Instead, her mind went spinning off into semidelirious images. The pain under his hand was like a hot iron pressed against her shoulder. It was as if she were being branded, marked as a criminal by the firm touch of the sheriff. The tears that seeped from between her lashes seemed to scald as they gathered in the hollows under her eyes.

"First time it happened, it was a couple of local boys looking for easy cash," he went on. "They got off with probation because they were juveniles. Betsy was pretty upset since the old man of one of the boys gambled away the money at the boats in Natchez and the families were too broke to pay restitution. She'll prosecute with a vengeance now. You'll do time."

The agony in Tory's shoulder and the implacable sound of the law officer's voice seemed to merge. Red-hot anger flooded over her. She clutched at it, since it helped clear her head. In husky tones, she said, "I won't. Not ever."

"You think you're immune because you're female?" He clamped down even more on the wound, as if to emphasize his ability to enforce punishment.

"Not immune. Innocent." It was amazing how much effort it took to form the words. Her tears spilled over again. They blurred her vision so the man kneeling at her side shimmered in a prismatic nimbus of light.

"Not likely, honey. Armed robbery, resisting arrest, endangering the life of an officer. You've got a long list to answer for."

As he spoke, he used his free hand to wipe at the wet track along her cheek. Tory turned her head away from the warm touch that seemed to linger with the disturbing feel of a caress. She didn't want him to see her crying, hated feeling so weak when he was so strong. "I'm not your honey, damn you. I didn't...didn't rob anybody. And I'll see you in hell before I serve a single day in your stupid jail."

"You'll wind up where it's hot tonight if you don't be still and let me take care of you."

"So you can throw me into solitary confinement, I suppose." She breathed in short gasps, knowing she should conserve her strength, but was too frustrated, too despairing, to keep quiet. She'd been through three harrowing days with Zits and Big Ears. For it to end like this was the last, unbelievable, straw.

"Oh, we'll get you some company. The creeps who abandoned you, your so-called friends, should make fine cell mates."

"If you can catch them."

Tory knew that the waspish taunt was a mistake as soon as the words left her mouth.

"Thanks for the reminder," he said, his tone clipped as he turned to speak again into the microphone attached to his shirtsleeve. "Sherry, update me?"

"The suspects haven't been located, Sheriff Benedict." The dispatcher rattled off the movements of a half-dozen police units along with numbered locations then ended with, "Unit 120 from town is covering the east section."

"That's Cal tonight, right?"

"Affirmative."

"Have him check out Fire Tower Road."

"Acknowledged."

Tory listened to the byplay with a sinking feeling. She needed to revise her knee-jerk impression of this lawman as a dumb hick. His quick actions and up-to-date equipment, not to mention the clear, assessing power of his gaze, suggested something very different. He'd allowed Zits and Big Ears to get away from him, true, but that was her fault. He could easily have left her lying in the road while he chased them down. It said something for him that he had not.

It wasn't like her to think in terms of stereotypes or to misjudge people. Or was it? Harrell had certainly fooled her with his quick grin and outgoing habits. She'd been taken in enough that she'd even promised to marry him. Not that she wanted to think about that now. Her ex-fiancé wasn't someone she wanted to waste time on ever again.

"So you've lost them," she said, her tone as even as she could make it.

The sheriff lifted a shoulder, a movement that caused the muscles under his shirt to bunch and flex. "Could be. This Horseshoe Lake area is a maze of old logging and oil well sites and tracks that lead to fishing camps. If they have sense enough to cut their headlights, hide out a couple hundred yards down some overgrown trail, we may never see them."

"You don't seem too concerned."

"Turn-Coupe is a close-knit community. We watch out for our own. Everyone knows everyone else. Strangers stand out." He flashed a tight smile. "Someone will spot them and give me a call. They always do."

She felt sure that was true. The sheriff was a man to be trusted; even she could see that. The authority in his voice and air of command had drawn her toward him the minute she stumbled from the van. It had been a mistake, in her case. And she wasn't sure what it was going to take to make it right again.

"Here, hold this." As he spoke, he caught her good arm and pulled her hand across to keep the bandages in place on her shoulder. She flinched as he brushed the raw strips on her wrists where her tape bonds had been pulled away. He paused, then turned his upper body to allow the light from the patrol unit's headlamps to fall across her arm. A frown drew his brows together. "What's this?"

Tory glanced from her blood-crusted skin to his narrowed eyes. "What does it look like?"

"As if you'd been tied up."

"Give the man a prize." Her wrists should hurt, she thought in morbid fascination, but the blazing torment in her shoulder and throbbing at the front of her skull made the scrapes seem trivial.

The sheriff studied the patrician slenderness of her fingers, the once perfect sheen of manicured nails, and the smoothness of skin that had rarely seen a pan of dishwater or done a day's work. He surveyed the expensive white silk that covered her before meeting her eyes once more. "So," he said in grim understanding. "Been indulging in a little bondage play?"

Her gasp was so sharp that it hurt her throat. "Do I look like...like someone who would enjoy such a thing?"

"You look—"

He stopped abruptly, and Tory was startled to see his skin darken, a change visible even in the uncertain light. For a brief moment she was far more aware than she wanted to be of his long fingers brushing the curve of her breast, the breadth of his shoulders as he hovered above her, and the firmness of his touch. Her stomach muscles tightened and she drew a ragged breath. In bald explanation, she said, "I was kidnapped."

"Sure you were."

His disbelief hurt, which was strange. Why should she expect this Louisiana lawman to believe her? She wasn't even sure her stepfather would accept her version of what happened, and he knew her better than anyone, was the only person in the world who might care whether she lived or died. As the realization sank in, she felt her anger seep away, leaving misery and weariness in its wake.

"Hold this," the sheriff instructed again as he placed her palm over the bandaging on her shoulder. He paused a second, then released her and picked up the scissors once more. He cut the neck of her top across to the shoulder and down to the armpit, severing the sleeve, then peeled the blood-soaked material away to expose the miniscule lace bra underneath. He paused again.

Tory clamped her jaws together to hold back her protest for both his tactics and the wave of pain that they caused. He glanced at her face, then, but made no comment, for which Tory was grateful.

With relentless efficiency, he ripped open more packages, applied a fresh compress, and then wrapped it with a wide strip of elastic bandaging to hold it in place. Her grasp on consciousness loosened, ebbing and flowing like the waves on the beach at Sanibel Island, her favorite place in the world. Sometimes, when she felt most attuned to the sea, she lay with her feet in the surf, waiting for the tide to come in. Gradually, the waves reached higher and higher until they broke over her head, submerging her. She felt that possibility now, as if a dark tide were rolling toward her. If she let go, didn't fight it, she thought she might be taken out to sea.

Her lashes flickered down, remained close. Distantly, she

felt the sheriff wiping the blood from her skin, taking care
not to touch the wound. The pungent smell of alcohol hovered on the air, then began to fade.

"Sherry? Where's that ambulance?" The voice of the
man who knelt over her carried a new hardness.

"Sorry, Sheriff," the dispatcher answered promptly, as
if she also noted the difference. "I'll patch them through
so the driver can give you an ETA."

Silence descended, broken only by the low hum of the
night creatures and the rustle of paper and plastic as the
sheriff gathered up bandaging trash. Then the radio sputtered again as the driver came on to say he was five minutes
away.

Tory heard the sheriff rise, then crunch across the gravel
to the patrol car. The blue-and-white strobe lights flared
into the night with blinding intensity even behind her
closed eyelids. He had turned on his flashers to help the
ambulance locate them.

The sheriff didn't return. Tory grew aware of a vague
sense of having been abandoned. She tried to ignore it, told
herself that she was lightheaded from all that had happened,
that the man wasn't her anchor or her guardian angel, far
from it. He'd done his duty toward her, and that was all
she had any right to expect. Anyway, she didn't know him,
didn't need him, and certainly didn't care if he went away
and left her to die alone.

It didn't help.

Alone, she was always alone, she thought with a shiver.
No real friends or close family, no one who understood or
cared who she was inside. It had been this way for as long
as she could remember; she should be used to it by now.
She had learned to hide her fears, to pretend to be harder
and more sophisticated than she really was, to use invented
personalities like the playgirl, the socialite, the princess as

masks to hide her insecurities. She'd become so adept at it that she sometimes wondered herself what the real Victoria Molina-Vandergraff was like.

The sheriff was coming back after all; she could hear his footsteps. Hurriedly, she wiped at the wetness under her eyes then lowered her trembling hand to her side. The sheriff of Turn-Coupe seemed to notice things that others might miss, she thought, and felt a shiver crawl up her spine at the idea.

"Are you cold?"

He hunkered down beside her again and reached to smooth his fingertips along the goose bumps that beaded her bare forearm. That touch triggered a fresh shudder that seemed to have no end.

"No," she whispered. "Yes…I don't know. The night is warm, but I feel so…so cold inside."

"Shock from trauma," he said softly, almost to himself. He turned to stare down the road with his head cocked to one side, as if listening for the ambulance. As the seconds passed with no sign, he breathed a soft imprecation and swung back to her.

He eased to the ground beside her with care, lying along her injured left side. Rolling her gently away from him, he slid his arm under her head and nestled her back against his chest. He circled her waist, then drew her closer, so she was tucked into his body from her shoulder blades to her ankles.

"What are you doing?" she whispered.

His warm breath brushed her cheek as he answered. "Sorry. It's the best I can manage until the ambulance crew gets here with a trauma blanket."

Tory knew she should reject the intimacy, but it was impossible. His body heat was so welcome, seemed so necessary, so right. Still it set off renewed shivering that made her shoulder ache with fresh intensity as the damaged muscles contracted to retain warmth. She huddled closer, accepting his strength, absorbing it as if it were life itself.

He held her carefully, shifting only to bring his long length into even firmer contact. He was so close that she could feel every button on his shirt, the hard metal star pinned to his chest, even the steady throb of his heart.

Tory focused on these things in an effort to block out the pain. Her breathing deepened and slowed to match the rise and fall of his chest. Each deliberate inhalation and sighing release of air seemed to take her deeper into the sanctuary he represented. Her gut-wrenching shudders slowed, became an occasional hard tremor.

By slow degrees, a singular sensation replaced her distress, the intimation of a state she almost didn't recognize, had come close to forgetting. She opened her eyes and stared blindly at the stretch of dirt and gravel in front of her as she circled the odd perception in her mind.

She felt safe.

It was strange beyond belief. It was improbable, impossible, unacceptable, yet it was also true.

Safe. At last.

No one knew where she was, at least no one who mattered. No one knew who she was or where she'd come from. No one wanted anything from her, or expected anything of her. She had nothing and no one to fear. At least for a short while, a few brief, lifesaving moments, she was truly safe.

She released the last vestige of mental resistance to the sheriff's aid. She could stop fighting, at last. Sighing with relief, she surrendered to the thought, and to the embrace of the sheriff of Turn-Coupe.

The sound of the ambulance began as a distant whine that was as persistent and annoying as a circling mosquito.

It could be heard for what seemed a long time before it rounded the bend with its red lights blending with the blue-and-white strobes of the patrol car until it seemed the woods would catch fire with the brightness. The sheriff didn't release her as Tory half expected, but stayed with her even when a paramedic stepped down from the vehicle and came toward them.

"Glad to see you, James," he said over his shoulder then in what sounded like strained displeasure. "She needs a blanket."

"Sure thing." The attendant turned and issued a low-voiced command. Seconds later the silver covering of a thermal blanket settled over Tory. From somewhere above her head, she heard the attendant speak again in calm assurance. "We've got her now, Roan. We'll take care of her."

Roan. It was an odd name with an old-fashioned ring to it. And the dispatcher had called him Sheriff Benedict, hadn't she? Roan Benedict, then. It was a name she would remember, she thought, as she felt the sheriff ease away, relinquishing her to the impersonal care of the others.

The rest was a blur of movement, voices, renewed cold and renewed pain as she was examined with brisk competence then loaded into the ambulance. It seemed she was leaving behind something important, but she couldn't think what it might be. Then she heard the low murmur of Sheriff Roan Benedict's voice somewhere nearby. She tried to push her hand free of the confining blanket, to reach out, but she was strapped down too well. The ambulance doors slammed shut and the vehicle started off.

She was alone once more.

2

The patrol unit's siren wailed as it hurtled toward Turn-Coupe ahead of the ambulance. Roan kept his eyes on the road, his hands on the wheel, and his mind on the business at hand. He didn't want to think about the woman strapped into the speeding emergency vehicle behind him. And he had no time for the sick regret that lay like a lead weight in his belly.

He'd never shot a woman before; it was definitely a first. He hoped it was also his last.

The lights of the town appeared around a curve. Seconds later, he flashed through the courthouse square, past the old Greek Revival building with its pediment-topped portico supported by columns, its wide steps and weathered bronze Civil War monument half hidden among the drooping limbs of a big live oak. With the official part of his brain, he scanned the row of low-budget shops that lined one side of the square. A light still burned in Millie's Beauty Salon. She'd been putting in long hours since her husband was diagnosed with cancer, probably needed the extra money. He made a mental note to send a deputy by to make sure she was all right and maybe escort her home when she was ready.

The hospital was about a mile on the other side of town, on land donated by its mayor of the past twenty years. His Honor had believed that the growth of the town would eventually overtake the hospital and it would be part of a prosperous business district. The businesses had turned out to be used car lots, garages and manufactured housing places, dotted here and there with a lumber yard, barbecue joint or rundown flea market. The town council tried hard to interest heavy industry, but the community had been passed over time and again. It seemed doomed to remain a small, sleepy place supported by a couple of medium-size sawmills and the sportsmen who visited the lake and stayed in Betsy's motel or bought beer, bait and sandwich makings at her convenience store. It was hard on the people like Betsy and Millie who had to make a living in town, and on the kids out of high school and college looking for jobs close to home.

Roan didn't mind. Small was good. Small meant clean streets, quiet nights and little in the way of a criminal element. At least, that was the way it had been until tonight.

He eased past the hospital's emergency entrance drive a few feet, then pulled over and stopped while the ambulance turned in behind him and made the short run to the glass doors under the steel-and-plaster portico. From that vantage point, he watched the technicians and nurses unload his prisoner. She looked so slight and pale on the sheet-covered gurney with its attachments of tubes and plastic bags. His eyes burned as he saw her being wheeled into the hospital's lighted interior. It was only as the doors closed behind her that he realized he'd forgotten to blink.

The additional patrol unit that he'd requested arrived just then. Roan radioed the officer, Allen Bates, to take over, instructing him to stick with the woman until she was out of surgery and safe in a hospital room then take up duty outside the door. Still, Roan didn't move on, even after he saw the deputy follow the stretcher inside.

He had escorted ambulances hundreds of times. Often they carried people he knew, friends, even family. He usually concentrated on the safety of the person in transit and also of the other drivers and pedestrians who crossed their path. Tonight was different. Tonight, he'd hardly known what he was doing.

He couldn't get the memory out of his head of the woman lying so still, with blood soaking into her shirt and his bullet in her shoulder. That endless time before the ambulance arrived was a nightmare in which he'd moved and acted like an automaton. Somehow, it blended in his mind with that other time, the night he'd found Carolyn lying on the floor of their bedroom, beside the bed they had shared for three years. Blood, there had been so much blood everywhere, even on the black shape of his extra handgun that she'd used on herself and the folded white note that she'd left for him.

He'd tended his wife as he tended the suspect tonight, had held her in his arms, willing her to live, during the short ride to the hospital. She had made it, mercifully, though their marriage had died that night. Since dying had seemed preferable to living with him for her, he'd given her the divorce she requested.

Roan shook his head to clear it. This woman tonight wasn't Carolyn, bore no resemblance to the fey, illusive girl-child who had been his wife. Life was almost too much for Carolyn, but it seemed nothing was too much for the woman he'd shot. She'd come at him out of the dark, a trim shape in shining white, tumbling with muscled grace and with deadly determination shining in her eyes. He'd been primed for many things, but she wasn't one of them.

To fire had been an instinct so basic that he couldn't even recall pulling the trigger.

He'd shot her.

God.

He'd been brought up to revere women, Roan thought. They were everything that was soft and tender and bright and good. They carried within them the promise of life itself, and to protect that promise was his honor and his privilege. The females who came through his jail didn't always fit the picture, but he never quite got over the feeling that they should, and might have if circumstances had been different.

He had that feeling now about his new prisoner. Which was crazy, since he didn't know her at all.

Still, he'd seen her, talked to her, and she bothered him. She didn't have the hard-edged bravado or unkempt carelessness of the kind of woman who operated outside the law. Women's fashions weren't exactly his strong point, but the outfit she'd had on looked high style, obviously expensive. She had the time and money for regular attention to her nails. Her hair shone with health and carried the tantalizing perfume of some expensive shampoo. Her eyes had appeared to be a mysterious hazel in the semidarkness, and she had glared at him with unselfconscious disdain. The cadence of her voice had been almost accent-free, like that of a trained actress or maybe someone who had attended a fancy school. Her body, when he held her, had been as slender and fine-boned as a thoroughbred's. The overall impression was that she should have stepped from a limousine instead of falling out of a rusty van.

She claimed she'd been kidnapped, the only information she'd offered. On the surface, it seemed plausible. But if so, then what was she doing cooperating with the pair of lowlifes shown on Betsy's security camera? Why had she wielded a handgun during the robbery? How come she hadn't been screaming for help at the top of her lungs when she came out of the van? Better yet, how had she been allowed to escape?

The whole thing didn't add up. It gave him a twisted feeling in his gut. It created chaos in his orderly world. It was a mystery, and he didn't like mysteries.

The best way to handle the problem was to get concrete answers as soon as possible. His immediate inclination was to stay at the hospital, partly to be on hand when the doctors indicated she was able to talk, but also to be sure she was all right. Still, no one would be allowed anywhere near her until her condition stabilized, not even him. His time would be better spent coordinating the search for the suspects still at large. Sherry had reported that Betsy had dropped off the tape from the robbery on her way home. If he could get a clear freeze-frame of the two men from it, he'd put out an immediate APB.

He'd get a frame on the woman, too, while he was at it. For purely professional reasons, of course. What else?

Leaning forward, Roan started the unit's engine and headed back toward town.

His dedication to the job lasted nearly two whole hours. At the end of that time, he headed back to the hospital. On the way, he swung out by the house on the lake to change his bloodstained uniform and make sure Jake was home from the movies; he trusted his son but a bunch of teenage boys could get into trouble without half trying.

As Roan approached the door of the operating room assigned to his prisoner, Allen Bates stepped from the waiting room next door. A question hovered in the deputy's eyes, though an easy smile lighted the rich, double-fudge brown of his face.

"Thought I'd see how it's going," Roan said in answer to that look of inquiry. "Any excitement?'

"Not so you'd notice. Nurse down at the surgical station said to tell you to come see her when you dropped by."

"I'll do that." That duty nurse would be Johnnie Hopewell, an invaluable source of information for what was going on under the covers, so to speak, in Turn-Coupe—since most of the results eventually showed up at the hospital. She'd been a Benedict before she married, so was also his cousin. Dark-haired, vivacious, and pleasingly plump, she was a favorite with patients and with him. Roan tipped his head toward the operating room doors as he went on. "I suppose the suspect is still in surgery?"

"Unless somebody wheeled her out the back way. A med tech stuck his head out a little while ago and said they'd be another half hour, give or take."

"That bad, huh?"

"It's not good, from what they say, but you know how it goes. Takes longer to get ready for the job than it does to get it done."

Roan nodded. "If you'll hold the fort here until after I see Johnnie, I'll relieve you."

"I thought you'd be heading home. Cal's got the graveyard shift, doesn't he?"

"He's still out chasing the bad guys. Besides, I wanted to keep an eye on progress here."

"Yeah," Allen said. "I can see how you would."

Roan appreciated the understanding in the deputy's voice, but it didn't exactly add to his comfort. He touched the brim of his Stetson in acknowledgment, then headed on down the hall.

Johnnie looked up when she heard his approach, then threw down her pen and came to meet him. "It's about time you showed up,'' she complained. ''What the hell do you mean, adding to my workload?''

''Sorry.'' He returned her quick embrace, and was in no hurry to break it.

''I'll just bet you are.'' Her smile faded as she drew back to study his face.

More sympathy was about to be offered, he thought. In an effort to avoid it, he said, ''Anyway, you like the excitement and you know it.''

''Some kinds, I can do without!'' Her voice turned wistful. ''Though I wouldn't say no to a good party about now.''

''That's Luke's department.''

The look she gave him was jaundiced. ''Not anymore, not since he got married.''

''I had noticed our cuz wasn't throwing as many shindigs.''

''Think he's afraid somebody, especially some other Bad Benedict, will steal his April away from him?''

Roan smiled. ''I think he's just, well...''

''Busy, huh?'' Johnnie laughed, a deep, rich sound. ''Guess they don't—didn't—call him Luke of the Night for nothing.'' She slid a quick gaze over Roan from head to heels while a reminiscent smile rose in her eyes. ''Of course, we were all pretty wild in high school, weren't we? Even you, before you started hanging out at the sheriff's department.''

Roan sighed and stepped back. ''That was then, this is now. What's the word on my prisoner?''

Johnnie sent him an intent look before she answered in the same businesslike tone. ''She's going to make it, no thanks to you. She lost a lot of blood but is stable, for now, as long as they don't run into anything too drastic. They're removing the bullet, repairing the damage. Recovery may take a while, so I hope you don't plan to haul her off to jail any time soon.''

He shook his head, aware at the same time of the easing of the tension inside him. He'd been half afraid Johnnie might have bad news.

She studied him for a second, as if not quite satisfied with his answer. Then she reached for a manila envelope that lay on the counter and passed it over. ''Your girl's been fading in and out. I tried to get a name, but it was no good. We removed all her personal effects before surgery. This was on her ankle, and I thought you might want to look at it.''

Roan turned the envelope over in his large hands. The words *Jane Doe* were scrawled across it in black marker. He had a strange notion not to open it, not to proceed further and to let it go, let the woman go, before he found out something he didn't want to know.

It wasn't possible. She was linked to one known robbery and might be implicated in others. His job was to find out who she was and turn her over to the justice system. As the parish sheriff, he had considerable authority, including some leeway as to who was or was not charged with a crime, but that power was a serious responsibility; abusing it was not in his rulebook or in his nature. He had sworn to uphold the law, and he would do it, regardless of who got hurt.

With an abrupt gesture, Roan thumbed open the envelope and poured the contents into his hand. He thought it was a bracelet at first, until he saw the extra length and realized it was an anklet. It was surprisingly heavy, a fine yet intricate chain with the deep burnish and minute scratches of well-worn eighteen-karat gold. Linked into it was a set of letters formed with channel set stones that glittered with diamond fire. As he straightened the piece of jewelry along his palm with a fingertip, it seemed to carry a lingering hint of the body heat of the woman who had worn it. Then he saw that the linked letters formed a name.

Donna.

Roan wasn't much given to New Age touchy-feely stuff or even to hunches. Still, holding the anklet to the light so the letters glittered up at him, he felt a shiver of premonition scrape down his spine.

Donna.

He frowned, a slow scowl that left an arch in one brow.

Johnnie, staring at him, put a hand on one ample hip as she demanded, ''What?''

''Nothing.''

But that was an evasion, if not an out-and-out lie. His prisoner didn't seem like a Donna. It was one more thing that felt all wrong.

Roan didn't like it. He didn't like it one bit.

''There's another problem,'' Johnnie said.

He looked up, alerted by something in her voice. ''Yeah?''

''She needs more blood, O positive. The hospital had half the units she needs on hand, and it may be hours before we can get the rest here.''

Roan's type was O positive. He didn't hesitate, didn't bother to even think about it. ''Why the hell didn't you say so?'' he demanded as he turned in the direction of the lab and began to remove equipment from his belt. ''Let's do it.''

''Donna? Donna, wake up.''

The voice was deep, quiet and masculine, the appeal urgent. Though it wasn't her name the man called, Tory felt she should respond. She lifted her eyelids a fraction, then snapped them shut again as bright light from directly above her sent a stab of pain into her head.

"Donna?"

The light was snapped off. Her hand was taken in a warm grasp. The touch seemed to lend her strength. She lifted her lashes again with slow care.

A man stood over her. His face was strained and somber in the subdued glow from behind vertical window blinds. The tan uniform he wore was familiar, as was the shiny badge on his chest.

The sheriff. She stiffened, tried to drag her hand free.

"Careful. You don't want pull out your IV."

It was a second before the words penetrated the drug-induced haze in her mind. Then she saw the plastic tubing that snaked from her hand up her arm and across the sheets to disappear somewhere above her. White sheets, pale-green walls, TV set placed high on the wall, faded cotton gown that smelled of bleach. She was in a hospital.

She returned her gaze to the man who stood next to the bed with his body partially blocking the light from the window. She moistened her parched lips, and began, "You. You're…"

"Sheriff Roan Benedict." He inclined his head in a brief, almost courtly gesture. At the same time, he released her and backed away a step, as if he felt he might be too close.

Tory appreciated that retreat; his tall figure looming over her had been unsettling. She took a slow, deep breath against the raw heaviness of her lungs and chest while she stared at him in the light of day, measuring what she saw against her impressions from the night before.

He wasn't what she'd call devastatingly handsome; his face was rough-hewn and weathered to a deep bronze, his lips were a bit too firm, and a half-moon scar indenting the end of one brow gave him a quizzical look even in repose.

Still, there was strength and inherent attraction in the alignment of his features. Like some western actor from the late-night movies, his height, square jaw and piercing steel-gray eyes bracketed by smile lines made him look like a man it would be easy to trust but dangerous to cross.

Her gaze dropped past his broad shoulders, touched briefly on the silver star pinned to his shirt pocket, and then came to rest on the wide leather belt that supported his holstered weapon.

''You're the one who shot me,'' she said in bald accusation.

The corners of his mouth tugged into a grim smile. ''That has a familiar ring.''

He was right; she'd said something similar before. For a second she glimpsed, like a dream on first awakening, the events of the night. The van. Zits. The shot. She'd been angry and confused. There was pain followed by the comfort of a firm voice and life-giving warmth of enfolding arms.

No, the last had to be a figment of her imagination; it couldn't have happened. Here in broad daylight, she could not picture this man, with his stiff stance, muscle-corded jaw, and shiny image of authority pinned to his chest ever unbending enough take her in his arms.

She met his gaze with a troubled frown. He was watching her, his expression shuttered, though some dark and not quite official awareness lingered in the gray depths of his eyes. She was so startled by it that she lay perfectly still, barely breathing, while feverish heat moved over her in a slow wave.

The door of the room swished open. A dark-haired nurse clad in a scrub suit of lilac and green bustled toward her. ''Well, so you're awake! How are you feeling?''

"She's fine, we're fine," the sheriff responded smoothly, before Tory could marshal her thoughts enough to answer.

"Let's see she stays that way, shall we?" For all her cheerfulness, the glance the nurse turned on the sheriff seemed to hold a warning. She reached for the stethoscope looped across her neck. "While I'm here, I need to get her vital signs."

It was a short drill without much entertainment value, but the sheriff seemed to find it interesting. He looked over the nurse's shoulder as she made notations on the bedside chart. When she turned to leave, he held the door for her, then stepped through it after her. It clicked shut behind them as if it had been given a firm push.

Tory could hear low-voiced conversation out in the hall. Since it was almost certainly about her and her condition, she strained to hear but could make no sense of it. She relaxed on the pillow again with a sigh.

This was the second time she'd been awake, she thought. She could remember being in recovery and parts of the gurney ride down long halls to this room. She looked around, taking stock in frowning concentration since she was half afraid that the hallway consultation meant she was more seriously injured than she seemed.

Both her wrists were wrapped in bandages to protect her duct tape injuries. Plastic tubes draped above her like Christmas garlands, including one connected to a machine that administered a high-powered painkiller in automatic doses. The bandaging that wrapped her shoulder and upper chest was bulky, but beneath it was only the natural soreness of any injury. She could flex the fingers of her hand and move her arm, a distinct improvement over the night before.

She was okay; she was going to survive pretty much

intact. That was a minor miracle, one she owed to first aid administered on a dark, gravel road.

But saving her life was the least Sheriff Roan Benedict could do after shooting her, wasn't it? No special gratitude was required. Anyway, he'd have done the same if she'd been a seven-foot-tall, three hundred pound male and guilty as sin.

She was innocent. She'd told the sheriff so and he hadn't believed her. That rankled. In fact, it made her even madder than being shot like a common criminal. The stiff-necked lawman out in the hall was so sure she was a desperado that he was standing guard over her. That had to be it. There was no other reason for him to be at her side.

Somehow, some way, she had to convince him. Surely there was some detail of what had happened that would prove her case? She let her mind drift back to be beginning, trying to find it.

She'd left the house on Sanibel for her run along the beach just as she did every evening. The sunset had been beautiful, with the last purple-and-crimson light of the day streaking down into the gulf. She'd passed well beyond the private Vandergraff beach area, racing past a hotel beach where tourists peered through cameras at the sunset, clicking off shots and rolling endless miles of videotape as they enjoyed their vacations vicariously through distancing lenses. She'd noticed the smell of frying conch scenting the wind, coming from a nearby restaurant. As the rustle of the breeze through the beachside palms and the deepening twilight soothed her frayed nerves, she'd run on and on, coming to a long stretch of winter homes whose owners had returned to cooler climes for the summer.

She hadn't been thinking, hadn't been watching. Her mind had been on her quarrel with Harrell. She'd given his ring back to him the weekend before, then he'd come

around that evening, just before she left the house. He'd
been so certain, being a supersalesman, that he could talk
himself back into her good graces. He hadn't taken her
refusal to listen to his spiel at all well. The words they
exchanged had left her rattled and upset.

That wasn't all. Her stepfather was also applying pressure, suggesting that she didn't know her own mind. He
seemed to think she was irresponsible and needed a husband to ground her. Or maybe he just wanted to be relieved,
finally, of responsibility for her.

Paul Vandergraff knew Harrell, had met him in passing
at the yacht club and on the occasional putting green. The
cheap furniture king of South Florida was an up-and-
coming man, Paul said, eminently suitable, for whatever
that was worth. That Harrell could be a new business ally
had been an added plus.

The reason it was so hard to persuade Paul she really
wanted out of the engagement, Tory thought, was because
she'd been so vague about her reasons. That was deliberate.
Harrell had been wheeling and dealing with his usual flam-
boyance, but this time he'd involved her. She had been so
depressed at the discovery and the fact that she'd been
taken in by him that she hadn't wanted to talk about it. She
didn't want to think, much less admit, that Paul might be
right about her since she'd drifted into the engagement with
little idea of how it had happened.

That lack of decisiveness was a grim reminder of the
pattern of her mother's life. Evelyn Molina, heiress to the
Bridgeman Department Store fortune, had been married for
her money so many times, beginning with Tory's titled
playboy father, that she'd ceased to change her name with
every wedding. She only added the current husband's sur-
name to that of her first husband's with a hyphen, just as
she had insisted be done for Tory when Paul Vandergraff

adopted her. Her stepfather seemed sure that Tory was just as flighty and irrational, had hinted for years that she would end up the same as her mother, fading away in an exclusive rest home for aging socialites dependent on prescription drugs. The broken engagement would give him more ammunition, make him even more positive that she was incapable of managing her own affairs.

The men came at her from the shadow of a stand of Australian pines. She ignored them at first, thinking they were just more tourists indulging in horseplay on the beach. They were close, too close, before she saw the danger.

The one she'd later dubbed Big Ears caught her with a flying tackle and dragged her down. Zits had hit her, a hard blow that sent her senses reeling. Before she could recover, she was flung onto her stomach with her nose pressed into the sand while her wrists were taped behind her back. She still had sand in her mouth when they gagged her. Within seconds, she was hoisted up and forced to walk to the stolen van. That short march over the sand with a gun to her head had been the longest of her life.

The click of the door dragged her back to the present. Tory turned her head as Roan stepped into the room again. Behind him was an older man wearing the white lab coat that marked him as a doctor, even before he stepped to the medication dispenser and began to adjust its flow.

"There now, Donna," the older man said, smiling as he surveyed her through the lower halves of his bifocals. "How are you doing? Not too much pain?"

She shook her head by way of an answer, though she lifted a brow at the same time. Moistening her lips that were suddenly dry, she asked, "Donna?"

"That's your name, isn't it? Leastwise, it was on the chain they took off your ankle." The doctor exchanged a quick glance with Roan before he moved to the bedside table to pour water, then handed it to Tory.

Her anklet, she thought, shielding her gaze with her lashes as she drank. It was a treasured gift from her mother, one of the few that meant anything. An expensive trinket, it spelled out a nickname her parents had used when she was a baby, a shortened version of the affectionate title, Little Madonna, given her by the old-fashioned servants of her Italian grandparent when she visited with them as a child. Her grandfather had been a prince, as had her father before he died in a plane crash, which made her a princess under the expansive rules of European nobility. The title had no more than social significance in democratic Italy, still Harrell had enjoyed introducing her by it, to her embarrassment. As if such a thing mattered.

"Well, my dear?"

The elderly doctor's eyes twinkled with blue gleams under his bushy brows, but they were still shrewd. Tory was also aware of the sheriff's concentrated interest in her answer. She couldn't think with her usual clarity for the lingering drug fog in her mind, still an idea was flitting around in the haze like a fly in search of a landing spot.

Stalling for time, she frowned at the older man. "I'm sure you know it's totally non-PC to call patients honey and dear?"

"Politically correct, you mean? Now, you're got me there. I've been told a hundred times not to get familiar with females, but damn it all—excuse the language—I like 'em and the habit of showing it is so old it's hard to break. Being semiretired, I get away with it most of the time." The grin he gave her was unrepentant.

"She wasn't happy about being my honey, either," Roan drawled from where he lounged with a shoulder propped against the corner wall of the private bathroom that jutted out into the room.

Heat rose in Tory's face, but she ignored it and the man who had caused it. "Semiretired," she repeated with a quick glance toward her medication dispenser. "I thought it was a different doctor taking care of me last night."

"That would be Simon Hargrove, a fine surgeon," he returned with the quick inclination of his white head. "I'm Doc Watkins, but don't get yourself in a stew. I help out around here still, now and then, and I wouldn't harm a hair on your lovely head. Roan says he needs to talk to you, so it must be important. All I'm doing is arranging it so he gets what he wants."

He had turned off her pain medication; it was there in his face, if not in his words. The most recent dose would wear off soon, then the heaviness in her chest and shoulder would become a consuming agony once more. Tory knew who to thank for this turn of events.

She shifted her head on the pillow to meet the steady gaze of the lawman. Her voice as cool and imperious as she could make it, she asked, "Torture, sheriff?"

"What I'm after is information. Torture will be a last resort."

"Suppose I have nothing to tell you?"

"I'm sure Doc and I can think of something suitable by way of encouragement."

Doc Watkins reared back. "Now, Roan—"

"Or maybe I'll wait until he leaves."

The sheriff was not impressed with her imprisoned princess act. She might have known. She wondered how good he was at seeing through other fabrications.

Time, that was what she needed, time to think, time to plan what she was going to say. If Sheriff Benedict didn't believe she'd been kidnapped, it was a safe bet Paul Vandergraff would have his doubts. Her stepfather would be even more incredulous when she told him that the man behind it was Harrell Melanka. And if he wouldn't take her word, who would?

Whatever charge the sheriff intended to bring against her would be dropped in due time; Paul would see to that. Her main worry was for what would happen afterward. Her stepfather might well send Harrell to take her home, since he disapproved of the broken engagement. There would be little to keep Harrell from trying to get rid of her again somewhere along the way. He might succeed this time, since she would be in no shape to stop him.

Paul Vandergraff was almost certainly unaware that she'd been abducted or where she was at this moment: though they lived in the same house while on Sanibel, their paths seldom converged. If he missed her at all, he probably thought she'd taken off for a few days as was her habit, joining friends for a sail in the Caribbean or a quick flight to Antibes or the Costa del Sol. He'd expect a call giving her whereabouts eventually, so would be unlikely to put out an alarm for another week, maybe two.

She had a little breathing room then. It was up to her to make the best use of it. The plan taking shape in her mind was simple, really, and the few extra days of recuperation it would gain her could be crucial.

She lowered her lashes and began to pleat the sheet that lay across her waist with her free hand. She willed tears to come, something that was surprisingly easy. "What if," she said carefully, "this name you've given me, this Donna, doesn't sound familiar? What if I say I don't know who I am?"

The sheriff was quiet for a seconds before he demanded, "*Is* that what you're saying?"

"I remember being shot," she answered, her gaze still

on the sheet. "Before that, not much—except for the accident and hoping I could use it to get away from the cretins who were holding me. And I seem to remember you taking me in your arms." She tried the effect of a helpless shrug and was instantly sorry. However, the hiss of her swift-drawn breath was almost blotted out by Doc Watkins's bellow.

"Gawd-a-mighty, Roan, what you been up to with this girl?"

"Nothing," the sheriff said with a harried glance at the elderly physician. "At least nothing that wasn't absolutely necessary and perfectly innocent."

Wounded bird: that seemed the best bet. She could do that one in her sleep. She murmured sadly, "That's what they all say."

"It's what you said, too, if I remember it right," Roan observed with grim dispassion as he stepped to the end of her bed and braced his hands on the high mattress. "I didn't believe it then, and I don't believe you now. I don't know what you're trying to pull, but it won't work."

"Don't browbeat my patient, son," Doc Watkins ordered. "She doesn't need this kind of hassle."

Roan gave him an impatient look. "I'm not browbeating her or doing anything else to her. Yet. But if you think you can do better, then have at it."

"Don't see how I could do much worse." The older man snorted his disapproval, then moved closer and picked up Tory's hand. Patting it a little, he said, "Now, look, love, it's like this. Roan's got a job to do, and he takes his work seriously. He needs a little cooperation from you. You owe him that, don't you think? I mean, he stopped to help you when he could have taken out after the bad guys. What's more, a nice percentage of the blood running through your

veins right now belonged to him yesterday morning. So
how about it?''

"He gave blood for me?" Tory couldn't keep the amazement from her voice.

"You're both universal donors, type O positive. You can
give blood to any other type, but only take type O your-
selves. The hospital was short, and Roan was willing.''

"And maybe feeling a little guilty as well?'' she suggested with a glance from under her lashes at the lawman.
The tips of his ears turned red as she watched. Whether it
was from embarrassment at being caught out in his good
deed, or anger that she'd guessed the reason, was impossible to tell.

It was Dr. Watkins who replied. "Oh, he might feel a
tad responsible, but that's all. Roan's a regular blood donor.
I only mentioned it because I thought it might make a difference in how you look at things. If you could just give
us some hint of how to go about finding the two creeps
who were with you, it would be a big help. The trouble
you've got yourself into can be worked out, I promise, if
you'll give us half a chance. But we can't help you if won't
trust us.''

It was masterly, that appeal. That it was undoubtedly
sincere made it even harder to combat. Trust didn't come
easy for Tory, however, especially now.

Harrell would be looking for her as soon as his goons
reported that they'd lost her. Her loving fiancé had ordered
her kidnapping, possibly even her death, because she'd discovered he had forged her name to legal documents. He
hadn't thought she'd mind, he said when she confronted
him; they were almost man and wife, after all. It was a
tremendous deal he was working on, the chance of a lifetime. He had to keep it hush-hush because the men he was
dealing with were heavy players. They were looking for

new capital and had agreed to let him in on the action, but wanted to see serious cash, like her old money inheritance, up-front. It was just a guarantee, the paper he'd signed for her; it didn't obligate her to anything. Anyway, the partnership would make them rich beyond imagining.

She'd refused to condone his act, had threatened to go to her stepfather with what he'd done. Then she'd returned his ring, to his flabbergasted fury. Shortly thereafter, she'd been abducted. It didn't take a member of Mensa to figure cause and effect. After all, a corpse couldn't object to a forged signature.

Trust them, Doc Watkins had said. She had trusted the sheriff for a few brief minutes while he lay holding her on a dirt road, but that was over and done. There was no one she could trust now.

"Donna, honey?"

She forced herself to meet the doctor's eyes. It was hard to lie to him in the face of his kindly concern, harder than she would have believed before tonight. Finally, she said, "I'll be Donna, if that's what you want, but I don't remember anything except what I told you. Please believe me, I really don't."

He sighed, then nodded, patting her hand again. "That's okay, then, don't you worry about it. Between the gunshot wound and the knot on your head, it's a wonder you're able to think at all. Things will work out, though, you'll see. We'll have you right as rain before you can get your foot back."

"I...hope so." A sudden constriction in her throat took her voice. She wasn't used to sympathy, much less the brand of kind acceptance that she heard in his voice.

"Doc," Roan Benedict said, a warning in his voice.

The physician and the sheriff exchanged a long look before Doc Watkins turned back to her. "Right. I think Roan has a few more questions, now. I know you probably don't feel up to it, but—well, he's been here since you were brought in last night, so maybe he deserves a hearing.''

How could she refuse without looking both ungrateful and as if she had something to hide? Which she did, of course. Regardless, she managed a nod of agreement.

''Good girl.'' The elderly man turned toward the door. ''I'll let you two get on with it, then.''

''You aren't leaving?'' The very idea of being alone with the sheriff made her stomach muscles clench.

''Don't worry. Roan's bark is worse than his bite. He won't be too hard on you.''

Doc Watkins sent the sheriff a stern look. If the lawman was affected by the warning, however, he gave no sign. He waited until the door had closed behind the white-coated figure of the older man, then he turned to pick up a black plastic case that had been sitting on the floor. As he placed it on the end of the bed, he said, ''The main thing I need from you is information about your friends.''

''My friends?'' She lifted an ironic brow.

''The two guys in the van with you.''

''Zits and Big Ears.''

''What?'' His face mirrored incomprehension.

''My names for them, since they didn't exactly introduce themselves.''

He sighed and looked fixedly at the wall above her head as if collecting his patience. ''So we're back to that, are we?''

''Always. Until you believe it.'' Her smile was bleak.

''You don't remember your name, but you do remember that you were kidnapped?''

She lifted her uninjured right shoulder to indicate the incomprehensibility of the brain's workings.

"It will go a lot better for you," he said deliberately, "and for this Zits and Big Ears, if you cooperate."

She met his gaze for the first time. "Are you saying you have a lead on them?"

"We located the van, which was hot, of course, reported stolen from Miami, though why anybody would bother to rip off such a piece of junk—but never mind. Your Zits and Big Ears dumped it in a parking lot outside town. The lot belongs to a company that runs a shuttle back and forth to the gambling boat over on the Mississippi at Natchez. A local timberman got off the bus after a day on the boat and found the stolen van siting where his brand-new red Ford pickup with big, expensive mud grips had been parked."

"Too bad." The comment was automatic as she searched his face. If he intended any added significance by letting her know exactly where the van had been abandoned, she couldn't tell it.

"If the pickup owner finds those two before we do, it will be worse than too bad. We won't have to worry about your pals anymore."

"Macho to the max," she said dryly.

"We call it taking care of our own."

"And you condone that? Seems strange for someone sworn to uphold the law."

His smile was grim. "I didn't say I condoned it. I just understand the impulse."

She shivered in an involuntary reaction to something she saw in his face. Looking quickly away, she said, "Yes, well, I don't see what all this has to do with me."

He stared at her a long moment, then straightened and raked his fingers through his hair so the thick, sun-bleached strands lay in ruffled rows. Finally, he gave a slow nod. "All right. Let's say, for the sake of argument, that you were kidnapped...."

"You mean you believe me?" She swung back to meet his gray gaze.

"I did say for the sake of argument. So we have a van that came from Florida. Is that where you live?"

She couldn't admit to that, she thought as she stared at the sheriff. If her stepfather should decide to file a missing person's report after a few days, the sheriff would be sure to spot it. "I don't know."

"When were you taken?"

"I'm not sure. Maybe three or four days ago?"

"That's a long time. Where were you kept?"

"No place in particular. At least, all I remember is the van."

He lowered his gaze to the mattress a moment, then his lips firmed. "The doctor who examined you says there was no sign of sexual trauma, no indication of intimate activity of any kind."

"So much for your bondage theory," she quipped, lifting a bandaged wrist by way of a reminder, even as hot color flooded her face.

"That isn't why I asked."

"No? Just curious, were you?"

"It's my job," he said with heavy emphasis. "The fact that you weren't molested could be important, especially now, with your memory loss."

"How so?" she snapped, stung as much by his grimly impersonal tone as at the suggestion for some peculiar reason.

"Few kidnap victims are spared, especially those who look like you. It means you were more valuable if left untouched, or else that the three of you were buddies trying the old scheme of squeezing money from whoever holds the purse strings."

"I have no need to squeeze money out of anybody, thank

you very much!'' The look she gave him should have
melted his iron man persona where he stood.

The sardonic lift of his right brow made the scar at its
end more prominent. ''You remember that, do you?''

She'd said too much, and knew it. She had to be more
careful. With a moody shrug, she replied, ''I don't know,
it was just there.''

''Fine.'' He studied her for a long moment, then a deep
breath swelled his chest, pulling the tan material of his shirt
taut across its muscled planes. When he spoke again, it was
on a different tack. ''So how much ransom were they asking?''

''I've no idea.''

''But they did make a demand of some kind?''

Phone calls had been made late at night, usually from an
open booth located outside a country store or some discount
outlet parking lot. Regardless, Tory was almost certain ransom had never been part of the plan. Not that she could
say so to the sheriff. With a helpless gesture, she answered,
''I don't know. It's all so...fuzzy.''

''Who would they have contacted? Who would have had
access to enough money to make them think kidnapping
you was worthwhile?''

Censure threaded the words. No doubt he was one of
those people who had little use for extreme wealth. He
looked like a man who had earned every penny he'd ever
made through his own hard effort, and was damned proud
of it. She respected that in him. It was a great deal more
attractive than Harrell's ambition to marry into old money
as a stepping stone to an obscene fortune.

As she remained silent, exasperation crossed the sheriff's
face. ''Right, let me guess. You just don't know. You've
no idea who might care enough about you to dig up a few
hundred grand, or maybe more.''

"Sorry…" The catch in her voice was real enough. It was possible no one cared that much.

"Sure you are," the sheriff answered.

The weary defeat in his voice touched her as nothing had until that moment. She looked at him closely, seeing, finally, the exhaustion that grooved the lean, bronze planes of his face and the creases in his tailored uniform that made it appear he might have slept in it. Doc Watkins had said he'd been at the hospital all night, and it was now almost noon. Had he been near her all that time as she lay sleeping? And was a part of the warm blood that coursed through her veins really his? It made her feel odd to think so, and yet there was a tenuous sense of connection, almost an intimacy, about it.

In defense against useless compassion and obligation, she said, "I might be of more help to you if you hadn't put a hole through me."

He let out his short, winded breath. The look he sent her was dark with anger and something more she couldn't define. Long seconds passed.

Abruptly, he threw up his hands. "All right," he said in rasping self-blame. "I'm sorry I shot you, okay? I didn't know you were a woman. I didn't know you wouldn't use the weapon in your hand. I had no idea what I'd done until I saw you lying there with my bullet in you, looking battered and bruised and so roughed up that you might have been pulled through a brier thicket backward. And even then, you were so…"

She stared at him as he stopped in midsentence and swung away from her. An apology was the last thing she'd expected. "So…what?" She asked, her voice husky.

He squared his shoulders, but didn't turn. "Nothing."

She lifted her hand to touch the scrape on her cheek, then ran experimental fingertips along the bruise on the line of her jaw. That damage, added to the knot on her forehead, blood loss, and long days in the back of the van without a bath or hairbrush probably had left her looking like warmed over death. But the simple truth was that it could have been worse. Much worse.

In brittle irony, she said, "You're forgiven. I think."

This time she had surprised him, or so it seemed. The look he turned on her was assessing, as if he might be rearranging his thoughts. Finally, he said, "I don't make a habit of shooting females, but I didn't have time to check for sex clues and you held your weapon as if you knew what to do with it."

"Maybe I do," she said, "but that doesn't make me a crook. Anyway, I doubt I was thinking straight or I wouldn't have pointed it at you. All I had on my mind, to the best of my remembrance was—getting away."

"You were still extremely lucky. I could have killed you, and might have if the light had been better or if you'd been moving even a fraction slower."

There was no bravado in his words, only a statement of fact impressive in its simplicity. "Yes. I imagine so."

"I'm glad I didn't."

She studied the taut contours of his face and the tucked corners of his firm lips, and thought that she needed to adjust her thinking. For him to apologize and take responsibility for what he'd done was a huge concession. Was it out of his personal code? Or did it stem from some Southern gentleman mentality left over from the previous century and kept alive in this Louisiana backcountry?

Regardless, she needed to take advantage of his brief moment of remorse. She couldn't afford to ignore any possible advantage.

Swallowing her reluctance, she reached up to wipe moisture from the corner of her eye in a gesture she was sure he couldn't miss. "I was just so glad to get away from those creeps," she said, allowing her voice to turn husky. "I thought I was free. Then to be shot was—well, it was a shock."

"I suppose it must have been."

"But it was so dark, as you said. I really can't blame you for thinking I might be one of the criminals."

His eyes narrowed a fraction. "I'm glad to hear it. Especially since there's something I need you to do for me."

"Oh?" It was possible she had laid it on too thick.

"Nothing major. In fact, it shouldn't hurt a bit." He tapped the molded black case he'd placed on the foot of the bed.

She glanced at the featureless box, then back up at him again. "I don't think I understand."

He smiled with a slow curving of his lips that banished the sternness from his sun-bronzed features and lit his eyes with silver glints. "Sorry. I thought you might recognize the drill. It's your basic identification process. You know, fingerprints?"

3

"**I**'m not a criminal." Tory curled her fingers into fists in a gesture of unconscious protection.

"People are printed for a lot of things that have nothing to do with crime," Roan answered as he began to lay out his kit. "It's part of the drill for high-risk jobs, plus the state of Louisiana requires it for liquor licensees and people connected to legalized gambling. Men and women have it done as a safety measure, and we go into schools every year to print kids for the same reason."

"None of which applies to me."

"You're sure?"

She looked away. "I think so. Who knows?"

"Exactly. If we run your prints through the computer and come up with a match, we won't have to guess anymore. That makes it worth a try."

He was so reasonable and so right. She hated that. In stiff tones, she said, "It's the principle of the thing. Besides, computers make mistakes."

"You have nothing to worry about if you've lived a blameless life."

"Right," she drawled in imitation of his dry certainty. She was being manipulated and she knew it. It was possible there was a reason. "Am I under arrest?" she demanded. "Is that what this is about?"

"I wouldn't say that."

"And I suppose you didn't stay here all night to make sure I didn't escape, either?"

"Not much chance of that." A smile creased his lean jaw.

He hadn't denied the charge. He'd just been doing his job then. "That's no answer," she said sharply.

His smile faded. "You're listed as Donna Doe for the moment, and you're in my custody. You'll be charged, or not, depending on what we turn up in the investigation of your alleged kidnapping."

Alleged. Nothing she'd said so far had made the least impression on the man beside her bed. The only way to prevent herself from becoming entangled in legal complications was to cooperate fully with him. Yet how could she?

For an instant, she let herself think of telling Roan Benedict everything for the pleasure of seeing his face when the phalanx of her designer-suited lawyers descended on this one-horse town with a veritable snow of writs and a private jet to whisk her away. But her fiancé would be on hand as well, with bushel baskets of flowers and murderous intentions. She might be coddled and petted and her every whim instantly gratified, but she'd be terrified to fall asleep on the journey back to Florida for fear that somehow, some way, Harrell would see to it she never woke up again.

No, she couldn't risk that. Not yet.

There was another possibility. She could explain, then throw herself on Roan Benedict's mercy. But what if he had none?

No, she had been right before. She needed time to get on her feet here in Turn-Coupe under the security that the sheriff provided. In a week or so, when she was more able to hold her own, she'd conveniently recover her memory. Surely she could put him off until then?

"So what's it to be?" he asked with strained patience. "My way or the hard way?"

She couldn't believe he'd risk reopening her wound by using force, but it was impossible to be sure. In any case, she had never been fingerprinted so no record of her identity should show up on computer. Her reluctance was instinctive rather than reasoned, something to do with the connection between fingerprints and Harrell's betrayal, she thought. It couldn't hurt anything, not really.

With a lift of her chin, she said, "Just get on with it."

He nodded, and moved his kit closer. At least he had the tact to keep his triumph to himself.

When he reached for the wrist of her good hand, the heat of his touch startled her. She resisted for a second, then surrendered to his control as he covered the back of her hand with his own and isolated her forefinger.

"That's it," he said quietly. "Don't try to help, just let me do it all."

It seemed a good plan. His grasp was sure, but gentle, and he avoided the plastic tubing of her IV solutions. She was aware of his palm pressed to the thin skin across the backs of her knuckles. Where their wrists came together, she thought she could feel the steady throb of his pulse and wondered if he could feel hers.

He was so close as he tried for the proper angle to place her finger on the inking pad that his elbow brushed the curve of her breast under her hospital gown. She focused her gaze on the musculature of his arm with its crisp coating of golden hair, letting it slide across the shirt pulled taut across his back and up to where deep, sun-burnished waves sculpted the back of his head and curled above his shirt collar.

She felt feverish, as if a flush were burning its way to her hairline. She shifted a little on the mattress, then dragged her gaze back down to where he was rolling her finger against the card that lay ready.

He turned his head to send her a quick glance. "You all right?"

"I...my head is beginning to hurt again."

"I'll only be a minute."

She didn't reply, but kept her gaze on what he was doing as he chose another finger and pressed it to the pad.

"Interesting that you remember the names you gave those two bozos with you when you can't think of your own," he commented without emphasis.

"The brain is strange like that, I suppose."

"Zits was one of them, wasn't It? I suppose for obvious reasons?"

She agreed. "The other had big ears like one of the little guys in *Snow White and the Seven Dwarfs.* He did the driving, so I mostly saw the back of his head."

It had been a protective measure, those names, she thought now, a way to make the pair seem less frightening. They'd been discussing what to do with her at the time, as though she wasn't a person to them but only a thing. Big Ears had wanted to buy a chain saw and cut her up the way he'd seen in some gruesome TV show. Zits, the brains of the two, had appeared to have other plans. Or other instructions.

"They never called each other by name?" Roan Benedict spoke over his shoulder, his manner offhand.

Tory hesitated. She didn't like the idea of those two getting off scot-free, even if it did protect her agenda. Finally, she said, "I seem to remember Big Ears calling Zits 'Chris' once, but it's all a little…"

"Fuzzy. I know," he supplied with heavy irony. "Zits would be the one with the build on him, while Big Ears was the tall dude, right?"

She gave him a taut glance, wondering if that was a leading question, then she remembered. "The security camera, I suppose?"

"Both men were on the tape. Your Zits character was beefed up, as if he might be a body builder on steroids. The acne could also be a sign."

"You have a point."

"Could be he makes a habit of shooting up during weight training. I can check with the Miami police, see if they'll take a photo around to area gyms."

"A good idea." The agreement was hollow.

"But it strikes me as odd that they'd let you get away— still supposing they kidnapped you. You were their meal ticket, their protection. The last thing they'd want would be to lose you."

She gave him a tart look. "They didn't lose me. I found a way to grab the pistol and make a dive for it. Anyway, I think Zits meant to use me as a shield. That's why he ripped off the duct tape, so I could be upright and mobile when he faced you."

"You remember all that?" Roan asked softly, and turned to pin her to the bed with his cool gray gaze.

She transferred her attention to her inked fingertips. "I told you the few minutes before I fell were fairly clear. I think—I'm almost sure I got this knot on my head while I was fighting with Zits. Maybe that has something to do with it."

The sheriff's snort suggested he wasn't convinced. He turned back to his job, completing the printing of one hand

and cleaning her fingers with an alcohol saturated towelette, then beginning on the other. He was carefully rolling her ring finger over the card when he spoke again. ''You have any idea where this Zits and Big Ears were headed?''

''Not really. Just away from Florida, I suppose.''

''You don't think they intended to wind up in Turn-Coupe?''

''I can't imagine why they would.''

''It's not a bad place to head for when you're in trouble, especially if you have family here.''

She frowned at his averted face. ''Is that possible? I mean, are you just guessing or do you know something?''

''Call it a hunch. The highway through town isn't exactly an interstate or even a main drag. Must be some reason they picked here to land.''

''But that would mean...''

''Exactly. They may still be around somewhere. Of course, other business could have brought them.''

''Such as?''

''We're in the process of deciding whether to call a special election, let parish voters say yea or nay to a gambling boat on Horseshoe Lake. Of course, it's a bit early for it to draw petty crooks like those two.''

''I see what you mean,'' she said. She also saw she had made the same mistake as Zits, in spite of her caution, of underestimating the sheriff of Turn-Coupe.

He glanced at her set face, but made no other comment. Retaining her left hand, he reached for her right again as he instructed, ''Both thumbs at once.''

It was a trick that she couldn't quite manage while flat on her back, at least not without pain. As he saw her difficulty, the sheriff reached to support her with a strong arm around her shoulder while guiding her with one hand to complete the imprint.

The semi-embrace was impersonal yet unbearably close. His strength supported her, enveloped her. His breath feathered across her forehead. The warmth of his body was a potent reminder of the evening before. She could feel a fine trembling start deep inside that was not entirely from the weakness of her injury. In an effort to cover it, she asked, "Have you lived here all your life?"

"Right here," he replied with one corner of his mouth curling in a smile. "And my dad before me, and his dad before him going back seven or eight generations."

"You have family ties, then."

"And then some," he drawled.

"But no wife?"

It was a moment before he spoke, "What makes you think that?"

Something in his face disturbed her, but she ignored it as she quipped, "No ring. Besides, you seem married to the job."

"Not quite. I have a family life, of a sort."

"That's why you stay here, family?" She couldn't keep the surprise from her voice. To the best of her remembrance, he hadn't seemed like a married man when he held her in his arms.

He eased her back on the pillow, then cleaned her thumbs. "It gets in your blood, small-town life. It's quiet, laid-back and easy. The pleasures may be simple, but they're real—long walks down tree-shaded roads, summer evenings listening to crickets and doves, or lying on a blanket sipping on a long neck and watching the moon come up."

It sounded remarkably like the life she remembered from summers spent with her grandparents in their small Italian village, except a robust Chianti had been the drink of choice. They had lived simply, close to the earth, regardless

of the ancient title. Those long days had been halcyon,
rising with the sun, sleeping away the drowsy afternoons,
tending the garden behind the crumbling palazzo while eating raw, sun-warmed vegetables off the vine, ambling down
dusty lanes to visit friends, listening to the voices of her
grandparents falling gentle in the twilight. She'd lived on
memories of those days during long, cold New England
winters, thought of them even when they journeyed to the
warmth of Sanibel.

A lifetime ago.

Tory had thought back then that she wanted to remain
in that small town always, had prayed fervently at the altar
in the ancient village church that her mother would never
come back for her. She always hoped that she wouldn't
have to return to being dressed up and paraded about for
the amusement of her mother's friends, to hearing her
mother's embarrassing secrets, or to be shuttled away to
the care of nannies and housekeepers while her mother
went out with men Tory despised.

Her mother always did return. That was, until she accepted the man Tory liked least of all as her fourth husband.
Soon afterward, there were no more summers in Italy.
Thinking of it now, Tory was invaded by longing so strong
it was like pain.

The sheriff studied her face an instant, then stepped to
the door and called down the hall. Moments later, Doc Watkins returned to restart her medication. He took her hand
and told her to ask for him if she needed anything Dr.
Hargrove couldn't provide. Then he left her alone once
more with Roan Benedict.

The sheriff picked up the fingerprinting kit and tucked it
under one arm, then reached for his hat, which sat on the
bedside table. Tapping the Stetson against his thigh, he

said, "I have to go, though I'll check back later. In the meantime, I've posted a man outside your door."

"I'm duly warned," she said, her tone cool.

His expression didn't change. "He's there for your protection as well as to see that you stay put. No one's allowed in here except the people that I designate, your doctor, and the nurse on duty."

"I get the idea." It was not a pleasant one, either, not when she was flat on her back and chained to the bed by medical hardware.

His gray gaze held hers as the seconds stretched. He looked as if he wanted to say something more. Instead, he gave a brief nod. "Right. Good night, then."

She watched as he let himself out of the room, then lay staring at the door. Almost, she wished she could call him back and start over. What she had just done—pretending to have amnesia—was so extreme and could go wrong in so many ways. She wasn't used to defying authority, nor was she used to dealing with men like the sheriff.

Oh, she knew plenty of men of power and position. Few were so certain of what they were and where they stood, however. Roan Benedict seemed to have no compromise in him. As he'd suggested, things were his way or the hard way. That bothered her. In fact, it scared the hell out of her.

It was ironic that the first thing he wanted was a set of fingerprints. She had discovered Harrell's forgery of her signature because of routine notification that her prints were missing from the paperwork involved in his business transaction. As the sheriff had suggested, a background check for criminal activity was a preliminary for a gaming license. She'd contacted the state agency involved, and they had explained exactly what kind of investment she was supposed to be making. It was then that she'd confronted Harrell. She wished, instead, that she'd gone to her lawyer. Things would have been different, she thought as she closed her eyes. So different.

Roan reached for the phone on its first ring. He glanced at the lighted display of his alarm clock as he spoke into the receiver. Two in the morning. Calls at this hour were never good news.

"Cal here, Sheriff."

"What do you have?"

"Incident at the hospital," the duty officer responded with the concise but unnatural wording he'd learned in police school and still favored, like he was in some damned police movie. "Two men infiltrated the premises. Believed to be the same two who robbed Betsy's convenience store."

A constriction like a steel band tightened around Roan's chest. He rolled to his feet and snatched up his pants in a single movement. "When?"

"Twenty minutes ago, sir. They gagged the prisoner and tried to drag her out of bed. Would have, too, if she hadn't managed to hit the nurse call button."

"Anyone hurt?"

"Allen has minor bruises from a scuffle with one of the men. Shots were fired, but he wasn't hit."

That wasn't what Roan wanted to know. Voice hard, he demanded, "And the suspect?"

"Secure."

"Damn it, Cal, was she injured again?"

"Negative. At least, no more than another bump on the head."

Roan's relief was so great he felt light-headed for a second. If Donna or anyone else had been injured it would have been his fault. He'd suspected Big Ears and Zits would be back. He should have posted more guards, inside and out.

He rapped out, "Where were the shots fired?"

"Outside the hospital. The felons discharged a few rounds as they headed for their vehicle. Some broken glass but little other damage. They got away in the same red pickup that was stolen from the drop-off lot."

"Pursuit?"

"Allen didn't leave the suspect, if that's what you're asking. He radioed location and direction, but the responding unit never made contact."

Roan frowned, holding the phone with a hunched shoulder as he fastened his pants and picked up his shirt. It was dumb to steal a vehicle, then drive it around in a small town where it might be recognized. Apparently, they weren't dealing with sophisticated criminal minds. On the other hand, Zits and Big Ears had vanished again. He didn't like the sound of that at all. Speaking into the receiver, he said, "I'll be there in fifteen minutes."

"Not necessary, sir. The problem is under control. There's nothing left to do but file the report. I only called to alert you to the situation."

"I appreciate your concern for my beauty sleep, Cal," Roan drawled, "but I want to keep a close watch on this case." His voice took on a deeper ring of authority. "Lock everything down tight and keep it as quiet as possible. I'll probably hear from the relatives of every patient in the hospital tomorrow, but I'd just as soon not see a report on the morning news."

"Affirmative."

"You did post a backup guard?"

"I didn't see it as essential for securing our prisoner. Besides, only Allen and I are here, sir."

Roan responded to the stiff resistance in the other man's

tone with silk-edged command. "It's essential to me, Cal. I suggest you order backup and stand guard until it arrives. If no one is available, take it yourself."

"But I'm the officer in charge."

"I know," Roan answered, and punched the off button for the portable phone. Cal Riggs could be such a pain with his stiff jargon, strict adherence to routine and protective attitude toward his authority as second in command. Sometimes, Roan had the patience for it. This wasn't one of those times.

He threw the phone into the center of the bed, then finished dressing with the speed of long practice. His wristwatch and his badge lay ready on the dresser. He slipped the watch on, then picked up the star. That symbol of his office had been on his chest for most of his adult life. It carried a tremendous responsibility; many of his decisions had to be made instantly with life or death in the balance. Still, it was seldom that he spent as much time weighing his options or making a judgment as he had in the case of Donna Doe.

The mystery of her nagged at him. He'd like to put her under a microscope and see what she was made of. Once he had that figured out, there were a few other things he'd like to discover about her, a few that required time, privacy and maybe a bottle of good wine to set the mood.

Jeez. Where had that come from?

Getting personal with the prisoner was the last thing he needed. It went against everything he'd learned about maintaining order in his town, against every principle in his private code. He didn't have time for it right now, probably never would. And that was if his prisoner was willing.

His prisoner. His, not Cal's. There was no "our" prisoner about it. The suggestion that Cal might have an interest in Donna raised hackles Roan didn't know he had.

He drew a ragged breath and pushed that idea back down where it belonged. Still, the obsession with her wouldn't go away. What was she, who was she? Poor little rich girl caught in an abduction scheme or well-kept call girl who knew something she shouldn't? Spoiled daughter out to wring money from Daddy before skipping with her abductors, or silly society chick out for thrills? She'd shown signs of a lot of things, including angel and witch. He needed to find out which she was, one way or another, before it was too late. She'd be gone the minute her memory returned—or the minute she saw that the game was up. She'd scream for a lawyer and bail like everyone else, and that would be it.

Or maybe not, if he decided it was important to keep her close. The case would come up at the parish courthouse. Judge "Pug" Miller was a cousin on his mother's side of the family. Settling legal questions between the two of them, often in a bass rig out on the lake, was a way of life.

To this point, the situation had disturbing echoes reminiscent of the incident with the Hearst heiress from back in the 1970s. Patty Hearst had been abducted at gunpoint. She later claimed she was raped and forced on pain of death to participate in the crimes of the political terrorists who captured her, but a jury had decided otherwise. Part of the reason was because Hearst had not only recorded political propaganda messages for distribution to the public, but was caught on film with a rifle in her hands. It was also, however, because she had no reason or coherent explanation for why she'd acted as she had, seemingly embracing the politics of her captors. If he remembered right, there'd been another factor at work. It appeared her greatest crime had been being born into an elite family that was bent on using its wealth to keep her out of prison. She'd expected too much of the legal system and it had turned on her. She had been, he thought, a lot like his Donna Doe.

Roan gave a snort of disgust, then pinned his star to his shirt with a practiced move. He was doing it again, grasping at every angle that might bolster Donna's kidnapping story. He wanted to believe her. That was the trouble.

He'd run her prints. Nothing. He'd compared the pictures from the surveillance tape against mug shots. Nada. He'd contacted the Florida Highway Patrol and Dade County Sheriff's Department where the old van had been stolen. Zilch. He'd even contacted the FBI for reported kidnappings, but they had no one approaching her description on file. The last hadn't exactly made him cry. All he needed was a swarm of uptight government types in button-downs crawling over his territory.

Regardless, Donna, if that was her name, was keeping something from him; he knew it. She had dragged just enough information from her tainted memory to keep him guessing, but nothing concrete to help nail the men with her. Was it the need to keep her lover out of jail or fear that held her back? Either way, Roan wanted answers, like an explanation for why Big Ears and Zits were so determined to get to her that they risked crashing the hospital. That was the first question on his agenda as soon as he saw Miss Donna Doe.

On his way out of the house, he looked in on Jake. His son enjoyed the heavy sleep of a teenager; the telephone hadn't disturbed him and Roan didn't wake him. He dropped a note on the kitchen table in case he wasn't back by morning, then left by the front door. Old Beauregard, lying near the edge of the high outside steps that descended from the second-floor living area to the ground, raised his head and turned up his dolorous bloodhound face as if in inquiry about the early exit. Roan bent to give him a scratch or two behind the ears, then ran lightly down the steps.

With one foot in the floorboard of his tan police unit, he hesitated while he patted his shirt pocket, making certain he had his cell phone with him. At the same time, he looked back at the house that was silvered by moonlight to a ghostly shade of gray. Built in the 1850s, Dog Trot, as the house was called for the carriage way cut through the center of the lower floor, was a bastard blend of Georgian and French West Indies styles. Four square and solid, two and a half stories tall with deep, sheltering porches, it had withstood searing summer sun, cold winter rain, the violent storms that sometimes spun across the heart of Louisiana, and hordes of kids as destructive as locusts. It had sheltered Benedicts since the day the last wooden peg was driven into the last hole, and it now protected Roan's son who slept so peacefully upstairs.

A few of his relatives, mostly female, made a fuss about Roan leaving a fourteen-year-old boy alone at night when duty called. He didn't much like it himself, but there was no other choice now that his dad, who'd lived with them when the boy was younger, was off on his great motor home adventure. Jake didn't want to be hauled out of bed several times a week to go to one of the neighbors' house, nor was he afraid of staying alone. Besides, Dog Trot was probably the safest place in the parish, much more so than the hospital, even without an armed guard. Few people wanted to risk the swift retaliation an attack on a sheriff or his family would bring, especially if the offence occurred on the official's home grounds. On top of that was the Benedict habit of protecting their own. This was their land, their home, their castle. Jake had once said when he was ten years old and into knights and dragons: Here, they were kings. Damned if his son wasn't right.

Roan grinned with a quick shake of his head, then settled
into the driver's seat and started the engine.

He saw the broken glass first, the remnants of what had
been the automatic doors leading to the Emergency Room.
It lay scattered across the polished floor inside, glittering
in the sterile brightness of the lights. Two EMTs dressed
for ambulance duty stood talking in hushed voices. They
looked up and nodded a greeting as he approached, their
expressions showing plainly that they'd like his take on the
situation. He only lifted a hand, however, as he crunched
glass under his boots on his way toward the main hospital
wing.

Cal met him at the nurse's station for Donna's room. A
young nurse garbed in lime green and rose, with a Walk-
man on her hip and black earphones nearly hidden by her
dark, curly hair, stood flipping through a chart. After a
quick look at Roan's face, she grabbed a cart and pushed
it out the door, muttering about making rounds. Roan let
her go. When she had vanished into a patient's room, he
summoned Allen from his position outside Donna's door.
Positioning himself so he could watch the corridor around
the suspect's room, he heard the reports of both Cal and
Allen.

When they'd finished, he asked, "What do you see as
the motive?"

"Who knows?" Cal answered with a shrug. "All the
suspect would tell me was that it was too dark to see her
attacker."

Allen put his hands on his wide hips. "You want my
opinion, her pals were trying to spring her."

"Then why the gag?"

"For show. To make it look like a kidnapping in case
they were stopped. Wouldn't surprise me to hear it was her
idea."

"You said her IV shunt was jerked out in an apparent struggle. I suppose she did that for the same reason?" Roan heard the hard anger in his voice with some surprise, but didn't bother to downplay it.

"An accident, maybe, because they were in a hurry or else didn't know how to remove the damn thing. I expect she fell because she passed out from the sight of blood."

Roan had seen no susceptibility of that kind on the night Donna was shot. Besides, women weren't as squeamish as men about that kind of thing in his experience. "So why hit the call button? Another accident?"

"Could be." The words were defensive. "We're dealing with amateurs here, seems to me, or they'd have made a better job of it."

"They almost pulled it off anyway, and might have if the duty nurse hadn't heard the scuffle over the intercom. Speaking of which..."

Allen didn't pretend to misunderstand him. "I swear I just walked off for a second. I needed a shot of coffee to stay awake."

"In other words, you didn't think there was any danger." Allen liked to talk, Roan knew; he'd probably leaned on the station door here, shooting the bull with the night nurses, since it was a habit during normal rounds. It wasn't surprising. The jail inmates sick enough to rate a hospital stay seldom required much watching.

"Who'd ever guess the two bad guys would come back, anyway," the deputy said, rubbing a hand over his face in tired bafflement. "Or that they'd be smart enough to hang around the side entrance until some visitor opened the door for them."

Allen was a good cop, Roan knew. He said in grim warning, "You will. Next time."

"Right."

Roan was satisfied. It was time to move on to other things. "So is the prisoner asleep?"

It was Cal who answered. "She wasn't last time I looked, but I could check if you want to know for sure."

"Never mind. I'll see for myself. Meantime, do you have somebody to take over for Allen?"

"No, sir. Allen's fine, ready to finish his shift." He glanced at the other deputy, who nodded dutifully.

Roan sighed. "You know how I feel about this, Cal, and you know the rule—any officer who has been fired upon is to stand down. You're the duty officer. It's your responsibility to arrange a replacement. Since you didn't, you'll have to take the rest of the shift."

"Yes, sir. I'll check the perimeter again while you're still here, sir." The deputy snapped a stiff and wholly unnecessary salute before he turned and strode away.

It was a shame Cal felt the need to buck him at every turn, Roan thought as he watched him go. He was young and gung ho, but most new officers were that way for the first year or two. Everything by the book, the newest book, of course. Rumor was that he might run for sheriff in the next election. He was well liked in a lot of quarters, went out of his way to curry favor in others; he might have a chance. If so, he'd have a race on his hands. Roan had served Tunica Parish as well as he knew how, putting long hours and all the heart and soul he had left into the job. If the voters would have him for another term, then he'd be around.

He'd had some conflict with the town council lately over this gambling boat business. Such things got around, and could be a factor. He was related to half the parish, however, and the Benedict clan was not only sizable but inclined to vote in a block to protect their interests. No, the real problem was that there were unwritten rules to elections in Tunica Parish that went with the legal and honor system little changed since France had ruled Louisiana. It wasn't considered good form for the loser in the sheriff's election to remain in the employ of the winner. If Roan won again, Cal would likely resign. And losing Cal's fresh approach and his interest in the latest technology would be a shame.

Roan dismissed Allen, then turned in the direction of Donna's room. He'd taken only a couple of steps, however, when he was hailed from the opposite end of the hall. He turned to see the hospital administrator, Hilton Darkwater, waving at him.

Another problem; he knew it. He waited impatiently for the thin-lipped, bespectacled corporate type to catch up with him.

"I'm glad I saw you, Sheriff," Darkwater said with a tight smile. "We need to talk."

"Can't it wait?" The need to look in on his prisoner had been riding him since he'd left home. It was so strong now that he was half inclined to tell the administrator to wait and see him in his office.

"I don't think so. You've got to get that woman out of here." He jerked his head toward Donna's door.

Roan put his thumb through a belt loop. "She's hardly in any shape to leave."

"I'm aware of that, but I'd prefer that you transfer her to Baton Rouge or New Orleans. This is a small community hospital. We have no facilities for this kind of case."

No restricted area with bars and locks, the administrator meant, Roan thought. "I realize there will be complaints, but…"

"You've no idea! I had to get out of bed to come down here and answer them. So many have come in that I had to turn off my phone." The other man inhaled audibly through his nose in agitation. "The hospital is barely breaking even now. If we lose patients because they're afraid they'll be assaulted in their expensive adjustable beds, then we'll hit red faster than a cheap thermometer in August. We might as well close the doors."

Roan didn't have a lot of sympathy, given that his phone rang constantly. Besides, the administrator had his own ax to grind. He'd been in his position for less than a year, but managed to cut waste and increase the occupancy rate dramatically. The scuttlebutt was that he was determined to perform magic in Turn-Coupe, not because he cared about the community and wanted to be sure its local hospital was kept open, but because he was bucking for a bigger job elsewhere.

Keeping his tone pleasant with an effort, Roan said, "I can't move her out of the parish without just cause, you know that. If one of the staff or another patient had been injured or even threatened it would be different, but that didn't happen. All we had was a little scare."

The other man's gaze held his for long, challenging seconds. Something he saw must have convinced him that arguing wouldn't help. His lips tightened again. "Could you at least post another guard at the hospital entrance?"

Roan inclined his head in acknowledgement of the reasonableness of the request. "I'll do that, though I doubt there'll be more trouble tonight."

"Let's hope not," the administrator returned with an almost visible shudder. Then as Roan turned away, he clutched at his arm. "There's also the damage to the emergency entrance. You bringing that woman in here caused it, you know. I don't see that the hospital should have to pay."

"Send me the bill."

Roan shook off the other man's hand, then turned and

moved down the hall. He felt certain the hospital's insurance would cover the damage, but it wasn't worth the fight or the hard feelings that refusal would cause. He'd find funds in the budget somewhere for it. If not, he'd pay for it out of his own pocket.

At Donna's door, he gave a quick rap with his knuckles then pushed inside. He stopped abruptly as he saw her lying pale and still, with her eyes closed and her hair spread around her on the pillow. The door, pulled by its automatic hinge, closed behind him with a soft thud.

She flinched at the sound. Her long eyelashes lifted, and she turned her head on the pillow in slow motion. She seemed to focus on the star on his chest as it reflected the glare of the light above her bed. Then her gaze moved upward to his face with the warm strength of a laser burning through his uniform and tracking over his skin underneath. It focused on the Stetson that he hadn't yet removed. A drowsy smile curved the tender lines of her lips. Then it was replaced by a frown.

"Where've you been, cowboy? You left me here alone, and look what happened."

He was an idiot. He had to be, because he suddenly felt tall in the saddle and ready to take on the world.

And Roan, watching the woman in the bed as she closed her eyes and drifted away again, knew exactly what he was going to do about Donna Doe.

4

"**I**'d rather go to jail!"

The defiant words hung in the air. Tory searched the set planes of the sheriff's face, but could see no sign that she'd made the slightest impression. In fact, he didn't even look up as he answered.

"That's not an option."

"You can't just take me home with you." Her protest was instinctive. She hadn't seen Sheriff Roan Benedict since the attack four nights ago. To have him walk in and announce that she was being removed from the hospital and placed under house arrest—in his house—left her breathless and disoriented.

"I can. This is my jurisdiction. I make the rules here."

"That's barbaric!"

"Isn't it?" He had the nerve to smile, as if the edge of panic in her voice amused him in some grim fashion.

"It can't be legal. I mean, you call it house arrest, if you want, but..."

"That's what it will be, and all it will be," he answered. "If you doubt the legality, call a lawyer. But be sure you can give him a full legal name and show how you mean to pay his bill."

That was unanswerable, at least while she kept to her present pose. It crossed Tory's mind to wonder if the sheriff knew it and was testing her, expecting her to confess to the charade. But why would he? She'd given him scant reason to think her amnesia wasn't genuine.

The effort to puzzle it out made her head hurt again. She'd refused the high-powered painkiller in the dispenser after the visit from Zits, opting for an occasional pill by mouth instead. It had been fine, until now.

"I don't believe I'm well enough to leave here," she said with a querulous weariness that was not entirely feigned.

"Doc Watkins says otherwise. You're a fast healer, according to him, and you've already been up and around on your own. Besides, the hospital administrator wants you gone. It's been all I could do to keep you here this long."

The daytime duty nurse, Johnnie, had told her much the same thing. Shifting ground, Tory said, "I suppose you take in all your injured prisoners as boarders?"

"By no means. But I think you'll find accommodations at Dog Trot a lot more comfortable."

"Dog Trot?"

"My house."

It sounded like a backwoods shanty. She had a momentary vision of a place crawling with hound dogs and with an actual "path to the bath" like some hillbilly movie. In tones edged with irony, she said, "I'm sure it's…lovely."

"It may not be the Ritz, but it's a lot better than the jail. The town lockup was built on the top floor of the courthouse before the turn of the century, also before such niceties as central heat and air. We have two cells designed to hold four prisoners each. Five short-timers are in residence now, all men. I could double them up so that you'd be alone, but the cells are side by side. There'd be nothing between you and the male prisoners except steel bars. And bathroom facilities are open to view for security purposes.''

''You mean they could see me...''

''All the time. Exactly.''

''Good grief!''

''And they'd talk to you twenty-four hours a day. It could be a fast course in the down and dirty instincts of the male animal.''

She digested that in silence for a long moment. Then she gave him an oblique glance and lowered her voice to a husky, suggestive timbre as she asked, ''What about your instincts? What's to curb them when we're alone at this house of yours with no steel bars, no witnesses?''

Roan cocked a brow. ''Let me guess. Mae West this time, all world-weary and sultry?''

''Lauren Bacall,'' she said in irritation at being called on the role-playing. ''Not that it matters.''

''Right. What's the famous line about whistling if I need you? It's a thought, but not something to keep you up nights. For one thing, it wouldn't be a good example for my son Jake. For another, I don't operate that way. No one at Dog Trot is going to molest you. Least of all, me.''

''And I'm supposed to accept that.'' Curiosity laced the annoyance in her tone.

''You have my word.''

He meant exactly that, she thought. The pledge was in the depth of his voice and the unwavering intensity of his gray gaze. The shocker was that she believed him. Not that she'd give him the satisfaction of knowing it.

To stay out of sight somewhere deep in the boonies had a certain appeal, on second thought. Roan Benedict would make a competent and extremely convenient protective shield against Zits and Big Ears, or even Harrell. She would have more freedom of movement in a less structured environment like a private home, more opportunity to arrange things so she could skip out if the going got too rough. In the meantime, it would be best if the sheriff didn't realize how cooperative she was suddenly prepared to be since he was smart enough to wonder why.

"I still don't like it," she said finally.

Roan Benedict gave her a level look. "You're a prisoner of the Tunica Parish Sheriff's Department. What you like or don't like isn't a priority."

"Or even a concern?"

"You could put it that way."

She didn't care for the inflexibility in his tone, but could see little way to change it. "Suppose I file a complaint?"

He chuckled, a soft sound of real amusement. "By all means, if you can figure out where to send it or and who might pay attention."

"You have it all figured out, don't you?" She stared at him, the perfect picture, she hoped, of frustrated reluctance.

"Maybe," he said in laconic agreement. "Get your things together. We're out of here in an hour."

He didn't wait for a reply, but turned and left the room with the free-swinging strides of unconscious athletic grace. He didn't look back.

Tory watched his broad shoulders and narrow flanks until the door closed behind him. It had never occurred to the man that she would do anything except exactly as he'd ordered, she thought. And he was right. For now.

She pushed up in the bed, supporting herself on one elbow while she punched the nurse call button. The door opened then and the deputy from outside, Cal Riggs, stuck his head through the opening. "Roan says you're being discharged. If you need Johnnie, it'll be a second. She and the other gal at the nurse's station had to go down the hall to help with some kind of emergency. I'll tell her you need her when she comes back by.''

She thanked the deputy with a smile. The men stationed outside her door had bothered her at first. She'd developed a distinct appreciation for them, however, since the attack. The two who showed up most often, Cal and Allen, had become friendly after a fashion. They hailed a nurse when she needed one, brought coffee, juice and soft drinks, and loaned her their newspapers. She thought sheer boredom played a big part in their helpfulness, but the rest seemed to be small-town friendliness. At least, she couldn't imagine such bending of regulations in a larger place.

''Anything I can do?'' Cal asked as he edged a bit farther into the room.

''Not really. I don't have that much to get ready.'' She waved in the direction of the few toiletries provided by the hospital and robe and slippers the sheriff had brought from the local discount store. ''But you might tell me if Sheriff Benedict has the right to detain me at a location other than the jail.''

The deputy's thick brows drew together above his hazel eyes. ''Like where?''

''Dog Trot, I think he called it.''

The deputy gave a low whistle. ''That's a first.''

''But is it legal?''

''It's not exactly by the book,'' he drawled, ''but Roan does pretty much what he pleases. He *is* the law in Tunica Parish.''

Cal's voice carried a shading of envy with, possibly, a touch of rancor. The comment was also fairly indiscreet. He'd been gradually thawing over the last few days. It was a good thing, since his stiff manner had been tiresome in the extreme.

She tilted her head as she asked, ''How long can he hold

me there, do you think? I mean, shouldn't I appear in court or something?''

"The circuit judge comes through every Tuesday, but court has recessed for two weeks while everybody goes on vacation." Cal shrugged. "It'll be a while before Roan can get an arraignment, even if he wanted one."

"Circuit judge?" Shades of the Old West, Tory thought, where a single judge handled an entire territory and the hangings had to wait until he was in town. Not that she had any intention of complaining.

"We don't have a whole lot of crime in the parish." Cal's tone was almost apologetic. "Half the folks are related, one way or another, and the Benedicts keep their fights to themselves out around the lake and its swamp waters. Roan goes out and takes care of it, usually without bringing in anybody. I think sometimes that's why they elected him sheriff."

"Has he been in office long?" Since she had Cal going her way this morning, she might as well make the most of it.

"Eight years, give or take, though he was on the force quite a while before that."

Cal made it sound as if he considered Roan ancient. That was almost funny, since the sheriff appeared to be in his midthirties and more fit than average. It was just as well that Cal, possibly ten years his junior, didn't realize how young and inexperienced he seemed by comparison.

"Roan must have started when he was a kid," she suggested.

"Not long after he got out of high school, around the same time he got married. He was hand-groomed for the job by the man before him, Sheriff Johnson. They say he ran the department for nearly two years after Johnson had a heart attack, helping him stay on long enough to draw his pension. Next election, Roan won by a landslide. No one's had the nerve to run against him since.''

It sounded much as she expected. Entrenched in his office, Roan answered only to the voters. There'd been countless movies and television shows about his kind, lawmen in small communities who bent the rules when it suited them.

''A law unto himself,'' she murmured, more intrigued than she wanted to be.

''Could be he's overstepping his place.'' Cal threw back his thin shoulders as he spoke.

''You mean by taking me home with him?''

''And whatever he does when he gets you there.''

''What do you mean?'' The last thing she needed was more trouble.

''People keep an eye on their public officials. They like them to be upstanding, God-fearing citizens who have the good sense to carry on in private.''

''Thank you,'' she said in glacial displeasure, ''but I'd like to point out that it takes two to 'carry on,' as you put it. If you think I'd cooperate in any funny business, you're mistaken.''

''Right, sorry,'' the deputy said, flushing to his hairline. ''Forget it, will you? Hey, I think I hear Johnnie out in the hall...''

It was a blatant excuse to get out of the room, Tory thought. No doubt Cal was afraid he'd said too much. But she was sure he really wasn't sorry for any problem Roan might be creating for himself.

She lay staring at the door for long moments after it had closed behind him. She was bothered, more than she could remember in a long time, by the idea that she might cause trouble for Roan. It had seemed so easy to pretend she didn't remember, to let herself drift while he took care of things, took care of her. After all, she'd been taking the easy way for years.

Dutiful stepdaughter and hostess, empty-headed party girl, cosmopolitan socialite: she could trade quips in three languages and kiss air with the best of them. She fooled everyone, even herself, into believing the many masks that she wore were real. Still a certain emptiness always remained, one she'd thought to fill with a husband and family.

Harrell had breezed into her life at the right time. He could be charming, when he put his mind to it, and very good at blending in with whatever crowd he joined. He was also salesman enough to draw out the image in the minds of those he met and make the product he was selling fit it. With her, it was himself as a prospective bridegroom.

It had been a while before Tory realized that his true tastes were not the more subdued choices of Old Money, but ran instead to red Ferraris, flashy gold jewelry, and neon midnights. If she hadn't been so determined not to be a snob, she might have dropped him then. Instead, she'd thought she could change him. She should have known better, and might have if she'd bothered to really look at the commercials that he ran for his business. The Cheap Furniture King of South Florida, he'd named himself, complete with jeweled crown and curvaceous queen perched on his lap as he ruled from one of his own easy chairs. Typical.

Where was Harrell now? Probably with her stepfather on the golf course at The Sanctuary or playing beer tennis at The Dunes, winner to buy the first round of imported brew. He would be offhand and unconcerned about her absence. Prenuptial jitters, he'd say with a shrug. The coming wedding was too much for her to handle, so she'd run off to visit one of her boarding school friends. She'd be back in a week or two, when her nerves settled down.

Paul Vandergraff would understand completely. Tory's habit of running away had begun after he became her step-father. She had watched him manipulate her mother with chill disapproval and ready access to prescription drugs un-til an exclusive rest home was the only resort. Afterward, he'd made it clear to Tory that her normal teenage mood fluctuations could well be taken as a sign of the same in-stability. Flight had become safer, always, than confronta-tion. Small wonder that she'd followed the same pattern with Harrell.

Of course, Harrell might not be so calm, after all, if Zits and Big Ears had worked up the nerve to call him. He was probably wondering why he hadn't been visited already by the Florida police. How long would it be before he discov-ered that she wasn't talking, and what would he do then?

For a brief instant, Tory felt a strong urge to tell Roan everything so he would know what he might be up against with Harrell. It wasn't fair, or safe, to keep him in the dark. But no, she couldn't take that chance. The second he learned who she was, he'd wash his hands of her. That was the last thing she wanted.

"Lord, hon, you look like you've going to your execu-tion instead of out to Dog Trot."

Tory forced a smile for Johnnie. At the same time, she recalled that the nurse was Roan's cousin, so not a good person to confide in about him. She said, "Cal told you, I suppose."

"Roan, rather, on his way to the business office to settle your account. What Cal said was that he hopes Roan knows what he's doing. What he meant, though, was that he hopes it all blows up in his face." Johnnie gave a cheerful laugh. "That boy's a sad case—high ambitions in a job where there's no ladder to climb."

"Except the one with Roan's badge at the top?" It had

become natural to refer to the sheriff by his given name when speaking to Johnnie.

Johnnie shot her a droll look as she picked up the blood pressure cuff that hung on its electronic monitor. "Cal's not likely to take over Roan's job."

"Because Roan is so entrenched?"

"Because he's too good at it." Johnnie wrapped the cuff around Tory's arm and inflated it. "Can't blame Cal, though. Being sheriff pays pretty well, and there's not much else for him to do around here."

"Oh?"

"Most of the young folks go off to college, then find work in bigger places. Men used to make a living in wood hauling or offshore oil drilling—my husband was a driller before his job went the way of so many back during the oil crisis. He's an air-conditioning repairman now. Folks have to stay cool, no matter what else happens."

"According to Cal, a lot of Benedicts are still around town," Tory said.

"Including me, huh?" The nurse gave a rich chuckle. "Yeah, well, they were some of the first settlers around here back before the Civil War, and managed to hold on to their land. They've got deep roots, not to mention timber and mineral rights to tide them over the hard times."

Land, tradition, her mother had been big on those things, as had her Italian grandparents. Tory said in dry appreciation, "Roan comes from old Southern stock then?"

"You could say so, though he'd laugh himself silly if you suggested he was plantation gentry or anything like that." Johnnie paused long enough to put a temperature probe in Tory's mouth. "There are actually four branches of Benedicts here, from the four brothers who left England in the late 1700s. Folks claim the guys had to leave, something to do with the death of their sister's snake-mean husband. I guess the Benedicts took care of their own even way back then.''

Tory raised a brow, since she couldn't speak. Any insight into the life of the man she'd be spending time with over the next few days could be valuable.

''The brothers were freebooters in the Caribbean for a while, but didn't take to the pirate trade. They landed in New Orleans and made their way up the Mississippi, settled around Horseshoe Lake. They each took a wife, though in their own sweet time. The oldest brother married a Scotswoman with red hair and a bad temper. My cousin, Kane, comes from that line. He's an attorney in town who just got married a year ago to a woman with red hair, though she's sweet as sugar cane, just like him.''

The temperature probe beeped and was removed. Tory asked, ''And the others?''

''One married the Indian woman who had guided them to the lake. That would be Cousin Luke's side of the family.'' Johnnie rolled her eyes. ''Now if there was one of my cousins that I wished I wasn't related to, it's Luke. Talk about tall, dark and dreamy. We used to call him *Luke-de-la-Nuit*—Luke of the Night—though I guess that's over now that he's married to April. That's April Halstead, you know. She writes romance novels. Ever read any of them?''

The name was familiar; Tory thought she might have picked up one of her books at an airport newsstand. She nodded as she asked, ''She lives here?''

''She likes the peace and quiet. Some folks do.''

''What about you?'' Tory asked. ''How are you related to Roan?''

''I was a Benedict before I married. Roan and I are actually from the same line. Our great-great-however-many-grandfather still had a little pirate left in his blood, I guess, because he kidnapped a Spanish woman from over toward the Texas border, one he fell in love with at first sight. Story goes in the family that she was about to be married off to a man twice her age, so being kidnapped was a mighty convenient way of avoiding a family wrangle.'' A conscious look appeared on her round face. ''Not that I mean to imply anything about what happened to you.''

''No, of course not.'' Tory gave her a wan smile.

''Still, here you are, heading home with Roan on account of a kidnapping. Now wouldn't it be something if...''

''Please!'' The nurse was obviously a raving romantic.

Johnnie sighed. ''Sorry. I guess stuff like that only happens in April's books.''

It seemed best to get away from that subject as quickly as possible. ''You haven't mentioned the fourth brother?''

''A rogue of the first water, that one. He found a Frenchwoman wandering in the woods. He never knew how she got there or where she came from and didn't care. He took her home with him and kept her there for over fifty years. Cousin Clay's from that line. He and Roan are good buddies.''

''Fascinating,'' Tory commented, since it seemed something was expected.

''We were all quite a gang in our younger days, Kane, Luke, Roan, even Clay and his brothers from time to time. We were a little wild but we stuck together. We watched each other's backs, kept each other from breaking our necks with dumb pranks. They were good times.''

''But none of you are all that closely related, right?''

''Fifth or sixth cousins, something like that, though some are related by way of other family lines. I mean, Turn-Coupe was isolated for a lot of long years. Intermarriage was common because there wasn't much choice otherwise.'' She moved to the end of the bed and scribbled on the chart hanging there. ''Doesn't happen much any more.

I remember I started going around with Todd Carlson in middle school. My grandmother freaked, since Todd was my third or fourth cousin or something. She made such a fuss that it scared me off of dating for a while.''

Tory tipped her head. "So is lack of choice the reason Roan hasn't married again?''

Johnnie grinned. "Not so you'd notice. I think he's just so busy, not to mention so modest, that he doesn't notice the women chasing after him. He's a hunk, though, isn't he? Not bulked-up-macho like a body builder, but quite a package. And such a cute butt!''

The pinching motions the plump, motherly woman made with her fingers to go with that last comment were so unexpected that Tory gave a spurt of laughter. Immediately, she caught her breath and clapped a hand to her shoulder. "Don't do that, it hurts,'' she pleaded with a heartfelt groan.

"Sorry. Anyway, that's the saga of the Benedicts. The brothers homesteaded good-size tracts of land, hunted and fished and trapped around the lake, raised cows and cotton and lots of kids the way most people did in those days.'' She opened her arms in a wide gesture. "And that's how we all came to be here.''

Tory couldn't help smiling at the pride and affection in Johnnie's voice. "It must be nice to have such a big family.''

Johnnie's expression turned droll. "Sometimes I wish I were an only child of an only child and lived in a city where I didn't know a soul. You can't run to the food mart for a gallon of milk around here without seeing a dozen people you know. If you go in your work clothes or without makeup, they say, 'What's the matter with Johnnie? She looks so bad. Think she's having family troubles?' I mean, honestly!''

"At least it shows they care," Tory said quietly. She actually *was* the only child of an only child. None of her mother's many flings at matrimony, after the gala first wedding to her Italian prince, Tory's father, had produced children. It was just as well, perhaps, since her mother had never been the maternal sort in any case. Only with her grandparents, in the little town tucked into the hills of Tuscany where the Princes Trentalara had lived for a thousand years, had Tory felt part of a family. Life there had been much like Turn-Coupe sounded, with such intense interest in everyone's well-being and close relationships that it was like living in the middle of a soap opera.

In some ways, then, her grandparents had provided the greatest security she'd known as a child. For a few precious summers from age six to fourteen, she had been sent to Mama Sophia's at the Trentalara estate. There, along with two older female cousins from Rome, she had been coached in manners and deportment so she was capable of meeting anyone of any station. The three girls had roamed Italy with Mama Sophia and Papa 'Vanni, learning about art and life and how to speak extremely idiomatic French and Italian. And they had escaped to romp with the gardener's children and range the hills with the village boys and girls. Those had been the best days, before Papa 'Vanni had a stroke and Mama Sophia fell and broke her hip and died of pneumonia, and it all came to an end. Afterward, it was a succession of nannies, butlers, boarding school counselors, and college deans who had shaped her life.

Tory, lost in thought, looked away toward the sunlit window as she began in soft tones, "I remember..."

Johnnie's head came up and her friendliness was replaced by sharp professionalism. "Yes?"

Tory stopped abruptly. She could feel the color draining from her face as she realized the mistake she'd almost made. She'd slipped earlier, too, when she'd suggested by inference that she had no near relatives. Had Johnnie noticed? Would she report it to Roan? Dear God, she was going to have to be more careful.

She tried for a confused look, followed by a sigh. "Oh, I almost thought—but no, it's gone."

"Too bad. Maybe next time." Johnnie moved to the bedside table and began to gather the toiletries there. "Right now, we'd better get you ready to go, since Roan will be back any minute. He's a lot of things, but patient is not one of them."

Tory didn't doubt that at all. And she wondered just how far he could be pushed before his control snapped.

5

"This is Dog Trot?"

Tory could hear the hollow disbelief in her own question as she sat staring at Roan's home from the front seat of the police unit. The house was an antebellum mansion with thick, bell-bottomed columns lining the broad front and wrought-iron railings in lacelike patterns stretched between the tall supports on the upper porch level. Wide front steps protected by more iron railings mounted to solid entrance doors on the second floor, giving the ground floor the appearance of a raised basement. These lower brick walls were nearly eighteen inches thick, and faded to a mellow rose-red under their tracery of vines. The most outstanding feature, however, was the tunnel-like porte cochere that cut through the center of this ground floor. Sunlight and shadow made interesting triangular patterns on its interior walls, while the flowering plants of a private rear garden could be seen through the wide opening. The whole place was well maintained, with an indefinable aura of quiet grace and solid comfort.

"It's home," Roan said.

"But it's huge!"

"Not really," he answered as he got out of the car, then

moved around to open her door. "That is, not until it's
time to paint. Then I swear it becomes a monster."

Tory had seen larger places: the Vandergraff winter
home on Sanibel Island, though thoroughly modern and
without noticeable character, was spread over more acre-
age. Her father's family home in Italy had been bigger as
well, a beautiful old villa of golden stone with a brass lion's
head on the ancient, hand-carved front door. Still, there was
something about the house in front of her. Dog Trot's
sturdy walls and thick doors promised peace and safety. It
had the look of a sanctuary.

She eased from her seat and stood. Roan put his hand
under her elbow in a quick gesture of support. It was then
that a great mud-red dog came trotting out of the shadows
of the center carriageway. He paused and stretched his back
haunches as he reached the sunlight. Then he tilted his head
back and gave a deep bark that had the sound of rolling
thunder.

"Good lord," she said under her breath. "What is that?"

A corner of Roan's mouth lifted in a smile. "Don't
panic, it's just old Beauregard—Beau to his friends—doing
his duty as guard dog."

"He's not a...bloodhound?" It was all she could do to
keep from shuddering, the direct result of too many movies
featuring such canines.

"Purebred and pedigreed, though he's too lazy to trail
much more than a rabbit."

The sheriff's voice carried a strong hint of affectionate
insult that suggested the opposite was true. No doubt the
animal was a trained man-hunter. He didn't seem vicious,
however, as he trotted up to have his head rubbed, then
leaned against Roan's pant leg in beatific enjoyment.
Watching Roan's hands smoothing over the dog's sleek pelt

and floppy ears in rough tenderness caused an odd, heated sensation in the lower part of her body.

"Does he bite?" she asked, her voice sharper than she'd intended.

Roan barely glanced at her. "Only when I say so."

"What a comfort."

"You don't like dogs?" Roan asked as he straightened.

"Little ones are fine." She'd had a poodle as a child that she'd adored, but Pierre had vanished from his carrier during a flight between New York and Fort Myers. She'd never wanted to invest that much caring in a pet again.

"But not big ones? Then you could be in trouble." He nodded in the direction of a barn that lay behind the house.

He was right. A pack of dogs loped from that direction. Black and tan in color, they had the raw-boned yet racy look of the hunting hounds in old English prints.

"Let me guess," she drawled. "You're a hunter."

"I suppose you don't like that, either."

She lifted her good shoulder in a careless shrug as she kept a nervous eye on the hounds that swarmed around them, sniffing her ankles as if in search of lunch. "It's nothing to me if you enjoy killing defenseless animals."

"What I actually enjoy is breeding and training dogs like my dad, my granddad, and great-granddad before me. Dog Trot hounds have been blue ribbon winners for generations. They're the best in the country."

"Therefore the name of your house," she said in her best bored, finishing school accents. "Charming."

He laughed, and rubbed Beauregard's big head as the bloodhound shouldered aside the other dogs and leaped up to plant saucer-size paws on his chest. "Hear that, boy? We don't impress her. We won't tell her the passage under the house is known as a dog trot."

Tory, plastered against the passenger door, saw nothing

comical in the situation whatever. Its only good point as
far as she could see was that Zits despised dogs.

Roan ordered the dog pack out of the way, then started
to close the car door. Tory stepped to one side. A sharp
piece of the gravel that covered the driveway pressed into
her foot, and she stumbled.

"Steady." Roan shot out a strong arm to circle her waist.
The close physical contact was so unexpected that she
swayed, losing her balance. He shifted his feet and caught
her closer against him.

She was pressed to his lean length from breast to knees,
and enveloped in the scent of starched uniform, mint-fresh
aftershave and heated male skin. His hold was rock steady,
the muscles under her fingers firm and unyielding. The
sense of power that he carried with him seemed to surround
her, enclose her. She could feel the quick rise and fall of
his chest, sense the thudding of his heart. His eyes behind
the shields of his thick lashes shimmered with gray appraisal, and something more.

"Sorry," he said in clipped tones. "I should have realized that you might be shaky."

"I'm fine," she answered, her voice as cool and distant
as she could make it as she exerted pressure with her hands
to break his hold. "If you don't mind?"

His lips tightened and he stepped back at once. He didn't
touch her again as she made her way slowly toward the
flight of wide steps that led up to the double front doors
on the main level. He stayed at her side, however, moving
with her in unnerving watchfulness that made her wish he'd
thought to provide her with more to wear than a lightweight
bathrobe.

Tory clenched her teeth and held firmly to the iron stair
railing as she climbed. She was determined that she
wouldn't stagger, wouldn't so much as hesitate. She might

have to accept Roan Benedict's dubious hospitality, but she didn't have to take anything else. She was concentrating so hard on reaching the top of the steps that she flinched when he spoke.

"Actually, you might want to be careful around Beau."

"No joke." The words were more than a little breathless. She was weaker than she'd realized, or else the steps were higher than they looked from ground level.

"He takes his guard duty seriously. If he feels you're headed where you shouldn't be, he might try to stop you."

"By taking off a leg, I suppose?"

"He wouldn't hurt you, necessarily, but he could make it hard to get around him."

"How convenient to have him around. One less deputy you need to pull from regular duty."

"Don't worry, Cal and Allen will still be at your beck and call during the day."

So he knew his men had made themselves useful. It almost sounded as if the sheriff disapproved though she couldn't think why. "Good," she replied shortly. "I was wondering what would happen when the kidnappers find out I've been transferred here."

His laugh had a dry sound. "You think I should have kept it secret?"

"Seems reasonable to me."

"Not much point. Everybody in Turn-Coupe will know by dark."

It was entirely possible that he was right. She'd noticed the level of gossip among the hospital staff. It had reminded her of her grandparents' village where no one could sneeze before breakfast without the rest of the town asking after their health by noon.

She was so hot. So was the railing. It was also slick; her fingers slipped on the smooth metal that had been polished

by countless hands over endless years. She could feel perspiration beading on her forehead and gathering between
her breasts, in spite of the dense shade from the great oaks
that flanked the house on either side. Her wound itched
under its bandaging, while its center ached as though a
white-hot poker was stabbing into her.

"Are you all right?" Roan asked. "Do you need to rest
a second?"

His voice seemed to come from some distance away. She
refused to look at him or the hand he held out to her.
Through dry lips, she answered, "No, thank you."

"Especially from me, you mean?"

"Whatever you say."

"I say you'll be lucky if you don't take a header down
these steps."

She glanced back at the dog called Beau who followed
at their heels. "Keep that animal away...and I'll be fine."

"You don't look it."

She tilted her chin. "So kind of you to mention it."

"Nice," he commented with a trace of exasperation in
his voice. "So who are you now, an aristocrat on the way
to the guillotine? Or maybe a princess with a heavy date
with the headsman?"

He was so close to the mark that she swung her head to
stare at him. The quick movement was a mistake. Her grip
on the railing slipped. She gave a soft cry as she realized
there was no way she could keep from falling.

She never struck the steps. Roan swooped, and a moment
later she was swung high, then carried quickly up the last
few treads and into the house.

Air-conditioned coolness, blessed and reviving, enveloped her along with the faint intimation of lemon oil polish
on old wood and an elusive hint of spice as if from some
forgotten bowl of potpourri. The smell was so like the scent

that hung in her grandmother's villa that she felt an odd shift of déjà vu, as if she might have been in the house before.

She caught a brief glimpse of a long and rather austere hallway furnished with antiques before Roan mounted the stairs that rose on one wall. The journey upward seemed endless. Then he pushed into a bedroom and crossed to a high tester bed piled with pillows. It felt soft and incredibly inviting under her, but the movement as he pulled away his arms jarred her shoulder. She drew in her breath with a quiet hiss.

"Sorry," he said, then reached to catch the lower edges of her robe that had fallen open, closing them over her exposed legs. He straightened and stood staring down at her with a frown of consideration between his brows.

She looked away from his steady regard, letting her glance slide around the room. The walls were painted a yellow so pale that it must have been white until age and the smoke of countless fires under the marble mantel had given it its present patina. Beneath the wide chair rail with its egg-and-dart pattern was a striped paper in white, yellow and gold that seemed to echo the sunlight glowing behind the lace curtains. The bed she was lying on was of rosewood with a massive tester supported by fluted columns. The gold silk of its inset overhead was pulled taut from the sides in sunburst fashion and pinned in the center by an intricately carved cupid. The sweet, glazed face of that doll-like figure was crackled with age and painted in colors that had faded to appealing pastels.

Without meeting Roan's steady regard, she said, "I should thank you for catching me just now."

"Don't bother."

The words had a hard, tired sound. Tory felt the rise of heat to her face, partly from the knowledge that she'd been less than gracious, but also from his close scrutiny. He was entirely too intelligent, she thought, too knowledgeable about people. He saw too much, penetrated the disguises she hid behind far too easily. She closed her eyes as she lifted a hand to her shoulder, pressing her palm against the bandage. "I mean it, really. I don't think I could have stood it if I'd fallen."

"Hurting again?" he asked, his voice altering. "Doc Watkins gave me enough painkillers to last until I can fill the prescriptions he wrote for you." He fished a small bottle from his pants pocket. "Hold on. I'll get a glass of water."

His instant response to her need made her feel even less gracious and more guilty than before. She opened her eyes again in time to stare after him as he disappeared into what seemed to be a connecting bathroom. He really was a disconcerting man.

A buzzing sound came from inside that bathroom, one she recognized as the discreet signal of his pager. No doubt it signaled some rural emergency: a cow escaped from its pasture, a drifter trying to stiff the local café for his meal, or maybe a little old lady racing through town at thirty-five miles per hour in a twenty-five miles per hour zone. Whatever it was, Roan would no doubt respond.

She'd discovered in talking to Johnnie and Cal that the sheriff took a personal interest in the welfare of Turn-Coupe's citizens, that he cared about them and their problems. In turn, every person in town seemed to need his help and advice on a daily basis. Roan never seemed to mind the calls on his time, even on his days off, they all said. It wasn't just that it was his job; he seemed to get real satisfaction from helping people.

She'd heard about men with that knight-errant streak. She also knew that the basic need to be needed was a part of the mental baggage carried around by a lot of males. Maybe if she played the dependent invalid to the hilt, then Sheriff Roan Benedict might be more inclined to be her protector rather than her jailer.

In some distant corner of her mind, she knew that her attitude was self-serving and more than a little condescending, but she couldn't help it. If Roan wouldn't accept the truth, then she had to try another tactic.

She could hear water running in the bathroom. A moment later, the sheriff stepped back into the room. The crystal glass he carried looked fragile in his large brown hand. He should have appeared ridiculous, perhaps, but instead seemed amazingly competent and at ease. She wondered, briefly, just how much experience he'd had in tending females in bedrooms. Then she pushed the thought away as being as irrelevant as it was distracting.

She allowed him to help her to a sitting position and swallowed the capsule he handed her. As she passed the glass back to him, he failed to take it. His gaze was on her throat, she discovered, as if he'd been watching her swallow. Warm color flooded to her hairline as he lifted his gaze and his eyes met hers.

She held that clear, gray gaze for endless moments, trying to see past the rugged features, the aura of command, the badge of his office. She wanted to know how he thought and felt, to penetrate the normal defenses of human beings to see the man he was inside.

It was impossible.

Embarrassed that she'd tried and a little depressed and confused, she let her gaze slip away. It fell to the holstered gun clipped to his wide leather belt. A shudder, completely involuntary, rippled over her.

"It's there for your protection."

"Right. I'll try to remember that while I'm having my

stitches removed in a couple of days.'' Attack was always her defense of choice against unwanted emotion.

''I didn't start this merry-go-round you're on,'' he answered in the same even tone, ''but I intend to see that it stops, one way or another.''

''A miracle worker, are you?'' The words were husky and not quite even.

''If that's what it takes.''

Tory wished that she could believe him, that she could tell him everything and let him take care of it. To do that, however, she would have to unravel all the events that had led her to Dog Trot, would have to reveal the person she really was behind the facade of attitudes and disguises she'd perfected over the years. How could she do that when she wasn't sure who that woman was herself?

''Dad?''

The voice from the open door had the pliant, uncertain cadence of adolescence. A boy stood there, obviously Roan's son since he was almost as tall and his features so nearly identical that it was almost humorous.

''What?'' It was a second before Roan withdrew his gaze and turned toward the doorway.

''Truck coming up the drive, probably Kane. Thought you might want to know.''

Roan dipped his head in acknowledgement, then reached out in a beckoning gesture. ''As long as you're here, come meet Donna.''

The boy slouched into the room with the leggy awkwardness of a half-grown colt. His sandy hair was cut one length at chin level and his eyes were more hazel than gray. As his father laid a hand on his shoulder, he glanced at it but made no attempt to move away.

''My son Jake, Donna.''

''Hello,'' Tory said, extending her good hand. The boy

gave her a quick inspection as he took it, but remained mute. He held her fingers a bare second, as if uncertain what to do with them. Then he broke the contact and stuffed his fists into his pockets.

She tried the effect of a smile. "I'm sorry if my being here is an inconvenience. I'll try not to be too much trouble."

His gaze slid away again, though whether from shyness or discomfort because she was in a hospital gown, she couldn't tell. He said finally, "It's okay. It's Dad's idea."

"So I imagined, but still."

Jake nodded, then looked at his dad. "About Kane? You coming, or you want me to ask him to step up here?"

"I'm coming." Roan glanced at his watch. "I have to check in with the office anyway, and Donna needs to rest."

They left without another word. Tory lay staring at the light beyond the lace curtains, watching the light fabric waft in the draft from the air-conditioning and listening to the faint whistle of the cool air blowing out of the floor vents. It was so quiet, so peaceful, and so very comfortable compared to the hospital. She could almost feel her nerves unwinding, feel herself drifting into medicated contentment so great she thought she could sleep forever. She had such a sense of being surrounded by absolute security. Why was it that only Roan Benedict could make her feel that way. Why?

Kane was waiting for Roan at the foot of the outside staircase. He leaned against the sturdy end post of the wrought-iron railing in the shade provided by the big oak that had sheltered them as they played cops and robbers when they were kids. It had been a fine way to pass a long summer's day. They were a hell of a lot busier now, both of them.

Beau, fawning around Kane's feet, abandoned him without visible shame as soon as Roan came down the steps. Roan gave the bloodhound a quick pat before reaching over the dog's head to take his cousin's hand. They exchanged greetings and mutual assessments, all in the space of a few seconds.

"So how've you been?" Roan asked at last in his capacity as host.

"Fine, fine."

"And Regina?"

"Finer." Kane grinned, his blue eyes bright. "Getting bigger and more impatient every day. And blaming me for the whole thing."

Kane had changed, Roan thought. There was a relaxed set to his shoulders that hadn't been there before his marriage to Regina, and his smile was quicker and more frequent. He looked almost as carefree as he had in their teenage years when the whole gang of Benedict cousins had raced boats, played baseball, tinkered with cars, and shared secrets and half-raw fried fish around roaring bonfires on the lake's edge. Roan had little doubt as to what had brought about the change. Kane was a happy man, and his Regina was expecting their first child.

"You're not trying to deny responsibility?" Roan said with mock sternness.

"God, no," Kane said fervently. "It's all my fault, even if I did have cooperation."

"Remember that, and you'll be fine."

"So they tell me."

"Who, Aunt Vivian and Miss Elise?" It was usually the older women who gave the best advice, in Roan's experience.

"And Granny Mae. Yes, and even April, for crying out

loud, though she's never been any closer to pregnancy than helping deliver a litter of kittens.''

Roan lifted a questioning brow. ''She and Luke trying, you think?''

''I didn't ask and don't intend to, since I'd like to live to see the birth of my child,'' Kane declared with a grin. ''But we're none of us getting any younger.''

Roan replied with the grunt such a crack deserved. A small silence fell, and he filled it by offering his cousin a cup of coffee. Kane declined, saying that Regina was making lunch and if he didn't get home soon, he'd hear about it. Roan acknowledged the excuse with a wry look of masculine compassion. At the same time, he felt a twinge of jealousy. No one was cooking lunch for him.

Stepping over to Kane's truck on the circle drive, he put the base of his spine against the front fender and crossed his booted feet. The visit was not entirely social, Roan was sure; it was too early in the day for that. They had finished the polite ritual that had to be taken care of before they could get down to business. Now it was up to his visitor to state his case.

Kane was a lawyer, so used to choosing his words with care. He was also dressed for the office, in slacks and a well-pressed dress shirt. Regardless, he followed Roan's lead, propping his expensive shoe leather on one of the tall black truck tires and studying it as he spoke. ''Regina called me at the office. She said Betsy telephoned her with a story from Johnnie about you being on your way to Dog Trot with a special guest. That wouldn't be true, would it?''

Roan sighed. The Turn-Coupe grapevine was fast, but it was nothing to the jungle drum swiftness employed by the Benedict clan. He supposed Kane had a right to be concerned, however; he and Regina lived in an old Greek Revival mansion just down the road.

"If you're worried about your wife…"

"You know better than that. It's you we're worried about, your safety, that is. Well, and maybe your sanity."

"Neither is at risk. I'd invite you in for an introduction so you could see for yourself, but the trip from the hospital was a bit rough and my prisoner is resting just now."

The look Kane gave him was grim. "You have a female prisoner here in your home, a possible felon, with no security measures?"

"You're forgetting Beau." The hound, losing interest in their discussion, had flopped down onto the walk and put his head on his paws. At the sound of his name, he gave his tail a sleepy thump.

"So I was. A huge oversight. Unless she takes a notion to murder you in your bed while Beau's outside howling at the moon."

"She's not going anywhere. She was shot, damn it."

"By you, right?"

Roan agreed with a curt nod.

"I'd heard it, but couldn't believe it. Not much fun, I'd imagine, for either one of you."

Kane was silent as he held his cousin's gaze.

"No," Kane answered himself, then added. "I hope you know what you're doing."

"I have a prisoner under house arrest here until her court date. That's all there is to it."

"Except you've never done it before. You sure it's not guilt that's riding you?"

"So what if it is? She still needs help."

"And I guess it has nothing to do with Carolyn?"

Roan shrugged. The remorse over the past was unremitting, but bothered him most on Jake's birthday when he was reminded that the boy had grown up virtually without a mother. Hell, he wouldn't know how to act without it on his shoulders.

"You weren't responsible for what your ex-wife tried to do. A lot of people felt you were probably the only reason it didn't happen sooner. Besides, you saved her life." The sun caught in the iridescent strands of Kane's dark hair as he tilted his head slightly, eyes narrowed against the reflection off the truck's windows. "But that woman in there isn't Carolyn. The way I hear it, she pulled a gun on you. You were justified in taking her down."

"I'm not confusing the two, if that's what you think," Roan said, his voice blunt. "Besides, Donna never fired."

"But you don't know that she wouldn't have, given the chance."

"Maybe, maybe not. Anyway, I screwed up and the suspect got hurt. Now I'm taking care of her the best way I know how. And that's it."

Kane gave a slow nod, then glanced away as a blue jay screeched in the oak tree at the far corner of the house, warning all comers away from his territory. Roan, following the same line of sight, wondered if maybe that wasn't what he was doing, too, in his own way.

When Kane spoke again, his voice had the smooth cadence it carried when he was presenting a case. "What about the legalities? For instance, has this woman even been booked? The D.A. will expect to see charges come across his desk soon. You know what a stickler he is, almost as much as you are yourself."

Roan refused to meet his cousin's intent gaze. "It's not easy to decide on charges since she can't remember enough to answer questions. According to Doc Watkins, her amnesia may clear up as she gets better, but it could be days, even weeks. Or never."

"You're the sheriff," Kane said in dry tones. "But I still

think I'll do a little research into the acceptable standards for holding a suspect with amnesia. You may need the info, especially if she escapes or her pals manage to snatch her out of your house." He hesitated for a moment, as if he expected a response, but it didn't come. Then he added, "What about Jake?"

Roan pushed away from the truck. "You actually think I'd put him in jeopardy?"

"Not intentionally, but you'll have to admit…"

"I admit nothing. The woman upstairs is not dangerous. I'll stake my reputation on it. I'm fully aware that the men she was with may pose a threat, but I can, and will, stop them. That's my job, if you'll remember." Kane was echoing the family concern, Roan knew, and he was even right in his way. Still, it rankled that his cousin would question his control of the situation.

"You'll post extra men?"

"Cal will take the duty. He wasn't too happy at first, but he's getting more gung ho by the minute. He'll probably show up tomorrow in camouflage and with black grease under his eyes like some commando. Anything to play the hero for Donna."

"Donna?"

"My prisoner."

Kane stared at him. Then a slow smile curled a corner of his mouth. "You know something, you almost sound…"

"What?" Roan couldn't keep the snap from the voice.

"Possessive."

His answer was profane.

"Or maybe you're the one playing hero. April always said you were a sucker for a damsel in distress."

"It runs in the family, I'd say." It was a plain reference to the way Kane had met his Regina. A single mother, she'd been sent to Turn-Coupe to spy on Kane's family with her son held as hostage to insure her compliance. Kane had fallen in love, in spite of his suspicions. He'd broken quite a few laws while riding to the rescue, and even taken a bullet in a desperate rescue of Regina's son from her crooked cousin who'd held the boy. It had ended in a messy legal battle in which Kane was the prosecuting attorney. Luke's romance with April Halstead hadn't exactly been a picnic, either.

"Oh, I'll grant you that," Kane agreed with a wry twist of his lips. "But that doesn't make keeping a possible felon cooped up in your house an intelligent decision, even if she is drop-dead gorgeous."

"Johnnie again?" Roan said with resignation.

"Betsy. She got a good look at her during the robbery, if you'll remember."

"I suppose there's not much use saying that what my prisoner looks like doesn't matter?"

"Not much."

Roan sighed. He took off his hat and ran his fingers through his hair, then settled the headgear into place again. "It's just that she's so damned alone. She drives me nuts with her playacting and high-class airs and prickly, in-your-face bravado, but other times it's all I can do not to pick her up and rock her like a kid. Something is going on with her, something she's not telling, and until I find out what it is, I'm not letting her out of my sight. She's my responsibility and I'm taking care of her. Nothing else matters."

"Oh, hell," Kane said with a slow shake of his head. "That's it. You're done. You're gone."

"What are you talking about?"

"If you don't know, then far be it from me to explain it. I still wish you'd send her to the hospital ward in the Baton Rouge lockup until the judge comes back from recess. But I see that's out of the question."

Roan shook his head. "I can't just turn my back, Kane. I have to do what's right, no matter what this town, or the family, thinks about it."

"Fair enough," Kane said, clasping his shoulder. "But you know you can call on the rest of us if need be. You don't have to do this alone."

"I know." All the same, Roan realized it was unlikely that he'd be asking his cousins for help. He had been alone much too long to relish the thought of family intervention in his life or his decisions.

Kane released him, then moved around to the driver's side of his truck. With one foot on the running board, he looked back. "You heard from your dad lately?"

Kane's tone was so casual that Roan almost missed the hint of purpose behind it. As it was, he couldn't quite figure the cause. "Pop? Still in Vegas, last I heard. You know how he is, doesn't call or write, just shows up when you least expect him."

"He hasn't taken up a new hobby out there, has he? They had a special on TV the other night about the seniors who get hooked on gambling. Seems they start out with Bingo as a way to pass the time. First thing you know, there goes the grandkid's inheritance."

"Dad's not that gullible."

"I'm glad to hear it."

"You getting around to asking about the gaming boat?" Roan said to hurry things along.

"I hear the mayor's trying to speed up the vote before the opposition can get organized."

"Seems to be."

"I don't much care for that idea."

"Ditto," Roan agreed. His dislike of the operation was not a moral stance; he'd defend to the death any man's right to throw away his money in whatever fashion he saw fit. What he objected to was any attempt to weight the scales on one side or the other. He also cared who was behind the deal, since that could directly affect the level of criminal activity that went with legalized gambling. Turn-Coupe was a decent community where it was still possible to bring up kids in a sane and reasonable manner with fewer than average problems from alcohol, drugs and gang warfare. He'd like to keep it that way.

Kane nodded. "I had dinner with the D.A. over in Natchez the other night. Since the casinos were allowed, their crime rate has jumped several percentage points, mostly in armed robberies."

"The town council is supposed to hold an advisory meeting a few days from now. I could use a little backup from the legal eagles in town."

"Melville and I will be behind you. I'll see what I can do about the rest."

Melville was Kane's law partner, and his cousin's influence with the rest of the courthouse crowd was strong. "Can't ask for more."

"You don't have to." Kane settled on the driver's seat of his truck, slammed the door and leaned out the open window. His gaze met Roan's for a long moment, then he grinned. "She's really beautiful, huh?"

"Unbelievable."

His cousin laughed, then stared past him a second before returning his gaze to Roan's. "I heard Regina on the phone early this morning, talking to April. They were hatching a plan to come over and check on you. Something about a pot of chicken soup or sausage gumbo, though they thought they'd better cut down on the spices for your guest."

Roan noted that his female prisoner had graduated to the status of company. Kane definitely knew when to shift his position. "Head them off at the pass for me, will you?

Donna's still a bit too under the weather to appreciate company. Maybe next week.''

"They're having a baby shower for Regina at Luke and April's house soon. Everyone will be there.''

Roan tipped his head. "That would play well, wouldn't it, showing up with a woman in handcuffs? I don't think so.''

"With the family habit of kidnapping our women—for their own good, of course—it might be a natural. Your Donna should fit right in.''

"She's not my Donna,'' Roan answered with grim emphasis.

"Have it your way.'' Kane turned on the ignition, then pulled away down the drive. But as he drove off, he was still grinning.

6

Roan didn't return to town. He had no security schedule set up for Donna just yet, so he took the duty himself to avoid reassigning a deputy in the middle of a shift. Anyway, he needed to catch up on his paperwork, and this looked like a good opportunity.

He gave it a valiant try, shuffling papers from one side to the other of his desk that was set up in a corner of his bedroom. Every time he managed to gather his concentration, the mutter of the police scanner or jangle of the telephone scattered it again. Several times, it was Sherry, informing him in her usual gravelly tones of minor occurrences that had already been handled by his deputies. Once it was the duty officer with a question. That their dependence was his own fault, Roan knew; he kept too tight a rein on his staff. Today, it seemed like a great idea to delegate a little authority so he needn't be quite so mired in details.

The focal point of the room, the traditional master bedroom at Dog Trot, was a Civil War era painting of Roan's great-grandmother and great-grandfather of some five generations back. Roan let his gaze rest on that couple, posed with the lady seated in a brocade-covered slipper chair with a hound asleep on her spreading skirts, and her husband standing stiff and protective beside her. They looked so formal and proper that it was almost impossible to imagine them unbending enough to indulge in the activity that produced descendents. Yet indisputably they had, since nine of their eleven children had survived infancy to continue his particular branch of the Benedict clan. It just went to show, Roan figured, how difficult it was to see beneath the facade that people presented to the world.

Take Donna, for instance.

He could easily imagine her in the full skirts and low-cut bodice of an antebellum ball gown and with her heavy, chestnut hair swept up in an elegant twist. She'd fit right in at the River Pirate Ball that took place every summer. Too bad it had already been held, since there wasn't a chance in hell of Donna being around for it next year. She'd be truly stunning in anything with a low-cut neckline, as he could attest with no problem after cutting away her silk top the other night. He'd barely registered the sweetly symmetrical curves of her breasts at the time, but the memory had haunted his dreams since then.

Roan swore and sat up straighter in his chair as he realized what the images in his mind were doing to his body. It had been a while since such involuntary reactions had been a real problem; he'd learned to bury his physical needs under tons of work. He went to his office at the courthouse, handled problems, rode his surveillance routes, came home to look after Jake, slept, then went back to the office. He'd got in the habit of thinking of himself as too uptight to have much of a life, much less inconvenient sexual cravings. He'd been wrong. His female prisoner had proved that without even trying.

In sudden irritation, Roan flung down his pen and scraped back his chair. What he needed was a cup of coffee.

On his way to the kitchen, he stopped to look in on Donna. She was still sleeping, lying in such unconscious grace that it made his chest ache just to look at her. The constant hassle at the hospital must have left her exhausted. Here at Dog Trot she could finally rest. It was a nice thought, even if her comfort was not his concern.

The original kitchen at Dog Trot had been in a separate cabinlike building out back, a typical arrangement in the old days when fire danger from cooking in an open fireplace was a constant threat. Roan's great-grandfather had renovated a portion of the brick-walled raised basement for kitchen facilities when wood-burning ranges became cheap and readily available in the 1890s. Nowadays, appliances were electric but the kitchen was still in the same place, at the bottom of the stairs that led down from the rear of the main hallway.

Jake was standing at the kitchen table when Roan came into the room. He was making a man-size sandwich using Texas Toast and hunks of ham carved off the shank that Roan had brought home the day before from the barbecue place in town. Glancing up, he raised an eyebrow and waggled the knife he held in a silent offer to make another sandwich. Roan declined with a shake of his head and a smile.

"She still out of it?" Jake jerked his head with its bowl-like shag of hair in the direction of the floor above.

Roan nodded as he picked up the coffeepot. "Had some catching up to do, I guess."

"Too bad. If you wanted to talk to her, I mean."

Roan filled his favorite mug, one Jake had given him for Christmas when he was six years old. It had a cracked handle and the slogan World's Best Dad was faded, but he still liked the familiar feel of it in his hand. Over his shoulder, he said, "We talked a little."

"She remember anything else?"

"Not that she's admitting." Instead of returning upstairs, Roan took a seat across from his son at the old butcher-block table that was scarred by the mealtime gatherings of generations of Benedicts. Jake had something on his mind, he thought, and was working around to it.

"She's a cool-looking lady."

"Think so, do you?"

"Sure. Don't you?"

Roan looked up in time to catch the boy's quick grin before it disappeared behind his sandwich. "As a matter of fact," he said deliberately, "she strikes me as a bit more than cool-looking."

"Figured."

"How's that?"

"Your type—high-class, independent, got problems."

Roan looked up, startled. "I didn't know I was that obvious."

"You're not," Jake said easily as he slung his hair back from his face with a quick, practiced gesture. "Except maybe to me."

It was a typical Jake observation. He was a great kid, Roan thought, though it was a mystery how he'd turned out that way. With no more idea of how to raise a child than a billy goat after Carolyn had left, he'd done the best he could, calling often on the wise older women of the clan and of course his own parents who'd lived at Dog Trot back then. Other than that, he'd applied the general Benedict theory of what turned kids into decent adults: regular work and responsibility, discipline when needed, free rein outdoors, and lots of love.

In self-defense, he asked, "So what's your type? Cyndi Frazier?" Cyndi was the daughter of the local horse trainer and breeder, and Roan had noticed that Jake usually found an excuse to make the Saturday night livestock auction in town. He showed every sign of having inherited the Benedict talent for zeroing in on the best-looking female in the crowd.

"Aw, Dad," Jake said in disgust.

"You know that actions count as much as looks, though?"

"Yeah, sure. Cyndi's neat, likes animals as much as I do."

Roan let it go at that. Jake had had firsthand experience with the concept, after all. His mother had been beyond lovely, a fragile, almost fey girl who looked as if life with its problems would be too much for her. They had been, too, or very near it. Though to give her credit, Carolyn hadn't abandoned her son so much as made a gift of him to his father. Jake was a Benedict, she'd said, and deserved to be brought up as one. Roan was grateful to her for that, in spite of everything.

Now and then, he wondered if he should have provided a substitute mother for his son. Jake didn't seem to feel the lack, though he was quiet sometimes after talking or visiting with Carolyn. Other than going to school and to church on Sundays, his life was spent with animals. He'd been tending them since he was seven or eight, with the help of his granddad in the early days while Roan's dad was still living at Dog Trot, by himself since Fredrick Benedict hit the road. Right now, he had a menagerie of seven beef cows, a nag that he and his friends rode on hot summer days; a bunch of laying hens, two goats, a hog that ate the table scraps, and the pack of hounds that was Dog Trot's claim to fame. Profit from breeding, training, and selling the hounds went into his college fund. He wanted to be a veterinarian like his cousin, though Clay had veered off into nature photography in the last couple of years. The local horse doctor had been making noises about retiring. If Jake could take up his practice, he'd be able to stay in Turn-Coupe. The long line of Benedicts living at Dog Trot would remain unbroken.

Jake swallowed a bite of sandwich and topped it off with a deep draught of milk. As he considered his next bite, he returned to the previous subject. "Now that this Donna Doe is here, how long is she staying?"

"I don't know—as long as it takes."

"She doesn't look like a crook to me. You really charging her?"

Roan had explained the situation in detail, since Jake would be exposed to it. Now he gave the boy a straight look over the rim of his cup, before he said, "Not me, personally. It's up to the court."

"But you're the one who'll put her in jail."

"She was involved in a crime. The evidence is all there."

"Right. It's your duty." The tone of Jake's voice said he'd heard it before.

"That's about the size of it."

Jake gave him a straight look. "What if your gut feeling says she didn't do it?"

"My feelings don't come into this."

"Yeah, right."

"I mean it," Roan insisted. "My job is to uphold the law, not to twist it to fit my own ideas of what's good or bad, right or wrong. Once you start down that road, there's no place to stop."

"Suppose she's innocent like she says? Suppose she's had all this bad stuff happen to her, and now you're going to make it worse by seeing she does time? How are you going to feel if you find out when it's too late?"

"It doesn't matter how I feel. The law protects the wel-

fare of the many over the good of the few. It's not a perfect
system, but it works most of the time. The court may turn
her loose, either because the D.A. decides she was under
duress or because he thinks he can't get a conviction, but
she'll have to go through the process.''

His son watched him for a long moment. Then he shook
his head so his hair fell into his eyes, hiding his expression.
''Tough on you.''

''Yeah,'' Roan said in tight agreement as he heard the
understanding in his son's voice. ''There are parts of this
job I really don't enjoy.''

''But some you do? Like maybe taking care of this
Donna Doe?''

The point at last: Jake wanted to know why he'd brought
this particular prisoner into their home. Roan answered, ''It
could have its compensations.''

''Like I'm supposed to think you'd take advantage?'' His
son made a rude noise. ''Anyhow, she seems pretty helpless
to me. You'll have to fetch and carry for her, help her
change clothes, maybe even help her take a bath.''

The rush of goose bumps across Roan's shoulders and
upper arms at the suggestions was as uncomfortable as it
was unexpected. This was getting out of hand. With deliberation, he said, ''The main idea is to keep her secure and
comfortable. Though I agree that it will be extra work for
us.''

''Us?'' Jake knew his father well, it seemed; his gaze
was suddenly wary.

Roan inclined his head. ''Cal will be here while I'm in
town, starting tomorrow, but I don't expect him to play
nursemaid. What do you think we should do?''

''Call Aunt Vivian?'' The suggestion was hopeful.

Roan shook his head, a slow movement he emphasized
with a steady grin.

"Aw, Dad."

"Just think of her as you would any of your injured animals. See she has something to eat and drink, make sure she gets her antibiotics, and keep her company if she's needs it."

"I notice you didn't mention the bath."

"You notice too much," Roan said with asperity. "Especially for your age."

His son grinned, then a cunning light appeared in his eyes. "If she was really one of my animals, I'd call Clay."

"I don't think so," Roan said. Clay was not only unattached and passable in the looks department, he had a wild-swamp-thing air about him that drew the women like honey. He'd caused quite a stir, recently, at book signings for his tome of photographs showcasing the ecology of Horseshoe Lake and its swamplands. Besides that, he was a thoroughly nice guy. Too nice, in fact.

"Come on, he'd get a kick out of it."

"I don't doubt it," Roan drawled, "but we'll keep this little chore in the immediate family. She's only one woman. We can handle it."

Jake heaved a gusty sigh. "I guess."

A small silence fell. As it stretched, Roan felt the rise of disquiet inside him. It was an instinct he'd learned not to ignore. The source wasn't that hard to find. Setting his coffee cup on the table, he said, "All jokes aside, son, this is serious business. The guys that were with Donna may come sneaking around when they find out she's here."

"I'll keep my eyes open and the doors locked."

"Fine. But it may not be enough." Though outdoor exercise had made Jake strong for his age, he'd be no match for a grown man with experience and ruthless inclinations.

"Cal will be in charge of the firepower during the day,

and you'll be here at night," Jake argued. "I don't see the problem."

"I don't really expect any," Roan said candidly. "If I did, I wouldn't risk it. These guys got scared off from the hospital, and they strike me as being followers, unlikely to risk another try unless ordered to do it. But I need you to be aware of the danger."

The boy polished off his sandwich and followed it with the last of his milk while his gaze remained fixed on the view outside the kitchen window. Giving his mouth a final swipe with his napkin, he asked, "I'm not grounded, am I? I can still ride my bike?"

Jake loved the woods and lake near the house, often hiking or riding his dirt bike through narrow trails to favorite haunts or the houses of friends and relatives. Roan nodded. "If you're careful. And if you let me or somebody else know where you're going and when you'll be back."

"You got it."

Roan thought he'd impressed his son with the seriousness of the situation, enough for reasonable safety, at any rate. Now all he had to do was convince Donna.

Tory knew Roan was up to something the moment he appeared with her dinner. His manner was too smooth and pleasant, for one thing, and he was much too solicitous. She accepted the tray he offered with its roasted chicken, green salad and iced tea, but refused his offer of more pain medication. She thought she was going to need her strength and a clear head.

He made no particular move while she ate, but stood leaning against the bedpost, talking in a desultory way. She encouraged him as much as she could without being obvious about it. The Southern slant of his tales was fascinating in its way, and listening passed the time with less awkwardness than she might have expected. She relaxed by slow degrees, until she could almost believe she'd been mistaken about his intentions. Then he sprang the question.

She choked on her tea, and went into a coughing spasm. When she could speak again she asked, "Do I what?"

"You heard me. I offered to help with your sponge bath before bedtime."

A sponge bath. Lying supine and vulnerable while the sheriff ran a warm, wet cloth over her naked body in that most intimate of rituals. She hadn't even allowed the nurses at the hospital to do that.

"I don't think so."

"It's a perfectly reasonable suggestion," he said, a defensive inflection in his voice. "You may not be able to manage, and there's no one else to lend a hand. Unless you'd prefer Jake."

"What I'd prefer is doing it myself, thank you very much," she said plainly. "Though what I really want is a nice, hot shower and shampoo."

He shook his head. "Doc Watkins will kill me if I let you get your bandage wet."

"I don't see why he has anything to say about my bath."

"You don't know Doc then. He's old-fashioned, thinks patients should be kept in bed and waited on hand and foot for ages, that modern hospitals push people out the door too soon. His instructions are for sponge baths over the next few days."

"And you're supposed to see to it."

"Not exactly. But lending a hand is the least I can do after bringing you here."

His voice carried a trace of mockery, she thought, as if he dared her to accuse him of wanting to see her naked. She looked away, unable to sustain his steady gaze. "All the same, I'm having a shower."

"Then I'll have to join you."

"Not in this life!" She swung toward him once more.

"Can't have you getting light-headed and falling again. You could hurt yourself."

He was teasing her, she thought, and enjoying it. She tilted her head. "It will only take a few minutes, and I'll be careful."

"What about your shoulder?" he objected. "There's no way you can shampoo your hair."

"I do have one good hand, you know." She raised her uninjured arm and waved her fingers at him to prove the point.

Roan's gaze rested an instant on the scabs left by her rope burns. Then he laced his long fingers together and reversed them, stretching them out before him until his knuckles popped. "I have two good hands. Does that make me twice as good at it?"

"That would depend," she said.

"Yeah? On what?"

"Your experience?" She was appalled the instant the words left her mouth. The last thing she was interested in was his past history with other women.

A look of diabolical yet smoky enjoyment rose in his gray eyes. "My experience may be limited, but I think I can manage. Let's see now, how would I go about it? I'd start, I think, with your face, nice and easy, so I wouldn't hurt your bruises." His gaze rested on her cheekbones a moment then moved slowly downward over the curves under her faded hospital gown. "From there, I'd glide my nice, warm, soapy cloth over your neck and throat, and down to your—"

"That's all right," she said hastily. "I'm sure that one body is pretty much like another when it comes to the bathing process."

"Wrong." He chuckled, a low sound of real amusement. "Yours is nothing like mine."

He had a point. "Well. But still."

"You doubt my ability?"

"It's just that—I don't know!" This mood change of his was so disconcerting that she hardly knew what she was saying.

"No? Where was I then? He pushed away from the post and stepped to take a seat on the edge of the mattress. Reaching out, he tucked the obscuring swath of her hair behind her ear then let his fingers trail along the curve of her neck and down her good arm to her hand. Picking it up, he continued, "I did your face, but what's next? It would be a shame to miss a single spot. I should use the cloth to lather every inch of skin, your fingers, your palm, wrist, arm...."

Tory could feel her heartbeat quicken, was aware of heat gathering inside her, pooling in the lower part of her body. She watched with lowered lashes as he followed the path he spoke of, slowly stroking each fingertip, then over her palm to the throb of the pulse in her wrist. Avoiding the healing scabs there, he trailed upward over the sensitive bend of her elbow to her upper arm, letting his soothing touch linger at the turn of her shoulder and full curve of her breast directly below.

Abruptly she came to her senses. Catching his hard wrist, she said, "Stop. Go much further, and you'll get your uniform wet."

He studied her while the amusement died slowly from his face. Finally, he said, "I can change the uniform."

"But not the man inside it."

He pushed abruptly to his feet. "I'll run you a bath."

It was a victory of sorts, but somehow it didn't feel like one. She waited until she heard the water filling the tub, then pushed upright and adjusted her nightwear. She was seated on the edge of the bed, patiently waiting, when he emerged from the bathroom a short time later.

Before she could speak, he said, "I'll wait out here. Just in case."

She'd been ready to make the same suggestion. That it wasn't necessary was such a relief she felt weak with it. That was, possibly, the reason she wobbled as she stood up.

"Can you walk?" he asked, moving forward a quick step to take her arm.

"I've been managing the hike to the bathroom for days," she said sharply.

He made no comment, but neither did he release her. They moved into the large, old-fashioned bathroom furnished with a claw foot tub. He eased away only after he'd seated her on a wicker stool beside it.

"Everything you need is laid out except the shampoo," he said. "I really don't see how you'll be able to manage that."

It wouldn't be smart to push too hard, Tory thought. "This is fine. Thank you."

He nodded, then retreated into the bedroom, though he left the heavy oak door ajar. She heard him settle into the brocade-covered armchair that sat in a corner.

The water was hot and heavenly. The slanted back of the old tub was just right for lounging, far more ergonomically designed than most modern tubs. She lay back with her eyes closed and the water lapping around her waist while tension melted from her like ice under a tropical sun. She'd needed this more than she realized, she thought. The only thing that would make it better was a water jet or two to swirl the water around her. She could easily spend the night here except for the certain knowledge that Roan would be checking on her if she didn't make bathing noises in short order.

The soap provided was strictly utilitarian but served the purpose. The urge to use it first on her hair, after all, was strong, but she resisted. Johnnie had helped shampoo her hair at the hospital a couple of days back, and she'd have to be content with that for a little longer.

It had been so long since she'd felt really clean that she soaped and rinsed once, then started over again. As she glided the wet bath cloth over her neck and shoulder, she could not help thinking of the gentle yet electric slide of Roan's hand over her skin. The sheriff had a sensual streak it seemed. That was intriguing, to say the least. She wondered what else he was hiding behind his badge and his notions of duty and honor.

It didn't matter of course. She wasn't interested in Roan Benedict, the man, just as he wasn't interested in her beyond her needs as an invalid and her welfare as his prisoner. She was another duty that he was attending to as efficiently as he took care of everything else.

It could get depressing if she let it.

She sat upright, setting off a tidal wave of soapy water, then started to push to her feet. Somehow, she put too much weight on her bad arm. Pain surged through her shoulder. Her elbow buckled and she toppled to the side, then her knee slipped on the slanted porcelain bottom of the tub. The splash she made as she went down was like a fountain. She felt water soak her bandage and aching wound. She choked out an imprecation, but there was no time for decent recovery. Immediately, she scrambled up and reached for the towel that lay on the wicker stool. She jerked it toward her.

The door crashed against the wall. Roan stood framed in the opening. "What happened?" he demanded, then stopped. The rich oak-brown of his skin took on a deeper stain.

Tory could feel her own color rise slowly from somewhere under her towel to flood her face. And she saw the sheriff's gaze follow it with burning attention. For long seconds, neither of them moved. Then Tory snatched the towel closer so it covered her from neck to knees. "Nothing's wrong. I just had a little problem getting up."

"You fell."

The look she gave him smoldered. "If you say I told you so, I swear I'll…"

"It's a little late for that." His voice was as grim as his face when he stepped toward her. Thrusting one arm under her knees and the other behind her back, he lifted her from the tub. He swung around, then carried her into the bedroom where he placed her on the bed. He dried her with movements so fast that she barely registered them, then reached for the top sheet and jerked it high, letting it billow upward before settling over her. The instant it touched her, he snatched away the damp towel she was still clutching. And there she was, naked under the sheet.

She'd known he'd be efficient.

He was also wet across the front of his uniform shirt so that it molded the sculptured ridges of his chest in dark-brown splotches. She'd tried to warn him.

"I might have known you'd need help getting out of the tub," he said as he stood over her with his hands on his hips. "It's too high off the floor."

"I didn't ask for any." It was the best answer she could think of at the moment.

"I should have been there anyway."

She frowned, disturbed by the shadow of pain deep in his eyes. Whoever said that he took his work seriously knew what they were talking about. "It wasn't your fault, okay?'' She struggled up to support herself on her good elbow. ''You warned me. I didn't listen. End of story. Except that my bandage is wet. I suppose you'd better call Doc Watkins so he can kill us both.''

He stared at her a moment longer, then a slow smile tugged one corner of his mouth. ''Not on your life. I can change it. If you don't tell him, I won't.''

''Deal.'' She stuck out her hand in an offer to seal the bargain. He took it briefly. Then he turned on his boot heel and left the room.

He returned seconds later with a first-aid kit that he placed on the bedside table. Seeing what he intended, she swung her feet off the bed and, holding the sheet to her, pushed upright.

''Careful,'' he said. ''We don't want any more damage than you have already.''

Of course they didn't, Tory thought in grim agreement. His goal was to get her well so he could put her in prison. Hers was to heal and get out of this antiquated house in this one-horse town. To do that, she needed Roan Benedict but, afterward, she could do without men in her life. She didn't need a stiff-necked sheriff with a hard heart and gentle hands.

''This may hurt,'' he said, as he began to pull away the tape stuck to her skin.

''We've been here before, if you'll remember,'' she said with irony, then added, ''You've had emergency medical training, haven't you.''

He gave her a brief glance as he peeled away a tape strip and started on another. ''How did you know?''

''The way you act, I suppose, as if it's all in a day's work.'' What she meant was that his manner now, in the midst of the semi-emergency, was noticeably less personal than it had been before the bathtub fiasco.

"The parish has a First Response team, police, firemen, voluntary emergency personnel who are first on the scene at fires, accidents, and so on. I'm usually one of the first people there anyway."

She didn't doubt it. "So how many lives have you saved? Besides mine, of course."

"Oh, dozens."

The answer was in bland exaggeration, as if it were a joke, but Tory wasn't fooled. The tips of the sheriff's ears were red, an indication that she'd embarrassed him again by forcing him to admit his skill. She rather enjoyed the sense of power that gave her, perhaps because she was so powerless otherwise in this situation. She said, "Tell me about some of them."

He shook his head. "Too boring."

"Let me be the judge of that."

His expression was still wary, but he complied, probably as an alternative to the strained quiet. As he talked, he stripped away the wet bandaging and replaced it with a dressing that was considerably lighter and more useful.

He'd pushed the sheet lower on her chest so that he could apply tape. The movement exposed the curve of her breast until only the rose-colored aureole of her nipple was covered. She felt decidedly exposed, but tried to ignore it. No doubt he was used to naked bodies if he made a habit of tending wounds, she thought; he'd certainly seemed to take in stride the glimpse he'd had of hers earlier.

She fell silent, but so did he. Glancing at him, she saw that his gaze was focused on the skin near her armpit, just under the side of her breast.

"This looks like an old scar," he said, meeting her gaze with a look of perplexity as he touched the faint line that curved from under the shallow fold where her breast met her chest wall.

What he'd found was something most men of her circle would have accepted without question. She'd have expected, with his Southern gentleman mentality, that Roan would have been too polite to show his curiosity, much less comment, but apparently not.

"It is a scar."

"It hardly shows at all," he continued. "The surgeon did a good job."

He continued to trace the path of the old pale incision from the edge of the sheet to the middle of her underarm area. The ticklish sensation brought on a ripple of gooseflesh that also hardened her nipples so their peaked outline became plain, mere inches away from his questing fingertips. She reached to shove his hand away so she could replace her sheet.

He didn't resist, but met her gaze while his own slowly darkened from curiosity to something more personal, and more vital.

He wanted her. The impulse was rigorously controlled, but plain in his widened pupils and tense features.

Her breath caught in her throat. Her fingers were suddenly nerveless so she fumbled as she pulled the sheet up and tucked it in above her breasts.

"It was cosmetic surgery, wasn't it?" he asked, his tone carefully neutral.

He wasn't going to give up. She swallowed, tempted to avoid the subject by pretending complete failure to remember. But she'd stretched her luck already with this man. It wasn't worth the risk. With an edge of bravado, she said, "Breast augmentation, at a guess."

"A boob job?"

"Crude, Sheriff. Lots of women do it these days, and most men seem to appreciate it."

"You mutilated yourself to please some man?"

She lifted a shoulder. "Who knows? Though isn't bigger always better in the male view?"

"Not in mine," he said with finality.

"Really." Her voice held dry disbelief.

"My dad always says much more than a handful of anything is pretty well useless. I figure he's about right."

"Now there's a thought," she drawled, in spite of the heat in her face. It was also a revelation, but she didn't intend to let him know that.

He watched her a considering moment before he said, "You can't have been very old or the scar wouldn't be so faded."

"Probably still in high school," she answered, giving him the truth without actually indicating remembrance.

"Jesus," he said under his breath.

She tended to agree with that comment. The surgery had been a fashion trend among her classmates, a way of aping their mothers, joining the world of the sophisticated and the beautiful. She had always been a part of the popular crowd, ready to go along with the latest fad, anxious to keep up with her friends. They were all she'd had those long years in boarding school. Of course, Paul Vandergraff had considered it an excellent idea. Anything to keep her happy and out of his way.

"I suppose I did it to feel better about myself," she said finally, "like most women."

"More attractive?"

"Something wrong with that?"

He stood and picked up his first-aid kit. "You're a beautiful woman, and must have been a pretty girl. I can't believe you ever needed artificial help." His voice deepened to a velvety pitch. ''You don't have to be perfect. The rest of the world sure isn't.''

It was an unexpected insight from a country sheriff. It was also a little behind the times. Voltaire had claimed that perfection was attained by slow degrees, requiring the hand of time, but that had been in another era. Most people today believed that youth and beauty were perfection and time demolished them. She could defend herself by claiming immaturity as her excuse, but that hadn't been all of it.

She had wanted attention. It hadn't mattered whether it came from her stepfather, her friends, or from the boys who had started hanging around the boarding school gates. She had craved it and would have done anything to get it. She'd outgrown that impulse, she thought, though it was impossible to be sure.

Roan was watching her through narrowed eyes, his gaze assessing. Critical. But what did she care what he thought? He wasn't a woman. He'd never been faced with the choices she'd had to make or the expectations.

''What are you staring at?'' she demanded in acid tones. ''Wondering if I've had a face lift, too. Well, I haven't. At least there are no scars to show it.''

He shook his head in slow negation. ''I was just wondering if it's possible to find the real you under all the pretension.''

She sincerely hoped not. The real woman was a confused bundle of nerves, unsure what to do with the next few days of her life, much less the long years ahead. Not that she'd expect him to understand, of course. He didn't know her fear that she would turn out like her mother, locked away until she died of despair because no one loved her for what she was inside instead of what she looked like and what she owned.

Tory took a deep breath, then exhaled slowly as she said, ''I doubt it.''

Roan hefted his first-aid kit, then turned and walked to the door. With his hand on the knob, he said quietly, almost to himself, ''Now that's a shame. A real shame.''

7

The click of the light switch and sudden brightness dragged Tory from a sound sleep. She opened one eye. Roan stood just inside the room, looking freshly shaved and pressed and more alert than any man had a right to at that hour of the morning. She gave a heartfelt moan and reached to drag the sheet over her head.

"Coffee time," he announced in grim good humor as he stopped beside the bed.

"This is the torture part, right?" she said from under the cover. "You think if you wake me every half hour, I'll break down and tell you all I know."

"It was only a couple of times during the night."

She flipped the sheet back to stare up at him. "You've got to be kidding. You marched in and out at least every hour."

"It's my responsibility to see you get your antibiotic," he answered in tones of supreme reason. "Besides, I had to check on you."

"To make sure I was still here, I suppose." As if she were going anywhere any time soon.

"And to be sure you weren't bleeding from where you

jarred your wound, that you haven't developed a fever—or fallen in the bathroom again.''

That reminder didn't exactly thrill her. ''Thank you very much,'' she said in muffled tones as she closed her eyes and turned on her side to burrow into her pillow. ''I'm fine. Now go away.''

''Exactly what I'm about to do.''

An odd panic rose inside her. She was quiet long seconds as she fought it back. Then she opened her eyes again. ''You're leaving?''

''I have a job to do. But don't worry. Jake will be here, and so will Cal. All you have to do is yell if you need anything.''

''I'm not worried,'' she said automatically. It was a lie. She felt as if she were being deserted. And she didn't like the immediate realization of just how dependent she was becoming on this man.

''Good. Then you'll be all right.'' The coffee cup he held rattled on its saucer as he set it on the bedside table.

She eased to her back again so she could see his face. His features were closed in, giving nothing away. He seemed different this morning, however, more reserved and official. It was a definite change from the man who had padded barefoot into her room during the night, with slumberous eyes, tousled hair, and wearing only a pair of jeans low on his hips. She liked that one much more than this buttoned-up lawman with his badge on his pocket and his weapon on his hip.

After a moment, she asked, ''When will you be back?''

''Hard to say, depends on what's going on downtown. I'll check in from time to time.''

No doubt he would. But that didn't do much to help her feelings. ''You have to go, I suppose?''

He tipped his head, studying her. "That almost sounds as if you'll miss me."

His voice had an edge, she thought, as if he might suspect her of putting on another act. Whatever she had gained in the way of belief the day before was apparently gone this morning. Veiling her gaze with her lashes, she answered, "I didn't say that."

"No, you didn't, did you?"

"Please," she said, sighing as she ran the fingers of her good hand through her hair, "I'm not a morning person like you. I can't manage word games this time of day."

"I'm a morning person only after a full a pot of coffee," he returned. "Speaking of which, you'd better drink yours before it gets cold."

With supreme effort, she pushed up to a sitting position. Roan moved to support her and put the extra bed pillow behind her back while she settled more comfortably. His courtesy made her feel ungracious. She murmured a polite thank you, adding as she took the cup he held out to her, "I do appreciate this, and all the rest during the night, even if I am grouchy about it."

"Not to worry. Anyway, that'll be Jake's problem today."

So it would be, she thought as she brought the coffee to her mouth. Somehow, playing the brave, beleaguered heroine with only the teenager for audience didn't promise nearly as much interest. Of course, she'd vowed to be the injured and helpless female around Roan, but that plan had lost its appeal. The bathtub incident had revealed unsuspected dangers to it.

"I think I ought to warn you about getting too friendly with Cal."

The polite, even way he put it made it seem almost normal, but the taut line of his lips and determined stare at a point ten inches above her head gave him away. "Do you indeed? What are you afraid of, that I'll seduce him?"

Roan dismissed that with a quick gesture. "What I'm saying is, Cal could be susceptible. You don't want that complication."

"You're telling me I should be on guard against him, then."

"I'm telling you not to try any tricks. Running them by me is one thing. Doing it with Cal might be something else again."

She wanted very much to ask if he wasn't susceptible, at least a little. She didn't quite dare since the answer might not be good for her ego. At the same time, she had an almost uncontrollable urge to ruffle his neatly combed hair, loosen his tucked-in shirt, something, anything, to make this automaton more like the man she'd glimpsed now and then, the one who smiled and joked and made her feel better. It was almost as if he had two personalities, she thought; she wasn't the only person good at alternate identities.

As she remained silent, Roan went on. "Cal will be stationed outside the house. He shouldn't bother you under normal circumstances. Jake will bring your meals and medicine, don't worry about that. He's dependable, for his age."

"Good for Jake."

His gaze rested on the clamped set of her jaw a second. "I suppose I should ask if you had any revelations during the night?"

"Revelations? Oh, you mean about who I am."

"Who you are, name, age, phone number, father, mother, brothers and sisters, anyone or anything else that might be useful."

She pretended to search her mind before slowly shaking her head. "No one and nothing."

"Not even a glimmer of a memory of the kind you almost brought back for Johnnie?"

She'd wondered when that slip would turn up. It seemed best, however, not to act as if it were a big deal. "Nothing."

"Too bad. If you think of something, or have any other problem today, let me know immediately."

He reached into his pocket and drew out a card, dropping it on the sheet beside her. Of quality white stock, it carried the contact numbers for his office in dark-blue lettering. She glanced at it, thinking it was just like the man who carried it: cleanly designed, straightforward, and without a shred of ostentation.

Speaking almost at random, she asked, "Are you expecting some kind of trouble?"

"I'm saying be careful, no more, no less. Cal's a good man. If he weren't, he wouldn't be on my team. But he needs no distractions. He's here for your sake, yes, but he's also looking out for Jake."

The grim tone of the sheriff's voice carried a warning. He had arranged matters to prevent his son from being endangered by her presence in his home, and if she did anything to change the situation, the consequences would not be pleasant. She hated to think, then, what Zits and Big Ears might do if they found out that she was alone at Dog Trot with only a boy and a single deputy as guards.

It was a strange sensation, thinking of someone else's welfare. She wasn't used to it because there'd never been a need; she had no one to care about or protect. More than that, the majority of the people she knew thought only of their own comfort and convenience first as a matter of course. Any altruistic inclinations were satisfied with money; they didn't sacrifice their comfort, would certainly never compromise the safety of their children.

"Maybe it would be best," she said slowly as she watched the steam rise from her cup, "if I went with you, to your jail. After all."

He was quiet so long that she risked a glance at him. A frown rested between his brows as if he were testing what she'd said, looking for reasons. As he met her gaze, he said, "I don't think so. Anyway, I'll be back in the middle of the afternoon, if not before."

He turned and walked toward the door. She let him get halfway across the room before she called out, "Roan?"

He paused, turned slowly to face her again.

"Why are you doing this? I mean, keeping me here in your house, taking care of me?"

"I thought we settled that."

"Did we? I remember something about unsuitable quarters at the jail and an irate hospital administrator, but that doesn't really explain it. Not many people would put themselves out this way."

"It's nothing."

"You take in all the people you shoot, is that it?"

His lips tightened. "There haven't been that many."

"But I'm not the first. Why?"

"Maybe I feel responsible. Maybe I don't want you on my conscience if it turns out, by some off chance, that you're telling the truth. Maybe..."

"What?" She was gripping her coffee cup so hard her fingertips were numb, though she couldn't make herself relax.

"Maybe I'm a sucker for a hard-luck story and a pretty face."

She laughed; she couldn't help it. The idea of him being

soft in any way was simply too far-fetched to credit. "Not likely."

"Fine, what do you think of this?" he said, his gray eyes narrowing, "I just like the idea of keeping you as my private prisoner. I'm waiting for you to get well before I tell you exactly what I want with you."

Something in his voice touched off a deep, internal shiver. What was it Cal had said? *Roan is the law in Tunica Parish*—Yes, that was it. But he didn't mean that literally. Did he?

"Sure you are," she said in derision. "More than likely, you get paid more this way."

His smile held no humor. "You'll have to wait and see, won't you?"

He swung toward the door once more as if he'd had enough of the conversation. It closed behind him with hardly a sound.

Disturbance lingered in Tory's mind as she went back over what they'd just said and also the events of the night before. Something was there, some intimation of truth, but she couldn't quite grasp where it began or ended.

She couldn't believe Roan Benedict was seriously attracted to her, a woman apparently everything he most despised. If he ever married again, it would be to some squeaky-clean country girl who wore Peter Pan collars, taught Sunday school, and knew ten ways to make meat loaf. He'd have no use for a poor little rich girl who couldn't make up her mind who she was and what she wanted, even when not pretending amnesia, and who had studied Cordon Bleu culinary arts so she could communicate with her stepfather's chef.

No, Roan's only purpose was to keep her secure; it wouldn't look good to the electorate if he lost a prisoner, especially if she escaped or was abducted from his own home. He didn't trust her, didn't buy her story. He'd be considerate enough while she was under his roof, but that was merely to prevent her from making difficulties for him by trying to leave.

But what did his reasons matter? The result was the same; she was safe for the moment.

A wry smile curled one corner of her mouth. It was peculiar, when she thought about it. She felt more protected than she had in years while shut up here at Roan's house, when her greatest fear had always been that she'd wind up like her mother, locked away in an expensive rest home for the loony well-to-do. For a brief instant, she pondered the idea that she might have hit on the reason her mother had failed to protest her fate. Maybe she'd felt more secure in her rest home than outside it with her husband and daughter and fast-living friends. But no, that was impossible. Wasn't it?

Tory drained her coffee cup and turned to set it on the bedside table. As her gaze fell on Roan's card, she picked it up and sat tapping it against her bottom lip. So the gentleman thought he had her number, did he? Well, she also had his, as he'd soon discover. He'd made a serious error in bringing her here; he'd opened the door to his private life. She was getting better by the minute, her body stronger and her mind clearer. She was sure that she could worm her way into his home and family until he found it impossible to either indict her or return her to Florida. He would be her refuge and her shield for as long as she needed him. And afterward could take care of itself.

Jake brought her breakfast a short time later. As he plopped the tray across her lap, she waved him to a seat on the end of the bed. "Have you eaten? Join me, why don't you?"

"I—yeah, I already ate," Jake said, wiping his hands on

the legs of his pants and looking as if he might break and run.

"Stay and talk with me, at least. I'm tired of staring up at the dumb-looking cupid in the tester."

The expression on the boy's face retained its wariness, though he flicked a glance up to the ornament that secured the swath of heavy gold material above them.

"It's supposed to be old, the cupid, I mean. My granddad from back before the Civil War brought the bed all the way upriver from New Orleans. Lots of things were kind of dorky back then, but I guess they liked them that way."

"Very likely," she said, impressed by his matter-of-fact acceptance of the Victorian heirloom. "Actually, I was wrong to call it dumb. It's a nice enough cupid, or would be if I had something else to do besides go eyeball to eyeball with it."

"I could maybe bring you some magazines," he offered, flinging a glance at the door at the same time in a clear indication that he saw the errand as a means of escape.

"That would be wonderful. What kind do you have?"

"Huh, that might be a problem…"

Tory hid a smile as she watched the dull-red color creep up his neck. "Not girlie magazines?"

"Lord, no! Dad would ground me for life. Just stuff that wouldn't interest you." He lowered his voice to a near mumble. "Livestock magazines, fishing, bow hunting. Like that."

"Guy-type things."

Jake agreed, then his expression brightened. "But some of my grandmother's old magazines are still up in the attic. She used to read about gardening, sewing, decorating, stuff like that."

"Much more my type of…stuff," Tory assured him.

"Be right back," he said, and whisked himself out the door.

She watched the opening where Roan's son had disappeared for long seconds. Then she shook her head with a wry smile and turned her attention to the tray he'd brought her.

The food was surprisingly good, slices of a wonderful smoked ham served with fluffy scrambled eggs, wheat toast and blackberry jam that tasted of homegrown fruit. She'd have preferred a half a grapefruit and an English muffin, but was in no mood to be picky. It was possible that she needed the protein to rebuild her strength, anyway, though she might have to hit the gym when she was well again.

Roan was right about his son; Jake was dependable. He brought the magazines he'd promised and piled them on the bedside table after wiping the dust that coated them with his shirt. They were practically collector's items with a fair amount of entertainment value in their dated pages. When he had gone, taking her empty tray with him, she flipped through one or two. Nothing seemed to hold her interest long, however, maybe because she was keeping one ear open for the sound of a car on the drive. After a while, she let the magazine fall open on her chest and closed her eyes.

By the time she woke, a variety of cabin fever had set in. She lay staring at the smirking cupid above her for a few minutes, then sat up and reached for her robe. Roan had not said, directly, that she couldn't leave her room. House arrest implied that she had the run of the premises as long as she didn't try to leave, now didn't it?

The house was quiet. The floor shifted occasionally with an arthritic creak of aged wood as she moved over it. There were few signs of life: no voices, no radio, no TV. The clutter of modern living, the headphones and remotes, newspapers and full wastebaskets, boxes of tissues and glossy photographs, were conspicuously absent. In spite of the cool air that streamed through the floor vents, she felt almost as if she were in another century. The antique pieces that lined the walls and Oriental rugs that made islands of color along the polished river of the hallway floor would have been just as perfect a hundred years ago as they were now. The mellow light that came through the French doors at either end of the hall must have fallen just so for generations. It was a strange sensation yet comforting in its aura of permanence. She wished, for just a moment, that she could hold on to it. And she wondered if this was what Roan and Jake felt when they thought of how long Benedicts had lived and loved within the walls of this place they called home.

She looked into the formal parlor to the right of the front entrance. With her bare toes sinking into the rug, she stared up in appreciation at the ornate cornice moldings and carved center medallion that supported the crystal chandelier. Years of relentless summer sun had faded the heavy drapes at the windows but had not dimmed the luster of their silk. One of the chairs had threadbare corners on its brocade seat as if it were a favorite; still the room felt unused, as static as a museum. The little things that might have made it more inviting were missing, the potted plants, table scarves, interesting bibelots or memorabilia. Apparently, this household of men thought they were just fine without them, but Tory fairly itched to bring the place to life. That was one thing she was good at, decorating strange surroundings to make them more welcoming. She'd had plenty of practice, after all.

As she moved back out into the hall, she glanced through the glass of the entrance doors. A patrol car was parked on the drive in the shade of the huge oak. Her heart thumped in her chest before she realized that it must be Cal's unit, as Roan called the police vehicles. For a single second, she'd thought the sheriff was back.

She saw no sign of Cal, however. He must be patrolling the grounds, or else had taken up a post in the cool breezeway provided by the carriageway under the house. Given the heat that flowed through the old, wavy glass, she could hardly blame him. Of course, it was also possible that he'd stepped inside downstairs to cool off.

She turned sharply at the thought, raking the corners of the hall with her gaze. Nothing moved. No uniformed man emerged from the shadows, no ghosts of former residents floated down it length. Only tiny particles of dust danced and gleamed in the air she had stirred with her movement. Her small laugh ended abruptly. This creeping about in a strange house was making her jumpy.

A dining room lay on the opposite side of the hall. She glanced in, but saw little of interest. Beside the door, however, was a speckled mirror from the Directoire period. It wasn't the beauty of the gilt frame that caught her attention, however, but her own reflection. In the clear light, she could see how wild she looked, with unkempt hair, shadows under her eyes, scraped cheek and a yellowish bruise on the edge of her jaw. It was a wonder she hadn't scared off the occupants of Dog Trot, she thought. Still, concern for one's appearance was supposed to be a sign of returning health, wasn't it? In that case, she must be getting better by leaps and bounds.

Three bedrooms other than her own took up space on the second-floor level. She identified one as Jake's from the rock music poster and photos of hounds at field trials. The other looked as if it might have belonged to his granddad. The master bedroom was easy to identify as well, due to its back location with lake view, expansive size, massive

antique bed and armoire, and the ancestral portrait that
topped the marble fireplace. The police scanner that sat on
the desk in the corner was also a dead giveaway. It was a
handsome room in a traditional, utilitarian manner, as modern as it needed to be, but not an iota more. Tory didn't
bother stepping inside. What the man who occupied it was
like was all there in plain sight.

At the end of the hall was a stairwell. Since most of the
activity she'd heard while in bed had come from that direction, she expected to find the kitchen at the bottom, and
she wasn't disappointed. Next to it was a family room.
Here, at last, was all the sprawling masculine comfort that
she'd half expected to see upstairs; the leather armchairs
and sofa, braided rug, and big screen TV.

Jake looked up from where he lay in an overstuffed
lounge chair playing a handheld video game and watching
a music video on TV at the same time. Surprise widened
his eyes. He scrambled to his feet, even as the big bloodhound lying on the rug made a growling sound deep in his
throat that warned her not to come any closer.

"You need something?" the boy asked.

"I— Lunch, maybe?" She tried the effect of a smile to
go with the spur of the moment request. It didn't seem
politic to admit she was snooping.

"Sure." He set aside his game and reached to give the
big dog a reassuring pat. "What do you want?"

"What do you have?" she countered.

"Don't know, but we can look. I'm hungry, too."

She was grateful, at that moment, for the insatiable appetite of youth; it certainly made things much easier for
her.

The dog followed them into the kitchen and flopped
down near the door. As Jake stuck his head in the refrigerator in quest of inspiration, Tory sank down onto one of

the ladder-back chairs pulled up to the scarred butcher-block table that centered the kitchen. It felt good to rest; she'd used more of her small store of strength than she'd realized.

The floors in this part of the house were of red brick, handmade, she would guess, and glazed in recent years with some type of protective finish. The old bricks were cool and slick under her feet, though the surfaces were uneven. She rubbed her toes back and forth in the grooves where they were grouted together as she watched Jake take out cheese, peaches and what appeared to be a whole ham.

"You're pretty good at this," she said. "You must be used to taking care of yourself while your father works." She tried to keep her tone light, hoping the boy would think she was just being polite, not trying to pry information out of him.

"I guess they think I'm old enough now."

"They?"

"Dad and my grandfather. I think I mentioned that Pop lived with us until a couple of years ago."

"Yes, of course, the traveling man." Tory said with a whimsical smile.

"Yeah, well, sort of." Jake shook back his hair as he took out a knife and began to carve generous slices of ham. "Pop was pretty broke up when Grandma died six years ago. It was a long time before he was interested in anything except taking care of me. Then he bought an RV. Now he's seeing the world—or at least the United States."

"Sounds like fun."

He glanced at her with a grin. "He especially likes it out West, like Nevada, Utah. He promised to come back and get me before school starts again. We'll head for the Grand Canyon, stop where we want along the way, see what there is to see. You want a pickle?"

Tory shook her head in answer to the tacked-on question. At the same time, she felt the slightest twinge of envy. The highways in South Florida were packed with RVs, especially in the winter as visitors made their escape from the cold up north. Funny, but she'd always thought more about the cramped living space than the freedom. It was one more thing on which to adjust her thinking.

Jake slathered bread with mayonnaise, piled ham on it, stacked fresh tomato and cheese slices on top of the ham, then added a second piece of bread. He slid the plate in front of Tory with a flip of his wrist, then brought a huge glass of milk to go with it.

"Anyway, we're not just going to look at the canyon when we get there," he went on as he turned to make his own sandwich. "We're going to hike from rim to rim. You start real early in the morning, spend the night in the canyon."

The touch of male bravado in his voice made Tory smile, as did his valiant attempt not to let his excitement show. "That will be a change from Turn-Coupe, won't it? I suspect nothing much happens here in the summer."

"Oh, I don't know," Jake said grandly. "A houseboat blew up at the River Pirate Days Festival last year. That was cool."

Cool. Right. "Was anyone hurt?"

"Not too bad," he answered as he sat down and pulled his own snack in front of him. "Dad and Cousin Luke jumped in the river and pulled out a bunch of people, so no one was killed. Oh, and a bunch of yo-yos kidnapped a woman out on the lake last summer, too. Luke's wife, she is now. Sometimes we have to run treasure hunters off our land, too, especially around festival time when people start thinking about pirate gold."

"I can see I was wrong," she said gravely. "You have

a lot of thrilling things going on. But what was that about pirates?''

''River pirates, not the ocean kind. They're supposed to have buried the stuff they took from travelers back in the old days, gold, silver, jewelry and so on. We don't allow anybody to come around digging for it, though. It leaves holes all over the place, and lord knows the dogs scratch out enough already.''

Tory was almost as fascinated by the boy's willingness to chat now as by his tale of buried gold and other adventures. He'd apparently decided that she was acceptable company, or else he was bored with being alone. Had she perhaps found an ally? If so, forging a bond was a major priority.

She asked, ''Have you looked for this treasure? Is it really there?''

''We used to dig all the time, me and my buddies, when we were kids.''

Tory drank from her milk glass to hide her smile. Jake wasn't exactly Methuselah. ''But you didn't find anything?''

''Few old square nails and horseshoes. Then we decided it just wasn't enough sugar for a dime.''

''What?'' She looked up him in perplexity.

He met her gaze, his own surprised. ''One of Pop's favorite sayings. Means not enough return for the work.''

''Oh. Well, why not make it easier? They have great metal detectors these days.'' She'd seen people with them on the beach all the time.

Jake shrugged with a trace of red in his face. ''It's just not that much fun anymore. They say old Mike Fink buried his treasure in the Indian mounds down by the river. We've played on them all our lives, picking up arrowheads, pieces of pottery and bits of bone. A couple of years ago, some guys came out from LSU in Baton Rouge. They told us the hills were burial mounds, and sacred to the Native Americans, sort of like digging up the Benedict family graveyard. Seems best to just let the mounds be.''

It was an endearing attitude. With more warmth than she'd expected to feel toward Roan's son, she said, ''I once read that pirates buried their gold near dead men so the ghosts would protect it. Guess this Mike Fink must have been pretty smart.''

''Dad says he was just so lazy he took the easy way out, if he ever buried anything at all. He figures the old coot spent it as fast as he got it.''

That sounded like Roan. ''You mentioned a festival?'' she asked.

The boy's face brightened. ''It's really neat. Luke is one of the pirate leaders. They come up the river on a boat and invade the town, grab prisoners and hold them for ransom. Just pretend, of course, but Luke said I could be a pirate on his boat next year.''

Tory tipped her head with a crooked smile. ''Wouldn't be someone you'd like to kidnap, now, would there?''

''Who me?'' he asked, his eyes a little too wide.

''Do you have a costume? You'll need something really neat, with a wide sash and a sword.'' Something to impress the girl he apparently wanted to kidnap.

''A bunch of stuff like that's up in the attic. I used to drag it out for Halloween.'' He shot an appraising glance over her. ''You could probably wear most of the women's costumes, long dresses and hats and stuff, though they're kind of small. Grandma used to dress up every year for the festival ball, and my mom, too, sometimes. I have a picture of her looking like Cinderella or something.''

''A recent one?'' She was frankly curious to know how

long Roan had been divorced, though she wasn't sure why it mattered.

Jake gave her an odd look. "No way. She left when I was two."

"That long ago." She couldn't imagine leaving a child that age behind.

"It wasn't her fault. She was real depressed. The shrink she went to told her she was stifled, or something, that Dad was part of her problem and she needed out of the marriage. So she took off. Now she's got a new husband and lives in France."

Tory wasn't sure which was more startling, that Roan's wife had opted out of marriage so easily or Jake's casual manner about it. He'd been much younger than she was when her own mother died, of course, so had fewer memories and regrets for what could have been.

In tentative tones, she said, "Sometimes a divorce can be a good thing."

"Yeah," Jake agreed. "My mom had a rough time growing up. Her mother was sick all the time, and her dad never kept a job more than a month or two—too high-tempered and set on doing things his way. He ran around with other women, too. One night he went out and never came home again. Her mother didn't have much of a way to make a living, so after a while she went to live with a brother. My mom didn't like it there, so she asked my dad to marry her. Then when she was pregnant with me, her mom died. That same year, they found her dad in the woods, nothing but a heap of bones—people figured he got too friendly with somebody's wife and the husband fixed the problem. Anyway, Mom got worse after I was born. They called it post-something."

"Postpartum depression," Tory supplied.

"Yeah. She just never got over it, not for years."

Tory was silent as she digested this bit of family history. Somehow, it seemed odd to think of Roan with a woman who had such mental scars. He was so strong and secure within himself; surely he would have chosen someone similar? Of course, he might not have realized how disturbed Jake's mother was; clinical depression could take many forms, going unrecognized until it was too late.

"People don't get to choose their parents or the kind of life they have as a child," she said quietly. "It's what they do afterward that counts. That's when they get to make life the way they want it to be." It was a lesson she'd learned the hard way, and was still learning.

Jake dipped his head in agreement. "That's what Dad says, too."

It was nice to know she and the sheriff agreed on something.

They finished their snack, and Tory helped Jake put the dishes in the dishwasher. She was replacing the pickle jar, when he said, "So, about the clothes in the attic, you want to look? Might be something up there you could wear around the house here."

She lifted a brow, then stuck a model's pose while holding the pickle jar in one hand. "You don't like my outfit? It's hot off the Paris runways."

"Yeah, and so becoming, too," he quipped. "Especially the way it makes you look broad across the back."

She twisted her head to glance over her shoulder. "Now that you mention it, I suppose there's room for improvement."

"Also room for a herd of elephants," he muttered.

"I heard that. But I don't know if I'm up to climbing any more stairs than it takes to get back to bed."

"Even after resting and refueling?" Concern overlay the hopefulness in his eyes that were so like his dad's.

"I don't know. It's the first time I've been up very long, you know."

"We'll only stay a minute then."

His tone was so coaxing that she didn't have the heart to refuse. Besides, she thought it might be worth the extra effort to keep him friendly. It bothered her to be so calculating, but she had a lot at stake.

The costumes were wonderful. Carefully enclosed in a huge armoire placed along one wall of the open attic space and smelling of mothballs, they spanned more than a century and a half. There were elegant evening gowns with whalebone-stiffened bodices and wide skirts that would require a crinoline, straight-skirted walking dresses, long-tailed men's coats and even a smoking jacket with velvet lapels. Nothing was fake or reproduced; the satins had the burnish of age, the lace was handmade; the men's shirts were collarless, and the stiff material of the trousers had faded streaks along the creases.

It was a fascinating glimpse into the lives of the Benedict family. Tory could easily imagine Roan and his cousins sneaking up to the attic on rainy days to touch the sumptuous fabrics and play dress-up, or a mother during the hard times of the Great Depression searching among the gowns for something to re-style for a daughter's special dance. Though she asked Jake about different items, he seemed to have little idea who had worn them or for what events. It made her sad to think that his grandmother had known, perhaps, but the knowledge had been lost with her passing.

Jake soon lost interest. He wandered away from the clothes to a collection of large wood-and-leather trunks that lined the wall near the stairs. Tory followed, looking over his shoulder as he lifted the lid of one of them. It was filled with cans and tin boxes painted a dark olive green.

"Rations from the Second World War," he told her.

"You're joking." She leaned closer to make out the faint white lettering on the sides of the cans in the dim light from the exposed bulbs overhead. "Why do you keep them? Surely they aren't edible?"

"This stuff is nearly indestructible." He picked up a can, throwing it up and catching it in his palm. "I don't know that I'd eat the meat ones like the beef stew, but my friend Teddy and I opened a can of chocolate cookies one time. We didn't get sick."

Tory made a face, though more to see his swift grin than in disgust. Moving on along the line of trunks, she asked, "What else is in here?"

"Papers, lots of paper," he answered as he lifted another lid. "Letters, receipts, farm records like the sales slips on cows and horses bought at auctions, or supplies and machinery from when Dog Trot was a working farm. It's sort of interesting to see how cheap things were seventy or eighty years ago."

"Or longer," Tory murmured as she saw the date on the top letter of a bundle that lay in the trunk's tray.

A collection of framed photographs left sitting on top of an old dresser next to the trunk drew her attention. She glanced over them, the children in school clothes or posing with football helmets or in karate *gi*s, young men and women enjoying picnics and vacation outings, all with similar facial shapes and large, expressive eyes. Obviously, the Benedicts had strong genes.

One photograph in particular caught her interest. She picked it up, wiping the dust from the glass to see more clearly. It showed three young men standing beside a stock car that looked like an awesome classic Plymouth Super Bird in Plum Crazy Purple. The one in the middle was definitely Roan, though he appeared leaner and more open-faced, barely twenty, if that old. The companion on his right had darker coloring with a hint of Native American in the height of his cheekbones. An engaging grin tilted his lips, but the expression behind the intense blackness of his eyes hinted at a steady flow of thoughts both clandestine and unsettling. The man on Roan's left had more refined features, and stared at the photographer with a gaze in which confidence and intelligence mingled so thoroughly that it bordered on arrogance. This third man was dressed in a fireproof driving suit and carried a bright-yellow helmet under his arm, though the other two wore jeans and jackets with emblems on the pockets.

Jake, moving to peek over her shoulder, said, "That's Dad with Kane and Luke, back when they spent a summer on the NASCAR racing circuit."

"Who'd have ever thought?" she murmured.

"Right," Jake answered with humor in his voice. "The old man has a wild side that shows up now and then."

"So I see." Tory couldn't help smiling at the picture the three men made together. Young and full of life, they appeared ready, even anxious, for the challenge of the race that was obviously about to begin. Pride, self-reliance and conviction in their ability to win was in every line of their bodies. Vitality seemed to flow from them, along with a hint of reckless audacity. They knew who they were, those three. They also knew what they wanted and would stop at nothing to get it.

They looked like great guys to know. Too bad she wouldn't be around long enough to find out. She sighed a little, as she reached to replace the frame.

It was then that she heard the scrape of a footstep behind her. A voice boomed out from the head of the stairwell. *"What the hell is going on up here?"*

8

"Deputy Riggs!"

For one brief moment, as she'd caught a glimpse of the uniform, Tory had thought it was Roan standing near the stairs. A large part of the shock in her voice was for the discovery that she was disappointed it wasn't him.

"I've been looking everywhere for you two," Cal Riggs said with a frown. "I was about ready to send out an APB. The sheriff wouldn't have been happy about that."

The one time she'd seen Roan angry, on the night she was shot, had been more than enough. She said hastily, "We were just looking for something else for me to wear."

"You must be feeling better. It's funny I wasn't told about that." He tipped his head to one side as he waited for an answer.

"Funny how?" she asked with a trace of irritation.

"I'm responsible for you. I need to know where you are at all times."

"Lighten up, Cal," Jake recommended as he stepped closer to her. "You found us, didn't you?"

The deputy turned toward Roan's son. "No thanks to you, boy. This wouldn't have been your idea, now would it?"

Tory couldn't let Jake get in trouble for trying to help her. "It's my fault, really. I was bored with staying in bed, and decided to find something more exciting."

"Were you now?" Cal narrowed his eyes.

He'd taken her remark, she saw, in an entirely different way from what she'd intended. "Well, it is quiet, you'll have to admit, not to mention pretty deep in the boonies."

"Something wrong with the that?"

Now she'd offended him, the last thing she wanted. Jake also looked less than pleased with her. She needed a way out of this situation, and the one that came to mind wasn't entirely fake. Putting a hand to her head, she swayed a little where she stood. "Oh. I really don't feel well. So dizzy. All at once. I need to…lie down."

"I knew you were overdoing it," Cal said, starting toward her.

"Jake, please?" She reached out to Roan's son in a strategic move to forestall the deputy. Jake played up beautifully, taking her hand and draping her good arm across his shoulders, then putting his arm around her waist as if supporting fainting damsels were an everyday affair. He was going to be quite a ladies' man one day.

"Here, let me," Cal began.

"I've got her." Jake made clearing motions with his free arm as he began to walk her toward the narrow stairs. "You go ahead, help catch her if she starts to fall."

It was a fine plan. It worked, too. In a few short minutes, Tory was back down on the main floor and ensconced in her bed once more. She tugged down her short hospital gown and tucked it under her thighs before slipping out of the robe and handing it to Jake. He took it, then helped her pull up the sheet.

"You think you need Doc Watkins?" Cal asked from where he hovered in the doorway.

"No, no," she said hastily. "I'm fine."

"Maybe I should contact Roan, let him decide."

"No, really, it was just the heat."

"Maybe, but it's my hide he'll nail to the barn door if I let anything happen to you."

"Please, I know when I need a doctor," she insisted.

She might as well have saved her breath. Swinging toward the hallway, the deputy said, "I'll call from the patrol unit."

"Jerk," Jake muttered under his breath as they heard the front door slam.

"Interfering idiot," Tory said at exactly the same time.

Their eyes met and they laughed. It was a rare moment of pure agreement.

Jake sobered first. "He thinks you're something, you know."

"The deputy?"

"Good old Cal. I saw him watching you."

"Oh, come on!"

"Promise." He crossed his heart, though there was a twinkle in his eyes. "He wanted to carry you down here in his manly arms. No telling what he might have done if you'd been dressed even half decent."

"Good thing I wasn't then," she said tartly.

He ducked his head so his hair swung over his face. "Yeah, I was thinking about that. We didn't find anything for you to wear, but shorts and T-shirts are pretty much the same whether they're made for guys or girls, aren't they? I could let you borrow some. That's if you wouldn't mind that I've worn them."

The offer was an honor, and she knew it. "I wouldn't mind at all. In fact, I'm grateful you thought of it."

"No problem." His grin was brief. "I'll see about it

right now. I mean, you might rest better in something less…drafty.''

She smiled at that teasing comment. ''You're really very thoughtful.''

''Nah,'' he said as he moved toward the door. ''Just trying to help.''

Tory stared at the door as it closed behind him. She liked Roan's son. She liked him a lot.

The black shorts Jake brought were a decent fit; the ''Kickin' Country Y106'' T-shirt was bright red and somewhat roomy, but that made it easier to pull over her bandaged shoulder. Still, the effort to get into them made her wound ache and took the little strength she had left. She thought about taking a pain capsule, but opted for plain aspirin instead.

She was drifting off when she heard Roan's car on the drive. Minutes slipped past, and he didn't put in an appearance. He must be talking to Cal, she thought, or else had come in the back way, through the kitchen, and stopped to question Jake. Since he wasn't, apparently, concerned enough to come and see about her, she made herself more comfortable and relaxed with a sigh.

She was almost asleep again when the bedroom door hinge gave the small creak that signaled someone had opened it. The now familiar electric charge she felt in the atmosphere told her it was Roan.

Tory didn't feel like being put on the defensive yet again. She didn't want to see disapproval in his face, or have more rules set out for where she could and couldn't go in the house. She kept her eyes closed and breathed in as deep and even a rhythm as she could manage.

The cloth of his uniform rustled as he moved closer. She could almost feel his gaze moving over her, coming to rest on her face. A small shiver of sensual awareness threatened, and she controlled it with strenuous effort. When was the last time she'd been so attuned to a man? She couldn't remember, wasn't sure she'd ever felt such a strong connection. Not that it meant anything, of course. It would be hard not to be supremely conscious of a man on whom she was so dependent just now. Once she was up and around again, the feeling would go away.

She half expected him to say something, put out his hand to wake her. He didn't, but neither did he move away. The minutes stretched and so did her nerves. Her heartbeat increased, pounding against her chest. It was all she could do not to keep her lashes from quivering.

Then she heard him turn, heard his footsteps retreating. The door closed behind him.

Tory opened her eyes and stared at the far wall while her pulse slowed to normal again. It was a long time before she slept.

It was Jake who brought her dinner. Padding along behind him was the bloodhound, Beauregard. As Jake placed the tray on her lap, the dog reared up and put his huge feet on the bed and gazed at her plate as if starving.

''Down, boy,'' she commanded hopefully as she shrank back against the pillow. ''Good dog, get down now.''

The big animal only wagged his tail with his tongue lolling out.

''Jake?'' She didn't look at the boy for watching the dog to be sure he wasn't going to clamber up on the bed. ''Make him stop?''

''Down, Beauregard,'' Jake said casually.

The dog looked shamefaced, then removed his paws and settled to the floor. Tory turned a suspicious gaze on Roan's son. ''I thought that monster canine stayed outside.''

Jake shrugged. ''He does, most of the time. Dad gave

old Beau a flea bath and let him in because he thought he might be company for you.''

''I'm sure.'' It was far more likely that the dog was meant to help keep her confined to her room since Roan knew she was nervous of him.

''Aren't you going to eat?''

There was an odd note in the boy's voice, as if he were trying to be offhand and not quite able to carry it off. He was eyeing her tray with expectation, as well, though his nostrils flared as if he were trying not to breathe too hard. Tory glanced down at the plate he'd brought her. It appeared to be country fare: mashed potatoes with onions, boiled green cabbage, corn bread, and a large helping of something she couldn't identify.

''I don't know,'' she said with foreboding as she indicated the mystery meat. ''What might this be?''

''Chitterlings.'' His shrug was elaborate. ''Us backwoods boonies types eat 'em all the time.''

''Chitterlings,'' she repeated, while dark suspicion revolved in her mind.

''You got it.''

''And what, precisely, are chitterlings?''

''You mean you've never eaten any?''

''I can't say that I have.''

''Well, after the Civil War, see, all us poor folks down here in the South had to learn to do without. Hog meat was popular because pigs could run free in the woods, eat acorns and things like that. But we didn't have anything to waste, so we learned to eat the whole hog. If you know what I mean.''

''Hog's head cheese,'' she said wisely, since she'd run across that in France as well as at a soul food restaurant in New York.

''And chitterlings, which are made from the—''

"Let me guess," she interrupted as she saw the gleeful anticipation in his face. "Intestines?"

"I was going to say guts," he replied with relish. "But whatever."

She gave him a dangerous smile. "And who cooked this culinary masterpiece?"

"Dad, of course. He does most of the cooking around here—except when one of the church ladies gets to feeling sorry for us bachelors and brings over a chicken casserole or a pound cake."

"I see. Thank you very much, Jake."

"Welcome," he said cheerfully, and turned to leave. *"Bon appétit!"*

Bon appétit, indeed. She was being had, she was sure of it. She ate the cabbage and potatoes, but gave the chitterlings to Beau, who had remained behind after Jake's departure. The bloodhound seemed to appreciate them, though Tory shuddered as she watched him eat.

It crossed her mind to get up and go see what Roan and his smart-alecky kid were having for dinner, since she'd be willing to guess it wasn't chitterlings. The only thing that kept her from it was the disinclination to give either of the wise guys the satisfaction.

Breakfast next morning consisted of a bowl of grits.

"Well, grits grow on these bushes about as tall as your knee, the best variety, that is," Jake said when invited to explain the origin of this latest dish. "Though I've heard about grits trees that grow so tall down around New Orleans they have to pick them with ladders. I've never seen one of those, of course, since I've never been more than ninety miles from Turn-Coupe in my whole, entire life."

"Right." Tory forced a smile in response to the folksy, cornpone humor in his voice. "I could have sworn grits were some kind of corn."

"Yeah? Well, we grow ours on bushes. We have to get down on our knees and pick each one of those little bitty grains off. Talk about hard work! But it's worth it, don't you think? We do love our grits, out here in the backwoods. I hope you enjoy yours."

Wallpaper paste would have been more delicious. Tory had seen grits on breakfast buffets at fine hotels throughout Florida, and knew for a fact that they were made from hominy, which came, in turn, from corn. They were usually served with real butter, and often with jelly. The bowl of them that made up her breakfast had no salt much less anything else to make them palatable. She tasted them, then put her plate on the floor for Beau who had spent the night in her room. At this rate, he'd soon be fat, but she was starving.

She waited until Roan left for town and she heard Jake go out the back. Stepping out of her room, she moved to the front door and peered through the glass until she'd located Cal, sitting in his patrol unit reading a newspaper. Then she made her way quickly to the kitchen. There, she scrambled two eggs, made toast, and sat down at the table with her plate and a huge glass of orange juice. As she crammed down the food, she kept watch out the back window. She could see Jake, just barely, through the trees. He had someone with him as he fed the hunting hounds down in the pen, a friend she thought, since the visitor looked about the same age and straddled a dirt bike as they talked.

As she put the dishes from her hurried breakfast in the dishwasher, she noticed pots and pans left stacked in the sink. She made dishwater and scrubbed them, then dried them and put them away. Afterward, she wiped down the cabinets and the fronts of the refrigerator and other appliances. Feeling virtuous, and amused at herself for the conceit, she started back upstairs toward her room.

She'd taken only a couple of steps when she heard the sound of not one dirt bike, but two. She reached the kitchen window in time to see Jake head out along a lakeside trail with his buddy. It was nice to see him get away for a while; still, it left her alone with Cal. Funny, but she felt like calling him back.

She was so at loose ends with nothing to do with herself, no place to go and zilch to occupy her mind. At home, she might have painted with watercolors or picked up a piece of needlework, or taken a boat out on the water, but here there was nothing. At the same time, her appetite still wasn't completely satisfied. She often ate when she was bored or upset and it didn't seem to matter that she knew the reason; the compulsion pushed her anyway. Rummaging in the refrigerator and freezer, she came upon a container of chocolate ice cream. She scooped a serving into a bowl, then took it outside to the brick-floored porch just beyond the kitchen door that was shaded by the overhang of the second-story porch.

Nothing happened, no sirens went off, no one seemed to notice or care. She had escaped, at least for a few minutes.

Settling on the porch swing, she enjoyed the shade while she gently pushed herself back and forth with her toes. It was hot and quiet, the only sound the buzzing of bees in the overgrown kitchen garden at the edge of the brick terrace that stretched beyond the porch. Farther away, on the other side of the barns and through a small stand of cypress trees, she could see the blue-black glint of Horseshoe Lake. The water seemed to beckon, as it did when she was on Sanibel.

The annual trip to the island for the winter and spring had always made her wild with excitement. She'd loved the big, rambling old place there that had been built by her Bridgeman relatives, her mother's grandfather back in the twenties. Paul Vandergraff had torn that house down and erected a slick, modern villa. It was one of many things she held against him.

Dog Trot reminded her of that original Sanibel house, now that she thought of it. It had the same spreading porches, same air of grace, and yet the solid strength that would allow it to weather whatever storms came its way.

It was too bad the lake was so far from the house here at Dog Trot, though. It would probably seem much closer if the view was more unobstructed. Maybe she could suggest to Roan that he cut a few trees? She sighed with a slow shake of her head. That probably wouldn't go over too well coming from his prisoner.

She wondered how deep and wide the lake stretched, but it was farther away than she wanted to walk just now. Besides, the hunting hounds were down there, and she didn't want to set them off. That would bring Cal running, no doubt, and he might feel it necessary to end her moment of freedom.

As she sat enjoying her creamy treat, she experimented with holding the bowl of ice cream with the hand on the injured side of her body for a second or two. The weight and grip caused a pulling sensation and slight ache, but no excessive pain. She was truly healing. Doc Watkins had been pleased with her progress when he'd dropped in the evening before, though she'd tried to prevent him from discovering the extent of it. Her strength was returning a little more every day. She would be well enough to go soon, though she was no closer to an answer on how to deal with Harrell. She couldn't seem to make her brain grapple with the problem.

Behind her, there came the sound of fast breathing. She stiffened, while her heartbeat accelerated to warp speed.

It was the big bloodhound that came trotting from behind

the swing and across the porch. Good old Beau, with his face like that of a woeful old man and his big nose that could sniff a sock and find the person who'd worn it among a million others.

"Beauregard, you big, dumb mutt, you nearly scared me to death," she scolded.

The dog stopped and sniffed the air, eyed her and her bowl thoughtfully and then approached. She sat perfectly still, since she was half afraid the least movement on her part would bring on a growl like an alarm. Though she'd been feeding him, she didn't really trust him not to take a bite out of her if it crossed his mind. He was, she thought, supposed to be guarding her and Jake; she'd heard Roan instructing him in his duties in a fashion only half playful before he left for work this morning.

The snuffling sound of the dog's breathing increased as he moved closer. He swiped his large, pink tongue around his lips with a tremendous lapping. He edged nearer.

Tory's breath caught as the dog's moist, panting breath fanned her fingers. Then he dropped his head, hunched his powerful shoulders, and slurped at the melted remains of ice cream in the bowl that she held in her hand.

Tory had some idea by now of Beau's intense appreciation for food, still she smiled as she watched him polish off the ice cream, chasing the spoon around in the bowl until the last gooey drop was gone. Then he turned his attention to her fingers, licking them one after the other until he decided the job was done. Plopping in a pile of bones and loose skin at her feet, he settled his massive head between his paws and closed his eyes.

Tory wiped her fingers on her shorts with a wry grimace then echoed the dog's sigh as the quiet settled around them and the hazy heat of the morning soaked into her tense muscles. Peaceful, it was so peaceful here. She couldn't remember when she'd ever been so relaxed.

After a while, the heat grew oppressive. She flapped at the neck of her T-shirt, but it didn't help. Perspiration gathered at her hairline. It dampened her shirt around her bandage, causing an itch that she couldn't reach. At the same time, she began to feel self-conscious, with an uneasy tingle between her shoulder blades as if she were being watched.

Tory turned her head, staring around at the woods that encroached on the barn and one side of the house, and the thick undergrowth that carpeted the ground in their shade. Anything could be hiding there, or anyone. She felt exposed. The house behind her suddenly seemed more a refuge than a prison.

Bending, she reached to run her fingers over the short, silky smooth hair of the dog's big head. "Good dog, good Beau, time to go inside, don't you think?"

She was whispering, though she didn't quite know why. It wasn't too surprising, then, that the bloodhound didn't move except to lift heavy eyelids so his forehead wrinkled.

"Really, old buddy, old pal, let's go. Don't you want to head inside where it's nice and cool? You can sleep in my room, if you want."

The dog didn't budge, even when she pushed at him with one foot. He was so big that he left her little room to step over him without tripping, especially since her stiff shoulder affected her balance.

"I promise, Beau," she wheedled, leaning to scratch behind his ears. "Come on, boy, move it. Hey, you can sleep anywhere you like. I'll even let you nap on my bed if you'll just let me get up."

"Now there's an offer I wouldn't refuse if I was in his place."

She whipped around to see Cal standing at the corner of

the house. He rested one shoulder against the old bricks of the raised basement while he hooked his thumb through a belt loop of his uniform pants. How long had he been standing there? She wished she knew. She glanced toward the woods again before she spoke, "I have a feeling Beau thinks he's on duty."

"No doubt of it. Want me to move him for you?"

"Could you?" she asked.

The deputy looked at the dog and gave a piercing whistle. "Up, Beauregard."

The big animal gave him a look of apparent disgust, but heaved himself to his feet and ambled off a yard or so.

"Thank you," she said, her voice cool as she slid from the swing. For some reason, she wasn't particularly grateful.

"You seem to be getting around better today," Cal noted as he watched her.

"A little." She wished, suddenly, that her underwear had not been discarded at the hospital along with the rest of her blood-soaked clothes. Her breasts felt entirely too conspicuous under the loose T-shirt.

He stepped forward, indicating the kitchen door with a wave of his hand. "I was about to go inside for something to drink, myself. Shall we?"

It was couched as a courtesy, but his manner implied that he didn't trust her to remain outside without supervision. He was within his rights, of course, still, walking ahead of him back into the house made Tory feel more like a prisoner than at any time since she'd arrived at Dog Trot.

In the coolness of the kitchen, he said, "It would be mighty nice if you'd stay and talk to me."

She almost refused, but thought better of it. It was foolish to let irritation stand in the way of gaining knowledge, and she thought it might be easier to get answers from Cal than from Roan.

Finding an opening wasn't easy. The phone rang three times while they were pouring iced tea from a pitcher in the refrigerator. One call was for Jake; the other two for Roan. He was apparently out of the office, and might or might not be on his way home. Cal took care of one questioner, but the other got a promise that Roan would call if he came by the house.

"He never has a minute's peace," she said as Cal replaced the receiver for the last call.

"True, but that's the way he likes it."

"I don't believe it."

Cal shook his head. "Folks know he has no wife or young kids, so few obligations at home. They're used to the idea that he's always available, always ready to drop everything at a second's notice and solve their problems for them. It's become a way of life."

"There's such a thing as delegation."

"He could do that, if he would. But he knows people want to see the Main Man coming when they've got trouble. That's Roan."

"It doesn't leave him much of a life."

"It *is* his life."

It sounded bleak to Tory. Full, maybe, but bleak. "As long as he keeps it up he's not likely to find time for anything else."

"What's it to you?" the deputy asked. "Don't tell me you're interested in the sheriff."

"Hardly," she answered, though she could feel heat rise in her face. "I just don't have much else to think about, I suppose."

"I don't notice you asking about the rest of us around here. Jake, for instance. Or me."

"I was glad to see Jake doing something this morning besides hang around the house," she said without emphasis.

It was a moment before the deputy answered, as if he were considering forcing the issue he'd raised. Then he said, "Don't worry about Jake. He seems to get a kick out of having you around."

"Meaning?"

"Never had much exposure to feminine company, you know. Because of the divorce."

It was good that he didn't mind having her around, not that it mattered. "His mother doesn't have him to visit her?"

"Not so you'd notice. The boy takes after his old man too much to suit her, reminds her too much of past mistakes. At least, that's the way I hear it."

"That's a terrible thing to do to a child." She heard the pain in her voice, but could do nothing about it. There had been times when she'd felt her mother had been happy to see her off to some new school or visit.

"I guess we all do the best we can."

It was an unexpected viewpoint from Cal. It made her wonder. "Did you know her?"

His smile was wry. "She was my cousin by marriage."

Tory frowned in concentration. "But you're not a Benedict. Are you?"

"Heaven forbid! I mean she was kin on my mother's side. Hey, we're all related around here. So be careful what you say, or you may find yourself in more trouble than you know what to do with."

It was good advice. She decided to take it. Changing the subject, she asked about the progress in finding Zits and Big Ears. They'd been reported twenty miles away in one direction and thirty in another, he said, but with no real leads on either sighting. The sheriff's office was proceeding on the assumption that the two were hanging around the vicinity for a reason, and were taking every precaution based on that assumption. What that meant, exactly, Tory didn't know, but it sounded impressive.

Since he had her interest, Cal gave her a rundown on his accomplishments and hobbies, including a couple of unlikely fishing tales. It was less of a hardship to listen to him than she'd thought; he had an unsuspected comic streak and even a certain degree of humility beneath his outward show of confidence. By the time he finally left the kitchen to make his rounds, she was halfway resigned to having him around, after all.

It was the middle of the afternoon when Roan finally returned to the house. Tory was lying on the den sofa. She had a magazine spread out beside her. She flipped a page, now and then, when she wasn't staring at the ceiling and trying not to think about what was going to happen when she could no longer pretend to be an invalid. The first she heard of Roan was the bass rumble of his voice and Jake replying as they spoke outside the kitchen door.

They talked quite a bit, those two. It was possible that would all change as Jake got older, more into the teenage rebellion stage. For now, they seemed to genuinely like and appreciate each other beneath the surface of their daily routine. It said something for the sheriff that he was able to maintain that close relationship, given his work routine. Not that she was interested in that part of his life, of course, or in the least inclined to look for good qualities in the sheriff as well as his deputy.

A short time later, she heard the kitchen door open and close. By the time she looked up, Roan was standing in the doorway. He appeared as tired as she felt, Tory thought.

The lines around his eyes had deepened in the last few days, as if his nighttime vigil with her had taken its toll.

"How are you feeling?" he said in polite inquiry.

Her smile was rueful. "Tired of sleeping, but not quite energetic enough for anything else."

"I understand you did a little cooking this morning."

So she'd been found out. She should have known Jake would notice. "Yes, well, I was hungry."

"We didn't mean to starve you, but your plate came back empty both last night and this morning."

"You actually thought I ate that mess you served? My plate was empty only because Beau doesn't gross out very easily."

He glanced at the big dog that lay beside the sofa. "That explains his sudden affection, then. I did wonder."

"What it doesn't explain is why you felt called upon to ply me with pig intestines."

"Chitterlings are considered a treat in some corners. But you made it so obvious that you considered us backward hicks that it seemed we should live up to the image."

She looked away. "Sorry. Knee-jerk reaction, I guess."

"Big cities have no particular magic that guarantees intelligence and culture for the people who live there," he said evenly. "Talking faster, thinking faster, isn't a sign of superior mental activity, but often means skimming the surface, dealing with the obvious instead of looking for what's underneath. It's about jumping in with your own ideas and needs first, or tuning out and going on to the next person instead of listening to the one you're with so you hear what they mean instead of just the words they're saying."

"I do see the object lesson," she returned in dry acceptance.

"Maybe, but teaching it wasn't my place. I shouldn't

have let the attitude get to me, since that makes me as—''
He stopped, closed his lips tightly on the words.

''As arrogant as I was,'' she finished for him without
inflection.

''As judgmental, I meant to say. Because it assumes that
I know why you feel the way you do.''

''I don't feel that way,'' she said abruptly. ''At least,
I've gained a little different slant on things lately.''

They watched each other for long moments there in the
cluttered, homey room. Finally, he said, ''I'm glad to see
that you're well enough to stay out of bed most of the day.
Do you feel up to having dinner with us?''

She tilted her head to one side. ''No more chitterlings,
tripe, organ meats or other such delicacies?''

A tight grin curled his lips. ''Promise.''

He looked so much like Jake at that moment that she
couldn't help grinning back at him. It would be fun to help
the two of them with the cooking and be included in the
banter and laughter between them as if she were a member
of the family. She answered simply, ''I'd love to.''

''Good. Let me change, then we'll see about it.'' He
swung around and walked away. Seconds later, she heard
him whistling as he went up the stairs.

She should have refused the invitation. Accepting it, getting closer to Roan and his son, was dangerous. For one
thing, it was much more likely that she'd slip up. For another, it would be fatally easy to become accustomed to
their warm human interaction, their companionship.

There was powerful attraction in Roan's hard strength
and bedrock dependability. He represented permanence as
solid and enduring as the house he lived in. Here with him
was the comfort, peace and ultimate safe haven that she'd
been searching for, unknowingly, since she was a child. She

wanted those things, needed them so much, that she ached with it.

That wouldn't do.

It was going to be hard to leave this temporary sanctuary, harder than she would have dreamed. There was no point in making it worse on herself by getting more involved with Roan and his son than necessary. She needed to cool it after tonight, she really did.

It was entirely possible, in fact, that she would be better off leaving Dog Trot and its owner behind as soon as possible. One way or another.

9

The call came while Roan was stretched out in his favorite chair with his eyes closed, the newspaper spread over his lap, and Jake's TV program droning in the background. Jake answered, then brought the portable phone over to the easy chair. His Honor the mayor was on the line. He and the group of good buddies who ran the town council were holding an informal bull session at Betsy's coffee shop, but they'd like his input. They wouldn't keep him long. Could he be there in a half hour?

The impulse to refuse was so strong Roan could taste it. This was bound to be another useless round of discussion about the gambling boat and its impact on the town and the parish, since they talked of little else these days. He didn't need this, didn't want it, wasn't sure he could hold on to his temper while he endured it. He was tired, and his primary obligation at the moment was to see to his son and his prisoner. He was off official duty, but still had a private responsibility. Either someone didn't know, or they'd forgotten.

If it had slipped their minds, however, it might be best not to remind them. He didn't want interference in his arrangement just because somebody got ticked off. Besides, he told himself as he heaved out of his chair and stepped into his boots, Zits and Big Ears hadn't shown up since the move out to Dog Trot. That they'd pick the next hour to stage an offensive was about as likely as a pair of rattlesnakes showing up at the back door.

"Lock up behind me and don't let anybody in that you don't know while I'm gone," he instructed Jake as he left the house.

"Got it," his son answered without looking around.

"I mean it," Roan insisted as he paused with his hat in his hand.

Jake finally gave him his attention along with a crooked grin. "I know."

He did know, Roan thought; he'd seen to that. Jake had long ago been taught all the rules needed by a boy who often stayed alone, and he'd been reminded to stay on guard about Donna every single day. Regardless, Roan hesitated. Donna was upstairs taking a shower. He knew that because he knew every sound in the old house, but also because he'd developed mental radar where she was concerned. He really didn't think she had any intention of leaving, or that she'd be able to get too far on her own. With any luck, he'd be back before she realized he was gone. This short trip should be okay then, but he still didn't like it.

Roan whispered an oath directed at the mayor and his friends, as well as his own habit of making himself accessible. Then he crammed on his hat and headed out the door.

The motel coffee shop smelled of brewing coffee, hamburger, mustard and onions, and the vanilla-scented sweetness of the homemade pies that were a regular feature. The unofficial town council meeting was being held in a corner booth. After a semigenial start, it went just about the way Roan figured.

"What you got against gambling?"

That question, with its trace of belligerence, came from "Tubby" Michaels. The wheezing, potbellied reprobate ran the lumberyard and was known for chasing his female bookkeepers around the counter. That he stood to gain directly during the construction phase of the big gaming operation shaded his views considerably.

"Nothing," Roan answered on a suppressed sigh. "It's not a moral issue. I don't care who plays or who doesn't. More than that, I know there's enough gambling north and south of us and across the river so any addict can get his fix without much effort—and that these folks could be leaving their money in town instead of taking it elsewhere. My concern is practical. What I care about is who we're inviting into Turn-Coupe and what the town is going to become afterward."

"These consortium guys swear they'll keep everything nice and quiet, that we'll hardly know the boat's out there on the lake."

"Except for the four-lane highway we're supposed to build through the courthouse square for them," Roan answered with irony. "Or the half mile of lake frontage they want to turn into a parking lot."

"They're only asking us to study the feasibility of those things," the mayor put in with exaggerated patience in his voice. A tall dandy with a handlebar mustaches, he sang in a barbershop quartet on weekends and considered himself a cut above most Turn-Coupe citizens in sophistication because he'd served a large portion of his army hitch in Europe.

"But it's important enough that they're willing to fly in here to talk about it." Roan glanced at his watch. The meeting was running too long. He should have sent a backup out to Dog Trot while he was gone. The need to get home only added to his irritability now.

"Yes, though that doesn't seem unreasonable to me," the mayor returned with a judicious frown.

"I certainly can't stop them, but I don't think we ought to be pressured into making a decision by the fact that they'll be showing up here in their private jets and limousines." This was the point of the meeting, that some of the gaming consortium members would be paying them a visit in an effort to stampede the council into calling a special election to decide the issue.

"He's right about that," Jensen, president of the local bank, interjected with a slow nod. *Caution* was his watchword. It was a good, conservative attitude in a banker, one Roan was pleased to see at this moment.

"In any case," Jensen went on, propping his elbows on the Formica coffee shop table and making a steeple of his fingers, "I thought increased tax revenue, increased jobs, was our reason for considering this venture. It makes no sense to obligate ourselves to spend big sums up-front that may take years to recoup."

"You and the sheriff are just antiprogress," Michaels said with a wave of one pudgy hand. "You like things exactly the way they are out on the lake and don't care what happens to the rest of us who don't have it so good."

That had a familiar ring to it, like something Cal had said the other day, Roan thought. "I care," he said firmly, "and so does Tom Jensen. We just don't happen to think this Florida consortium has the answer to our problems here in Turn-Coupe."

"Could mean more patrol units and better equipment, like computerized fingerprint scanning, even a new jail," the mayor said. "You might want to think a little harder."

"Could be we'll need all that and more if this thing goes through. Studies show the incidence of assaults and burglaries rise dramatically about three years after a casino goes in, as hardcore gamblers max out their credit cards and resort to illegal ways to get cash.''

"You saying you don't need to modernize down at your office?''

"Our equipment is sufficient for our current level of crime,'' Roan insisted, though he felt a little beleaguered. He'd hoped that Kane and his law partner, Melville Brown, would be here. They hadn't been called for this unofficial gathering, it seemed, probably because the mayor knew they would side with Roan on this issue.

Michaels grunted. "Is that so? The way I hear it, you've got a woman prisoner out at your house because you don't want to house her in a jail that has no provision for females.''

Cal had been talking all right. "That's true, as far as it goes.''

"And how far does it go, sheriff? If our jail is so fine, why don't you put this woman in it? Or do you have other reasons for using your own house as a lockup?''

Roan rose slowly to his feet and leaned to rest the palms of his hands on the table on either side of his coffee cup. His voice was flat and gaze steady as he asked, "Just what are you suggesting?''

"Why, nothing.'' Michaels glancing around the table for support. "It's a logical question, don't you think?''

"This particular Jane Doe is a special case.''

"I'm sure she is.'' The man's lips formed a snide smile.

"The main problem is the injuries she sustained during her arrest.''

"Injuries you caused, right? I know things have changed, that the setup was weird and all that, but it still strikes me as downright pitiful to see a woman shot. We don't need that kind of thing around here. Why, there's no telling who you and your deputies might go shooting next. Could be one of our kids.''

Michaels didn't have kids, but that didn't make his comment any less painful. With sardonic emphasis, Roan said, ''I'll try to control the urge.''

''And another thing. You've been sending a deputy out to your house every day for special guard duty. Where does that leave us here in town? I mean, ain't you spreading your force kind of thin? What if the two that robbed Betsy decide to come back and see what the rest of us have in the till?''

''You worried about the lumberyard?'' Roan asked softly as he studied the other man. ''Or are you just throwing mud so no one will listen to what I have to say against this gaming venture? Either way, you have no grounds for complaint. The chief of police and I can handle it.''

''Now, Roan,'' the mayor began, his tone placating.

Roan straightened, his gaze hard as he met the stares of the town officials one by one. ''In case there's any doubt, let me make my position clear. I don't like this gaming invasion, and no amount of fancy equipment or fast-stepping logic is going to shift my views by so much as a millimeter. If it happens, fine. Then I'll do my job to the best of my ability. But you can leave me out of the welcoming committee for your slick visitors. I'm sure the crowd will be big enough that I won't be missed.''

''Fine,'' the mayor said in stiff acceptance. ''As long as we can count on you to keep security tight while they're here.''

''As I said, I'll do my job.''

Roan was still steaming when he pulled up in the driveway at Dog Trot. As he got out and headed for the back door, he heard the dogs barking in their pen down behind the barn, where they'd been relegated full-time since

Donna's arrival. He'd check on Jake and Donna, then ease down there and see what had set them off. Could be something as simple as a skunk or armadillo rambling around in the dark nearby, but it was best to be certain.

The house was empty. The lights were on, the television still played, provisions for a snack were on the kitchen table, but Jake didn't answer his call. Donna wasn't in her bedroom, and Jake's bed had not been disturbed. Beau wasn't around, either, and didn't answer when Roan whistled. But what sent a shaft of pure terror through him was that the den gun cabinet stood open and the twenty-gauge shotgun Jake's granddad had bought him for Christmas was missing.

Where the hell were they? What could have been important enough to take them out of the house and into danger. He could think of only one thing. Zits and Big Ears had shown up, and Donna had persuaded Jake to let them in.

His heartbeat was so loud it deafened him. Cold sweat trickled down the back of his neck. He paused for a moment, listening, afraid of what he might hear. He could just catch the barking of the hounds in their pen. Somebody was out there.

This was too much. Nobody invaded his property, nobody touched those who belonged to him. He didn't allow it, wouldn't allow it. He spun around and sprinted for the back door.

Once away from the house, it was clear that the barking was coming from two different directions now. The hounds yodeled from behind the barn, but he also recognized Beau's deep, distinctive baying off to the left, in the deeper woods that circled the lake. Its urgency signaled that he was on a trail.

Roan whistled through his teeth, a piercing note that all

the dogs recognized instantly. The big bloodhound's yelp-
ing picked up speed and intensity, as if he thought the hunt
had turned serious. Was Beau with Jake, or did it mean the
dog was following the boy and Donna and whoever had
come to the house for them? One thing was certain, he was
after human quarry. Beau was trained to disregard lesser
game.

The urge to plunge headlong into the woods was strong,
but Roan fought it back. He eased among the shadowed
trees, circling toward where he'd heard Beau. He knew this
land like he knew his own bedroom, could walk it blind-
folded without a misstep. Whoever was out here was on
foreign ground, bumbling around in the dark. Roan had the
advantage and he intended to use it.

He circled a stand of tupelo, heading toward an opening
thirty feet ahead. Then he halted with every muscle tensed
and ready.

A shape moved in the dimness, became two people. They
were coming toward him, moving with stealth and keeping
close together. He couldn't be sure, but he thought one
carried a weapon. He quietly released the flap of his holster.

The pair stopped. One of them turned, looked back, before swinging around and staring straight toward where he
stood. For a second, he thought he'd been spotted. Then a
sibilant whisper, exasperated and distinctly feminine,
sounded on the still air.

"You sure you know where we're going?"

Donna. Donna's voice, Donna's outline in the dark. She
was safe. She was still here.

"That was dad's whistle, I swear. I'd know it anywhere."

Jake.

They were safe.

They were both safe.

The rush of relief was so great that Roan felt light-headed with it. Following on its heels was adrenaline-fueled rage so strong that he closed his eyes while he willed it back under control. Only then did he step from the black strip of shade cast by a cedar tree.

"Here, Jake," he called in a hail so low it barely disturbed the night stillness. "If you can manage not to shoot me."

The two gray shapes stiffened. Jake gave a soft exclamation. Then he released the hammer on his shotgun and started forward to meet him while Donna followed more slowly.

"Man, but we're glad to see you," Jake said fervently.

"Ditto," Roan said. "But what the hell are you doing out of the house?"

"Beau set up such a ruckus that I had to see what was going on."

"You should have called me." Beau was still yodeling in a continuous bellow, though he didn't seem to be moving as fast, if at all.

"You were busy."

That was unanswerable. "Did it occur to you that you could have run right into whoever is out here?"

Jake's only answer was to lift the shotgun that he'd rested against his shoulder.

"Great," Roan said in taut sarcasm. "And while you were blasting away, what about Donna?"

"She wanted to come with me," his son protested.

"I'll just bet she did."

Donna stepped closer, almost nose to nose with him in the darkness, as she said, "I didn't come out here to meet whoever was sneaking around, if that's what you think."

"You just felt like a midnight stroll."

"No, I felt..." She stopped and looked away.

"Come on, you can do better than that."

Her face was unreadable in the dark, still he could feel her resentment. "If you must know, I didn't want to be alone. In case they doubled back and I was trapped inside."

Sympathy was the last thing he needed to feel. Roan shook it off, asking after a moment, "Why isn't Beau on a leash if you two had him on a scent?"

"He got away from us," Jake answered quickly, almost as if he wanted to divert the heat away from Donna. "We circled down to the lake, hoping he'd come out of the trees where we could see him. Then we heard you whistle and headed back this way."

"And you heard nothing, saw nothing?"

"We'd have told you," his son protested in injured tones.

Roan accepted that with a short nod. "Head on back to the house, both of you. If anything looks or sounds unusual, don't go in. Sit in the patrol unit and wait until I get back. If I'm not there in fifteen minutes, radio for help."

Jake didn't move. "What if it's Zits and Big Ears out there? What if...?"

"I'll take it from here," he answered, letting the hard finality of his tone speak for him.

It was enough for Jake; he swung in the direction of the house. Donna looked as if she'd like to argue, but finally followed the boy.

Roan came upon Beau in an elm thicket with his leash caught among the limbs of a deadfall. The big bloodhound was frantically glad to see him. Almost before Roan could get him untangled, he was off again, baying as he ran. He headed straight for the lake.

Roan kept up with the dog as best he could. He leaped briars, ducked under tree limbs, was almost jerked off his feet by Beau's hard tug on the leash. Short minutes later, a Native American mound loomed ahead of them. The long earthwork pile was covered by a thick stand of oaks that had been untouched by an ax for over a hundred years, with an understory of dogwood, wax myrtle, palmetto and endless kinds of briars. Beyond that natural rampart lay the open lake.

Roan gave a quiet order, and he and Beau scrambled up through the undergrowth along the mound's southern edge. He paused and reined in the dog at that vantage point, using the Spanish-moss-draped branches of a big oak for cover. As he stood there, the night sounds returned: the squeaky songs of crickets, the calls of frogs, the distant hoot of a barn owl. A limb of the tree overhead creaked with the lift of a breeze that died away almost before it began.

He heard them then, heard a low curse followed by a dull, metallic thump. As he spun toward the sound, he saw two figures silhouetted against the light-gathering surface of the lake. One was tall and thin, the other shorter and more muscular. They were bent over what appeared to be a lightweight aluminum boat beached on the lakeshore.

The pair might be campers. They could be treasure hunters using their summer vacation to sneak in and sink a few holes in search of Mike Fink's hidden gold. They could be after Indian artifacts and wary of being caught on what they knew was private land.

Roan was certain they were none of those things. He'd worried in the last few days about why there had been so little sign of Donna's cohorts and what they might try next. He didn't have to worry any longer.

Approaching the house by water had been logical. A boat was quiet, left no trail, and was hard to identify because of the similarities between models. In addition, visitors to Dog Trot from the water were common; Clay came and went that way all the time. But the two men had been spooked by Beau and all the commotion he'd caused. They were in full retreat, already launching the cheap boat and splashing out to climb on board. A few seconds more and they'd be gone.

Roan unsnapped Beau's leash. "Go," he ordered. "Hunt!"

The big bloodhound took off in a flying leap. Roan plunged after him.

Underbrush hid his view, but he could hear Beau's excited baying, catch panicked yells. Water splashed and one of the intruders shouted a curse followed by a hollow thud, as if he'd dived headfirst into the boat. An outboard motor cranked with a rumble, then sputtered and died. It roared again, and was slammed into gear so fast it backfired.

Roan broke into the open in time to see the boat swerve away from the shallow shoreline. Beau was in the lake, splashing after it with his ruff standing like a lion's mane. The man crouched on the forward seat pulled something from the waistband at his back, something that caught a dull gleam from the starlight. He brought it around, leveled it at Beau.

In a single movement, Roan slid to a halt, pulled his handgun, steadied it and fired. The shot cracked out, and a furrow skimmed across the water directly in front of the boat. The two men yelled and ducked. The speeding craft fishtailed, then straightened with a churning wake and zoomed away toward the safety of the lake's deep-water channel.

Roan narrowed his eyes, following the boat as long as he was able. The men in the boat were blurred with darkness and movement, but appeared to be the same two caught by the convenience store camera. The boat was probably a rental from the bait stand at the public landing. He'd have that checked out first thing in the morning.

Roan lowered his weapon. It would have been easy to pick off those two instead of shooting ahead of them. It wasn't an option. For one thing, he might be wrong, and the last thing he needed was the death of some teen delinquent on his conscience. Most of all, it wasn't his way.

He whistled to Beau, but still stared after the boat with brooding anger. He wanted his hands on Donna's pals so bad he ached with it. They held the answers to all his questions about his houseguest. Coming so close to collaring them was so frustrating he wanted to stomp up and down and curse and kick stumps like the most backward redneck who ever lived.

He should be used to coming up empty; Lord knows it happened often enough in his line of work. This time was different; it was personal. Why it should be that way, beyond the fact that the men had been on his land, he wasn't prepared to explore. It was just the way he felt.

Beau emerged from his plunge in the lake and gave himself a mighty shake that sprayed water like a cold shower. Roan launched into a half bitter, half humorous complaint while giving the hound the rough caresses and praise that made him happy. Then the two of them turned back toward Dog Trot.

The dog scouted ahead in a weaving pattern, his nose to the ground. Just before they broke from the cover of the trees into the yard at the back of the house, Beau growled low in his throat and stood at point.

"Aw, jeez, Beau," Jake drawled from out of the night. "Don't you know Donna yet?"

Roan thought the dog was being more dutiful than anything else, since he was wagging his tail. As the bloodhound moved on again, he followed to where Donna and Jake stood at the edge of the brick patio with light from the kitchen window spilling over them.

"Did I lock you out or something?" His voice was hard, even in his own ears, but this second failure to follow instructions was even less acceptable than the first.

Jake ducked his head an instant, but didn't retreat. "We were in the house until we heard the shot and were afraid something happened to you. What was going on?"

"I fired as a warning because they drew down on Beau." He should have known they'd be worried. And it took a second for Roan to realize he'd included Donna in that, maybe because she was so pale and silent. He'd give a lot to know what was really going through her mind. And he was going to find out, as soon as he could make an opportunity.

"They were hightailing it, huh? You see who it was or what they were after?" Jake asked.

"Not exactly."

"You can bet it wasn't any treasure hunters. They came too close to the house." Roan's son frowned as he glanced at Donna. "You think they'll be back?"

Roan tightened his hold on the weapon he still carried, but replied only, "Hard to say."

"I mean, they could try sneaking in again tonight if they thought we weren't on guard because we'd already run them off. They have to be mighty brassy to risk coming in here. Or mighty desperate."

Sometimes Jake was too bright for his own good, Roan thought. With a nod in the direction of the dog pen, he said, "If they do come back, it won't be any time soon. Why don't you take Beau and go let the other hounds out for the night?"

"Now?" Jake asked in an incredulous tone.

"Now, as an advance warning system." Roan didn't raise his voice, but his tone said plainly that he was in no mood for argument.

Jake looked from him to Donna, then back again, as if he suspected there was more than one purpose behind the order. Still, he went without further argument.

Roan followed the boy with his gaze, partly as a safety precaution, but also to be sure he was out of earshot. But before he could turn back to Donna, she said, "It was Big Ears and Zits again, wasn't it?"

"Looked like it to me."

"It also looks as if they waited until you were gone to make their move."

Her tone was taut but composed. Where was the panic at this second attempt to retake or even kill her? He said, "And that shows they've been watching the house."

She gave a short nod. "I'd say it also means that Dog Trot isn't safe."

She was right, but that didn't mean he had to like it. At least she hadn't blamed him directly. Nor did she need to, since he could take care of that just fine all by himself. In his own defense, he said, "I might have a better idea of how to guard against them if I knew what was going on. And if I didn't have to worry about my son acting as your knight protector."

"I'm sorry if you think I should have kept him inside. He said he'd had weapon safety training and that you arranged for him to practice on the rifle range set up for your deputies and the town police. He seemed to know what he was doing."

"Feeling guilty are you?" he asked, his tone silky. It was interesting that she might. He hadn't expected anything of her, which made it interesting that she expected something from herself.

"By no means, Sheriff. Moving in with you wasn't my idea."

Was that how she thought of her sojourn at Dog Trot,

moving in with him? "So whatever happens is on my own head? Even if I'm left fighting shadows in the dark?"

"I could tell you that I'm as much in the dark as you are, but I doubt you'd believe me."

Her tone was moody and not particularly hopeful. It was just as well, since she was right.

In the faint light of the moon, he could just make out that she was wearing shorts and a red T-shirt. She had on no underwear; that much was plain from the way the soft cotton knit draped over her breasts, outlining the tight buds of her nipples. The knowledge of her nakedness under her scant clothing acted like an aphrodisiac. Combined with the adrenaline still pumping in his system, it gave him impulses that he had no business entertaining.

He needed to get away from her, to let his temper cool before he said, or did, something that he would regret. But something was driving him, some deep-seated fury that was directed at her, yes, but also at himself and the whole impossible prisoner-jailer situation. He hated what he was having to do, but he had no choice. He hated what she was, but it couldn't be changed. Somewhere beneath all that was virulent attraction that was getting harder and harder to control.

It had begun the minute he knelt beside her and saw the face of the woman he'd shot, and had grown every day since. He'd stood at her bedside for countless hours as she slept, memorizing every inch of her face, inhaling her scent, fantasizing about the contours of her body under the sheet. He felt responsible for her in some primitive way that he didn't even try to understand. Still, it was more than that. He wanted her with a useless ache of the heart that he hadn't felt since he was a boy longing to believe in the magic of Christmas morning while knowing that Santa Claus was a lie.

The clothes she had on were the same ones he'd thrown in the dryer just before supper. She must have retrieved them after he left. It was a sign that she was getting around a lot better than he'd thought, better than he might have expected. He latched on to that idea like a lifeline.

"You were too tired to sit up this afternoon, but now I find you out chasing after Beau. A miraculous recovery, wasn't it?"

"Amazing what a little rest can do."

The words were flippant enough, but the edges of her voice were taut with strain. He tipped his head toward the black stand of woods around them. "You sure there was no midnight rendezvous?"

"With Jake along for kicks? What an opinion you have of me, Sheriff—bondage play and seducing a teenager, all based on a piece of film that doesn't mean a thing because I was coerced."

"Were you, though? Or were you along for the excitement? If that's what you need, you don't have to settle for the kind supplied by lowlifes like your Zits and Big Ears."

The light from the kitchen windows slanted across half her face. In it, she looked suddenly wary. "Meaning?"

"It can be supplied a lot closer to home," he answered in tight challenge.

"If you think for one minute…"

"I'm not thinking at all," he answered, his voice dropping to a lower note. "Which is the problem."

Hard on the words, he reached for her. With instinctive care for her injured shoulder, he brought their bodies together in exact alignment. His senses filled with the heat of her skin, her sweet distinctive fragrance, her quick breaths and the way her breasts molded against his chest with delicious, resilient pressure. The sudden onslaught made his mind reel. She fit the hollows and hard planes of his body as if made for him alone. Nothing had ever been so right, so perfect.

He wanted to take her away somewhere and kiss her for a million years, to taste the deep recesses of her mouth and trace the tender curves of her lips with slow, honeyed care. He wanted to know every inch of her, to fill his hands with her, surround her, hold her, until this deep hunger inside him for possession was appeased. He wanted never to let her go.

God, he was going crazy.

Her face was upturned, the silver glint of moonlight touching her cheeks but leaving her expression unreadable. A waiting stillness seemed to hold her, or perhaps it was reluctance to move for fear of pain. He lowered his head and took her smooth, cool lips with his hot, hot mouth.

For long moments, she remained quiescent in his arms. Then the fingers of her good hand slowly closed on the taut muscle of his upper arm. She made a low murmur in her throat and moved closer against him, into him, as if in need of the contact. She allowed the briefest of access, the most tingling of brushes from his tongue against hers, permitted an elusive taste of her sweet essence.

Then she clenched her fingers on a fistful of his shirt-sleeve and shoved at him. He was forced to either let her go or hurt her. As he stepped back, she demanded, "What do you think you're doing?"

It was a good question. Before he had time to answer, he heard the panting and thudding footfalls of the dog pack Jake had released. Suddenly they were encircled by dogs that pushed and jostled them in their pleasure at being free of their pen.

"Down!" Roan ordered as he caught Donna's arm. The dogs tucked tail and subsided, backing away to give them room. Roan turned with his prisoner toward the oblong of light that was the kitchen door. At the same time, Jake strolled out of the darkness with his weapon over his shoulder.

"Good grief," Donna said in shaken tones that might have been from distress over the onslaught of hounds, but could have been from something else entirely. "Dogs, guns, weird food, and late night visitors—is it always this way?"

"Nah," Jake answered with a crooked grin, when Roan failed to comment. "Sometimes it gets really strange."

"I hope I'm not around to see it!"

She didn't wait for more, but pulled away from him and walked into the house. Roan watched her go with narrowed eyes.

She would be around, because he was going to make sure of it. She'd be around whether she wanted to be or not; she was a prisoner, not a guest, and it was time she realized it. He had an idea, one it might take a few day to put into action. When it was in place, their relative positions should be crystal clear.

It was time, and then some. They were going to have to start playing this strictly by the rules. Before it was too late.

10

Tory spent most late afternoons over the next few days on the screened porch on the upper floor of Dog Trot. It faced southeast, so was protected from the westward slanting sun and caught stray breezes off the lake. From its second-floor elevation, she could watch the rippling water through the trees, catch sight of an occasional blue heron or silver-white crane. The screen that kept out flying insects and wind-borne trash also gave the illusion of a private retreat from which to view the world.

She'd brought a book she'd found on forensics with her to read this afternoon while stretched out on the chaise longue that, with a collection of wrought iron chairs and tables, made the porch like an outdoor room. It lay beside her, however, as she stared out over the water. She couldn't concentrate on its pages for thinking of that night nearly a week ago. It wasn't the puzzle of why Zits and Big Ears were so determined to get to her that they'd risk prowling around the sheriff's house that troubled her, but something else entirely.

The sheriff had kissed her. It was the last thing she'd expected.

Oh, she'd felt the awareness between them that told her

he was attracted to her in a purely physical fashion. Still, he had said plainly that she had nothing to fear from him while at Dog Trot. She'd believed him, had truly thought the restraints of his office and his dedication to duty would prevent him from touching her.

Did she mind? She wasn't sure.

Roan Benedict had kissed her. He had touched his mouth to hers, and she'd felt the world shift on its axis. This back-country sheriff with his unbending rectitude and old-fashioned manners packed more punch into a single kiss than any man she'd ever met, certainly more than poor Harrell had managed in all the weeks they been together.

A part of the reason she'd ended her engagement was because she'd decided she couldn't take a lifetime of Harrell's paint-by-numbers attempts at foreplay, had never been quite stirred enough by it to go to bed with him. Not that she had much to compare it against, really. Indiscriminate sex was seriously stupid these days from a health standpoint, but it was also true that not many men moved her. She felt that if she didn't care for the way they kissed, she wouldn't care much for the rest of it. She'd tried to be satisfied with Harrell because she wondered, finally, if she hadn't been too particular.

What did it mean, the sheriff's kiss? Or did it have any meaning beyond the impulse of the moment? He had suggested once that he had a hidden motive for bringing her here. Was this it?

And if it was, did she want to do anything about it? Or should she encourage him in hope that he'd be more likely to accept that she was kidnapped and release her? To use the physical attraction between them went against the grain, but it was the only possible advantage she had at the moment.

The endless questions circled in her head as she watched

the sun drop down behind the trees and sunset colors streak the sky. Added to everything else, they made her tired beyond words. She closed her eyes, trying to shut them out.

The brush of something warm against her ankle roused her from a light sleep. Beauregard, she thought. The big dog was fast becoming a nuisance, though secretly she had to admit that she was fond of his company, especially the ambling walks they often took around the grounds near the house in the evening. How he had managed to find his way out onto the porch, she didn't know. She was sure she'd closed the door behind her.

The warm breeze off the lake was pleasant as the sun's heat faded. She didn't want to be disturbed. Not yet, anyway. Draping her forearm across her eyes, she said, "Go away. That's a good boy."

The pressure on her ankle firmed. It was hard and encircling, nothing at all like Beau nudging her for attention or the friendly lick of his tongue. She jerked away. At the same time, she snapped open her eyes and pushed herself upright.

Roan knelt at her feet. The evening light beyond the screen burnished his sandy hair to gold, and caught bronze gleams from the hair on his arms. His gray gaze was steady, and his mouth firm with purpose. His arm was braced on one flexed knee, and from his fingers dangled a thick ring of black plastic.

"What are you doing?" she asked, her voice suddenly husky.

"Installing a monitor."

She eyed the device in his hand that appeared to have a small LED display with a blinking light set into the plastic. "To monitor what?"

"You. Your comings and goings."

She pulled her feet up and wrapped her good arm protectively around her knees. "I don't think so."

"It's just an electronic device. It won't hurt you," he said, the planes and angles of his face stern as he dangled it in front of her. "A guy who used to be one of my deputies sells the things now. This is his latest model."

It was a little like a scuba diver's watch, only bigger, Tory thought, with holes evenly spaced in the plastic cuff-like band to allow for air circulation. With a tight smile, she said, "And I suppose you want to test it on me?"

"Something like that." He waited, his gaze watchful.

"It's like a gadget out of a James Bond movie. Does it shoot laser beams or use radio waves like a walkie-talkie?"

"Neither." He hefted the device, his gaze shuttered. "It's more like...an electronic handcuff."

"Like kind of space-age bondage sex toy?" she asked, the words dry.

A slow red tide rose in his face. It was fascinating to watch, though she couldn't tell whether it was from embarrassment or anger. Even his eyes appeared hot as he said, "You should know."

"Only because I've seen pictures," she corrected with asperity. "I told you what happened to my wrists and ankles, but you're too stubborn to recognize the truth when you hear it."

He pointed the monitor at her. "If you think you can get out of wearing this by that kind of accusation, you're dead wrong. I need to know where you are at all times. I especially need to know when you go wandering off at night."

She stared at him a long moment. Then abruptly something clicked in her mind. She'd read a magazine article a while back that had described devices like this being used for paroled convicts to confine them to a limited area in and around a halfway house. With this thing on her ankle, she'd have no chance to run, no way to get away from Dog Trot without its owner, the good sheriff, knowing it before she was out of sight.

She swung her legs off the chaise and surged to her feet. Fighting to keep the panic from her voice, she said. "You can keep your monitor."

"It's for your own good."

"Sure it is. You're taking this way too far. Just because you're the law doesn't mean you can do whatever you want."

Roan rose slowly to his full, commanding height. "What I want has nothing to do with it."

"Doesn't it? You control where I sleep, what I eat, what I can and can't do. Now you want to control every move I make. I think you like having me helpless and under your thumb." He'd shown that he could be affected by what she said. Since words were her only weapon, she had to use them regardless of how much she hated it.

His high color receded, leaving a white line around his mouth. "You're about as helpless as a stinging scorpion. But it's my job to keep you safe. I can't do that if I don't know where you are."

"Isn't having me under surveillance around the clock enough? I can hardly go to the bathroom by myself. You've even set your son to watch me!"

"You're a prisoner," he said with deliberation as he moved around the end of the chaise. "What do you expect? Or is something else going on here? Maybe you had plans to slip out on me, maybe that's why you're so set on avoiding this substitute ankle bracelet."

She backed away a hasty step. "Don't be ridiculous. Where would I go? I just don't like the invasion of privacy. Would you want someone following your every move?"

"No, but I don't make a practice of holding up convenience stores."

"Neither do I!" He was closing in on her. The door to the hall was somewhere behind her. She risked a quick glance over her shoulder to locate it.

"Don't," he warned, his voice hardening. "Don't make me hurt you. This is a fight you can't win, I promise."

"You promise?" Her rejection of the word was scathing. "You also swore you wouldn't touch me while I was here. So much for promises."

"You haven't been harmed so far. But I can't vouch for what might happen if you force me to pin you down for this little ceremony."

That he would admit to such a thing was so startling that she made the mistake of meeting his eyes. The pupils were wide and dark, almost obscuring the gray of his irises, and layered with bitter self-knowledge that was more disturbing than all his implied threats.

Her poise deserted her, as did her arguments. She spun around and dived for the door.

He was upon her in two long strides. Fastening his fingers on her good arm, he jerked her to a halt, and swept her around so she stumbled toward the chaise once more. He tripped her then with a quick hook of a booted foot behind her knee. As she tumbled to the cushioned surface, he fell with her, supporting her so his elbow took the jar as they landed, instead of her shoulder. Still, the fast movement took her breath. As she lay winded, he covered her with his body, holding her immobile with a long leg across her knees and her good arm pinned uselessly under his armpit.

"Now," he said softly. "Where were we?"

No triumph was reflected in his face. Still, outrage feathered along her nerves and settled in some deep, untouched corner of her brain. No one had ever dared treat her like this in her life. That this hayseed sheriff had the temerity made her long to do desperate things to him.

"Let me up," she said in a hoarse whisper.

He eased away from her a fraction. "Are you all right?"

"Other than being crushed and having all Doc Watkins's good work undone, you mean?"

"I did warn you," he said, his voice even. At the same time, he glanced down to where her bandaging lay under her T-shirt, as if checking for damage.

There was none, and Tory knew it. The fall hadn't exactly made her shoulder feel good, however, which added to her resentment. "Do you treat all your women suspects this way, or is it just me?"

"A few have hinted that they'd like to be handcuffed to my bed. I've never been tempted before, but I might make an exception." His voice dropped a note and his drawl lengthened. "Who knows? It could grow on me."

"You're not scaring me." She lifted her chin in bravado as she spoke, but it was a lie. Hard purpose made the planes of his face look set in stone. She straightened her pinned arm behind him and pushed against the lounger, trying to shift from under him. He tightened his muscles to remain in place, and settled his weight more firmly against her lower body.

"Funny, but I think maybe I am scaring you a little. And that's interesting."

"I'm so happy you think so," she said in strained derision.

"I'd halfway expected a different reaction."

She was still for an instant while she accessed the expectant look on his face. There was nothing salacious about it, she realized. He was waiting for the light to dawn. "You expected...you really thought I might enjoy this?"

"It was a possibility."

"So the whole thing was a test. To see how I would react to being forced, to see if I'd like it." She'd been angry before, but that was nothing to the rage that burned through her veins now.

"I wouldn't say that, exactly. It was more a question of seizing the moment."

"Because I said your stupid monitor looked like a sex toy?"

"Something like that."

She closed her eyes. The word she called him under her breath was not a compliment.

"Agreed," he said shortly. "But I'd say you passed. So tell me one more time how you got the marks on your wrists."

"Duct tape and the kind of prickly plastic rope used to tie up boats. And there was nothing the least enjoyable about it." Did he believe her? She lifted her lashes, meeting his gaze once more in the hope of some sign, some tiny indication that he might. All she saw was her own reflection in the dark mirrors of his pupils. Then that was gone as he looked away from her.

"For the record, I despise the kind of lawmen who take advantage of female prisoners," he said. "I'd never do that. Never. The other night was..." He stopped, took a breath so deep that she suddenly felt, where his chest pressed against her, the points of his star and the hard thud of his heartbeat. When he spoke again, his voice was brisk and authoritative. "Let's call it a mistake. Now, if we've cleared that up, we can go on the next problem. Are you going to cooperate, or do we continue as we started here?"

What had he been about to say? She'd give a lot to know. "Your methods of persuasion need a little work. So does your technique with women," she said in her best, bored socialite voice. "A few lessons in manners might not hurt, either."

"Manners," he repeated. "You mean as in, *'A gentle-man always rests his weight on his elbows'*? I'm not sure what you're complaining about, since I'm doing that."

"I mean like having the courtesy to get off me now that you've won," she answered with indignation caused, in part at least, by the fact that it was her turn to flush. His manners as a lover were not something she'd given much thought to, but his quip opened new vistas.

"Yes, well, I expect my mother would have agreed with you about that one."

"Your mother." The words were blank.

"I learned my manners at her knee, of course, as most Southern good-old-boys do. Well, most of my manners. Not the—"

"I get the picture," Tory said in some haste, since she really did not want or need to hear more about his habits in bed. "So?"

"So what?" The question was distracted, as if his mind had slid off on a tangent.

"Are you going to get off me or not?"

"When I'm ready."

"And when might that be, do you think?" she demanded.

He gave her his full attention. A slow smile curved his lips. When he spoke, his voice had a deep, silken glide. "Maybe when you agree to do exactly as I ask?"

Her eyes widened. This was not blustering male bravado, but pure intent. Still, it was tempered by something else, a half-tender enticement that invited her to see the humor of their position, and also its unacknowledged dangers.

The problem was that she did see. She felt it as well, felt the slow shift of change within herself that made the weight of his body less a burden and more a source of sense-gratifying contact, less a means of domination and more an intimate and alluring physical intrusion into her space.

He couldn't do this to her. It wasn't right or fair when he had such power over her freedom. Still, he was also susceptible to her appeal; he'd as good as admitted that much, hadn't he? If he used sexual attraction as a weapon, he could hardly complain at retaliation in kind. How risky could it be when he'd just explained why he'd never go too far?

She lowered her gaze to the star on his shirt that was mere inches from her breast. Shifting her injured arm, she touched a fingertip to its engraved surface, warm from his body heat, then traced its points one by one. In tentative tones, she said, "I don't know why you're so set on making me wear the stupid monitor. It's not as if I have anywhere to go or any reason to want to get away from you."

He was quiet for so long that she thought he wasn't going to answer. When she looked up, he was watching her with a suspended look in his eyes. Then he gave a slow shake of his head while irony tugged a corner of his mouth upward. "I seem to have made a strategic error."

"What?" She kept the word as innocent as possible without overdoing it. Roan Benedict was an intelligent man, much more so than Harrell who had never seen through her little ploys or realized how well she understood him. But even intelligent men had been known to underestimate feminine cunning.

"Never mind. The monitor is mostly about protection."

"Why would I need it when you're around?"

"I'm not always. I can't be, and that's the problem."

She studied the slash of his thick brows, his square jaw and chin. Protection, he said. As she lay there against him, she could almost feel it surrounding her, enclosing her with him in a cocoon of safety. It was a sensation she could grow to depend on if she let herself, just as she could get used to reaching out to him, touching him of her own will and purpose.

Lowering her lashes, she let her gaze rest on the firm curves of his lips. Her voice a mere thread of sound, she asked, "But who will protect me from the inside threat?"

"That," he said, lowering his head so that his breath teased her lips, "is something you'll have to figure out yourself. But if you need a test, I don't mind."

An alarm bell went off in Tory's mind, but it was too late. He stroked her lips with his in the lightest of caresses, tasting the smooth and moist delicate corners, then returning to their center. With gentle courtesy, he enticed her to open to him. It was impossible to resist. She flowed against him, into him, with her lips molding to the firmer contours of his, seeking their heat and gentle abrasion. His kiss was golden fire, desire and persuasion, endless persuasion. That he wasn't more domineering triggered surprise, then even that disappeared in the sweet magic of joined mouths.

She smoothed her palm across his star and the resilient planes of his chest beneath it, then reached behind his neck to draw him closer, deeper. The crisp feel of his hair between her fingers sent a shiver of pleasure over her. Feeling it, he tightened his hold. She could ignore the incipient pain in her shoulder, but not the hot firmness of him against her thigh. That sign of his involvement was an incitement, and she pressed closer with a soft murmur in her throat. Lost, she was lost in the pure fascination of this backcountry man.

The peal of a bell-like tone somewhere under Roan startled Tory so much that she jumped. He withdrew by slow degrees and with reluctance in the last clinging touch of his mouth. Releasing her, he sat up and put a hand to the pager clipped to his belt, tilting it to read the display. His chest lifted with a sigh that might have been from resignation, but could also have signaled relief.

"Sorry, but I have to cut this short."

He didn't mean their embrace, but rather the campaign to attach the monitor. Hard on the words, he clamped a hand on her ankle and slid the black plastic cuff around it. She jerked against his hold, but he pressed tighter, holding her down, while he turned his head and met her gaze with firm purpose. She stared into the faceted steel of his eyes, but could find no relenting there, no hint that anything she'd said or done had moved him an inch or ever would. She swallowed hard on a sudden knot of tears, but resisted no more.

The rest of it took scant seconds. While she stared at his broad back, he fastened the cuff with a special tool he took from his pocket, tested it for fit and the possibility of chafing, and then gave a satisfied nod. He reached to touch her other ankle briefly, perhaps looking at the few remaining scabs that marked it. Then he pushed to his full height and stood looking down at her.

"I'll be back," he said quietly. "Soon."

Was it a threat or a promise? She couldn't tell. And what did it matter anyway? He did what he wanted to do, always, and nothing and no one could stop him.

"Don't hurry on my account," she answered, forcing the words through the tightness in her throat.

He hesitated, watching her. At last, he said again, "I'm really sorry."

She turned her head, staring out over the water, and did not look around again until he swung away and his footsteps faded down the inside hall. A minute later, she heard his car heading down the drive.

He was sorry.

A hard knot formed in her throat as she digested that idea. Any other man would have been ablaze with satisfaction over his conquest, but not Roan, the almighty Sheriff of Tunica Parish. He was sorry that he had forced his will on her. He was sorry that he had crossed the line with a prisoner, an act unacceptable in his book of restrictive codes and outdated notions.

Roan Benedict held himself to a higher ideal of what a man should be. He was a Southern gentleman, with all the pride and strength and sense of duty implied by that title. The question was, where did that leave her?

She had not acted the part of a lady. She had tried to trick him, to use physical attraction to get what she wanted, and it hadn't worked.

She had been hiding behind Roan Benedict for some time now, using him to keep her safe while endangering both him and his son with her lies. He deserved better.

She didn't like herself all that much just now, especially with her body cooling from the sheriff's heated weight and with the last, drugging seductiveness of powerful emotions fading from her veins. When had she grown so unscrupulous? When had she ceased to care about other people? Had she always been this way, or was it the effect of being around Harrell and her stepfather? Did she really think, as some said, that the rich were different? Did she believe, deep down, that she could get away with anything?

Wrong, wrong, wrong.

Still, what could she do? If she told Roan the truth and threw herself on his mercy, would it be any different? Would he believe her, or only think it was another trick? If he looked into her background and discovered what she said was true, would he not feel duty-bound to protect her all the more?

She couldn't allow that. No, her first plan was still best.

She needed to get away the first chance she saw, needed to get to Paul Vandergraff and find out where he stood in this fiasco. Once she had straightened out her life, then maybe, just maybe...

Maybe what? There was no place in Roan's quiet, useful, honor-bound existence for someone like her. No place at all. The sooner she got used to the idea, the better off she'd be. So what was left, then, except to go on as she had been, to use whatever means she could to lull him into relaxing his vigilance?

She glared at the black plastic band around her ankle, then lifted her foot and kicked experimentally to test the weight. She hated the thing, not only for the loss of freedom it represented, but for the memories that were now attached to it.

As she set her foot down again, the band scraped over her opposite ankle. The contact grated across her skin with much more roughness than she'd expected. She frowned as she sat up and leaned to inspect the damage.

It wasn't the monitor that had scratched her. It was the chain of her ankle bracelet. Roan had returned it, slipped it on her ankle while she was too distracted by the monitor cuff to notice. It glittered up at her, bearing the name that he knew her by, one as false as she was: *Donna.*

She had missed it. But what did it mean that Roan had given it back to her? Had he decided it had no value as evidence? Did it indicate, perhaps, that he understood her need to have something of her own? Or had he simply returned it as recompense for making her wear the monitor?

As she stared at it, Tory wondered what Roan would think when he knew her by her real name. Would he understand her pretense or despise her as a fraud and a coward? Would he ever learn who and what she was inside? It didn't look hopeful.

Depression and disquiet warred inside Tory over the next few days. She stayed in her room, reading, pacing, watching Roan come and go; refusing to admit, even to herself, that she was hiding. The cause, she decided finally, was embarrassment, yes, but also injured feelings. She had almost forgotten that she was not a guest at Dog Trot. The reminder hurt.

She wondered if Allen and Cal and the other deputies in Roan's office knew about the monitor. The idea made her uncomfortable, something to do with privacy, she thought, but also with a feeling that this was a personal issue between Roan and herself. She wasn't wild about Jake being aware of it, either, though she knew he must.

Roan's son brought up her meals as he had before, though he seldom stayed to talk. While it was a relief not to have to deal with his unspoken sympathy, his avoiding her seemed like a slap in the face. Roan himself hardly came near her. He had seen to it that she was unable to escape without detection, had assured himself that she was fairly well recovered, and was no longer interested in her or what she needed. Even Beau deserted her at times, loping off to follow Jake about his chores or on his dirt bike trips. That the solitary confinement was largely her own choice made little difference, Tory still felt like a burden, an unwelcome addition to the routine at Dog Trot.

If Sheriff Roan Benedict thought he could hold her like this forever, he was mistaken. She was going to leave as soon as she figured out how to escape without alerting the world.

She began her campaign near noon of the next day. It had been a sultry morning, with distant thunder that promised to shake a storm out of the gray sky before long. Jake was home instead of out riding or visiting with friends; she'd heard the beep and chime and ear-grating music of the video game he was playing earlier. Dragging on a pair of cutoff jeans and a "Kickin' Country Y106" T-shirt, she set off in search of the boy. The cuff set off no alarm as she descended the stairs, so she concluded it was all right to leave the upper floor, at least. Not that she'd been in much doubt.

She found Jake in the kitchen, frowning into the pantry as he swung the door back and forth from one hand to the other. He looked up with an uncertain smile as she came into the room, but seemed happy enough to have someone else to help decide what was for lunch. They settled on homemade vegetable soup canned by Cousin Kane's Aunt Vivian the previous summer. Jake introduced her to the delights of floating small cheese crackers shaped like fish in the soup and drinking milk over ice with it. It was comfort food at its finest, and went far to banish the constraint between them.

They talked of this and that, the fish he'd been catching on the lake, the baby shower given for Cousin Kane's wife, Regina, the excitement over the coming baby. All the while, Tory mulled over the best way to approach the teenager about what she wanted to know. At the first lull in the conversation, she said, "You know, this cuff thing on my ankle is really starting to get to me. I can't imagine having to wear it for months."

Jake's slim face mirrored relief, apparently because she'd brought up the subject. Until then he'd looked everywhere except at her leg. It was as though the cuff embarrassed him almost as much as it did her.

"I don't see why you have to wear it at all," he said. "It's not as if you're going to welcome the creeps who had you with open arms if they do show up again."

"I think your dad is more worried about my running off

to find them,'' she pointed out in dry humor. ''He doesn't exactly trust me.''

''I tried to set him straight about that, but got the 'You'll understand better when you're older' lecture. Man.'' He shook his head in disgust.

His partisanship was gratifying, but also disturbing. She studied the flush of color on his cheeks with distinct misgivings, wondering if he'd developed more than a mere liking for her company. He was at a susceptible age, old enough to feel the first stirring of infatuation, but too young to realize its brief nature.

Compunction, uncomfortable and unwanted, touched her just as it had that day on the porch. To rope in this boy, maybe to pit him against his father, made her feel on a level with an earthworm. And yet, what choice did she have? She needed help, and there was no one else.

''It's like being watched,'' she said with a small, brave smile. ''Like some perverted little man is following me everywhere I go.''

''Nobody can see you,'' Jake said in earnest reassurance. ''It's not a video camera or some fancy eye tied into a satellite surveillance system. Want me to show you how it works?''

Tory couldn't have asked for a better offer.

The control center had been set up in the den as a central area with an available telephone line. She might have missed the simple white plastic box holding its computerized module if Jake hadn't pointed it out. Set up on the end table beside the sofa, it received a radio signal transmitted by the cuff on a designated frequency, then sent data relating to all activities to the monitoring station in Baton Rouge via phone line. According to Jake, personnel at this station could tell if the monitor and its wearer were out of range, if the transmitter had been tampered with, if the battery was low, or if the phone line was out because it had been cut or from bad weather. Range for the unit was 150 feet. If she and her cuff moved farther than that from the house, the control center would dial up the monitoring center and another computer there dialed the phone number of the house. Voice recognition software could identify whether the person answering the phone was the wearer. If it wasn't, or if the wearer didn't reach the phone in a given length of time, the monitoring center immediately notified the sheriff's office.

"And that's when your dad comes running," Tory said, and compressed her lips.

"Exactly." The boy nodded in approval at her quick grasp of the mechanics.

"What I don't understand is how the computer is supposed to recognize my voice when it's never heard it," she said after a moment.

"Yes, well, you're a special case, according to dad, since you don't have a criminal record. The control center is set up to okay a specific command in his voice instead of yours. He's the only one who can call off the alert."

Roan had left nothing to chance. She could almost admire him for that, even as it made her more determined to find a way to circumvent him.

Glancing at Jake, she mustered a sigh. "I know your Dad means well, but he has no idea what wearing this thing is like. I mean, it gives me the willies, flashing when I move, sending every little thing I do somewhere so strangers can keep up with me. I don't suppose there's some way to take it off now and then, say when I'm in the shower?"

"No way!" Jake exclaimed. "You have to use the right tool or they can tell you're messing with it. Besides, water doesn't hurt the thing a bit."

Now they told her, Tory thought in irritation for her uncomfortable baths lately that she taken with one foot resting on the tub rim. At the same time, she frowned over the problem. The tool Jake was talking about was undoubtedly the little wrench device Roan had taken from his pocket to attach the cuff. Finally, she suggested, "I suppose your dad is looking after that, too?"

"Not exactly."

It was in the house, then, or else there was a spare. Jake knew so much about the monitor that she had little doubt he also knew the location of the tool.

She turned her best and most cajoling smile on the boy. "Where it is? Give me just a tiny hint, please, pretty please, Jake? I'll find it myself. You can look the other way. No one will ever know. I promise I'll only slip the cuff off for relief, no more than a few minutes at a time."

"Dad would have a spitting fit!"

She didn't doubt that for a second. "He won't find out, I promise. It would be our secret."

Roan's son looked away. He chewed on his bottom lip. Then he squared his shoulders and faced her again. With a shadow of condemnation in his eyes, he said, "I don't keep secrets from my dad. That's not the way it works around here."

That was that. Forced to choose loyalties, the boy had sided with his father. She should have known that he would. He had been well brought up. Truth, justice and honesty forever, amen. It was, no doubt, the Benedict way.

"Never mind," she said with her best attempt at a careless shrug. "It doesn't really matter. Forget I asked." She paused. "So. What shall we do this rainy afternoon?"

"Nothing. That is, I can't right now," Jake mumbled with hot color flooding his face as he looked away from her. "Got to go check on a dog that's been off his feed the last couple of days."

It was an excuse, Tory thought. He didn't want to be around her, didn't like her quite as much anymore. That it would happen some time was inevitable, especially when she left Dog Trot, still, regret for it weighted her chest. It had been nice to have Jake's uncomplicated approval. She was going to miss it.

The rain began not long after he left for the barn. Tory wandered from window to window, watching the swaying trees and warm downpour that splattered from the eaves, until she saw Allen sitting in his patrol unit on the drive, watching her. She waved as he lifted a hand in recognition, then retreated into the upstairs hall. Her bedroom held no interest, nor did reading or television. Idly, she climbed the steps to the attic again and wandered among the ancient keepsakes.

Rain pattered on the slate tiles overhead. The humid air through the eave soffits brought out the smells of dust and decay, mothballs and ancient sweat. It wasn't hard to imagine ghosts of the Benedict ancestors hovering in the corners, whispering among themselves as they tried to determine who she was and what right she had to pry into their former belongings.

She glanced through boxes of old Christmas decorations and newer ones for Christmases she never expected to see. She smiled over ancient baby clothes and kids' toys going back at least three generations, and flipped through stacks of 78 rpm records and eight-track tapes. The dust she stirred up caused her to sneeze, then sneeze again. With that reaction, and bothered by a feeling that she was poking around again where she didn't belong, she turned to go.

Near the stairs, she caught sight of a collection of boxes that were unmarked and shoved helter-skelter into a nook formed by supporting rafters. They were in such contrast to the rest of the carefully stacked and organized attic storage that curiosity made her stop.

Inside the boxes were the discarded mementos of a married life. They had been thrown in without wrapping or noticeable concern for their value, sentimental or otherwise. There were the dried remains of what might have been a cascade wedding bouquet, a pair of champagne flutes tied with stained white ribbons and engraved Bride and Groom; a twisted garter, napkins stamped with names and a date, and a wedding photograph in a tarnished silver frame. The smiling bride was a fragile-looking blonde and the groom was Roan.

She was definitely prying, delving into Roan's life just as she had the day she'd found the racing photo, but she couldn't resist. She reached for the silver-framed wedding portrait and tilted it toward the overhead light. As it caught the full glare, she rocked back on her heels with a small winded sound.

It was silly, of course. The items so carelessly discarded were obviously from his wedding, perhaps put away after his wife left them behind. She'd known somewhere in her mind that there'd been a ceremony, guests, and all the other details that went into the celebration of a marriage. Yet holding proof in her hands made it all so much more real somehow. She had to force herself to relax her grip on the frame before she bent it out of shape.

The photo was a formal portrait like a thousand others, taken in a church with ribbon-decked candelabra flanking the couple and a stained glass window in the background. Still, as Tory stared at it, the sense of something not quite right prickled at the edge of her consciousness.

The girl was pretty in a winsome fashion, with the slender shape and undefined features of a teenager. She appeared almost doll-like in her floor-length white gown overlaid with lace, with her bouquet held tightly at her waist and a nervous smile on her lips. Roan was tall and stalwart, staring at the camera with a near defiant air. His tux was white and, though doubtless rented, fit him to perfection. Frozen in time and place, the couple seemed so young, yet at the same time strangely mature.

The pair must have shared dreams for the future and hopes of eternal union to go with the promises they'd made, yet they had been disappointed. The marriage was over, the promises ended, the hopes and dreams gone forever.

Sighing, Tory replaced the frame in its box, then closed the cardboard flap. It was as she left the attic, heading back down to her room, that the niggling puzzlement over the wedding picture was solved.

The problem was the expression on the face of the groom. If his wedding day had been a joyful occasion, he hadn't let it show.

11

As time for the early dinner hour kept at Dog Trot neared that evening, Tory sauntered into the kitchen and took a seat at the butcher-block table. Roan looked up from where he stood over the stove frying chicken. Tory held his gaze, her own straight and inquiring. He tilted his head, as though considering. Then he calmly asked Jake to set another place. She felt as if she had won a major skirmish in an undeclared war.

While they ate, Tory took careful, if furtive, note of the enemy, mentally comparing Roan to the attic photograph. His expression gave little away as he talked with Jake about the sick hound and a truck-car accident in the center of town. She came to the interesting conclusion that Roan had a solemn personality, or at least he didn't smile too often.

She had thought that he was somber around her because of her invidious position as a suspect, but perhaps it was simply that he didn't find much pleasure in life. It was a side effect, possibly, of constant exposure to the seamier side of human nature through his job. But it might also be that he was simply unhappy or unfulfilled in some way important to him. She could understand that all too well.

She offered to help with the dishes, but was firmly refused. Either Roan didn't want her underfoot, or he was wary of letting her get too close. Whatever the reason, it made her feel useless and in the way, especially as he and his son moved back and forth in a choreographed routine, as if they'd cleared away together a thousand times. They didn't need her help, didn't need her; that was plain to see.

Still, she hovered near the door, uncertain whether to go or stay and unwilling to say good-night and retreat once more to her empty room while it was still daylight. As she stood there, Beau heaved himself up from in front of the window and padded over to her to nudge his big head under her hand. She accepted the hint, smoothing her hand over the short, silky hair on his head and scratching behind his ears as she considered the idea that Roan thought her incompetent. She might lack something in the housekeeping department, but she was more than proficient in the kitchen. There was a lot she could show him about his battering and frying techniques for chicken, for instance. Telling him wouldn't work nearly as well as showing him, she suspected. She just might do that, too. If she stayed around that long.

The bloodhound, watching her with soulful eyes and a mournful mien, reached out with his nose to sniff her wrist, then gave the palm of her hand a slurping lick. She wiped the wet patch on the side of her shorts, but smiled at the big dog anyway. At least somebody at Dog Trot approved of her and was willing to offer a little companionship.

"Come on, Beau," she said. "Let's take a walk."

"Don't go too far," Roan said from where he was drying the frying pan.

She hadn't realized he was watching. His words, she thought, were a reminder, or possibly a warning, as if he sensed somehow that she might be planning something.

The look she gave him was cool as she opened the outside door. She didn't bother to answer.

Roan stepped onto the back porch and walked to the railing, leaning to brace his hands on it as he scanned the garden and wooden areas between the house and the lake for Tory. She hadn't gone far, even if it had been a while since she left the kitchen. He'd known that, of course, since the monitor's control box remained silent. That didn't keep him from being relieved to catch sight of her and Beau among the trees.

She was leaning against the trunk of a pin oak with her fingertips thrust into the pockets of her cutoff jeans. Something about the slope of her shoulders and tilt of her head made her look pensive, remote and, yes, even lonely. Then she sensed his presence or possibly recognized that the closing door meant someone had stepped outside. Calling to Beau, she pushed away from the tree and started toward the house.

He wasn't going to have to drag her bodily back into the house at least. He wouldn't have put it past her to force that on him for the principle of the thing.

She wasn't happy with the monitor and he didn't blame her. At the same time, she'd been mighty quiet about it so far. He'd like to think it was because she held no grudge, but that seemed unlikely. It made him uneasy, rather like holding a firecracker with a burned-down fuse. He couldn't decide whether it was going to go off in his hand or turn out a harmless dud.

The rain had stopped an hour or so after he got home. The storm clouds were trailing off to the northeast, leaving behind a few streamers that caught the pink and purple of the last evening light. The orchestra of insects was just tuning up for its nightly performance. He breathed deep, inhaling the rainwashed freshness of the air and rolling his shoulders in an attempt to relieve the tension in his neck.

What the hell was he going to do with his prisoner?

Donna was disrupting his routine, stealing his sleep and complicating his life. He'd checked in with Allen a dozen times today by radio. That was in addition to talking to Jake. He'd also fielded messages having to do with her all day long. A few callers had expressed civic concern, but a couple of elderly women had almost hyperventilated with curiosity over the sleeping arrangements at Dog Trot. That was in addition to a former teacher of Jake's troubled over his being exposed to the "criminal element." Aunt Vivian had rung him up to ask if he needed a casserole brought over, and the mayor had reminded him about the police escort from the nearest airport when his gambling consortium guests arrived. For all the work he'd got done, Roan thought, he might as well have stayed home where he could look after his prisoner and his son himself.

He was going to have to make a decision about Donna soon, since he was fast running out of time and excuses. Somehow, he just couldn't do it, couldn't bring himself to hand her over to the legal process. Not yet.

As she came up the steps with Beau, the bloodhound almost tripped her as he pressed against her knee as a strong hint that he expected to be petted for serving as her escort during her walk. Roan, watching them, said, "I didn't know you and Beau were so thick these days."

She gave him a tight smile. "We came to a mutual agreement. I feed him ice cream and he doesn't bite my leg off."

"Makes sense. You hit on his fatal weakness."

"Not by trying," she said sharply.

She apparently thought he was accusing her of sabotage. "No, if you want to know the truth, I think he's partial to women as well as ice cream."

"Is he?" She moved past him to settle in the porch swing then set it in easy motion with the toes of one foot, avoiding Beau who followed her and plopped down so close that the swing passed back and forth over him.

"He was orphaned at four weeks old," Roan went on as he turned to face her. "Carolyn, Jake's mother, bottle-fed him every four hours until he was weaned."

She gazed at him a second before she said, "He must be getting on in age then. I hadn't realized."

"Yeah." He had nothing to add to that comment, mainly because he was sorry he'd brought up the subject. He crossed his booted feet at the ankle as he leaned on the railing.

"I somehow got the idea that your wife didn't much care for the dogs."

His reluctance to talk about past history was more than just a matter of privacy or even the normal male inclination to avoid personal problems. It was bone deep, something he'd learned at his father's knee: family business was discussed only with family. Still, he didn't want to cut Donna off just now. He was proud she was talking to him at all, since he'd expected her to hold a grudge over the monitor much longer. Though he was also aware that his concern about such a thing was a bad sign.

"Carolyn liked puppies and babies fine just as long as they were helpless and happy," he said as he crossed his arms over his chest. "It was when they began to have minds of their own that she had problems. But Dog Trot and Turn-Coupe were what she really couldn't stand. And me, of course."

The only sound on the porch was the steady creak of the chains on the swing. Just when Roan was beginning to think Donna had lost interest in his personal life, she spoke again.

"I saw a wedding photograph of the two of you when I was in the attic. Wouldn't it be more natural to have it out where Jake could look at it instead of putting it away as if his mother were never here?"

This was why you didn't discuss family affairs, he thought. People always figured they knew better than you what was best. He asked, "Find anything else interesting while you were snooping?"

"I wasn't snooping, just…exploring."

"You and Jake."

"He wasn't there. Anyway, I didn't think you'd mind."

"You were wrong." It touched him briefly that she would exonerate his son, even as he wondered what kind of idea she had of him that she figured Jake needed protection from his father.

She halted the swing and extended her ankle toward him. "Take this off and you won't have to think about what I'm up to while you're gone. I'll have something to do besides poke around in your business."

"Such as hightail it out of here."

"I'm not that stupid."

"I wouldn't have to worry if I locked you in your room, either."

"You wouldn't!"

He wasn't at all sure of that. This woman had an uncanny ability to touch him on the raw, so he said and did things that were less than rational. He fixed his gaze on the toes of his boots while he breathed through his nose. Finally, he sighed and uncrossed his arms, bracing his hands on either side of him on the railing. "Maybe not," he said finally. "At least, not tonight."

"But you might," she said, her voice flat. "Especially if I tried to make this place a little more like a home instead of a museum."

"Dog Trot is fine as it is," he answered a shade defensively. "We don't need gewgaws catching dust and cluttering up the place."

"Most people don't consider family keepsakes clutter."

"Anyway, Jake broke a couple of collectible figures and a vase or two playing ball in the house. That was after my Mom died. My dad and I figured anything of value was safer put away in the attic."

"He's not a child anymore," she said.

"Your concern for his welfare is touching, or would be if I believed it. Unfortunately, I don't. So what are you getting at? What is it you want now?"

"Nothing," she protested. She started the swing again. "I was just thinking, for obvious reasons, about memory. Photos are one of the best aids we have for recalling the past. They also help kids to feel connected, so they understand the things that happened. If a picture or two of his mother were sitting around, she might not be such a mystery."

"There aren't that many," he said shortly.

"One, then. Jake's mother was pretty in her wedding photo, but so young and...fragile-looking."

That was an astute observation. "Exactly. She wanted to be married, but it was like a fairy tale to her. After the big deal of the wedding, she hated everything about it, especially being pregnant and having a baby. She liked playing with Jake well enough when he was smiling, but handed him to someone, me, my mother, my father, every time he cried. So how is it supposed to help Jake to be reminded that she tried to commit suicide after he was born, then deserted him while he was still in his so-called terrible twos?"

Her eyes were dark as she stared at him. "Jake said she was depressed, but I didn't realize she tried to kill herself."

"With my handgun," he said with repressed savagery.

"I...I'm sorry."

"Sorry that it happened, or sorry that you brought it up? Never mind. Since you know so much, you might as well hear the rest. It happened here in the house, in the room where you're sleeping. We were living with my parents—it's a big house and Carolyn didn't much want the responsibility of a place of our own. I was off duty so my holster was hanging over a chair in our bedroom. Dad and I were working with the dogs down behind the barn, training a new leader. I heard the shot and started running. When I found her, she was lying on the floor in the white nightgown she'd worn for our wedding night. She'd tried to shoot herself in the head, but botched it, and I..." He stopped, not quite sure how to go on, or why he'd been so determined to give her the grisly details.

"You had to apply first aid," she finished for him in sharp understanding. "That's why you were so upset when I was shot."

"When I shot you," he corrected. A shudder rippled over him, leaving goose bumps in its wake. He stared beyond her at the evening shadows lengthening under the trees, though what he saw were bright-red splotches on white. Blood, so much blood.

The swing jerked and swayed as she left it. Moving to his side, she put her hand on his arm. "It wasn't your fault, any of it."

He met her gaze with its sympathy and instinctive women's wisdom. In rough rejection of it, he asked, "How do you know?"

"You were right about the way I came at you out of the van that night. I was just so determined to get away, to get to you, that I didn't think how it might look. Afterward, it was such a shock to have my escape turn into a nightmare that I wasn't responsible, said things I didn't mean. It's the same with Carolyn. Jake mentioned that she'd had a difficult time of it before you married. You couldn't help that, or her problem in dealing with it.''

"I used to think I could," he said, then gave a humorless laugh. "I thought I could slay all her dragons.''

There was more comfort in the feel of her palm on his skin than he would have believed possible. The low timbre of her voice seemed to ease some sore spot deep inside him. Strange, but he had a real need to make her understand how the thing with Carolyn had all come about, maybe because Donna was a stranger without preconceived notions, maybe because the two women were connected in his mind.

After a moment, he went on. "When we were young, twelve or thirteen, I used to help Carolyn sneak out of the house so that her dad couldn't find her and beat her when he came home drunk. It was worse on Friday nights, so we'd camp out in the fort we built down by the river. Carolyn was a bookworm. She lived in a sort of fairy-tale dream world. She used to call me Sir Roan, tell me I was her knight in shining armor and she knew I'd always protect her. It felt good to be looked up to like that, but it was scary, too. I tried to be what she expected, I really did, but sometimes I think it was the wrong thing to do. By fighting her battles for her, I kept her from standing on her own feet.''

"Weren't things better after her father left?''

"Not really," he answered, wondering at the same time what else Jake had told her. "Her mother wasn't able to work, and the public assistance they got didn't go very far. She and Carolyn were too proud to accept help from the church groups, much less ask for it. They always pretended things were better than they were, or that their circumstances were going to change somehow, some way. I tried to help. I drove Carolyn and her mother to town to shop or to keep doctors' appointments. I mowed their yard and kept their old house painted and repaired. One year I planted a garden for them, but they didn't gather the vegetables because that might have looked as if they needed to grow their own food. Carolyn would accept a few dollars from me when her mother needed medicine or some other comfort. That was all.''

''So you had both Carolyn and her mother leaning on you then,'' Donna said in tentative tones. ''It must have been a heavy burden.''

Surprise held him silent for a moment. He'd never looked at it like that, but simply accepted it as his duty to help a friend. ''Anyway, everybody noticed how close we were and sort of assumed we were a couple. I guess we did, too. She liked coming here to Dog Trot, being with my mom and dad. After she and her mother had to move in with her mother's brother, it seemed like a good idea to get married. We did, and I thought everything would be all right.

''But it wasn't.''

No, it hadn't been, for all the reasons he'd given before. Roan turned his head to meet Donna's gaze. Something in his face must have unsettled her, or else she realized she was still touching him, for she lifted her hand and stepped back. He studied her features, her eyes with their hint of compassion behind their coolness, the yielding softness of her mouth, the self-possessed tilt of her chin. She had her problems, but she was nothing like Carolyn. Nothing at all. Thank God.

The shift of a breeze across the porch brought her scent to him. He breathed it in before he could stop himself, that soap-clean fragrance tempered by a mind-stopping whiff of warm woman that had haunted him for days as he sat beside her bed. The involuntary tightening of his body was inconvenient, but no surprise. He'd been in a state of semiarousal for so long now that it was beginning to feel natural. What was new was the sudden ferocious need to bury his face in the tender curve of her neck and draw long breaths of that special scent, to burn it into his memory.

His changed mood seemed to communicate itself to her. She tilted her head and lifted an inquiring brow. When he said nothing, she asked, "So was it really postpartum depression that triggered the suicide attempt, as Jake seems to think, or was it something else?"

"Both, I guess. Her mother died, they found her father in a shallow grave, and she was never the same. It was as if she figured out, finally, that things were never going to get any better unless she did something about them."

"So when she didn't die, after all, she left. Tragic."

"Maybe, maybe not." He pushed away from the railing, putting distance between them. The last thing he wanted was her compassion. What he did want was her hands on him again, touching more than his arm, occupying his thoughts to the exclusion of all else, bringing him the peace that was always just beyond his grasp. The impossibility of it ever happening made his voice harder than he'd intended as he added, "Could be it was for the best."

"Meaning?"

"Carolyn needed professional help. I never realized it, wouldn't admit that I couldn't make everything right for her. That I wasn't all she needed."

His voice died in his throat as he heard what he'd just said. He'd acknowledged that he was partly responsible for his wife's problems. That was something he'd never done before.

"I think you're taking too much of the blame," Donna

said, her tone pensive, as if she might be thinking of something other than his dismal history. "It was your wife's decision."

"In a manner of speaking. Her therapist told her she'd never find herself while she was clinging to me as a lifeline, that she needed to let go. I guess it was true, since that's more or less what she did." Roan turned his head to study the woman beside him. "I don't suppose that's what you might be doing here, would it?"

A short laugh left her. "Finding myself? Hardly. But I thought you were sure I was a hardened criminal."

She was right. Had his thinking shifted, or was he just considering possibilities? He couldn't let her know he'd weakened even that far, or there was no telling how she might try to use that advantage. Anyway, it was the law that mattered, not what he might or might not think.

With an offhand shrug, he said, "I meant maybe that was the reason you took up with your pals, Zits and Big Ears. Maybe you're a poor little rich girl with problems that you're trying to solve by chucking everything for a life-style with no rules or obligations."

The look she gave him was dark. "Would that be so bad?"

"It has its appeal for all of us at times, but it's no remedy. At some point you're either forced to turn around and come back or else you run full circle. Either way, the problems are still there waiting for you. So what's the answer?" He waited to see if she would respond with the truth, or if the curtain would go up on another scene of her endless playacting.

She shifted uneasily, then moved further along the porch railing. Without thinking, he followed, wanting to be close, cursing himself for the weakness. She was under his protection. He had to keep that in mind at all costs.

"Maybe I'd rather not remember," she said in compressed tones.

It was marginally possible, but he wouldn't bet on it. He let silence stand as his answer.

"Actually, I don't care if I never do. I think I could get used to being in the country like this, to following the seasons, working in the garden, being able to watch the stars at night."

"Judging by your anklet, I'd say the stars in your world have a bit more glitter," he offered with deliberate irony.

Her laugh sounded forced. "From rhinestones?"

"Not according to the local jeweler. He says the stones are blue-white, finest quality diamonds. A photo of the anklet is circulating in the national network, but nothing has turned up on it."

"You mean it hasn't been reported stolen or missing."

"And no one's taking credit for being the designer."

"You think of everything," she said flatly.

"I try." He paused, then went on. "There are aids to memory, if you agree. Hypnotherapy, for one."

She straightened with a challenge in her gaze. "You expect me to let you poke around in my memory?"

"Not me, personally. Dr. Watkins is certified, and you couldn't be in better hands."

"I don't think so, thanks."

"Afraid of what we'll find?"

"As I said, I prefer my memory as it is, even with its glitches."

She had an answer for everything. He had to admire that. "You might remember something that would clear you."

"My, my, Sir Roan, are you trying to solve all my problems now?"

He flinched; he couldn't help it. He'd known that telling her about his private life was like handing her a weapon, but had expected her to have more scruples than to use it. He must have come too close to whatever it was that she was hiding. That was a promising idea though he allowed nothing of it to show on his face.

"I'm trying to do my job," he said evenly. "That includes solving your problems, since they impact the case."

"In other words, you want to be rid of me as soon as possible."

"Your stay at Dog Trot was always supposed to be temporary," he said without emphasis.

Her lips twisted at the corners. "So it was. Too bad."

"Meaning?"

Her lashes came down and her gaze rested on the star pinned to his shirt, as if it fascinated her. For an instant, he thought she was going to reach out to touch it, as she had before. As she spoke, her voice was low and not quite steady. "Given enough time, we might have come to a better understanding."

Did she mean what he thought? It didn't bear thinking about. In rough denial, he answered, "I think we understand each other well enough."

"Do you? But there's always room for...improvement."

It was a test of his willpower and sworn avowal that he wouldn't touch her. She was tempting him, even taunting him, because she knew very well that he wanted her. She thought she could use the oldest trick in the book to make him forget why he was holding her prisoner, forget everything except the sweet, sweet pleasure of tasting her, having her. And she was right, damn them both to hell.

"Don't," he commanded in hard, self-directed contempt.

"Don't what?"

"Don't look at me like that, don't say another word. Go into the house now, before you get in more trouble than you can handle."

She lifted her chin, her gaze meeting his in clear challenge. "Suppose I'd rather not?"

He didn't intend to move; there was no recognizable order from brain to muscle and bone. One moment they were standing with their backs to the railing, and the next he was upon her in a smooth glide of extending muscles. He lifted her with easy strength to seat her on the railing then hold her waist while he stepped between her spread thighs until he was firmly, mind-blowingly wedged against the softness at their apex. She gasped and clutched at his shoulders. Then they were still.

"If you don't," he said, his voice a jagged rasp of sound, "then you'll find out how easy it would be for me to forget what and who I am. You'll find out what it's like to be loved in hot, Deep South fashion, holding nothing back. And you'll discover that the experiment won't make a damned bit of difference, because I won't let it. I can't, not and live with myself."

She swallowed hard, for he watched the movement under the golden skin of her throat with burning eyes. She whispered, "I thought…you had no objection to a test?"

"I said it, but I was wrong," he answered, his breath coming so fast and deep it made his lungs ache. "Call me oversensitive, but I do object when it's a lie. I object when it's to throw me off the scent. I object when it isn't me you want, but what you can get from me."

"That's what you think this is about?"

She was shaking; he could feel the tremors under his hands, against his body. It affected him as nothing else could have, so that it was all he could do not to slide his hand under the soft cotton of her T-shirt, to cup her breast and put the pad of his thumb squarely on the spot where her heart pounded.

She was no streetwise call girl as he'd thought possible

at first, but a woman in over her head and not handling it well. Fear did that to some people. It made them react rather than think. Once they'd chosen the wrong path, it was nearly impossible for them to turn away from it. He'd give a lot to know where she had miscalculated, and how far gone she was at this minute. If he knew, he might still be able to set her right. She was far too straight in her ways, in how she talked and how she fought, for her mistakes to be too critical.

Excuses. He was making excuses for her again. It might have been funny, if it wasn't so pitiful. And who would make them for him if he went back on his word?

It took wrenching, gut-tangling effort to step back, to set her on the floor and support her until she was steady on her feet once more, and then to let her go. Still, he did it. It was that or else make love to her there in the gathering darkness, have her with fierce tenderness and no thought or hope of tomorrow, then take her up to his bed and have her again. And again.

"It doesn't matter what this was about," he said with grim care. "It's over."

He put his hand on her elbow and turned her toward the kitchen door. She went with him into the house, then moved obediently toward the stairs to the upper floor as he headed her in that direction. At the foot of the staircase, however, she turned back. Her eyes were huge in her pale face and shadowed with secrets as she stared at him across the room. Then the lovely curves of her mouth tilted in a smile.

"Over?" she said, her tone quiet, almost contemplative. "I think it's just begun."

12

Tory heard about the impending arrival of the gaming consortium members on the police scanner. It was an accident. She was walking past the open door of Roan's bedroom when the scanner on his desk blared out static and police code. She glanced in, but didn't stop and back up until she recognized Roan's voice in answer.

She was alone in the house and more than a little bored, since Jake had gone to hang out at his friend Terry's house for the day. Eavesdropping on police messages would prevent her from wandering around like a lost soul, or inviting Cal, on guard duty, inside for coffee just for company.

The bit about the consortium had come in a message from Roan's office to him where he was on his way to attend a funeral out in the country for a former police juryman. The mayor wanted Roan to swing by the mayor's office on his way back into town to discuss the impending visit of a couple of the gaming bigwigs, Evan Battersea and Harrell Melanka. Tory, listening to the exchange, longed to have her boredom back again.

Harrell was coming to Turn-Coupe.

It was obvious that Zits and Big Ears had reported, finally, they'd lost her. No doubt they'd also told Harrell that she had been injured and was being held under tight police security. If the two had listened around the area, they might have told him, as well, that she'd lost her memory and no one in Turn-Coupe had any idea of her identity.

Her ex-fiancé was coming. He'd find some trumped-up reason to see her, then stage a touching recognition scene. Immediately afterward, he'd produce proof of identity and request that she be released into his care while calling in a raft of high-powered lawyers to file all the necessary motions to have any charges dismissed. If that didn't work, he'd bring in Paul Vandergraff. With her stepfather in the picture, she'd be on her way back to Florida before the ink dried on the paperwork.

She wouldn't go.

Yes, but how could she stay? Roan hardly believed a word of what she'd said up to this point. If she conveniently regained her memory and tried to tell him now that Harrell was behind her abduction, he'd figure out what a consummate liar she was. How likely was he to believe a word she said then?

The message she'd heard made it sound as if the visit from the consortium had been pending for some time. For a brief moment, Tory wondered if Roan hadn't mentioned it to her because he knew of her connection and was stringing her along. Then logic kicked in. He hadn't brought up the subject because he had no idea she'd be interested. It was paranoid to think otherwise, though the situation was enough to drive anyone a little mad.

She couldn't just do nothing. To start, she needed to find out when Harrell was arriving. When she knew how much time she had to work something out, then she'd make up her mind whether she was going to face him or run. She didn't want to go like that, but running away looked like the most intelligent decision she could make. That was, of course, if she could figure out how to get rid of the monitor so the eternally vigilant parish sheriff didn't stop her before she was a mile from Dog Trot.

She returned to the scanner off and on the rest of the day, in between trips to the kitchen to prepare a steak-and-broccoli pie for dinner. She grew adept at making out the voices on the scanner and understanding what was going on in the parish. A part of it was the context of the messages, but the codes and numbers rattled off by the communicating officers were also very similar to those used on the daily reruns of one of Jake's favorite TV police programs.

She heard Roan again, reporting in from various points. It occurred to her that if she paid close attention to the scanner while he was away from Dog Trot, she'd always know his location and what he was doing. Not only would he have a much harder time dropping back by the house unannounced, but she'd know whether to try any doubtful activity she might want to undertake. That she now had a way to keep tabs on Roan, one almost as good as his method of tracking her whereabouts, gave her immense satisfaction.

She was concentrating so hard on the scanner late in the afternoon that she didn't hear the back door open, didn't catch the first quick footsteps on the stairs. It was Beau, lying at her feet, that alerted her. He lifted his head with a rumbling growl of warning.

Tory came erect as she tilted her head to listen. Beau wouldn't growl at Jake or Roan. Cal had orders to patrol the woods on a regular route, keeping the house in view but staying outside for the most part. No one else should have had access, yet the intruder seemed to know exactly where he was headed.

The big bloodhound heaved himself to his feet and stood

stiff-legged as he watched the door. The ruff on his neck rose as his growl deepened to a threat. Tory put a hand on his big head.

The even treads hit the floorboards of the hall, were deadened briefly by the hall carpet, then approached the bedroom without pause. If the intruder feared attack by the growling dog, there was no sign of it.

Tory looked around for an escape route. The windows of the bedroom opened onto the back gallery, but she'd never get them open in time. The brass doorknob was already turning, the door beginning to open. Beau's growl broke into gruff barking. Tory reached for a small brass statuette of a shepherd and shepherdess that sat on the bedside table.

The man paused in the doorway with his hand still on the knob. He was a stranger, with black hair cut close to his head to control its tendency to curl, and the clearest blue eyes Tory had ever seen. The combination of light and dark reminded her of a summer's storm as it blew in off the gulf, all calm clear skies on one side of the beach and somber darkness on the other.

Tory held her makeshift club in front of her as she demanded, "Who are you?"

The man flicked a glance at her, but concentrated his attention on the barking dog. "Down, Beau," he called above the dog's din. "For crying out loud. See if I bring you any deer bones this winter!"

The bloodhound subsided, looking away as if embarrassed while he wagged his tail. It was plain that he knew the man who continued to talk to him in half humorous, half exasperated appeal. Tory wasn't quite ready to relax, however.

The newcomer gave her a straight look, taking in her weapon, before he inclined his head in a truncated bow.

"Didn't mean to scare you, ma'am. I'm Clay, Clay Benedict. Roan gave me a call, said he'd be tied up at work a couple of more hours. Since Cal's shift is over and Jake's still out rambling around, he asked me to come over and take up the slack, so to speak."

"You could have knocked," she suggested.

"Did that, but I guess you were busy. Roan clued me in on what's been going on, so it seemed best to have a look-see, make sure you were okay. I let myself in with the extra key down at the barn."

"I'm supposed to take your word for this?"

He smiled, a slow curving of his mouth that rose to reflect in his eyes with real humor. As he spoke, his voice carried a deep, musical lilt. "I'd be obliged if you would."

He was a Benedict all right. The family resemblance was there in his height, his square shoulders, the thick brows and steady gaze from large, wide-spaced eyes. He appeared younger than Roan by a couple of years, possibly, but had the same confidence, the same audacity as the three men in the racing photograph Tory had seen in the attic. Still, she wasn't quite ready to relax her vigilance.

"Give me a good reason."

"Hmm. I could show you my driver's license, but didn't think to grab my wallet before I took off, since I skimmed over on *Jenny.*"

"*Jenny,*" she repeated, her voice flat.

"My airboat," he said in quick explanation before he gestured toward the bedside phone. "Give Roan a call, why don't you? He'll vouch for me."

Disturbing Roan at work was the last thing she wanted to do. Feeling suddenly ridiculous with the statuette in her hand, she set it back on the bedside table. Beau, as if taking his cue from her, flopped down on the rug beside her again. After a moment's thought, she said, "Maybe you could just tell me something about your cousin that would convince me?''

"Expose Cousin Roan's secrets?" Clay tipped his head to one side as a wry glint appeared in his blue gaze. "That could be a problem."

"Meaning?"

"I'm not sure he has any."

The stare she gave him was jaundiced. "I expect you can think of something."

"A challenge, huh?" He turned to set his spine against the door's frame, then crossed one booted foot over the other in a relaxed pose. "Let's see. He'll turn thirty-four next birthday. Since Jake's fourteen, Roan was barely twenty when his son was born. He's been sheriff forever, and he works too hard at taking care of everybody in sight. How's that?"

"Keep going." She crossed her arms over her chest.

Clay appeared to search his mind. "Old Roan likes to fish, at least when he can find the time. His favorite food is fried white perch. He hates light beer but loves light potato chips. His son is the most important thing in his life, but next in line is his 1970 Plymouth Super Bird."

"His what?"

"A Classic Car," Clay said with a pained expression. "Note the capital letters. An elegant machine of chrome and steel of a kind they don't make anymore—a symphony of precision mechanics and fine engineering that's such a vision of grace and positive motion that she looks as if she's racing even when she's standing still."

He was describing the car in the photograph she'd seen in the attic. "Color?"

"Purple. Some silly name. I don't know."

"Plum Crazy," she said, and smiled.

"That's it," he agreed, his gaze sharpening with interest.

"Original paint job?"

"Absolutely."

She took a step toward him. "Does it still have the rear wing?"

"The car's in perfect shape—not a scratch or ding, runs like a son of a gun, doesn't use a drop of oil." He stared at her. "But if you're so into Classic Cars, how is it you missed hearing about Roan's baby?"

She shrugged, shielding her gaze with her lashes as she tried to rein in her enthusiasm. "It never came up."

"It will, just wait."

She tipped her head. "You sound as if you might have more than a passing interest."

"It rubs off when you and your brothers tag around after three cousins wild about combustion engines. That was years ago, of course. None of us have time for it anymore, what with work and families. Anyway, I switched over to boats, well, boats and photography."

"And they're your current passion?"

A quick grin came and went across his face. "I guess that's one way to put it. Roan has a bass rig with a 150 horsepower motor that I've been trying to get him to sell me—Lord knows he doesn't need it, no more time than he has to fish. It's a classic of its kind, souped up so it outruns anything on the lake. He bought it not long after he lost a boat race to Luke and Kane and had to cook and serve breakfast to them in the buff."

She stared at Clay. "You mean as in...naked?"

"Boggles the mind, doesn't it?"

The image certainly had mental impact. "So he bought this superfast boat because he meant to win the next race."

"Did, too," Clay agreed with a nod. "Our Roan doesn't like losing."

She'd noticed. A slow smile tugged one corner of her

mouth as she stepped toward Clay and put out her hand. "All right. You convinced me."

He straightened and enclosed her fingers in a warm clasp as he grinned down at her. "Don't tell Roan I spilled the beans, will you? He also doesn't like people talking behind his back."

"I can tell you're really worried."

Clay lifted a shoulder. "I'm not above kidding him to his face, but he might consider discussing his misspent youth with you a different proposition altogether."

"I see." Coolness layered her voice again.

"I doubt it," he answered without quite meeting her gaze. "It's the kind of thing a man prefers to tell on himself." He turned toward the hall. "You don't suppose Roan has an extra beer in the fridge, do you? Since I'm taking guard duty for him, the least he can do is supply refreshment."

It was a diversion, but she decided not to call him on it.

Clay turned out to be a human database on the Benedict family, both past and present. He entertained her with tales of the brothers who'd settled Turn-Coupe, including his own family branch, enlarging on what Johnnie had already told her in the hospital. His close family included two brothers, Adam and Wade, and an artistic mother, though he mentioned a twin who had been killed in an accident a few years back. His stories sometimes seemed far-fetched, but were lively and sensitive. She found herself enjoying the easy camaraderie that rose between them. With a little gentle prodding on her part, he even filled in a few more gaps in her knowledge of Roan. He steered clear of anything too personal, but didn't seem to mind talking about his hobbies or his job and its responsibilities.

It was growing late when he started telling her about the way Roan souped up the engine in the patrol unit he drove, frustrating the local teenagers who liked to hot-rod their cars and race them on the street.

"You should have heard what Dale Rathson said after Roan pulled him over following a chase down the old lake road. He went straight home and started tearing the engine down on his brand-new Mustang, swearing he'd beat the sheriff next time. Dale's dad had a fit when he found out."

"You're supposed to be watching out for Donna, Cousin, not boring her to death," Roan said from the open doorway of the kitchen.

Tory swung to face him. How long had he been standing there, she wondered? Did he know that she'd been teasing information about him from his cousin? And did he realize that he'd made Clay's presence sound more as if he'd been sent to protect her than to guard against her escape?

Clay rose to his feet and reached to clasp his cousin's hand. "It's about time you got home."

"Figured you were about ready to leave," Roan said easily. "That's if you want to get home while it's still light enough to tell the lake from the trees."

"That's what boat lights are for, old buddy."

"No sense taking a chance."

Clay tilted his head to one side, sliding his gaze from Roan to Tory, then back again. "You trying to get rid of me? Say the word, and I'm gone."

"Don't go yet," Tory said before Roan could answer. "Stay for dinner. It won't take long to put it on the table." Roan's attitude seemed strange, almost possessive, she thought, especially when he was the one who had sent Clay to Dog Trot.

Roan compressed his lips, a sure sign of displeasure. "Who's going to cook? Jake's not back and I don't feel like starting a big meal."

"Dinner is ready," she said with a confident smile. "I made it earlier."

"You?"

"Including dessert."

He turned to his cousin. "You'd better stick around then, in case Jake and I wind up with accidental food poisoning."

"If I poison you," Tory said with ultra sweetness, "it will be no accident. Believe me."

Clay grinned as he looked from one to the other of them. "I don't think I'd better go, after all," he said to his cousin. "Sounds like you two need a referee."

The look Roan gave him had a slicing edge to it, but Clay met it with a lifted brow. After a moment, the sheriff laughed. "Let me grab myself a beer and another one for you and we'll sit outside, out of Donna's way. She can call us when the food's on the table."

Tory might have been annoyed at being treated like the hired help if not for a sneaking suspicion that Roan's main concern was to get Clay out of the house, away from her. That idea was so intriguing that she stood for a long moment, staring after the two men as they banged their way out the screen door. Then she shook her head, and moved to put the steak-and-broccoli pie in the microwave to reheat then set the table.

When Tory went to call the men a short time later, she paused at the screen door that opened onto the back porch. Roan and Clay were lying on lounge chairs out on the patio, the perfect picture of comradeship as they drank their beer. Jake was just returning; he called a greeting to the two men as he dismounted and cut the engine of the dirt bike, then wheeled it over to join them. There was something permanent and enduring about the small group, as if they were where they belonged, and knew it.

A warbling ring cut through the rumble of masculine

voices. Roan threw up his hands as if in disgust, then pulled his cell phone from his shirt pocket. He got up and walked away a short distance, asking staccato questions and nodding his head from time to time as he listened to the answers. Closing the phone with a quick slap, he turned back to the other two.

"Bad accident on the old iron bridge," he said. "I have to go."

Tory opened the screen and stepped outside. "Your plate is ready, if you want to grab a quick bite first."

"No time," he said, with only a brief glance in her direction before he turned to his cousin. "It's a messy deal, a carload of teenagers and an eighteen-wheeler with a load of chemicals." He gave a terse description and a comment or two which indicated that the ancient bridge, one of many in the state awaiting allocation of funds before replacement, was known for accidents. Then he added, "The First Response team has been called out. You can ride with me, Clay, since you don't have land transport."

"Can I go?" Jake asked, the gaze he turned on his father hopeful.

Clay didn't move, but only squinted up at Roan. "What about Donna?"

"Jake's here now, plus Allen will cover Dog Trot until I get back. They need every First Response teammate at the wreck."

"Aw, Dad," Jake said in complaint, the expression on his face showing plainly that he'd rather be in on the excitement of the wreck.

"And the time in between?" Clay asked.

"Won't be any. That was Allen on the phone. He's on his way." Roan leaned to offer his hand to Clay to help him off the lounge, a not too subtle hint that he expected him to get a move on.

"You've covered all the bases, haven't you?" Clay's voice was without inflection as he rose to his feet, but Tory thought she caught the gleam of amusement in the rich blue of his eyes.

Roan made no reply. Turning on his heel, he stalked toward his patrol unit on the drive that curved around from the front. He climbed in and cranked the engine, barely waiting for Clay to drop into the passenger seat before he put it in reverse. Seconds later, the two men were gone.

So much for wowing anybody with her culinary ability, Tory thought as she turned back inside the kitchen. Roan could eat later, but it wouldn't be the same; nothing would be as fresh or as good as it was at this moment. She'd gone to so much trouble, making the filling and the crust from scratch, even creating a special crème brûlée for dessert. A wrecked meal was nothing compared to helping save lives in a bloody traffic accident, of course. Still, she was disappointed. She'd really wanted to prove her usefulness.

Tory wondered, again, if she shouldn't tell Roan about Harrell, shouldn't lay everything on the line. That would be the Benedict way, wouldn't it? Everything honest and aboveboard, out where everyone could see exactly what was going on and know where they stood? It might even be the best way.

She didn't dare. She had too much to lose. Besides, she couldn't stand to see the disdain in Roan's face when he found out how she'd lied to him.

When had his opinion come to mean so much? Why did it matter at all?

It didn't, not really. Of course, it didn't.

With a quick shake of her head, she moved to the range where she dished up the meat pie for Jake and herself. Roan's son, still nursing his grievance over being left behind, slouched off into the den with his dinner. Tory put her plate on the table, poured a glass of merlot, and took a salad from the refrigerator. Then she sat down to eat, alone.

On a bright and sunny Saturday morning, Tory was awakened by a powerful roar. It sounded like someone playing around with a high-powered engine on the drive in front of the house, accelerating, then backing off the throttle as if listening to the tone and pitch. Flinging back the sheet that covered her, she slid out of bed and reached for her shorts and T-shirt.

Roan's Super Bird sat on the driveway. It was a beauty, sleek and trim, its Plum Crazy Purple paint job shimmering in the sunlight with an iridescent bloom like a perfect Santa Rosa plum. Looking as perfect as the day it rolled off the assembly line, it gave silent testimony to the loving care that had been lavished upon it in its lifetime.

Tory's footsteps crunched in the gravel as she circled to the front where Roan stood with his head under the raised hood. He straightened and turned to face her.

If he had not been in front of his own house, she might not have recognized him; he was that different. He looked younger, more carefree, in a pair of cutoff jeans faded almost white and with ravels hanging down over his muscular thighs, a T-shirt with ragged openings where the sleeves should have been, and ancient rubber thongs on his feet. His hair was rumpled and still wet instead of neatly combed, as if he'd done no more than rake his fingers through it when he stepped from the shower. A fine sheen of perspiration highlighted the muscles of his arms, calling attention to their smooth power.

Tory had never seen him jogging and there was no exercise equipment in the house that she'd noticed, which meant his physique had to come from pure hard work. She was duly impressed as she allowed her gaze to travel up the length of his long legs, past his narrow hips and flat waist to the width of his chest.

"Morning," he drawled with one brow lifted in inquiry.

She could feel the heat that swept toward her hairline for being caught at something perilously close to ogling him. To cover it, she stepped to his side and glanced into the engine compartment. Instantly, her embarrassment was forgotten.

"A 426 Hemi," she said, and whistled softly under her breath. "I'll bet she really flies."

He didn't answer. The silence lasted so long that she lifted her gaze to meet his. He was staring at her with a bemused expression. As he met her eyes, however, he blinked then shook his head. "I've had it up over the speedometer limit on the track, over two hundred miles an hour. They ran Super Birds on the NASCAR circuit, you know, though they had to replace the fiberglass nosepieces. They flew all to pieces in the races."

She reached over to rap with her knuckles on the cone-shaped nose of the car. At the metallic ring of aluminum instead of plastic, she said, "You were running it then?"

His eyes narrowed a fraction, perhaps in surprise at her knowledge. "For a while."

"How did you ever get hold of it?"

"Won it."

"You're joking."

A lock of hair fell into the middle of his forehead, softening the hard angles of his face, as he gave a slow shake of his head.

"How?"

The silver facets of his eyes shone with remembered pleasure as he told her about his summer spent on the NASCAR circuit with his cousins. The car they had run was named the Whirlwind, he said, because it was always spinning out, but it had given them the grand prize of the summer, the Super Bird.

"I saw a photo from that race in the attic, I think," she said when he paused for breath.

"Kane was suited up, wasn't he? He usually drove while Luke and I ran the pit."

"So you were the engine man." She couldn't help smiling at the idea.

"Master mechanic," he corrected, putting his hands on his hips. "Luke drove the truck and trailer between gigs, though we all took turns at everything."

"Kane and Luke let you have the Super Bird? Must be great guys."

"The best, though I paid them for their share."

He would, of course; he wasn't the kind to take anything at someone else's expense. Unaccountably, the idea made her chest feel tight. Turning back to lean under the hood again, she said, "Well, master mechanic, judging from the smell of fuel under here, I'd say your Carter Thermoquads need adjusting."

"The carburetors?" His shoulder brushed hers, bare skin against bare skin, as he stepped close to peer at the engine.

"Fire it up again, if you want proof."

"Oh, I believe it, since I just decided the same thing." He turned his head to look down at her. "What I want to know is how you came by your knowledge of performance cars?"

This was dangerous ground. Should she disclaim everything or pretend to the retrieval of some small chunk of memory? In a play for time, she did her best to look confused as she said, "I'm not sure. It almost seems…"

"What?" He turned to put his back to the fender, patiently waiting.

"I think I may have had a car something like this, only red, and there was...a man."

"There would be," he said under his breath. "What else?"

The quiet tone of his voice was like a friend inviting a confidence. It gave her the nerve to continue. "Somehow, I see it as maybe a birthday gift when I was a teenager?"

She'd been sixteen, actually, and the car had been a fire-engine-red 1969 Oldsmobile Cutlass with a white convertible top. It was a guilt gift, or maybe a bribe, from her stepfather after he'd had her mother locked away in her fancy nursing home. He'd known she enjoyed attending Classic Car shows and he'd thought that was the way to get her to agree that he'd done the best thing. It hadn't worked, but it was a long time before he realized it.

"This man you mentioned, could he have been the one who taught you about carburetors?"

He had been a tennis pro at the club, handsome, tan and on the take, especially when it came to silly young girls. What he'd taken had been her confidence and her car. He'd smashed both to smithereens, along with himself and her best friend, on the Key West Causeway. But she couldn't tell Roan that. She looked away, allowing a vacant expression to slide over her features, as she answered, "Who knows?"

"Right."

Did that laconic comment mean he accepted the lie, or that he didn't? She couldn't tell. One thing she did know, she'd gone far enough. If she wasn't careful, she'd be telling Roan Benedict everything. How they'd spent weeks, her and Mark, going through the motor on the Olds, souping it up with new rods, a stronger piston, even shaving the heads to improve performance. They'd been a couple, an item, among their group. He was everything all the girls wanted: fit, experienced, long sun-streaked blond hair pulled back in a neat pony tail, gorgeous turquoise eyes, lots of free time. And she'd had him. For a few brief weeks.

"This wouldn't be the guy you had the breast surgery for, would it?"

Tory looked up sharply, startled that Roan had made the connection from the little she'd told him before. She was really going to have to stop underestimating this man. And he was right, of course, in a way. The augmentation had come during Christmas break the following year.

She met his gaze for long moments, with her own open and vulnerable. There was such tolerance in his face, such calm acceptance of human frailty. For all the high standards that he set for himself, she thought, he didn't require others to be perfect.

Suddenly, she hated the barrier between them created by her lies. She longed to be able to say anything, tell him whatever she pleased. That she couldn't, that she had to leave him and soon, caused an ache so strong she felt the rise of incipient tears.

He was waiting for an answer. The best she could do was a shrug before she sought a distraction, then found one in her need to know when Harrell was arriving. "So, you're actually taking a day off," she said as she turned back to survey the engine again. "I guess that means nothing much is happening in Turn-Coupe, no robberies, no murders—no funeral processions to lead or parades to police?"

"Not today."

The man was closemouthed beyond belief. She'd have to make another attempt. "No excitement of any kind, huh?"

"Well, let's see. Bobby Crofton punched Joe Myers's son in the nose over a backyard ball game and their respective mothers got into a hair pulling because of it. The husbands of the two ladies then traded insults and a few swings at each other. Bobby's grandmother was so disgusted at the spectacle that she turned the water hose on the whole crew, which changed the fight into a big mud wrestle. Libby Myers not only fell down and got her white jeans dirty but ruined her new perm, so she charged the old lady with assault and…''

"You're making this up," Tory accused him.

"Happened. Cross my heart." He turned his head to meet her gaze with laughter in his eyes. They were so close that she could feel his body heat, feel her arm grazing his so the curling hair on his forearm tickled her elbow. The scent of the herbal shampoo he'd used surrounded her, along with those of clean clothes, warm male and engine oil. She could see herself reflected in his pupils.

Her awareness of him became visceral, a thing of instinct and burgeoning emotion that had nothing to do with what was best for either of them. She stared at him while her wayward thoughts went slipping down peculiar paths. What would it be like to make love to him? Was it possible that this nebulous content she felt in his presence would extend to the bedroom? Could she laugh and joke with him, trust him, while their emotions rose to fever heat and an exciting hint of elemental danger still sang in her blood? Somewhere in her mind where logic left off and intuition began, she thought it was possible.

It was an enticing idea, so enticing that she could almost hear the alarm bells going off in her head. Her situation here was getting much too precarious.

Reaching out to brush her fingertips over a section of plum-colored paint that was waxed and polished to a mirror shine, she said, "Maybe people will have something else to do besides squabble when the gambling boat gets here. Any developments on that front?''

"Some of the bigwigs are coming to talk to the town fathers, see if they can speed up the special election."

At last. "You'll have to be on hand for this powwow, I guess. When is it?"

"Couple of days."

Not long, not long at all. She needed a fast plan for escape. Growing suddenly aware that the vehicle in front of her might be useful, she trailed her fingers along the fender again. "So," she said, in careful nonchalance, as if reverting to the previous subject, "where do you keep this baby of yours that she stays in such mint condition?"

"In the barn," Roan answered with a cool silver glint in the depths of his eyes. "Under lock and key."

She should have known.

Their attention was caught just then by the sound of a vehicle slowing on the road. They turned in time to see a silver-and-turquoise behemoth of a motor home swing in the drive. It lumbered toward them with smooth power and pulled to a stop behind the Super Bird. The side door opened with a hydraulic hiss. A man stepped down and strolled toward them.

He was tall and lanky, with a head of dark hair liberally streaked with gray and the lean flanks and square shoulders of a man half his age. His eyes were a soft yet keen gray under bushy brows, and a smile split his sun-baked face.

"Don't tell me," Tory said. "Another Benedict."

"Give the little lady a prize," the newcomer said. "And I'll take a cup of java myself, while you're at it. I've been driving ever since I got your call, son, the best part of twenty-four hours."

"Whatever you want, Pop," Roan said as he walked forward and enveloped his father in a bear hug. "It's good to have you home again."

"Yeah, yeah, you have to say that after dragging me

away from the prettiest, sweetest lady I've met in some time, don't you?'' The older man cleared his throat and thumped his son on the shoulder a final time before stepping away again.

"I should have known you'd have something going.''

"So you should, since being a monk isn't exactly the Benedict way. Well, for most of us. But never mind that. If this is the lady friend you're calling in the clan to look after, coming home may just be worth it.''

"Calling in the clan?'' Tory asked with a lifted brow as she glanced at Roan. Clay had stopped by again, and just yesterday afternoon, Luke had dropped in and talked for a while with Jake while she was taking a nap. Did all these visits have a point?

Roan paid little attention other than to wave quickly in her direction. "Meet Donna, Pop.''

Roan's father was apparently a man who had spent a lifetime sizing up people; the once over the older man gave her was so fast and slick that it was done almost before Tory realized what was happening. There was nothing salacious in it, however, only a judicious weighing of the evidence of his eyes. If he noticed the electronic monitor on her ankle, he had the kindness not to linger on it.

"Donna,'' he repeated, reaching for her hand and carrying it to his lips while rich appreciation rose in his dark-gray eyes that were so like his son's. "The pleasure is all mine.''

"Thank you, Mr. Benedict,'' she said, then flushed at the absurdity of feeling grateful for the salute.

"Call me Pop, everyone else does.''

Something about his gallantry and the warmth of his smile made her want to respond in kind. "I'm sorry if you were put to extra trouble because of me.''

"No trouble at all.''

"It was just an excuse to get him here," Roan said in offhand explanation before he smiled at his dad. "How long is it you've been gone this time?"

"Not that long," the older man protested.

"Since just after Christmas. Long enough, in fact, that I think a little family get-together tomorrow as a welcome home is in order."

"Think so, do you?" The look Pop gave him was intrigued. "For a family council, would that be? Or you have something else in mind?"

"Might liven up the place," Roan said. "You know Donna surprised us the other night by turning out to be a good cook? She makes a great custard thing."

"Crème brûlée," she corrected. She might have been more impressed by the compliment if she didn't suspect its primary aim was to change the subject. She thought his father noticed the tactic as well. The way he narrowed his eyes was so much like his son's habit that it was all she could do not to laugh.

"Crème brûlée? Lord, she must be a gourmet chef instead of a mere cook," Pop said. Releasing her hand that he was still holding, he flung his arm around her shoulders in a casual embrace and swung around in the direction of the tall steps into the house. "Speaking of which, I've just remembered that I'm starved as well as in need of a cup of coffee. Let's get to be friends over a late breakfast, honey bunch. What do you say?"

"Friends?"

"By all means. Tell me you can make a decent omelet, and I may even adopt you into the clan."

Tory glanced back at Roan as she wondered how he would take the last suggestion. She could have sworn it was satisfaction that she saw in the stern lines of his face. But that was not possible. Was it?

13

The plans for the family gathering got underway at once. Before Tory knew what was happening, she was delegated to make garlic-baked brisket and blackberry cobbler, and cousins of all degrees, or their wives, were calling to see what they should bring in the way of covered dishes.

Pop or Jake answered the phone most of the time, but every now and then she fielded the questions. She could hear the curiosity in the women's voices as they discussed food and drink, but not one of them came right out and asked why she was in the middle of a Benedict clan gathering instead of shut up in jail where she belonged. She'd have thought it was her own distant manner that prevented it, except that she knew better. After hearing Roan and his son and father as they answered the phone, she thought it was respect that held everyone silent, that and the obvious protective cordon they seemed to be drawing around her. Their voices turned stiff and unresponsive when they talked about her. They invited no questions and answered none. Pop and Jake did it, she thought, because they had taken a liking to her, and also because they were following Roan's lead. Why Roan bothered was another question.

That mystery revolved in her brain until she thought

she'd go crazy with it. Was it simply a matter of principle? Could it be because some in town objected to the license he was taking in keeping her at Dog Trot, so he had to prove there was no danger in it? Or was it only the sanctity of his home he was protecting?

One other reason came to mind. He could be using her as bait to catch Zits and Big Ears. That would certainly explain his extra vigilance.

The trouble was that anything was possible with Roan. Anything at all. She found out how true that was late that afternoon while picking blackberries for the cobbler.

The berry patch was not far from the house, but out of the allowable range for the monitor. Roan gave his okay for the outing and arranged temporary override for the surveillance. Shortly afterward, he drove away to town for party supplies, leaving Jake to help her pick the berries and Pop on guard duty.

The blackberries were hybrids planted back in the fifties or sixties, according to Pop, and located in what had been a large kitchen garden and fruit orchard alongside the track beyond the barn. Roan apparently mowed between the rows from time to time to keep down weeds, but that was the extent of cultivation. The vines were huge, a tangled mass of arching canes loaded with thorns, and also with fruit in all stages from green to red to the near-black purple that signaled sun-warm ripeness. The fruit, as big as plums and of ambrosial sweetness, promised a wonderful cobbler.

Tory and Jake picked berries in companionable silence, accompanied by the drone of bees and the occasional squawk of a blue jay startled from its nest among the briers. Now and then, she caught a sweet whiff of summer honeysuckle that tumbled over a rotted stump. The old garden area was shaded from the late-afternoon sun by the encroaching trees, but it was still warm. Tory was hot, her fingertips were purple, her hands stung from raking against the thorns as she pulled berries from among the thick tangle, but she didn't mind. It was grand to be away from the house. She enjoyed being with Jake, and liked the idea of being useful. It was peculiar, but she was happy.

She was happy. How long had it been since she'd felt such near-euphoric content? She couldn't remember. A long time. The reason for it was not something she wanted to think about however, not now or any time soon.

Tory's berry bucket was less than half full when she heard the motor home start, then go trundling off down the drive. She looked at Jake with raised brows.

"Pop doesn't get it, I guess," he said as he frowned in the direction of the departing vehicle.

He meant Roan's dad was having trouble remembering that she was a prisoner. She'd noticed that, as well. It was nice that he was so unconcerned. "He said something earlier about delivering invitations."

"Yeah. Pop is probably going to shoot the bull over at Kane's house with him and his granddad, Pops Crompton. I heard him saying something about it on the phone a little while ago. But don't worry, Dad won't be gone long. And old Beau will let us know if anybody tries to sneak up on us."

That last assurance was well-meant, but since Beau was sprawled out asleep on the shady track, looking like a roadkill, it was hard to draw much comfort from it. In any case, her concern didn't run in that direction. She was without a guard, since Allen and Cal weren't around on weekends. Her monitor had been deactivated. Escape conditions couldn't have been better if she'd planned them.

The only thing she lacked was transport, and that was in the barn. All she had to do was figure out a way to get to it.

Enlisting Jake's help was out; she'd already established that he wouldn't go against his dad. The boy would probably feel he had to stop her if she tried to leave, too, and she wasn't sure she had the strength to fight him. He might set Beau on her if push came to shove, and though the dog had developed a fondness for her company, he was trained to obey working commands.

Tory wrestled with the problem as she continued to fill her bucket. Time was flying and it felt as if her brain and her will were paralyzed. She wondered in despair if her reluctance to leave wasn't making a fool of her. She should just break and run for it, letting the details take care of themselves.

What did she really need in order to go? The keys to the barn and to the Super Bird. Roan had put the car back under cover after washing and polishing it. When he decided to go into town, he'd changed out of his old shorts. The keys might still be in the pocket.

The only way she was going to find out was to look. The best time to do that was now. But first, she needed an excuse that would detach her present guard.

"My bucket's getting a bit heavy to hold without straining my shoulder," she called to Jake who had worked his way around to the back side of the front row, out of sight. "I think I'll go empty it and find us something cool to drink."

"Sounds good."

The words were offhand, as if his mind was on other things. Tory hoped it stayed there.

Moving at a casual stroll, she set out for the house. In the kitchen, she dumped the berries into a bowl, then sprinted up the stairs to Roan's bedroom.

The shorts and shirt he'd been wearing were nowhere in sight; he must have dropped them in the bathroom hamper.

It was doubtful the keys had been left in them then. They weren't on the desk, on the chest of drawers or on the dresser, nor were they in any of the dozen drawers she checked. Tory stood in the middle of the room, surveying it, while frustration beat up inside her.

The bedside table. Of course.

Short minutes later, she sat in the driver's seat of the Super Bird with her hand on the ignition key and the barn door open behind her. Her foot was on the brake, her free hand on the wheel. All she had to do was turn the key, put the car in gear, and go.

She couldn't do it.

Roan had taken her into his home when he didn't have to, and at considerable risk. He had nursed her, protected her and treated her almost like one of the family. To leave him now would be a gross betrayal of trust. She would be exposing him to the censure of everyone he knew, if not actually jeopardizing his position as sheriff. He'd be forced to chase after her. If he caught her, and he well might, he'd be forced to prosecute her for the escape attempt.

Where was she going to go, anyway? Back to her stepfather? Harrell would only confront her there, eventually, instead of here. She'd still have to deal with his lies and machinations, only she'd be doing it alone.

Tory released the key and leaned back, slumping down to rest her head on the low seat back. Grim-faced, she stared at her own reflection in the glass of the windshield. What she was running from this time, she saw clearly, was her own stupid pretenses that had evolved into this charade. If she'd told the truth from the beginning, she wouldn't need to go. No Benedict would ever have gotten themselves into such a mess because lies and pretenses were not the Benedict way. How much easier, in the long run, was the strict road of virtue.

What she should do was retrieve her bucket and go back to picking blackberries, then make every minute count of her time remaining at Dog Trot. A couple of days, and that would be it. Her curious idyll as a prisoner would be over. It had to be; there was no other way.

Abruptly, the door beside her was wrenched open. Roan stood with one hand on the handle and the other braced on the frame above her head. His voice harsh, he asked, "Going somewhere?"

"Obviously not," she answered, as she turned her head slowly to meet his hard gray gaze, "or I'd be gone by now."

Stillness invaded his features. For long moments they neither moved nor spoke. Then he said quietly, "But you thought about it."

"If thinking were a crime, the whole world would have a criminal record. But you're right," she added as the urge to try the Benedict method of dealing with problems crept in on her. "I did intend to go. I searched your room for the key, though I'm sorry about that, truly sorry."

"What stopped you?"

She moistened her lips, trying to find the courage to tell him everything, settling, finally, for a half truth. "I discovered that I didn't have any place to run."

He was quiet a moment. "Now what?"

"Now I go back to my berry picking, I suppose," she said, her smile uncertain as she swung her legs out of the car and stood up. "Unless you have other ideas."

He looked so stern, and it was so long before he answered, that she thought he was going to order her into the house. Then he replied with deliberation, "I have one, but I'm not sure you'd like it."

"What?" She waited, searching his face.

A deep, silent breath lifted his chest, then he shook his

head and stepped back out of her way. "Never mind. You've lost your help, you know."

"Jake? How is that?"

"That's why I came home, to send him over to Kane's house. Pop scared one of Aunt Vivian's kittens up a tree when he arrived in his motor home. She called, afraid Pop was going to kill himself trying to mount a rescue if Jake didn't come get the poor little thing down."

Roan sounded irritated by this task added to his day. She knew better than to believe it now. People wouldn't call on him so often if they didn't know he was always willing to help. It was his job, yes, but also his nature. The show of annoyance was to keep people from finding out what a pushover he was.

He was quite a guy, was Roan Benedict. If she could find the right words to explain just how alone and trapped she'd felt, and still did, would he understand? Would he look past his anger and forgive the lie she'd been living these past weeks? Would his precious honor allow him to help or would he abandon her?

The impulse to find out was like an ache. It would be such a relief to have it out in the open, to be herself. It should be such a simple act, to relax and tell him all the things she wanted to say.

It should be. But it wasn't.

He was watching her. She had to find some comment, some quip, before he demanded to know what was going on in her mind. Casting an eye over the pristine uniform he'd changed into for the trip to town, she said, "So who's going to take Jake's place? You?"

He sent a wary eye toward the berry patch along the track. "You don't have enough yet?"

"Takes a lot for cobbler for the whole clan," she informed him. The prospect of watching him try to remain cool and neat while helping her with such a messy job had irresistible appeal.

The look he gave her said he knew exactly what she was up to, but he'd let her get away with it for now. Turning toward the berry patch, he said, "The sooner we get started, the sooner we'll be done."

They worked for several minutes during which neither of them spoke. The ease Tory had shared with Jake was gone, however. The sun was just as warm, the bees just as busy, but the atmosphere almost vibrated with tension. Did it come from her, or from Roan, she wondered? Or was it from both?

After a time, he said, "How did Pop get out of this? I thought using blackberries was his idea?"

"Not quite, though cobbler is apparently his favorite."

"And you're willing to brave snakes and heatstroke for his sake? You and Pop hit it off, didn't you?"

"He's a sweetheart," she said lightly. "Besides, how could I not love a man who promised to buy underwear, makeup, and other such necessities for me while in town?"

"I meant to take you shopping when you felt up to the trip," he protested.

She suspected that he'd deliberately kept her wardrobe scant as another deterrent to escape, but had no intention of arguing with him about it. "Anyway," she went on, "your dad is different, a man so good that he sees only the best in people. Consequently, they probably show him the better side of their natures."

He stared at her, then gave a low laugh. "You know, you're right."

"It's a failing, what can I say?" She picked a berry and tossed it in the bucket he held. "I'm looking forward to meeting the rest of the Benedicts, to see what they're like."

"Some great, some so-so, some a real pain in the—a royal pain, just as in every other family."

She appreciated the fact that he refrained from using rough language around her. It put her on a different plane, even if she had been known to use a few words in moments of stress that would shock a pirate. "I enjoy listening to you and Jake and your dad. You're so comfortable together."

"Not something you're used to?"

She avoided his gaze, unwilling to let him see the pain that surfaced at the idea. "So it seems. I think maybe I don't have much family."

"Why do you say that?"

"They'd be looking for me if I did, wouldn't they?" Paul Vandergraff would surely be curious by now about where she'd gone, and possibly even a little anxious. They'd gone their separate ways too long, however, for any family closeness between them.

Roan paused a second, then reached for a berry so high that she'd missed it before. "I wonder sometimes what kind of home you came from, what kind of life."

An unaccountable tightness constricted her throat. She had nothing to share with him, nothing to use to make a bridge of any kind between them.

"Maybe I'll never know," she said finally. "It'll be like being reborn as a native of Turn-Coupe."

He looked up, scanning her features as if expecting sarcasm. Then he let his gaze wander in leisurely appraisal of her tank top and shorts. "Yeah? You don't look much like it, even in that Dixie Chick getup."

"I could fit in," she protested in spite of the heat that flooded into her face. "I'm getting a feel for country life. Fresh vegetables, animals, the great outdoors."

"It's a lot of work, unless there's a big family to share it."

"Like the Benedicts?"

"Like kids. You know, curtain climbers? Cereal slingers? Miniature people wanting to slobber in your iced tea at every meal and be cuddled every time you turn around."

"Oh, those." His derogatory description might have fooled her a while back, but now she heard the affection in it, and the longing. He must have enjoyed Jake's childhood, in spite of everything.

"Your kids would be something to see, beautiful smooth skin and big dark eyes," he said in a musing, half-reluctant tone. He seemed to have forgotten that he was supposed to be picking blackberries.

"Depends on the father, I'd think," she quipped without meeting his gaze.

"It does, doesn't it?"

The words were even lower than before, and freighted with meaning. Was he reading her mind? Or only testing to see how far she'd fallen under whatever spell he was weaving with his talk of babies? Too far, she realized with sudden clarity. She was entranced by the vision, just out of reach, of living in peace and security at Dog Trot, fishing on the lake, tending the garden and belonging to his extended family. Becoming a Benedict.

It was never going to happen. Even without the wall of lies between them, she was too different. She'd never fit into his world, nor would he ever consider leaving his home and community where he was so respected for the barren, artificial existence of hers. The idea of anything of the kind was like forbidden fruit, as unreachable as the sweetly ripe blackberries she could see hiding deep among the briers, too deep ever to be reached.

She leaned far into the brier tangle, trying for an especially big berry. It was just out of her grasp. She stepped closer, until a crisscrossed barrier of dried brown canes pressed against her upper arm. Still, she couldn't quite grab it, mainly because she couldn't balance that well while holding her injured arm close to her body. She inched a bit more.

Her sweat-damp rubber sandal slipped. Stinging pain bit into her arm as the briers caught her, clinging to her skin with their curving hooks. She drew breath on a quick gasp.

"Don't move!" Roan said sharply from behind her.

"I can't..." she began, but the words were never finished.

He snaked an around her from behind, then grasped the dead briers in his bare left hand and pushed them free of her skin. Before she could even breathe in relief, he swung her from the brier tangle and set her down. Then he shifted his grasp to her shoulder and bent to thrust his forearm under her knees. A moment later, she was swung high against his body.

The contact was so unexpected, and so close, that an involuntary shiver ran over her. His body was hot where it met hers, and his face was only inches away, almost against hers. She drew back slightly and put her hand against his chest, as if to put space between them. The berry juice on the tips of her fingers stained the smooth, tan fabric of his shirt. The purple spots spread as she watched. Funny, but she didn't like seeing him lose his neatness, after all.

She looked up at him with wide eyes. "Your uniform..."

"Doesn't matter," he said. "What about your shoulder?"

"It's all right. But this berry stain may not come out in the wash."

His lips twisted in a smile though the look in his eyes was stark. "A lot of things don't."

It wasn't berry stains he was talking about, she knew, but acknowledging it didn't seem like a good idea. "If you'll put me down, I can walk."

"Those damn thongs of Jake's are too big for you." Swinging around, he started toward the house.

"The blackberries!"

He turned slightly, and she saw the bucket where he'd set it down. He took the two long strides that brought him to it, then bent his knee enough that she could grasp its bail.

"This is ridiculous," she protested, even as she balanced the bucket on her middle.

"It's energy saving, your energy," he said, starting toward the house once more. "You shouldn't have been out here this long, anyway. It's too soon."

"Thank you, Dr. Benedict, but it isn't, you know. Doc Watkins says I can do anything I feel big enough to do."

"That covers a lot of territory, doesn't it?"

It did, of course, including activities that should not have been in her mind at all. In defense, she said, "I think you just like having me under your control. You want me back at the house and under monitor watch again so you'll know where I am at all times."

The look he gave her was straight. "Exactly."

At least he was honest, even if he did leave her with nothing to say. Lowering her lashes, she dipped into the bucket she held and took a berry, popping it into her mouth. The sweet-tart richness of it filled her senses and ran down her throat. She took another. As long as she was eating berries, she didn't have to argue with him or make bright conversation. She could let herself absorb the hard strength of his arms around her and the heat she saw in the silver-shadowed depths of his eyes.

On impulse, she selected the biggest, juiciest berry she

could see in the bucket, then put it to Roan's mouth. He
hesitated a moment before he took it. As he chewed, he
slowed his stride, though his gaze never left her face. He
stopped. His expression was suspended, taut with intima-
tions of rigorously controlled impulse. She lowered her
gaze while her heartbeat kicked into a higher, near-
suffocating gear.

The fruit had left a small stain on his full bottom lip.
She stared at it, mesmerized by that spot of moist purple.
The need to taste its sweetness combined with the warm
flavor of his mouth was so strong that her own lips tingled.
She saw him swallow, and could not prevent herself from
touching his sun-glazed throat with her fingertips.

She didn't decide to kiss him. There was no single moment when she said to herself: *This is what I want, what
I'm going to do.* It felt like compulsion, as if she had no
choice except to slide her hand behind the strong column
of his neck and draw his mouth down toward hers.

His muscles were tense so that he lowered his head by
stiff degrees, as if uncertain of the wisdom of complying
yet unable to combat the gentle pressure she exerted. Then
abruptly his resistance vanished.

Berries and fresh country sunlight and warm, clean male-
ness, he tasted of all those things and something more that
was simply Roan. He tasted perfect. She felt his chest swell
and his grasp tighten before he took the kiss deeper. The
smooth firmness of his lips sent gratification spiraling
through her. The abrasion of his tongue on hers was an
enticement past bearing. Tory didn't care if they stood there
mouth to mouth and oblivious, swaying in the warm Louisiana afternoon, until the final night came and the world
spun to a delirious end.

Why? Why did it have to be this man who matched her
needs so perfectly? Why did it have to be here, so far from

all she knew? Why did she have to find him now when everything was so wrong and might never be right again?

The questions had no answers. She pushed them from her mind while she let herself melt against him, let herself flow into him and around him until she wasn't sure where she ended and he began. And didn't care.

She felt it when he began to walk again, felt the long purposeful strides that took them swiftly back toward the house. Soon they would be surrounded by phones and all the other invasive stealers of privacy. They would be where the monitor was engaged, where she was once more a prisoner, and felt like it.

Dragging her mouth from his, she turned her face into the curve of his neck. With her lips against the salt-flavored velvet of his skin, she whispered, "Do we have to go back?"

For an answer, he swerved toward the barn they had left open. Seconds later, they were inside that big, open space, with the wide doors closed behind them.

It smelled of hay from summers past and animals that were long gone, of dust and mice, dried manure that had been ground to a powder, and a strong whiff of engine oil and rubber tires. Dirt-daubers whined like miniature concrete mixers in their mud nests among the rafters. Rays of sunlight streamed through holes in the walls to spotlight the purple paint of the Super Bird that sat glowing like some gigantic jewel in the cool gloom.

Roan set Tory on her feet before he opened the back door of the Super Bird and held it wide. He didn't urge her to climb in, made no attempt to persuade her, but only waited for her decision. She knew very well that entering the car meant acceptance of whatever might take place once they were inside. But she had vowed to make every minute count of her time left at Dog Trot, hadn't she?

She stared up at him a moment longer, then she set the berry bucket down and got into the vehicle, sliding across the seat to leave him room. The door, as he pulled it to behind him, shut with such a solid and final thud that a small shiver ran over her. Rolling down the windows for air, which he did in a few quick moves, didn't help. She shivered again as he settled back beside her.

"You can't be cold," he said quietly as he placed his arm across the back of the seat above her.

She shook her head. "Hot, instead. It's so hot."

"Not as hot as it may get. Do you mind?" His voice was husky, almost tentative.

"I like the heat," she said as she settled against him, then laughed a little at her careless word choice, perhaps from nerves. To cover it, she went quickly on, "Why do I get the feeling you might have done this before? Maybe in high school?"

"Not me, though I've bumped the siren at quite a few parking teenagers in the last few years."

"You should be ashamed," she murmured as she eased closer. At the same time, she rested a hand against his chest, spreading her fingers until her palm was pressed over his heart. She could feel its solid thumping against his chest wall. He was, she thought, as uncertain as she was about this chance they were taking.

She felt the brush of his lips across the top of her head, then along her temple to her ear. "Actually, I am," he said against her hair at her temple. "I might have to give them a little more time in the future."

"See that you do." The words were distracted. She was wrinkling his uniform by lying against him, and that wasn't good. With a marked lack of finesse, she found the buttons and slipped them from their holes, then pulled his shirt from the band of his pants while he eased away enough to help her. As his sleeve radio dropped down his arm, she caught it. "What about this?"

"Off," he said with the sound of satisfaction in his voice.

"And this?" She held up the pager as she unclipped it from his belt.

Roan took it from her without a word and put it together with the belt he'd unbuckled before tossing both into the front seat. Then he reached for her and dragged her across his lap, taking care not to strain her injured shoulder. At the same time, he eased back on the seat so they were half sitting, half lying on the leather upholstery, propped into the commodious corner of the boat of a car.

He brushed a hand along her arm, then caught the strap of her tank top and eased it away from the small bandage that covered her wound as protective cushioning. "Does it still hurt?"

"Only now and then, when I forget and do something I shouldn't."

"Like today?"

She shook her head. "It doesn't hurt at all now."

"Good," he said softly, and his breath feathered her skin as he leaned to brush his lips over the bandage, then trail a line of small, hot kisses to the mound of her breast, peeling away the thin knit that covered it to expose the nipple. He took that sensitive, rose-tinted peak into his mouth, wetting it, laving it with his tongue.

Tory made a soft sound in her throat as pleasure spiraled through her. She arched her back to allow greater access. At the same time, she grasped his waist, smoothing her hand along it, caressing the heated skin of his rib cage.

He made a low, hungry sound in his throat and pulled her nearer, until the heated weight of his body half covered hers. Tory caught his waistband, drawing him closer against her until she could feel the burning, pulsing evidence of his arousal, sense the hard pressure of his need.

Tory wasn't sure where all the boldness was coming from. She'd never been particularly aggressive in a sexual sense. Perhaps it was the heat and the lovely glide of her hands across his sweat-dampened skin. It could be desperation and the effect of her near-death experience, forcing her to reach out and grab for what she wanted, for the chance at life and love that she had been missing. Or possibly it was just the man himself.

Roan was everything she'd ever dreamed of in a mate. Strong, decent, honorable and caring, he attracted her on some deep, visceral level she couldn't explain, in spite of his unbending habits, or perhaps because of them. That she could have him here, in this moment, was an unexpected benefit to her captivity. A craving to capture him in her hands, to explore the rippling muscles of his back, to mold his taunt backside to her palms, to grasp the hot, silken length of him drove her. It was shocking, distressing, this reckless hunger to feel him against her skin, have him inside her, to absorb his essence deep into her body. She tugged at her own shirt, dragging it off over her head and dropping it to the floorboard.

The leather was hot against her back and Roan's firm flesh burned her breasts. To brush her hardened nipples against the light furring of hair on his chest gratified some deep inclination inside her. It fired her blood and created an ache in her lower body that demanded appeasement.

"Take it easy," he whispered against her lips. "Nice and easy does it."

He was right. Time slowed, stretched to accommodate them. With murmured words and encouraging hands, they moved together, searching for the sites of most perfect delight. Warm and deep, wild and free, their caresses mingled, spanned every millimeter of bare skin and eons of uncharted years. They sought the essence of each other, every taste, every firm curve and moist, silken hollow. Tory was hot, so hot, lost in the sensations of exquisitely sensitized skin, butter-soft leather under her, powerful male above her.

The remaining barriers of clothing were disposed of in a few languorous moves. A breeze shifted over them, flowing into the barn through a thousand cracks and drifting in at the open windows. It fanned their skins as Roan moved over her, parted her thighs. He pressed deep, twisting slowly to the last inch of penetration. She answered with her own involuntary surge, rising against him in mindless, virulent need.

He was perfectly still as his skin beaded with purest pleasure and he breathed a sound between a groan and a prayer. Feverishly, Tory soothed his skin while a deep, wordless breath signaled her agreement. Their eyes met as he paused, stretching the limits of her endurance and his own, pulsing within her to the rhythm of his heartbeat while her own internal muscles clamped down in slow, unstoppable possession. His gaze was smoke-gray yet fierce with concentration, as if his entire being were focused on the contact of their bodies.

"Roan."

The whispered word was at once a plea and a promise that she was with him, wanted him, needed him and could not bear not to have him. Now.

Dragging in a shuddering breath, he closed his eyes as if shielding his thoughts and feelings as he began to move within her. His palm closed around her breast, teasing the nipple with gentle abrasion. It was more than she could bear. She surged against him, imploring him with hands and lips to drive stronger, faster, deeper, fueling her urgent need to merge with him, to absorb his strength and hold it inside her for the rest of her days.

Together, they strove in primitive rhythm, reaching beyond the sweat-slick contact of their bodies, beyond time and place and into an ancient realm allotted to those who love with open hands. They found it, tumbled over the threshold and into the ultimate nirvana where in giving they received the only true wonder in the universe.

And afterward, they lay with the sweat cooling on their bodies and their hands ceaselessly caressing, trying to soothe away the pain of the coming separation. They had to part, to become two again instead of one. To live their different lives with all their problems and duties that loving could not change.

It was going to be hard, Tory thought as she stared with dry, burning eyes into the barn's dusty dimness. Hard beyond belief.

It was going to be so hard to leave him.

14

Luke and April Benedict were the first to arrive, but Kane and Regina, with her son Stephan, were close on their heels. Kane had brought along Lewis Crompton as well. With the elderly gentlemen was his wife, Elise, whom he introduced, with an endearing twinkle in his fine eyes, as his bride. Doc Watkins arrived and was taken off by Pop Benedict for a tour of his motor home and discussion of some mechanical difficulty with it. After that, came the onslaught. So many Benedicts of both sexes poured into the house that Tory lost all hope of keeping names and relationships straight. The only people she managed to single out from the crowd were Clay and the nurse from the hospital, Johnnie.

It wasn't her party, of course, but a homecoming for Roan's father. Pop, dragged out of the motor home by Jake, held court on the front porch, shaking hands with all the men and hugging all the women who flocked to see him. Everybody hugged everyone else, in fact, and generally seemed delighted to see them. There was much talk of this person and that who couldn't come, much catching up on all the births, marriages and deaths that had taken place since the last time Pop was home.

"Revolting, isn't it?" Clay asked with a grin as he

strolled to where Tory had taken refuge near a porch column. He took a sip from the long neck that he carried in his hand.

"What's that?"

Clay waved his beer toward Luke and April where the couple stood talking to Kane and Regina. "So much evidence of Benedict procreation, for one thing. That's on top of the public displays of wedded affection."

There was laughter in his eyes, and also a hint of envy that gave Tory an instant sense of fellow feeling. "You don't mean that," she said with a wry smile.

"Sure I do. Luke's so damn happy it's enough to set your teeth on edge. As for Kane, you'd think he invented pregnancy, or rather that his darling Regina had. That poor baby-child of theirs is going to stay hid out at least another six months from sheer terror at having to measure up to the expectations of its doting parents."

"Oh, I doubt that!" Tory's gaze lingered on Regina in her stylish aqua maternity dress. The lady was hugely pregnant, but beautiful with the serene and healthy glow the condition sometimes gave to women.

"Well, no, Kane probably won't allow it, come to think of it. Being a lawyer, he'll probably file an injunction to force the kid to appear."

"He's that much of a clock-watcher?"

Clay shook his head with a quick grin. "Just that anxious."

"I doubt he's any more ready than Regina. She was saying something just now about wishing it was only two minutes to go instead of two weeks."

"Like waiting for Santa Claus, can't wait to open the package and discover what they have."

"They haven't had an ultrasound done to find out?"

"And ruin the surprise? Who'd want to do that?"

It was an interesting attitude, one few of her friends would have understood, Tory thought, since *instant gratification* was their watchword. It was nice to come across a man who could savor anticipation. Come to think of it, Roan had something of the same quality.

"What about you?" she asked. "Any prospects in that direction?"

"Lord, no, love. I'm not married."

"I know that," she answered with some asperity. "What I meant was, do you have your eye on someone?"

"Present company excepted?"

"Of course," she answered at once, then was a little surprised at how easily the bland assurance was made. Clay was a good-looking guy, almost devastatingly so, if you liked the devil-may-care type. He wasn't for her. She preferred someone a bit more serious, someone rock-steady that you could depend on to be there, always and without question.

"Got your eye on someone else, that it?" he asked with a soft note in his voice.

"What?" She turned her gaze toward him, then as she met the knowing look in the rich blue of his eyes, the realization struck her that she'd been watching Roan. That was a bad habit, one she needed to break. Voice a little stiff, she went on before he could answer. "No, of course not. It would be foolish while I'm a prisoner, wouldn't it?"

"Doesn't hurt to dream."

"Doesn't help, either," she said under her breath.

"Meaning?"

"Nothing."

"Come on, out with it." He upended his beer bottle for the last swallow, then turned to set it on a convenient table.

"I just...feel out of place, I suppose." She shifted uncomfortably, since she knew very well what he was thinking. He was wrong. She had hardly spoken to Roan since the afternoon before. The sheriff had slept alone in his room while she stayed in hers, then spent most of today getting ready for the party. It was plain enough that the incident in the back seat of the Super Bird had meant less to him than she had imagined. He was giving her no chance to discuss it, much less repeat it.

"That's it. Really," she insisted as Clay remained silent.

"Yes, well, but you've been meeting people this evening, haven't you?"

"A few." They had all, Roan, Jake and Pop Benedict, presented her to one cousin after the other, but she had little to say to them, after all. It was no big surprise when they'd politely drifted away to join other groups where they had more in common.

She'd watched the cousins she'd heard most about from Roan and Jake, wishing she dared join them. But Kane had seemed as formidable in his way as the sheriff, and his wife, Regina, with her red hair in soft curls around her shoulders, freckles dusting her nose, and stunning set of antique cameo jewelry, was far too busy with people asking after her welfare to be approached. Luke was surrounded, as well. His wife, well-known romance author, April Halstead, in peach silk and with her golden-brown hair in an elegant twist, spoke with such flashing wit that Tory didn't feel up to her standard at the moment. Even Mr. Crompton and Miss Elise, with their gentle smiles and gracious manners, were so obviously the local gentry and beloved by all that she didn't have the courage to bring herself to their notice.

She finished a bit lamely, "I suppose the truth is that I have no right to be here."

"That's for Roan to decide, isn't it?"

"I'm not sure it's crossed his mind I might have a problem with it."

"Don't kid yourself," he said on a dry laugh. "Not much escapes old Roan, especially not much that goes on with you. For instance, he's wondering right this minute what we're finding so all-fired interesting to talk about, and how he can break it up without it looking as if he's riding herd on you. Or on me."

"You're joking," she began with a glance in the direction he indicated.

"Don't look!" Clay warned in an urgent undertone. "Not unless you want to bring him hotfooting over here. But maybe that's exactly what you do want?"

"You're certifiable, do you know that?" She kept her voice light with an effort. He was right, of course, though the last thing she'd ever do was admit it.

"Yeah," he mourned. "Nobody ever takes me seriously."

"Poor baby," she said, falling from sheer stress into the kind of mindless, cocktail party repartee that had once been second nature. "I expect they're happy to take you for any and everything else."

He stepped back as if in shock, his manner mocking though there was something close to discomfort in his eyes. "Why, Donna, sugar pie, sweetheart, my own honey child, whatever can you mean?"

"Nothing, nothing. Excuse me a second, will you? I need to check on the brisket in the oven and see if I can figure out some way to arrange all the pots and bowls of food people have brought."

"Coward," he called after her as she walked away.

She looked back with a smile. "You got it."

She was lifting lids and peeling back aluminum wrap, trying to separate meat dishes from vegetable dishes and salads from desserts, when April and Regina came into the kitchen. She divided a brief smile between the two women, but kept on with what she was doing.

"We thought you might need a hand in here," Luke's wife said, her gaze both bright and curious.

The expectant mother, Regina, seconded that with a smile that illuminated the softness in her face. "Just tell us what to do."

Tory felt a brief flash of a kind of acceptance that she hadn't known since the cliques and in-groups of boarding school. Was it just wishful thinking, or was there really something in the way the women looked at her, as if they thought she had something in common, knew there was something more than a jailor-prisoner connection between Roan and herself. For no good reason she could think of, hot color flooded into her face.

"I don't know, really. I'm not too sure how to go about this," she said. That was the truth. She was used to buffet meals for large groups, but her participation in the arrangements usually consisted of discussing the menu with the caterer and writing his check.

"Nothing to it," April assured her. "Just put all the meat dishes together with forks handy, and stand back."

It wasn't quite that easy, of course, but there was no great difficulty either. Logic was the key. Paper plates were stacked first, along with silverware and napkins, then followed in order by salads, meats, vegetables and desserts. Glasses for drinks were on a separate table so anyone who wanted could pick them up on a second trip without breaking into the serving line. April helped Tory lay out food and decide which dishes might need reheating, while Regina filled plastic glasses with ice and poured tea and other cold drinks.

They talked of generalities as they worked, though Tory

noticed April glancing at her once or twice with a quirk of amusement about her mouth. After a few minutes, Tory intercepted one of those quick glances and lifted a brow in inquiry.

"Sorry, it's nothing, really," April said with a quick shake of her head while she sliced a baked ham with deft strokes. "Only, the funny thing is that I warned Roan, a while back, that you'd come along one day."

"You what?"

"It was at Regina's and Kane's wedding reception. I was teasing Roan about having no steady woman. He said he had no time for one, and I made some smart remark about him making time when a female came along and held a gun to his head. Honestly, I think I must be psychic."

"Or Roan is," Regina said with laughter in her voice. "Tell Donna his answer."

April gave the other woman a quelling glance. "Oh, I don't think she wants to know that."

"I think maybe I do." Tory looked from one to the other.

April bit her lip an instant, then gave a quick nod. "He said any woman who did that would find herself flat on her back. To which, I said…"

"Maybe that's where she'll want to be if you're lucky," Regina put in with a chuckle.

"And he said then…?" Tory asked with dangerous calm.

"To the best of my memory, it was something like, 'Let's hope so.'" April glanced at Tory's set face. "Please, it was a joke. That's all."

"I'm sure." Tory turned her gaze to the pie she was uncovering. "Somehow, it doesn't strike me as very comical."

Regina came close to put a hand on Tory's arm. "We're sorry, really. The whole idea seemed so wildly improbable when April told me what he'd said, so out of character, that for it to actually happen is the kind of coincidence that makes you laugh. Roan may look stern, but he's probably the most tender and caring of the Benedict guys. Courting women at gunpoint just isn't his style.''

''Not by any stretch of the imagination,'' April added.

The gazes of the two women were so earnest that it was impossible for Tory to hold on to her annoyance. She looked away as she said, ''I think you've got it all wrong, anyway. Courting has nothing to do with why I'm here at Dog Trot.''

''If you think that,'' April said, holding her knife poised in the air, ''then you have a lot to learn about Benedict men.''

''Absolutely.'' Regina's agreement was dry. ''They fall fast and hard, and when they do, nothing stands in their way. They'll do whatever it takes to hold on to the woman they want—even if it means bending a rule or two, or even a few laws.''

''Oh, please. Roan Benedict is the most stiff-necked, law-abiding, unforgiving man ever born! He wouldn't bend one of his precious laws if his life depended on it.''

''No? Let's see,'' Regina said, a considering look in her green eyes. ''According to Kane, he's holding you here illegally since no charge has been filed against you—and no charge has been filed because he talked Cousin Betsy out of the notion. In the meantime, he's diverting sheriff's office personnel to his private use for your sake, a clear violation. And he's concealing the extent of your recovery from your injuries so no one will question his actions. That's just for starters.''

Tory stared at her. Finally, she said, ''He isn't endangering his job, is he?''

"Oh, dear," April said with a flashing grin in Regina's direction. "She does have it bad."

"Well, you have to admit she's in good company."

"Too right," April said, and sighed. Then she brightened. "Did I tell you another grand idea that came to me in the middle of last night?"

"You know you didn't," Regina said as she stopped to shake her fingers, apparently half frozen from the ice she'd been distributing among the glasses.

"History is repeating itself, at least it is in a strange sort of way. You remember the four Benedict brothers who first came to Turn-Coupe? One married an Indian woman who came here with them, another married a red-haired Scotswoman who came as a settler, the third kidnapped a Spanish woman who wasn't too averse to being taken away, and the last married a Frenchwoman he found lost in the woods?"

"So?" Regina's glance in Tory's direction seemed to invite her to enjoy the joke of April's intense concentration.

"Well, you're the stand-in for the Scotswoman who came from back East, and I'm the one that was kidnapped. And Tory, here," she ended in triumph, "was found in the woods with no memory of who she is or where she belongs, just like the Frenchwoman."

"Stretching, honey, stretching," Regina told her.

April took the ribbing in good part. "Maybe, maybe not. But you have to admit it's an interesting theory."

"I'll admit no such thing. Even if I am Scots on my great-grandmother's—"

"See!" April crowed. "And my great-grandfather eight or nine generations back was a Spanish merchant who wound up in New Orleans because he offended some grandee back in Spain and decided to travel for his health."

"All we need now is a Native American woman for one of the guys."

"Clay," Tory said without hesitation. She just couldn't resist. It was all a joke, anyway. Wasn't it?

"Perfect," Regina said with satisfaction.

"If she doesn't scalp him for being such a flutter-by."

"A what?" Tory was lost again.

"Male version of a butterfly. You know, a guy who flits from one woman to the next because he's afraid of being caught. Luke was a lot like that, once upon a time. In fact, Clay often reminds me of Luke—in his bachelor days, of course. Luke is so settled now he's practically set in concrete."

"Which is another thing about the Benedict men you'll have to guard against," Regina said wisely. "They are such homebodies, once they're married, that you'll be lucky if you ever leave Turn-Coupe again!"

"Thanks for the heads-up," Tory said tightly, "but I doubt it will be my problem."

April and Regina exchanged a quick look, but neither commented. Still, Tory, afraid they might, quickly zeroed in on the portion of what had been said that was of particular interest to her.

"Jake told me something about what happened last summer between you and Luke, but I never did hear all of it."

With a sparkle in her eyes that indicated how important the story was to her, April regaled her with the tale of how she had decided to write a story about the Benedicts. The family had been none too happy about being put under a microscope, particularly Luke. In the meantime, another sticky situation had developed. Prank calls, midnight shootings, and life-threatening boat explosions had been the result. Finally, Luke had spirited April away against her will, taking her far back in the swamp that lay beyond the lake, the only place he'd felt she might be safe.

The way the writer's voice softened when she talked of her days on the lake with Luke was a revelation. Tory was fairly sure this was another incidence of a Benedict hauling off a woman who wasn't terribly unhappy to be abducted as April had suggested. Or at least one who had come to appreciate it.

"I'm afraid Luke and I made life a bit hectic for Roan at the time," April said. "He had to step in at the crucial moment to help take the shooter, who happened to be someone we'd both once known."

"I don't suppose he minded," Tory answered with a touch of acid in her tone, "given his dedication to his job."

"He hasn't had much else to be dedicated to in the last few years," April answered.

"He has been a bit more extreme about it since you and Luke married," Regina put in with a troubled frown. "I get the feeling, sometimes, that he may be…lonely."

"He has Jake and Pop," Tory said shortly.

"True, but it's not the same."

Tory refused to acknowledge that as she fidgeted with the position of a cake taken from a plastic cover. "Then I'm sure there are plenty of women who wouldn't mind being the sheriff's wife."

"He told me once that he wasn't immune to women," April said in musing tones, "but didn't have much time for them. Besides, I think he intimidates a lot of them, especially those a bit younger."

"The last thing he needs is a silly young thing. She'd drive him mad in a week. Not," Tory added in some haste, "that his love life is any of my concern."

"Of course not," April said, her face perfectly solemn.

"Absolutely." The echo was from Regina.

And the two women didn't even look at each other.

A short time later, they called everyone to come and eat. A serving line formed as if by magic, and soon one and all had a plate piled high with the bounty and had spread out, seeking some corner in which to consume the food in comfort and safety. The main danger was the kids, ages four to around ten, who ran in and out of the house in a tight pack with a good half-dozen hound dogs at their heels. Harassed mothers corralled them, finally, and sent them to wash their hands before sitting down to plates that had been prepared for them. Someone called for a blessing, and abrupt silence descended for the prayer.

A period of relative calm followed as the serious business of eating got underway. The only sounds, other than the clatter of utensils and tinkle of ice in glasses, were the compliments, both wordless and fulsome, to the cooks. More than a few of these were directed toward Tory for her brisket and, later, her cobbler served with homemade vanilla ice cream.

Tory, sitting near Miss Elise and Mr. Lewis, watched Roan as he dipped his spoon into his dish of cobbler. For herself, she couldn't bear to taste it. Even the sweet berry smell of it brought a rush of memory that made her feel hot inside her skin. Then as Roan put the cobbler in his mouth, he closed his eyes. An instant later, he opened them again and looked straight toward where she sat. His gaze was opaque and his face pale. He turned and set the dish aside.

He couldn't bear it, either.

Clay was among the first to finish, mainly because he'd been first in the serving line. Setting his plate aside, he brought out a guitar with which he accompanied himself as he regaled the others with popular country-and-western ballads and old folk songs. He had a good voice, a rich baritone with much liveliness and underlying humor. His lengthy renditions of "Froggy Went A-Courting" and "There's a Knot on a Log" drew the children to him like flies, so they clustered around his feet and begged for more.

No one showed any inclination to leave after the dirty plates and glasses were collected and disposed of in big garbage bags. Someone went out to his vehicle and brought in a fiddle, another person produced an accordion. The parlor was cleared for dancing, with the chairs and the rug moved out to line the hall. Tory stayed in the kitchen, putting food away, as long as she could. When there was absolutely nothing else to do, she drifted back up to the upper floor and took a seat on the attic stairs, out of the way.

People came and people went. Teens holding hands whispered from a few treads above her, while a group of older women sat fanning themselves in the chairs against the hall wall. She felt conspicuous, with a crawling sensation along the back of her neck as if people were watching her, discussing her. She had no place here, and never would.

It was a relief when Clay found her again.

"Dance?" he asked, holding out his hand.

She looked up into his laughing blue eyes and was mightily tempted, if only for the sake of feeling a part of the gathering. Finally shook her head. "I don't think so."

"Come on. Your long skirt will hide the monitor cuff, if that's what you're worried about."

That had been the point of the matchstick skirt in rich turquoise and burgundy, of course, one that Pop Benedict had bought for her at the local discount store. She didn't remember ever wearing anything quite so thoroughly non-couturier in her life, or anything she appreciated more. Still, she shook her head. "It wouldn't be appropriate."

"Who cares for that? Fun belongs to everybody." He

reached to help her to her feet. "We'll stay out here in the hall, if you'd rather."

How could she refuse in the face of such logic? In any case, she didn't want to, not really. She longed to feel a part of the day, the moment and the family in some fashion, at least for a few minutes. It was ridiculous, but she couldn't help it. She put her hand in Clay's and let him pull her to her feet.

He danced well, but she'd never expected anything else. Anyone who played and sang as he did had to have music in his soul. She complimented him on his earlier performance, and watched in bemusement as his face shaded with color. That he wasn't blasé about such things was a part of his charm, however, and she liked him better for it.

They moved to the music of a Texas-style waltz only a few seconds, however, when someone tapped Clay on the shoulder. Tory looked up to see Luke waiting expectantly.

"Oh, come on," Clay protested as he came to a stop. "Go dance with your wife, for Pete's sake!"

"I did that," Luke said as he stepped between them and encircled Tory's waist with a long arm. "And now she's dancing with Pop, the man of the hour."

"Fine," Clay warned. "I'm going to go get in line."

Luke only laughed and whirled Tory away. After a moment, however, he glanced down at her. "I hope you don't mind. I couldn't let Clay monopolize the woman of the hour."

"Hardly that," Tory said in dry correction as she looked up at April's husband. "I feel more like the ghost at the banquet."

"And a gorgeous one, too—I'm speaking, you understand, as an objective, and very much married, bystander."

"Understood," she said with some amusement for his worry that she might take the compliment personally.

''Not that April would ever be jealous, since she knows she has no cause. Roan, on the other hand, is a different story.''

He had her sudden and complete attention. ''Did he send you to separate me from Clay?''

''Not exactly. It was my idea, since I'd rather not see two of my favorite cousins tie up and fight.''

Tory was growing a little tired of this preoccupation with her relationship with Roan. ''If your cousin is concerned, it's probably because he's afraid I'll talk Clay into helping me escape.''

''And would you?''

''Why not?'' she asked, drawing back enough to meet his dark eyes.

''Consideration? Gratitude?''

''Because Roan took me into his home? I didn't ask him to do it. Not that it matters. I doubt Clay would ever go against him.''

Luke's smile held approval. ''Smart of you. Which leads me to the interesting conclusion that Roan must be obtuse where you're concerned, or else he's putting himself in Clay's place and none too certain he could resist.''

''I don't see that at all,'' she said in flat denial. ''He's just covering all the bases.''

Luke tilted is head. ''That's possible, knowing Roan. But I doubt it.''

The best answer she could make to that was a dignified silence. Before the quiet between them could grow too strained, there was a movement behind her. A man spoke above her head. ''My turn, Cousin. You've been dancing with the lady long enough.''

It was Kane, whom Roan mentioned more often than the others since they both worked at the courthouse.

"It's the same damn—excuse me—darned, waltz," Luke said in exasperation.

"Sorry. Sheriff's orders."

Luke gave Tory a crooked smile as he relinquished her. "See what I told you?"

She still held to her own opinion as to Roan's reasoning, but returned his smile anyway. Even she could see that the situation had its droll aspect.

The music ended just then. A slow ballad began, a crooning tune about a cowboy falling in love with the sound of a woman's voice. "Much better," Kane said as he moved into the dance. "Now, which would you prefer? Shall I be discreet or fan the flames?"

"I'm not sure you have a choice," she said without pretending to misunderstand him. "Surely Roan trusts you, of all people."

"You'd think so, wouldn't you? I mean, if Regina doesn't present me with a son and heir in the middle of this party it will be a miracle. But I still have orders to keep it clean and make sure you turn into a wallflower again before too long."

A slow tide of anger began to rise in Tory. "The nerve of that man! If he doesn't want other people dancing with me, why doesn't he ask me himself?"

"He's somewhat occupied with His Honor the mayor, or I'm sure he would."

She hadn't noticed, not that she'd have recognized the official in any case. "How is that? According to Jake, they're barely on speaking terms."

"Seems the men with the gambling consortium swept into town without advance warning, so the big parade from the airport to Turn-Coupe that His Honor had planned came to nothing. Roan was asked to provide a police escort, understand, but had more or less refused to have any part of it. The mayor is convinced Roan either knew the men were coming and failed to sound a warning, or else he dropped the ball by not knowing.''

"This gambling consortium,'' she said, her voice tight, "how many men are involved? That is, how many are here?''

"A couple, I think. They checked into the motel about noon, so Betsy tells me. That's a cousin of ours who owns the motel and convenience—but I was forgetting. You know about her, don't you?''

"We met, so to speak,'' she said in distraction, hardly registering the apologetic smile Kane directed at her. Her thoughts were chaotic, a confusion of fears and impulses. If the men from the gambling consortium were here, that meant Harrell could be in Turn-Coupe already. Her time had run out.

Or had it? Maybe he wasn't here because of the report by Zits and Big Ears. Maybe he'd been coming anyway because of the gambling operation, which was why the two crooks had brought her to Louisiana in the first place. Maybe he had no idea that she had been injured and was in custody, so she was panicking for nothing.

At that moment, the front door swung open, letting in a blast of hot summer air. The late arrival was brash and beaming as she greeted everyone in sight, laughing as she made her excuses about being late. A pleasingly plump woman with streaked blond hair, she looked very different from the last time Tory had seen her behind the counter of her convenience store, passing over cash from the register with both hands. Then she turned to usher inside the man who mounted the steps behind her, saying something about a guest at the motel who'd been at loose ends on a hot Sunday afternoon.

The guest was Harrell Melanka.

15

Roan was preoccupied. He'd been short enough with the mayor that the man had stalked off in a snit. Now he allowed a mild baseball argument to flow back and forth around him without notice. He was off duty today and responsible for no one's welfare. It was a welcome change, or would have been if he could avoid thoughts of Donna and what she was doing, who was with her and what they were saying.

God, but she stayed with him. He couldn't make a decision worth carrying out, couldn't sleep or eat for thinking of her. The hot love they'd made in the barn haunted him; the need to go to her, to have her, to hold her against him in the night was so strong he shook with the effort to suppress it.

He couldn't give in. She was his prisoner, a woman under his protection. He'd been guilty of forgetting that once, and must not do it again. It went against everything he believed about the cool, unemotional exercise of his duty as a law officer. It condemned him in his own eyes as a man who took advantage of his position to enjoy the favors of a woman who had little defense against it. It made him the kind of dishonorable lowlife that he most despised.

And yet, the memory of Donna's surrender was as warm and delicious as the cobbler she'd made, and as tempting. They blended together so closely in his mind until the mere thought of blackberries could make him ache with need for her. He couldn't take the taste of them anymore; he'd learned that much today. They could be off his list for good.

The sound of a commotion brought his head up. It came from near the front door, where he'd last seen Donna. He'd put Kane in temporary charge, but his cousin had other concerns just now with Regina so near her due date. Roan started toward the noise.

Donna stood near the doorway in frozen immobility while Cousin Betsy introduced a newcomer. The man with her was well-dressed and urbanely self-assured, with the vapid good looks of a male model. He glanced around and saw Donna, and his mouth dropped open in a parody of shock.

"Tory!" he exclaimed, starting forward with his arms outstretched. "God, but what are you doing here?"

Triumph shafted through Roan. At last he was going to find out the real identity of his Donna Doe. Hard on the heels of that realization came something close to dismay as he saw all too well that it meant an end to having her at Dog Trot.

He transferred his gaze to Donna. Her face was as white as the sleeveless blouse she wore, and her eyes appeared wide and empty. It was plain she knew the smooth dandy, but she stepped away from his embrace, putting up a hand to ward off his approach.

Roan moved forward, barely noticing the friends and relatives who whispered among themselves even as they gave way for him. Infusing his voice with every ounce of authority he possessed, he asked, "What's going on here? Is there a problem?"

"Roan, thank goodness," Betsy exclaimed. "I didn't mean to upset anybody, or cause a to-do. But when Mr. Melanka said he'd never seen a country homecoming, of course I invited him along. I mean, it just seemed neighborly."

"Melanka?"

"Harrell Melanka, staying at the motel. He's from Florida, with the—"

"Gaming consortium," Roan finished for her, his voice grim.

"That's right," Melanka said with a lift of his chin. "And you might be?"

Betsy gave a loud laugh, a sign of her discomfort. "Oh, Harrell, this is our host I've been telling you about, Sheriff Roan Benedict."

To offer his hand was an engrained response for Roan. It was also a test. A man with the kind of quiet self-confidence that mattered had a firm, brief grip. He didn't feel the need to impose his strength on others or to make a contest of a simple greeting. Roan made a mental bet that Melanka wasn't that kind of man, and he was right. His handshake was too hardy and too hard. He was trying to prove something, but Roan wasn't impressed.

As he stepped back again, he said, "You know my prisoner?"

"Prisoner?" The other man's frown drew his brows together over his cosmetically straight nose.

"The lady you called...Tory." It was amazing how hard it was to make himself say the name.

"If she's your prisoner, there's some mistake," Melanka replied, his voice hardening as he took an aggressive step closer. "She's Victoria Molina-Vandergraff, stepdaughter of industrialist Paul Vandergraff, and the hereditary Princess de Trentalara of Italy. She's also my fiancée."

Roan felt as if he'd taken a hard right to the stomach. For a long second, he couldn't breathe for the clutching pain in his chest. He'd known that the woman he'd called Donna must have another life somewhere else, but he'd never dreamed of that kind of background. It was transparently clear that nothing and no one in Turn-Coupe could ever hold her now, least of all him.

"Ex-fiancée," she said.

That cold correction was made by his prisoner. It didn't exactly make Roan's heart bleed, though he had no intention of asking himself why. It was enough that he could drag air into his lungs again.

Then she turned her head in his direction. He met her soft hazel gaze, so defensive yet aware, and knew at once that he'd been right all along, that there had never been a moment when she hadn't known exactly who she was and what she was doing.

"Victoria." He tried the name in his mind, and was surprised to discover that he'd spoken aloud.

"Tory," she said. "The people I know best call me Tory."

"Good Lord, Tory," Melanka said. "Don't tell me you've been hiding out under another name? I don't know what kind of game you've been playing with these good people, but it's over. Let's go home."

She gave him only a fraction of her attention. "I'm not going anywhere. I'm certainly not going anywhere with you."

"I know you were a little upset with me, darling, but I promise that's all behind us."

"Not for me, it isn't."

It was time, Roan thought, to introduce the new arrival to the reality of the situation. "Excuse me," he said in

neutral politeness. ''But the lady is still in my custody. I'll
say where she goes, and when.''

''Is that right?'' Melanka asked on a short laugh. ''When
I let Paul Vandergraff know his daughter is being held in
some Podunk town instead of sunning herself on the Riv-
iera like he thinks, he'll have so many lawyers slapping
you with writs and injunctions you'll feel like a punching
bag.''

''That's his privilege, but I should warn you that it may
only ensure that formal charges are pushed forward so she's
put under lock and key.''

''No formal charges?'' Melanka said, picking up on the
one point Roan would just as soon he'd have missed.
''What are you trying to pull? Seems Mrs. North mentioned
some tale about you and your prisoner, a woman you'd
shot, even if I didn't know it was Tory at the time. If it's
true, damn you, I'll not only get Tory away from you, but
I'll see you stripped of your badge and run out of office.''

Roan gave a short laugh. ''You're welcome to try. But
let me get this straight. You're so concerned about your so-
called fiancée's welfare that you're threatening court action,
but she's been missing for weeks and you're just now discovering she was gone?''

''You don't know Tory. She does things like this, running off without a word to anyone. Then it blows over and
we're back to square one.''

''That's not true!'' Tory exclaimed. ''At least...I may
take off now and then, but I know my own mind.''

Was that what she'd been doing with the petty thieves
who'd hit Betsy's store, Roan wondered, running away
with them as a way of getting back at her fiancé? Roan
didn't like to think so, but it seemed to fit. At the same
time, he had nothing but contempt for a man who would

publicly brand someone he was supposed to care about as that spoiled and irresponsible.

"She claims she was kidnapped," he said deliberately. "I don't suppose you can shed any light on that?"

"Does it seem likely?" Melanka asked with a pained expression.

"You're saying it's not possible then?"

"I'm saying I don't know a thing about it!"

"Or about the robbery committed while she was with the men who are supposed to have abducted her?"

"Give me a break. Why in hell would she want to rob some penny-ante store when she has an annual income in the high six figures from her mother's estate? Does that make sense?"

"Penny-ante?" Betsy cried, even as he spoke. Behind her, somebody whistled, an admiring salute to such a hefty income.

"So no one has reported her disappearance, you or this Vandergraff?"

"Obviously," Melanka drawled.

That explained why he'd found no description on the police network, at least. "And that doesn't strike you as strange?"

"You have to know her."

Melanka was using condescension to try to make Roan look and feel like a fool. That only worked, Roan knew, if he allowed it, and he wasn't in the mood. "On the other hand, it could be that you didn't know because the lady's right, you're no longer in the picture."

Melanka seemed to consider, then gave a judicious nod. "I'm sure it may look that way. But the fact is, Sheriff, that you and I both know how this is going to turn out. Save yourself a lot of grief and just turn her over to me.

I'll take her home and her stepdad can handle it from there.''

''No!'' Tory stepped to where he stood, and put her hand on his arm. ''Please, Roan.''

''You heard her. She doesn't want to go with you. That's the end of it, as far as I'm concerned. Now, I'm going to have to ask you to leave.''

Melanka turned to the woman beside Roan. ''Tory, honey, this has gone far enough, don't you think? I know we had our differences, but come on, now. Let me take you home where you belong. You don't even have to talk to me if you don't want. Once we're back in Florida, everything will be fine. You'll see.''

''No,'' Tory said again, her voice tight.

''That's it,'' Roan said, moving toward the other man.

Abruptly, Melanka leaped to grab Tory's left wrist and jerk her toward the door. She cried out and clutched her injured shoulder.

Something snapped inside Roan. He sprang at the ex-fiancé, fastened hard fingers on his arm so he released Tory. Then Roan landed a hard right to the man's too handsome chin.

Melanka staggered back out through the front doorway, stumbled, regained his feet. Rage twisted his face. He lunged forward again. Roan met him, blocked his wild punch, and then connected with another smashing right. The other man grunted as he spun around with the force of the blow. He went down with a thud that rattled the porch floor and lay stunned.

Roan moved to stand over him. Melanka heaved to one elbow, as if expecting another blow. When it didn't come, he swiped a hand under his nose, then turned greenish as he saw blood. His laugh was harsh, breathless. ''So much for Southern hospitality.''

"Exactly," Roan agreed. "You have two minutes to clear out, or you'll discover what happens when a Southerner really gets a bellyful of uninvited company."

"You'll arrest me, that it? I doubt your fine mayor will appreciate the gesture, or the treatment, I've had from you."

"The mayor isn't the law here."

"You won't be, either, not for long. Once this place is dependent on gaming money, I'll see to it that there's a new sheriff."

"Fine." Roan reached down and picked up the man by his shirtfront, then shoved him toward the steps. "But do it far away from Dog Trot."

Harrell Melanka almost fell again, then caught his footing. He straightened his clothes with a jerk, while sending a look of pure spite, the refuge of the ineffectual man, toward all the Benedicts who had crowded out to watch the show. He swung around and marched down to his rental car. Slamming the door behind him, he sprayed gravel as he tore away down the drive.

"Gee, I'm sorry," Betsy said at Roan's elbow. "I didn't know who he was, honest, and sure didn't mean to stir up such a hornet's nest."

"Never mind," he answered, sighing as he ran his fingers through his hair. Turning back inside the house, he sent a quick glance toward Donna—no, Tory—where she stood in the hall.

April was beside her. "I'll see to her," Luke's wife told him. "You take care of your guests."

It wasn't what Roan wanted. He'd have much preferred to send his guests to the devil while he took Tory in his arms and held her until her pain went away. That would help no one, least of all a woman who apparently hailed from the rarefied parts of the world where people had gazillions and titles to go with the cash.

"Right," he said under his breath. Then he dragged air into his lungs and looked around at his relatives. "All right, folks, let's get back to the serious fun."

They didn't, of course. There was too much gossip and speculation going on. Those who weren't interested in talking had more consideration than to linger where everything was in such turmoil. People began to gather their dishes and their kids, to say their polite goodbyes and climb into their cars and trucks. In less than a half hour, the house was empty. Even Jake and Pop left, taking Clay's invitation for a fast spin in his airboat out to his place in the swamp. He'd promised them the high treat of watching the comic turns of a baby blue crane he'd rescued from a watery death and named Banty because the bird was convinced he was a bantam chicken.

Roan straightened the worst of the ravages left by the departing guests, mopped a couple of sticky puddles in the kitchen and hauled out the trash. When he could put it off no longer, he climbed the stairs to Donna's—Tory's room. He thought he might find her asleep, since April had reported giving her a couple of aspirin. Instead, she was sitting up in bed with a paperback novel resting on her knees while she stared at the darkened window.

She looked so enticing, so soft and warm and alone, that he felt a wild urge to forget what had happened a little while ago, to abandon all thought of right and wrong and duty, and simply climb in bed with her. He wanted to hold her, to feel her heart beating against his chest, to listen to her breathe and not get up again until he was a very old man.

Dumb. Impossible. Impossibly dumb.

She turned her head to meet his gaze across the room.

Her eyes were shadowed with watchful stillness. She didn't speak.

"How's the shoulder?" he asked as he closed the door behind him. "Any damage?"

She shook her head. "It's all right. I just…needed to get away from everyone. Are they all gone?"

"Finally." He moved toward the bed, stopping where he could lean a shoulder against one of the tall posts at the foot.

Her smile was faint, a token effort for the fact that neither of them seemed to be fond of crowds, or at least not for long. After a moment, she said, "I'm sorry if Harrell ruined you dad's homecoming."

"Oh, he was the icing on the cake," he said on a short laugh. "The Benedicts will be talking about this shindig this time next year." He paused, then came out with the question that burned in his mind. "Why? Why didn't you tell me?"

"What? That I used to have a fiancé?"

"That I had a princess living in the spare bedroom and scrubbing my kitchen floor. Think of all the fun I missed, not knowing it." He breathed deep, trying to calm the anger that simmered inside him.

"Supposing I remembered that little detail?" she asked, her voice husky.

The look he gave her was as level as it was hard. "You remembered. In fact, I don't think there was a time, from the very first, that it slipped your mind."

She held his gaze for long moments, her own crystalline with suspended thought. Then she looked away. "No. Though I wish it could have."

He swore, a soft sound that was loud in the stillness. He'd half hoped that she would deny it. It would have made things easier. "So what happened? Did you have a tiff with

Melanka and run off with the two thugs that brought you here? Or was it some kind of scheme to get more than just an allowance from this stepdad of yours?''

She compressed her lips, and the look in her eyes was hot as she swung back to face him. ''I told you what happened! I was kidnapped off the beach at Sanibel. Zits and Big Ears were hired to chase me down and haul me here. As far as I can tell, Harrell is the one who paid them to do it.''

Roan crossed his arms over his chest. ''Why would he do that?''

''Why do you think? I'm an heiress, you know, or didn't you get that part? My mother was the only surviving grandchild of Angus Bridgeman of department store fame. My stepfather benefited from marriage to my mother to the tune of the start-up fortune for his empire, so it was her money that put him where he is, her money that made him a big-time industrialist. Everybody thinks it's a huge deal that I'm his stepdaughter, but he's only controlled and grown the fortune that came to me when my mother died. And that's what Harrell wanted, that's why he was so totally pissed when I broke the engagement.''

''It was revenge then?''

''Also to make sure I didn't ruin the deal he'd put together with the gambling consortium. He used my name and our engagement as proof to his backers that he could deliver his portion of the money that would cut him in on the profits. When it came time to sign the papers, though, they wanted my signature. Harrell knew I'd never go for it, so he forged it. I found out, broke the engagement and was unwise enough to tell him I meant to contact his associates to make sure they knew I was out of the deal. He wasn't happy.''

''You handed over his ring because of a financial deal

gone sour? It couldn't have been much of a love match.''
The hollow feeling inside as he put that question was a
warning, one he did his best to ignore.

She gave a moody shrug. ''The sour deal was proof that
it was my money he was after and he'd do anything to get
it. Not that it matters, I'd already realized the engagement
was a mistake; Harrell seemed like a self-made man, a mav-
erick, but that was a sham. The minute he became a part
of my crowd, he did his best to be more supercilious and
Old Money than the most obnoxious Harvard grad. More
like Paul Vandergraff. He and I...don't get along. I made
it my purpose in life to offend him at least once a month
from the day my mother died in a fancy sanitarium where
he put her.''

Roan didn't like the easing he felt in the region of his
heart, but it was there all the same. ''Not exactly the most
mature or effective retaliation I've ever heard of,'' he offered.

''No,'' she agreed at once. ''I was a teenager when it
began, and I suppose it became a habit. I decided, recently,
that there are more valuable reasons for living.''

The need to ask her what that might be was so strong
he almost choked on it. But he wasn't going to be a part
of whatever future she might have, couldn't be, and the
sooner he faced it the better. ''All right, so Melanka had
you kidnapped to prevent you from talking to his business
partners. What then?''

''What do you mean?''

''You weren't likely to keep quiet about it later.''

''Oh, I was supposed to die, of course. A lot of kidnap
victims do.''

The dead calm of her voice made the hair rise on the
back of his neck. She must have faced that particular truth
long ago, perhaps even as a child, for it to be accepted with

so little emotion. The ache that caused inside him was nearly as strong as the knowledge that he'd shot her at the end of her kidnap ordeal. Almost, but not quite.

"Tell me about this kidnapping one more time, from the beginning," he said, his voice as even and official as he could make it. "I want every detail, from the time you left wherever you were staying to go for a swim, or whatever you were doing, to the time you fell out of that rattletrap van with a pistol in your hand. Leave out nothing. I want to know exactly what time everything happened, every single place you stopped, every time you ate, who the men with you talked to, when and where. Who they might have called, and every word they said to you or to each other. Start. Now."

"Does this mean that you believe me?"

"How can I, when you've been lying to me for weeks? The fact that you don't need money doesn't mean you weren't an accomplice in the convenience store robbery. Added to that, there's no proof Melanka is who he says he is. You could have called him, asked him to provide you with a background, as implausible as it may be. Sorry, but I'll have to look a lot deeper before I reduce the charges against you, much less drop them."

A twisted smile appeared on her lips. "At least you didn't take the word of the first man to back up what I said."

"Meaning I'm a stupid idiot, but not chauvinistic?" He pushed away from the bedpost and moved around to the end of the bed where he could put the carved footboard between them.

"Something like that," she agreed.

"I'll be anything you like, as long as you talk to me. Come on. I want the story of how you got here from Florida."

She gave it to him, talking nonstop for the best part of an hour. The words tumbled out in near incoherence at times, as if she'd been waiting for the time when she could lay them out for someone. He liked to think she'd been saving them for him alone, but her manner was too distant, too self-contained, to allow it. As he listened to her, he studied her face, noting the patrician nose, the delicate molding of the lips, the air of refinement in every line. He should have known she was someone special, he thought. Or perhaps he had, and preferred not to acknowledge it for all the reasons that made it impossible for him to consider her innocent, even now.

Finally, she came to a halt. The silence stretched between them as he turned over what she'd been able to add to the little he knew already. The one she called Zits had made a couple of calls, but she'd only heard the distant sound of his voice at the pay phone, not the actual words. They sometimes mentioned the Big Man who'd pay them, but had never called him by name. Zits had been pretty cagey, all in all, cagier than seemed likely if he'd intended to kill her. Of course, she'd offered the pair money, more than they stood to make from the man who'd hired them, if they released her. It was possible that was the reason she was still alive. Whether it would have been enough to save her life in the end was another question.

She was watching him, her gaze so intent on his face that it almost felt as if she were trying to read his mind. At last she said, "What do you think?"

"It holds together, barely."

"And that's all? Why would I make up something like that?"

"To stay out of jail after you got yourself into more than you could handle?"

"Oh, please. Have I done anything since I've been here

to make you believe I'm some kind of thrill-seeker or so mentally unstable that I'd get a kick out of pointing a gun at someone? It's crazy! I think you just don't want to accept that I was in that van against my will!''

He stared at her, his gaze moving from the quick rise and fall of her breasts under her blouse to the taut lines of her chin and mouth, and the accusation in her eyes. In trenchant tones, he said, ''You're right.''

Her face changed, softening, and a flush appeared on the ridges of her cheekbones. ''What? I mean—''

''If I believe you, then I'm guilty of something close to attempted murder.''

''No, only of doing your duty.''

''If I take everything for the truth,'' he went on inexorably, ''then I'll have to let you go.''

''I should think that's what you'd want. You'd be rid of me, rid of the problems I've caused you. Maybe you and the mayor could work out your differences....''

''Do you think I care two cents for what the mayor thinks, or for working things out with him?''

''You disagreed because of me, didn't you? At least, Jake said—''

''Jake talks too much,'' he answered in taut annoyance. ''I'm an elected official, a parish official, with nothing to do with the town of Turn-Coupe's mayor. He didn't hire me, and he can't fire me. If I choose to accommodate him for the sake of peace and getting things done, that's one thing. If we have different views of what's best for the town and the area, that's something else again.''

''I didn't realize.''

''Fine. Now you do. Maybe you'll also see that the problem of Melanka and this gambling consortium will remain whether you go or stay.''

''Yes,'' she said slowly. ''I think I do.''

Did she? Did she understand that so long as the man posed a danger to her, then Roan preferred to have her where he could protect her instead of worrying about her running around loose where the ex-fiancé could get his hands on her again? The last thing he needed was for her to be taken as a hostage for his cooperation. And that was something Tory could easily become if Melanka or anyone else figured out how important her welfare was to him.

"Good," he said, as if the subject was settled. As it was, indeed, in his mind. "It's possible that the news wires may get hold of your story—nobody in my office will leak the news, I think, but a lot of people have been speculating about you and the sensation of your identity may be too good to keep. You might want to consider letting your family know first."

"If you mean my stepfather, I've already called him," she said in low tones. "It seemed best to head off his lawyers, if I could."

"So are they coming or not?" If he was to be inundated by legal eagles before breakfast in the morning, he'd just as soon know it now.

"Paul agreed to wait, though he won't keep them leashed forever. In fact, he said..."

"What?" he asked, as it appeared she wasn't going to finish what she'd started to say.

Her chest lifted and fell in a sigh. "He said I had only to give the word, and I'd be free in a matter of hours."

"And why didn't you?"

"Give the word? I was so sure that you'd see reason, that it would be unnecessary."

Roan narrowed his eyes as he studied her. "You really expect me to believe that?"

"Why not? You're a fair man."

"Thank you. I think. But what bothers me is the question

of what took you so long to get in touch with Vandergraff. If he's so willing to spring to your defense with a legal team, why did you stay here pretending amnesia for so long? Why did you let Doc Watkins take care of the hole in your chest when you could have had the best plastic surgeons, best medical team in the country?"

"Because..." She stopped, compressed her lips.

"Because you were afraid Vandergraff was involved?" he asked. "Or is it something else? Did you maybe get a kick out of all of us running around at your beck and call, knocking ourselves out to see that you were safe and comfortable?"

She lifted her hand then let it fall again in a tired gesture. "What does it matter? It's over, or as near to it as makes no difference. I'll be gone before long, and you can all get back to your normal lives as if I'd never been here. In the meantime, I'd appreciate it if you'd at least take off the monitor. Even you will have to admit that I'm not such a desperate felon that you have to know my every move."

He stepped around to the side of the bed where her foot was stretched out in front of her in a pose of unconscious grace. He slipped his little finger under the collar of the device. Even as he tested for tightness and chafing, he was aware of the silken smoothness of her skin, and the certain memory that it was even silkier in other places.

He stepped back, abruptly, before he said, "I'd feel better if you kept the thing for another day or two, at least."

"You're not going to remove it."

He shook his head.

She watched the movement, watched him, while her features settled into grim purpose. "Fine, if you really enjoy keeping me in electronic bondage. But if it's a substitute for keeping an eye on me yourself, I don't think much of it. Satisfy my curiosity, will you? Tell me why you've been avoiding me since we picked the blackberries?''

''That shouldn't be too hard to figure out,'' he said, retreating another step and shoving his hands into the back pockets of his jeans.

''No? Well, I must be missing something, because I don't get it. Unless I did something wrong…''

''It isn't you,'' he said swiftly, even as alarm crawled over his scalp at the idea that she was blaming herself. ''It's me. I'm the sheriff, you're my prisoner. It's unethical for me to take advantage of you.''

''I don't remember that part, you taking advantage,'' she objected. ''I was perfectly willing.''

''I didn't mean it literally,'' he answered, trying to ignore the interruption. ''But it's my duty to keep my distance so there is no possible question of using my position to…''

''To force me to make mad, passionate love with you?''

''Don't make this any harder than it is already,'' he said without meeting her gaze. He couldn't remember the last time a personal discussion had been so uncomfortable, though he thought it was some time back in grade school. The problem was not embarrassment, however, but the powerful urge it gave him to overturn every ethical pledge he'd ever sworn in his life.

''I wouldn't dream of it,'' she returned. ''Nor would I dream of influencing you based on the aforementioned mad, passionate love. Even if I wanted to, and even if it was possible—and guessing that's the next place you might be going with this.''

''No, but it isn't enough to discount the possibility. I have to remove all chance of even the appearance of influence. Either way.''

''It's your duty to avoid me.''

"Exactly," he said, and felt a slight smile curve his mouth as relief for her understanding flooded over him.

"Two things are wrong with that," she said, her features solemn as she sat up and swung her feet off the bed.

Wariness gripped him, but he could no more have failed to ask than he could stop breathing. "And they are…?"

"Number one, I've been living under your roof for the best part of three weeks and, thanks to Cal, everyone already suspects that you had only one reason for bringing me here. And number two…"

"Number two?"

She slid off the mattress and padded toward him in silent, lissome menace on her bare feet. Her gaze was open and innocent, too innocent, as she answered, "Nobody's watching."

16

She was testing him, Roan thought. She was also torturing him. Did she know how much he would like to throw his damned Benedict ethics to the four winds? Did she have any idea how delectable she was with her bed-rumpled look of wrinkled skirt, smudged eye makeup and tangled hair? Could she guess that nothing in his whole life had ever been as hard as standing there and watching her when all he really wanted was to pick her up, put her back in bed, then crawl in beside her and hold her all night long?

He hoped not, or he was a goner.

"Doing what's right doesn't depend on whether anyone can see," he said, his voice vibrating deep in his chest. "It's a matter of personal integrity. And it has nothing to do with what I want, or what you might need. It's about what's best for everyone, including the people who voted me into office and have kept me there all these years."

"If what I need is you, then you'll sacrifice me as well as yourself?"

She reached out to put her hand on his chest, trailing her fingers over the oxford cloth of his shirt. The touch was as light as duck down, still he felt each fingertip as a separate spot of heat. "It's the way it works."

"For how long?" She lifted her fingertips to brush across the faint beard stubble in the hollow of his cheek.

"As long as it takes," he replied, or thought he did. His senses felt scattered, yet so attuned to the warmth and scent of her, to the feel of her breath on his throat and the brush of her skirt against his shins, that he was fast nearing overload.

"You won't kiss me or touch me, won't take me to some of the private corners of your home or your lake and its swamps?"

"Not on your life. If I did," he said deliberately, "I might never stop until we were both so sated with love that we couldn't move."

She met his eyes, though hers were not quite focused. "I like the sound of that."

This was, he thought, a game that two could play. He let his voice drop lower, to something just above a whisper. "So do I. If I could, I'd take you to the attic and make love to you at midday when it's dusty and dry, and so still and hot you can hear the roof shingles melting. Or I'd have you at midnight beside the lake while the bullfrogs call and the loons cry, and the moon sails above us on guard duty. I'd take you out in a boat and rock with you on windblown waves until we were lobster red and tender from sunburn. Or I'd walk with you down some path in the woods until I found a bed of pine needles. But most of all, I'd take you into my own big bed. I'd hold you while we both slept, and wake with you in the early morning to new dawn love that is often best, and always right."

She moistened her lips, a slow movement, before she asked in tentative wonder, "Would you? Really?"

"It isn't the most sophisticated program, but nothing could be more satisfying."

"I don't need sophistication."

The words were so stark that he thought they might almost be true. "No Eiffel Tower, no Paris in the rain? No Venetian gondolas or lavender-scented satin sheets in a five-star Mayfair Hotel?"

"Romance is where you find it, and love."

"As long as that's what you're really looking for," he answered.

She was quiet a moment, while she searched his face. "But you don't think that's what I want?"

"Here and now, maybe. But what about later, when the days are all the same, and the nights, and the only exciting thing that happens in a month of Sundays is old Mrs. Adams's Persian cat running off with the ugly tabby down the road? What about when you realize that there's not a single mall in Turn-Coupe, and that the best hairdresser is run by a woman who likes Twinkies and big hair, calls her place Millie's, and wouldn't do a pedicure on a bet?"

"I'd live," she said with a trace of defiance, "since I prefer shopping by computer and have done my own pedicures for years."

"It wouldn't work."

"Because I wasn't born a redneck?"

"Because you're a rich lady with a wide view of the world, and I'm a small-town sheriff with small-town ideas and small-town ways. You can't fit in, and you never will."

"And you're too afraid of being left alone again, afterward, to let me try," she said, and set her lips in a thin line.

"Low blow, Tory." Was it accurate? He didn't know. He hadn't thought about Tory in relationship to Carolyn and what had happened with his ex-wife. For one thing, there'd been no time and little encouragement as long as she was classed in his mind as a prisoner. But they were also far too different for any comparison. Tory, for all her insecurities, was a fighter. Carolyn had never been that; it just wasn't in her.

"I don't need fancy things around me, and I don't need change," she said. "What I need are things that *don't* change, and people who don't."

That was laying it on the line, he thought, at least to a point. The problem was that he was in no position to do the same. He wouldn't be until this was over, if it was ever really over.

"And what I need," he said with care, "is for you to let me do my job. I need your trust."

She removed her hand, looking away from him. "That's so hard."

He took a deep breath, his first since she'd touched him. "It's never easy, not for any of us. But it doesn't work without it."

It was an exit line if he'd ever heard one, especially since she didn't seem to have an answer for it. He stepped away from her, then stopped. "About this engagement of yours, was there a prenuptial agreement?"

Her gaze was remote as she faced him again. "What about it?"

"I was just wondering if it included a will, or anything about the distribution of assets if anything happened to you."

"It didn't, as a matter of fact. Harrell suggested a mutual agreement wherein anything he had became mine on his death, and vice versa. Since I was more likely to outlive him, statistically speaking, and didn't need his money, I didn't see the point."

Roan nodded. "And you didn't consider that he might need your money."

"He appeared to be on a sound financial footing at the time."

Roan digested that a second before he asked, "So who does inherit in the event anything happens to you?"

"Various charities, a few old friends, and my stepfather," she said with a careless shrug, or one that was meant to appear that way.

"Isn't that a little strange, since you don't care that much for him?"

"The will was drawn up by family lawyers, and is basically a copy of my mother's will. Besides, there's no one else."

"But you'd change the beneficiary if you married?"

"Of course, especially if there were children."

"That's what I thought," he said, and went from the room, closing the door carefully behind him.

It was twenty-four hours later, give or take, that the call came about the bodies. Since it was late, Roan was at home. His dad had gone fishing for the day with Lewis Crompton, and hadn't yet returned, which left only Jake to watch after Tory. Roan called Cal in for duty at Dog Trot and waited until he drove up, then he took off.

The accident was at the old iron bridge again. The vehicle was in the water, lying on its side and submerged so that only the right rear tire appeared above the surface of the deep creek-like tributary of the lake. The wrecker was already there when Roan arrived, and the driver was attaching a line. First Response and rescue squad members had made several dives. They reported that it was a pickup truck with two passengers, both males. As far as they could tell, neither had survived the crash.

Roan examined the skid marks and debris on the road with the aid of a spotlight, and talked to state police troopers who were taking measurements. From all appearances, the pickup had been traveling at a high rate of speed when it was hit from behind with enough force to send it through the guardrail. The skid had been minimal, indicating the rear-ending was unexpected. Paint flecks suggested the perp in the hit-and-run was driving a white vehicle, which covered a good 40 percent of cars in a state where light colors meant cooler interiors during the torrid summers.

Roan had a gut feeling about the occupants of the vehicle in the water. It came to him when he saw the mud grip tire that stuck up out of the water and learned it was a red truck hidden by the creek's murky swirl. The identification of the passengers as two males added to it. By the time the pickup rose slowly to the surface and was dragged ashore, he was ready for the news.

Zits and Big Ears. No doubt about it. He'd have recognized them from Tory's description, but he also had the still photo made from the video camera film. It was the two men who had kidnapped her, and they were very dead. Someone had not only run them off the road, but had stopped long enough to spray the van with automatic weapon fire before it settled to the bottom of the creek bed.

He was discussing the timing of the accident with the state police when a Jeep came barreling down the road and swerved onto the shoulder just short of the bridge. Luke and Kane got out, followed by Pop. Before Roan could ask about Jake, his son hopped from the back. They all strode toward him, as fascinated by the accident as a quartet of ambulance chasers. Roan stepped aside to let them get a good look at the carnage.

Luke whistled. Kane swore. Jake looked a little green, and didn't object at all when his granddad put an arm around his shoulder.

"That who I think it is?" Kane asked with a narrow glance in Roan's direction.

"Yeah."

''Witnesses?'' Luke asked as he deliberately moved to block the view of the boy as well as that of the female driver of a passing car.

''None that stuck around or felt the call of civic duty strong enough to report it,'' he answered. ''So where did you guys come from?''

It was Jake who spoke up. ''We got back from fishing maybe ten minutes after you left. Tory knew all about the wreck since she'd been listening on the scanner.''

He might have known, Roan thought. He tried to think if anybody had given descriptions of the victims or the truck. It was entirely possible, in which case, Tory would know by now that Zits and Big Ears were no longer around to trouble her. She'd also know, he hoped, that she might be in danger from whoever had whacked them. ''Cal was still at the house, right?'' he asked without even trying to temper the abruptness of the question.

Pop said, ''And royally pissed over being sent to Dog Trot instead of hightailin' it out here where the action's going on. Speaking of which…''

''If you want to know who did this, your guess is as good as mine,'' Roan said.

''Right,'' his dad said, though the look in his eyes was jaundiced. He was no fool.

''It has something to do with Tory, doesn't it?'' Jake asked.

''Jake,'' he said in warning.

''Well, it does,'' he muttered, though he didn't press it.

Kane did, however. ''If Jake's right, then it puts a whole new light on this deal with your lady prisoner. It looks as if somebody is covering their tracks, which means—''

''I know what it means,'' Roan said shortly. He just didn't want to think about it, couldn't stand to think about it.

"Somebody wanted our Tory out of the way before, and now they may want it even worse," his dad put in. "If they're willing to risk turning a couple of guys to hamburger with an assault rifle on a public highway, what would they do to her?"

Luke barely glanced at the others as he asked, "It has something to do with this gambling business, right?"

"So it seems." Roan filled them in on the details, as much as he knew of them, in a few short sentences.

"Reminds me of something," Pop said in ruminating tones. "You may have wondered why I agreed to come home when you called in the clan. It wasn't exactly a snap decision."

"Pop," Roan began, trying not to sound as impatient as he felt.

"Bear with me, boy, bear with me. Now I'd been hanging around the casinos, mainly because that's where the ladies like to hang out playing the slots. I fell into talk with a croupier who happened to be from Natchez, where he got his start on the gaming boats on the Mississippi. He told me how this bunch of bigwigs were wanting to put a big old boat like that on Horseshoe Lake, and of course I was all ears."

So was Roan, all at once. "Go on."

"Thank you, son. Well, seems this group of investors had mob connections, not exactly a huge surprise. But they had nothing to do with our Louisiana branch of the Cosa Nostra. Seems they were from Florida, where they'd made piles of cash running drugs. They'd been busy laundering a lot of the take, running it through furniture stores because of the high cash flow, not to mention all those shipping crates of stuff with great hiding places. They'd also turned their eye toward gaming, but felt places like Vegas and Atlantic City would be too hard to crack. They settled on little old Turn-Coupe because it was quiet and backward and they could run all sorts of rigs without anybody noticing until it was too late. Once they had that base, they could branch out into bigger things.''

''Why is it that I'm only just hearing about this?'' Roan asked, his gaze steady.

''Looked as if you had the situation under control—until people started turning up dead, like these two.''

Roan looked at Kane and Luke, and the repudiation he saw in their faces was a mirror for his own feelings. If this bunch of creeps thought it was going to be that easy, they'd soon discover their mistake. Their gaming operation was history in Turn-Coupe. They just didn't know it yet.

''The guy who showed up at the house, the man Tory was supposed to marry,'' Jake said with a frown between his brows, ''wasn't he supposed to be some kind of whoop-de-do-big-deal furniture dealer?''

''That he was.'' Roan wasn't certain how much of what his dad had said to take at face value, but it sounded as if Harrell Melanka was in bed with the mob, big-time, and trying to get an extra share of the mattress. He'd thought he could use Tory's money to buy his way into the gaming deal, and had turned vicious when it failed. Now it appeared he was covering his bases while doing his best to see that the venture went on as planned. The question was what he meant to do about Tory.

It was then they saw the headlamps and flashing light of an approaching patrol unit. The siren burped a greeting before the driver pulled over on the shoulder just behind the Jeep.

Cal. It could only be Cal. Roan felt his stomach muscles clench and his face set in grim angles.

''Kane,'' the deputy called as he stepped out and moved

toward them with his loose-limbed stride. "Just the man I need!"

Roan gave his cousin no chance to answer. In a voice of steel, he asked, "What are you doing here? You're supposed to be at the house."

"Don't get in an uproar," Cal said, lifting both hands in a gesture both defensive and calming. "It was your prisoner who sent me to find you. Seems like—"

"Why the hell didn't you say so?" he demanded, turning toward his patrol unit.

"Now, wait a minute, don't go off half-cocked," Cal protested. "It's Kane, here, that she really wanted found."

"Regina," Kane said, starting forward. "The baby, it's the baby. I *knew* I shouldn't have left the house."

"Everything's fine, but they couldn't locate you even after your wife got to the hospital. They tried to contact Roan then, of course, but got Tory. She sent me to tell him, so he could chase you down."

"God," Kane whispered, then took off at a run for the Jeep.

"Wait for me." Luke sprinted after him.

Any other time, Roan would have gone with them. Not now. Scowling at Cal, he asked, "Why the hell didn't you just call me, or have Sherry do it?"

"Everything was quiet, real quiet out at Dog Trot," the deputy said. "And it isn't as if your prisoner was going to run off. I mean she could have done that practically any time this—"

"That's not what bothers me. Suppose whoever hired the kidnappers came after her?"

"You're not back to that are you? No, really, I just thought I'd run out here because there was a chance I'd catch sight of Kane on the way."

"What you thought," Roan said in low fury, "was that

you were missing out, stuck on a surveillance job while everybody else was in the middle of the excitement. So you left your post like the most stupid, wet-behind-the ears recruit. And you think you have what it takes to do my job?''

Cal shoved his shoulders back and his face forward. ''Where the hell you think you get off, talking to me like that?''

''I'm still the sheriff of Tunica Parish, or was the last time I noticed. I'll talk to you any way it takes as long as you're on my force. The two men we just pulled out of the water are the creeps who abducted Tory, and whoever killed them may go after her next. That means you've jeopardized her safety. Didn't they teach you anything about that at the academy?''

Cal glanced from Roan to the dead bodies. The red in his face receded to gray. ''Yeah,'' he said finally. ''They did. Or they tried. I'm sorry, Roan. Real sorry.''

It was a beginning toward the responsibility needed for law enforcement.

Roan gave a hard nod. ''Right. Now get back in your unit and see if you can catch up with Kane and Luke, give them an escort to the hospital so Kane doesn't run over somebody or kill himself trying to get there.''

Cal took a step back, then snapped an awkward salute and took off at a run. Roan watched him only a second before he spoke over his shoulder. ''Jake?''

''Yeah, Dad. I think we'd better get home, don't you?''

Luke spoke up then with a nod toward his Jeep that was disappearing in the distance. ''I'll come with you, since I seem to be on foot.''

''You're not leaving me here, either,'' Pop said.

''Right,'' Roan answered. ''Let's move it.''

It was a relief to be rid of Cal, Tory thought. She hadn't exactly encouraged him to stick around after she saw how he was itching to leave. It had been weeks since she'd been really alone, with no one around to know or care what she was doing. It felt strange.

The house seemed unnaturally quiet as well. The rooms were cavernous with their ceilings so high that the light of a lamp hardly reached into the upper levels. Her footsteps echoed off the plastered walls as she walked. There were too many windows and the darkness crowded too close against them. The intermittent squawking of the scanner was so loud that it grated on her nerves.

Beau was disturbed by the absence of Jake and his dad, she thought. The big hound followed her around from room to room, curling up near wherever she settled. Now and then he lifted his head as if to listen, and twice he got up and went toward the door, barking in low and gruff inquiry. She thought he might want out, and opened the door for him, but he only stared into the night. When she shut the door again, he returned to her side.

It was perhaps a half hour after Cal left that Beau looked up from where he lay curled on the bedroom rug and barked a warning. Heaving upright, he stood with his big front feet planted and the hair on his neck raised in a ruff. Tory looked in his direction from where she sat on the end of Roan's bed, following the unfolding drama at the iron bridge. "What is it, boy? You hear something? Is it Clay again, or just April's cat teasing you?"

Luke's wife had told Tory about her big black tom, Midnight, that liked to roam around the lakeshore. Tory thought it might be the better part of valor for the cat to stay away from Dog Trot with all its hounds, but she'd promised April that she'd keep an eye out for him.

Beau growled again. Hard on the sound, a knock came on the kitchen door downstairs. Tory turned toward the sound with her nerves jangling. She'd heard no car on the drive. Of course, it could have been covered by the scanner noise.

The impulse to ignore the summons was strong. However, the door was locked, and she wasn't sure Pop or Jake had their keys with them. It could also be news of Regina. She liked Kane's wife and was worried about her, and Cal might be back with a report.

It was Harrell who stood on the back gallery. In the light that fell through the upper glass portion of the door, she could see him standing with his hands in his pockets and a pensive smile on his face.

"What do you want?" she called. Behind her, Beau rumbled a growl followed by a low bark.

"We need to talk, Tory. Open the door."

"I don't think so." It was the last thing she'd do, in fact, when she was fairly certain the bodies of Zits and Big Ears were being hauled from the wreckage of their getaway truck at this moment. Mention of multiple gunshot wounds were a strong indication that their deaths had not been accidental.

"I mean it, darling. You have to let me in. I know you have questions about the papers I signed, but I'm sure I can clear up everything if you'll just listen."

He'd always been sure he could talk his way around her. Once maybe, but not anymore. "Go away, Harrell. I'm not interested in anything you have to say."

"Fine, if that's the way you want to play it."

For a split second, she felt relief shift through her. Then she saw Harrell take a handkerchief from his pocket, shake it out, and then wrap it around his fist. He drew back then and slammed a hard blow at the door glass. The corner pane above the handle broke with an icy tingling, scattering shards across the brick floor at her feet. Then Harrell reached in, feeling for the lock. Two seconds later, he was standing in the doorway.

Tory took several steps back, but stood her ground since she saw no sign of a weapon. No doubt Harrell thought he needed none to deal with her. Beau padded forward to put himself between her and her ex-fiancé while his growl rasped like a buzz saw. She laid a hand on the big dog's head. "I'd stop there, if I were you. He's trained to hunt men."

Harrell had already come to a standstill. "We can talk here," he said, his gaze on the dog, "but I've been watching for a chance to see you, and don't intend to miss this one."

He'd been watching. She didn't like the sound of that since it meant he knew she was alone. "Make it brief."

"I didn't mean to hurt you before. You looked so normal and well that I didn't think…"

"Never mind. It wasn't permanent."

"Thank God. I'm so sorry, you know. More than I can say. I've wanted desperately to tell you."

"Harrell," she began.

"I'm really sorry for everything, though I know you don't want to hear it. You stopped caring, didn't you? I guess I'm just surprised at how fast it happened, how fast you threw in with the creeps who abducted you."

"I was never in love with you, Harrell. I told you that when I gave back your ring. It was mistake from the beginning, and there was no point in compounding it. As for throwing in with my kidnappers, as you put it, you know better. Nobody's here, now, so you don't have to pretend."

He laughed. "Right. You were too good to fall in love with me, weren't you, princess? But your sheriff is a different story. If I'd known half-killing you would do the trick, I'd have tried it long ago."

"Crude, Harrell. But why am I surprised?"

He turned dark red under his tan. "That'll play well in the press, won't it? I know a reporter or two who'd love to break the story of the kidnapped heiress shot by the hick sheriff. TV crews and news vans will swarm this town. Nobody will be able to go to the bathroom without having a reporter hand them the toilet paper. They'll crucify this rebel Rambo of yours, a man who shot you full of holes, scrambled your brain, and then locked you up in his own house with a kinky restraint so he could use you for his own little sex slave. What a story! I love it. Don't you?"

"You are revolting," she said, every syllable as distinct as she could make it.

"Do you think so?" His smile was snide. "But how can you tell, considering all you've been through? I mean, who could blame you for needing the services of a good therapist after all this terrible trauma? Maybe even a nice stay in a luxurious rest home would be advisable, say with a flock of high-priced psychiatrists in attendance?"

Beau, responding to the menace in his tone, edged forward with a snarl. Tory smoothed his big head to restrain him, and saw that her fingers were shaking. Her voice was not quite even as she said, "That's ridiculous."

"You know, I don't think so. I think you've played right into my hands with this little affair of yours. Your stepfather is going to just hate all the publicity. We've already agreed that you're too much like your mother, too flighty and frivolous, unable to cope with the pressures of your family name and position. I think he'll see my point when I suggest a long recuperation under sedation, lots of sedation. That is, of course, unless you'd like to forget all our little differences and marry me, after all?"

"You're crazy," she whispered.

"No, not at all, just determined to do things my way.

We can leave right now. I'll see that everything's kept quiet. No press, no announcements. We'll have a small wedding, maybe just a civil ceremony. You'll forget the papers you made such a fuss about before and we'll live happily ever after.''

She laughed. ''Oh, deliriously. With you in charge of my money and me in a rest home.''

''Darling, I'll always take care of you. Your stepfather and I will do it together.''

''I don't think you'll find it easy to persuade Paul Vandergraff to share.''

His face turned cold. ''Don't underestimate me. That's a big mistake, as I think you've already discovered.''

''It's a common failing, isn't it?'' she asked, tipping her head. ''Even you fell into it when you thought I'd go along with whatever you did.''

''Are you thinking of fighting me?'' His voice rang deadly hard. ''Don't. To have you as my wife isn't absolutely necessary. All I really need is for your signature on those papers to go unchallenged.''

He was threatening to kill her. He could stand there and do it because he thought she had no defense. The very idea sickened her. It also brought rage boiling up from inside her.

She'd been kidnapped, tied up and gagged, jerked around, shot, accused of being a felon, imprisoned, fitted with a degrading monitor, publicly revealed as a liar, and threatened with a mental institution. She was tired of it. She was damned tired of it, and she wasn't going to put up with it any longer.

''Listen to me,'' she said, narrowing her eyes to slits. ''I am Victoria Molina-Vandergraff, the Princess de Trentalara. You think you're a big man, but my Italian great-great grandfather once had his enemies cut to ribbons so my great-great grandmother could weave them into rugs. Mess with me, and I'll wipe the soles of my high heels on you. Literally.''

Beau snarled as if on cue. Harrell's eyes widened for an instant, then he gave a snort of derision. ''You scare me.''

''That's smart of you, because I mean every word.''

''Don't be silly, you aren't going to do anything. Come on now, let's go.''

He reached for her as he had before, but she was ready for him. She whirled away, put the table between them. The dog stood firm, with front legs planted wide and teeth bared. His barking was like constant thunder.

''All right, you little bitch...'' Harrell began.

Beau attacked. His big, long body made a powerful arc in the air as he leaped for Harrell's throat.

Her ex-fiancé threw up his arm, then howled as Beau's teeth sank deep into his wrist. Dog and man tumbled out the doorway and onto the brick patio. The fall broke Beau's hold. Harrell rolled, scrambling away, wide-eyed and cursing, while Beau snapped and worried at him.

''Beau!'' Tory called, starting forward. ''Down, Beau!''

It did no good. The dog couldn't hear her above his deep barking and Harrell's yells. Then Harrell grabbed a roof post and dragged himself to his feet. He flung a look of impotent fury in Tory's direction. ''You'll be sorry!'' he shouted. ''I'll make your life a living hell. I'll see you dead, and your hick sheriff, too!''

Hard on the words, he took to his heels, disappearing around the house with Beau after him. A moment later, Tory heard a car start and roar away into the night. Beau continued to bark for a few minutes longer, then he came trotting back to her for approval.

Tory crooned to the big bloodhound and scratched behind his ears, soothing him and herself as she smoothed out his ruff. At the same time, her thoughts raced like an overheated engine.

She couldn't stay at Dog Trot, not any longer. Her presence would bring a media feeding frenzy. She was a liability to Roan; everything he'd done for her, or tried to do, would be dragged in the dirt. He'd be held up to ridicule, or worse, accused of all the ugliness inventive minds could conceive. When it was over, he'd be notorious, him and his sleepy, peaceful little town. And the backlash against him would probably drive him out of office.

She couldn't do that to him, couldn't let it happen to his family that she held in affection and respect. They didn't deserve it, any of them.

And Roan didn't deserve to have his life endangered because of her, either. She couldn't stand it if anything happened to him, or to Jake or Pop if they got in the way. The problems she had with Harrell were hers to solve. It was time she faced them. It was time she went home.

The strange thing was, she was ready. She'd changed over the last few weeks, had become more her own person. She knew what she wanted out of life, had decided, finally, what was important to her. She was ready to stop drifting, stop letting other people make decisions for her. She was ready to stop running away.

Except, of course, for this one last time.

She knew where the tool that unlocked the monitor was located since Roan had returned it to where it was before. She knew, of course, where the keys to the Super Bird were kept. She knew the way back to Sanibel.

The only thing she didn't know was if she'd ever see Turn-Coupe again.

Or the man who was the sheriff of Tunica Parish.

17

Tory was gone.

No lights burned in the house when Roan and the others pulled up on the drive. The back door was locked. Beau met them just inside, whining and dancing around them as if disturbed and with the skin between his eyes folded into wrinkles. Roan flipped on the kitchen light at the same moment that he noticed the broken glass.

Jake pushed past him and loped up the back stairs, calling as he went. His voice echoed in the emptiness. No one answered, no one appeared.

Roan dropped a hand to Beau's big head as the dog leaned against him. "Where is she, boy?" he asked under his breath. "Where's Tory?"

"Son?" Pop called from the patio, his voice taut. "You might want to look at this."

Roan's dad had been the last one out of the car, the last one to head for the kitchen door. He'd paused on the patio. As Roan glanced toward him through the open door, he saw him staring down at something on the bricks in front of him.

A cold heaviness settled around Roan's heart. He stepped

to the switch beside the door and flipped on the outside
light. "What is it?"

Pop looked at Roan from under his brows. Then he nodded toward the dark stain at his feet.

Roan went to one knee and reached to touch the spot. It
was wet and a little tacky. Swiveling on his heels, he held
his fingers to the light.

Blood.

He felt as if somebody had kicked him in the stomach.
He couldn't breathe, couldn't think. His brain seemed hot
and too big for his skull. The fear and rage that gripped
him was so vast that he had to remain absolutely motionless
in order to contain it.

"Don't," his dad said. "It doesn't have to be hers."

It didn't have to be, no, but she had been alone. Who
else's could it be?

"Is there more of it?" he asked, his voice sounding
strange even to his own ears. The smeared stain in front of
him was small, the size of a quarter, with half dozen or so
drops scattered around it.

"Looks like a few over here, near the walk. Then they
disappear in the grass and the dark."

"Get a flashlight, will you? Mine's in the car." Roan
was already moving onto the grass as he spoke, scanning
the ground with his gaze. He was helped by the fact that
Jake had turned on some of the upstairs lights so their glow
illuminated the backyard.

"Dad? Dad, up here!"

It was Jake, calling from the upper balcony. Roan turned
to look up at him, narrowing his eyes to make out his son.
He was alone.

"You found her?" Roan waited, hands clenched into
fists, for the answer.

"She's not here, but..."

Jake's voice had cracked; that was one reason he'd stopped. His words were thick, and carried an undercurrent of fear, fear for Tory. He'd grown close to her in the last few weeks, Roan thought. But there was something else, something he couldn't quite say.

"Tell me!" Roan called, while his heart throbbed in his chest. "What is it?"

"This," Jake said, and leaned over the balcony to fling down something dark and heavy and circular in shape. Roan shot up an arm to catch it by purest instinct. The instant his fingers closed around it, he knew.

It was the monitor. Tory's monitor.

"Where was it?" he asked. "Her bedroom?"

"Nope, yours."

The answer was tight, and an instant tip-off that Jake had known where to look for Tory. The boy must have gone to her room first, Roan thought. Seeing no sign of her, he'd moved along to the next possible place where she might have been sleeping. He should have known it was impossible to keep what was between them a secret. If there was anything between them worthy of the name.

Roan swung around with the monitor and stalked to where he could see in the light from beside the kitchen door. He half expected the mechanism to be cut. It wasn't. The lock had been opened. He stared down at it, smoothing the ball of his thumb over the silky smooth leather that had been polished by Tory's ankle in an unconscious gesture.

Had she found the tool and released herself? But if it was that easy, why has she waited until now? What had triggered her release? Had someone forced her to do it? Had she been hurt? Where in the name of heaven had she gone?

The swinging beam of a flashlight approached from around the house. The gleam caught the monitor in his hand, steadied on it for an instant. Roan's dad said nothing until he was close enough to flip off the light and speak in a normal voice.

"You think Melanka was here?"

"I have to go with that idea, because—"

"Because the risk is too great otherwise. If you assume she left of her own accord, and do nothing, she may die."

"Exactly."

"And you couldn't take that."

Roan gave a short, humorless laugh, even as pictures of the mutilated bodies he'd seen earlier that evening flashed through him mind. "If he touches a hair on her head, I'll kill him with my bare hands."

"I thought so," his dad said with satisfaction. "Now then. What are you going to do?"

It was a good question. Roan closed his eyes briefly as he tried to sort through his options. The way he saw it, there were only two: he could go, following on Tory's trail, or he could stay put, send out an APB and wait to see what happened.

He wasn't much for waiting.

"Dad?"

The interruption came from Jake on the veranda above him. He cast an impatient glance in that direction. "Yeah?"

"I'm not real sure with the dark and all, but it looks from up here as if the barn door might be open."

The barn. The Super Bird was there.

It had been there. The dark interior was empty. His car, his pampered classic with unmarred paint, shiny chrome, and Hemi engine, was gone.

Tory had taken it this time. She had taken it and headed home, back to Florida.

But what if she hadn't? What if it had been stolen by whoever had come for her? It didn't matter. Either way, he wanted his Super Bird back. He wanted it, and he'd have it if it was the last thing he ever did.

There was no time to waste. With his mind made up, Roan began to click off tasks and duties in methodical order. He made certain Tory had not left a note, checked her closet to see what she'd taken with her, which proved to be nothing at all, and contacted her stepfather's Florida residence only to be told that he had no information. He talked to his office to make certain things would run smoothly while he was out of town, and also to ask for an APB on the rental car Melanka had been driving, since he'd made a note of the plate number. He left instructions with Jake and his dad, in case Tory got in touch, then he went back upstairs to load his pockets with extra rounds for his weapon and to throw a few things into an overnight bag. He was jerking the zipper closed when his dad appeared in the doorway.

"So what's the deal?" Pop asked, his voice gravelly with something that sounded a lot like concern.

"Why am I going? I thought we settled that."

"Oh, I know you're following after Tory for her protection, but then what? Are you going to straighten things out between you, or just drag her back out of sheer stubborn pride, because she got away and it's your damn duty to see she stands trial?"

"Hell, Pop!"

"Don't take that tone with me, son, because this is your old man talking. I may not be as young as I used to be, but I still know what's what. That woman meant something to you, just as you meant something to her."

"Yeah, I meant something to her, all right," Roan answered, his gaze on what he was doing. "I was her jailer."

"Because that's the way you wanted it, the only way that felt comfortable to you. As long as you controlled what was between you, you were all right. But the minute you began to lose that, you backed off so far you were near out of sight.''

"She doesn't belong here, Pop, she never did. She has a grand life somewhere else that she'll go back to eventually. The little we had together didn't mean anything. She was just marking time.''

"You figured she was going to leave you, just like Carolyn, so you bowed out in advance.''

"That's not so!'' He looked up, but couldn't quite focus on the man in front of him for thinking, wondering.

"Not all women need freeways and fancy shops and restaurants and lots of different things to do. Some happen to enjoy peace and quiet and a lake view. Not all women are like Carolyn, Roan. They don't leave without good reason.''

"Fine. So we'll talk about the future, if we get the chance.'' It wasn't true. But it was apparently what his dad expected from him, and Roan didn't have time to argue.

"Now you're talking! We'll be waiting, Jake and me, to hear from you. And from Tory.''

He didn't answer. What was there to say?

But he wasn't through with explaining himself yet, or so it seemed. Jake was waiting for him, leaning on the passenger door of the car, when he came out of the house.

"I want to go with you, Dad,'' he said, his voice so low it was little more than a mumble. "I can't stay here wondering what might be happening to Tory.''

First his father, now his son. Victoria Molina-Vandergraff had somehow managed to get under the skin of every male on the place, including Beau's. It was going to be a long time before she was forgotten. Roan threw his bag into the back seat and slammed the door. Then he turned to his son.

"Look—" he began with as much patience as he could scrape together under the circumstances.

"I know what you're going to say," Jake interrupted, his head coming up. "I'm too young, I'll just be in the way, you need to move fast, blah, blah. I don't care! I want to do something to help. She may be out there hurt somewhere, or maybe kidnapped again and tied up where she can't get away. She needs us, I know she does, and she's my friend. I have as much right as you do to go after her."

The boy had a point. More than that, Roan was proud of him for his protective instinct toward Tory. It showed that he was growing up, becoming a man and a true Benedict. All the same, he couldn't let him go.

"I know you're worried about her," he said, as he reached to put his hand on his son's shoulder. "So am I. But I don't even know if what I'm doing is worthwhile or a wild-goose chase. Somebody needs to stay here in case she calls, or to pass on any other news that might come in."

"Pop will be here."

"You're right. But there's another problem. I can't deal with a killer if I have to watch out for you as well as Tory."

Jake's lips tightened before he said, "I can take care of myself."

"In a fair fight, yes, but this guy doesn't fight fair. If I was forced to choose between saving you or saving Tory, I don't—" He stopped abruptly, unable to go on.

"Yeah," Jake said slowly. "I get it."

Roan nodded, cleared his throat. "If you have any problems here that Pop can't handle, call Clay or Luke. Kane has his hands full right now."

It was Jake's turn to nod.

"Fine." He turned to go.

"Dad?"

He glanced back with a lifted brow.

"You…take care of yourself."

Roan smiled. "Yeah. I'll do that. Don't worry."

"Bring Tory back."

He couldn't promise that, and didn't try. With a quick pivot, he caught his son in a bear hug, then stepped back, buffeted him on the shoulder in the traditional rallying gesture of males embarrassed by their own emotion, but acknowledging it anyway. A moment later, he climbed into his patrol unit and drove off. When he turned onto the highway at the end of the drive, Jake was still standing where he'd left him, watching him go.

On his way through town, Roan put gas in his unit and called the hospital to check with Kane, pausing long enough to congratulate his cousin on being the father of a fine new baby girl. Regina was tired, Kane said, but had done a wonderful job. Roan, hearing the preoccupation in his cousin's tone, didn't bother to explain what was going on with Tory but only congratulated him again and hung up.

As he pulled out on the road, he placed a final call to the office to check on the search for Melanka's rental car. It had been found; Melanka had turned it in at the airport. He had taken a flight to Florida, and he had been alone. Only one ticket had been charged to his credit card. No one by the name of Tory Molina-Vandergraff had been on that departing plane.

For about two seconds, Roan allowed himself the luxury of relief. Melanka had left town. Tory hadn't been with him.

But there was still the blood. What about the blood?

Suppose Melanka had killed Tory and hauled her body off somewhere to dump it? Suppose he had taken the Super Bird so the rented vehicle would be free of evidence, and had plunged both car and Tory off into the lake or the river? Or what if he'd hired some creep to do the job for him while he, the picture of innocence, dropped off his rental car and flew home? Tory would simply disappear. He might never know what happened to her, or what might have been between them.

God. He was going nuts, not knowing, but only guessing. Maybe guessing wrong.

Roan weighed the radio mike in his hand, about to put out a bulletin on the Super Bird. If Tory was driving it, heading for the sunshine state, he could have her picked up even if it was in Mississippi, Alabama, or in the Florida panhandle.

Yes, but hadn't he done enough to her? She didn't need to be chased down by some gung ho officer like Cal, one who might do a body search, cuff her without giving a damn about her hurt shoulder, then throw her in a tank with dope dealers and hookers where anything could happen to her.

No. He couldn't stand the thought of that, either.

If Tory wasn't in the Bird, what did it matter? If she was gone, lying somewhere in the swamps, then he wanted her killer. He wanted Melanka's head, and he'd have it if he had to drive to hell itself.

He ended the call, slapped the mike onto its hook, then plowed his fingers through his hair as he stared at the road unwinding in front of him. Why hadn't he believed her when she'd told him she'd been kidnapped and that the men who had done it had orders to kill her? He'd thought himself that she didn't seem the type to consort with the lowlifes captured by the security cams. If he'd only followed his instincts.

Still she'd been so evasive, so vague and changeable. Yes, and he'd been knocked off balance by a visceral and hormonal attraction of the kind he hadn't felt since high school. She'd got under his guard when he'd held her in his arms and felt her warm blood seeping into his shirt, and he hadn't liked it. He hadn't wanted her to be real and innocent because then he'd have to deal with what he felt. And that had scared him so much he'd preferred not to think of it at all. It had scared him because he'd known that he had to lose, that she'd either be found guilty and sent to prison, or else return to whatever fine and easy life she'd left. Either way, he'd be alone again.

Look where it had got him, that refusal to face facts. Tory had left because she couldn't trust him to protect her any more. He'd left her alone, and now she was gone. He had to find her, had to make her safe again, even if it meant losing her. It was better to know that she was alive some-where in the world than to think that she might have left it for good. He could not stand to think of her gone, dying in pain and horror while he was off about his duty. His eternal duty that meant nothing if she wasn't there. His duty that he was leaving behind, now, without a qualm or second thought or an instant's consideration for what anyone might think of his using an official vehicle for a semiprivate mat-ter. So much for how important it was, to him or anyone else.

He had to believe that she'd taken his car. It was the only acceptable explanation. Everything else was too damned hard to face. Impossible, in fact.

So where did that leave him?

If Melanka was flying, he didn't have her, couldn't touch her for the next—what, sixteen or seventeen hours that it would take for the drive to Florida? Or longer than that, if she stopped for the night. Maybe her ex-fiancé knew where she was headed and meant to get there ahead of her so he could be waiting when she showed up?

Tory was no match for Melanka. She wasn't wary enough, or as vicious as she'd need to be to best him. For all her attempts to be hard and cynical, she was too soft inside, too weak from her injury. No, she was no match for a killer.

Or was she? She'd fooled him, hadn't she?

She must have known where the release tool was for the monitor all along; she couldn't have got away so quickly tonight, otherwise. He could pinpoint when she must have found it, at the same time she found the car keys. The question that bugged him was why she hadn't taken it off as soon as she'd found the means. Unless it was the certain knowledge that he'd track her down, with or without the damn thing. She'd left now because he'd learned who she was and she'd known from looking at him how much difference it made. Because she didn't trust him, now, to keep her secrets or keep her safe.

Did it matter that she was an heiress and a bona fide princess? Did it really?

Of course it did. It changed everything. Everything.

Roan was, by his best estimate, two hours or less behind her. The Bird was fast but he had the advantage of an official vehicle with emergency lights and a siren if he needed to use them. He should be able to run her down. The greatest danger might be that he'd miss her in the dark or overshoot her while she was stopped for gas or a break.

He had no real authority in Florida or any of the states in between; his jurisdiction extended only to Tunica Parish. Once he passed that parish limit sign, he'd be just a man, like any other. No better, no worse. No special privileges.

It would have to be enough.

The drive passed in a blur of traffic, road signs and communities with the sidewalks rolled up for the night. He took back roads from Natchez to Hattisburg, then turned south and east on Highway 49 to I-10. The wide open interstate unrolled ahead of him with the broken strips of the white center line flashing past like blinking lights as he made time through the night. He stopped for gas and a package of salted peanuts that he poured into the neck of a cold drink bottle as an energy snack, then he hit the road again.

The sun was rising by the time he reached Mobile. He squinted into it as the click of his tires over the joints of the causeway kept pace with his thoughts and fears. He'd seen no sign of the Super Bird.

On through the stunted pine barrens of the Florida panhandle he flew, making time. On the other side of Tallahassee, he found I-75 South and the constant parade of billboards advertising suntan lotion, tropical gardens and retirement havens. With the increasing stream of cars and fifth wheels and motor homes, he entered tourist land and began to see the first bougainvillea, the first palms, the first Bermuda coral-colored villas, and the vast trailer parks like cities made of aluminum and fiberglass. He drove in what had become a semidaze, so it was almost a shock to see exits signs for Fort Myers suddenly appear and realize he had almost made it.

Sanibel, an orderly island with its precious trees and rampant vegetation sheltering private bungalows and beach mansions so large it wasn't always easy to tell them from the hotels. Most of them were shuttered and silent, however, deserted for the summer as their owners retreated from the humid heat of the rainy season, preferring cooler watering places like Bar Harbor and the Hamptons. Roan was briefly puzzled by the fact that Vandergraff had not left, but thought he might have reached an age where the semiannual move was too much trouble, or that he had overriding financial interests in the place.

Roan had asked his office to find and radio to him the

address of the Vandergraff house. It was midafternoon
when he finally located the entrance gates of the fenced
enclosure. Since they were standing open, he turned in and
took the snaking, shell-paved drive though arching jaca-
randa trees and under towering royal palms to the wide
front doors constructed of beveled glass. He pulled up and
slowly unfolded his stiff muscles from behind the wheel.
Standing with his arms braced on the car door, he took a
good look at the Vandergraff winter home.

It was an architect's dream of angles and wings, balco-
nies and cool, shady lanai, a spreading paradise of marble
and stucco wrapped around a Moorish style garden with a
spouting lion fountain and a shifting, glittering Olympic-
size pool. Blindingly white in the tropical sun, it whispered
of comfort and seclusion and money. It was a place that
would have every innovative convenience known to science
and imagination, every luxury of which the mind could
conceive. It was Tory's home, or one of them.

With a quick shake of his head, he shut the car door and
walked to the entrance. A maid or housekeeper in a black-
and-white uniform appeared, though she only opened the
door a crack, staring wide-eyed through it at him and the
star on his chest.

Sí, this was the Vandergraff residence, but Señorita Victoria, she was not at home. She had returned, *Sí, sí.* But
she had showered and changed, fast, fast, and gone out
again, driving the purple monster of an automobile across
the causeway to Fort Myers. No, she had not said where
she was going or when she would return; perhaps it would
be late. Señor Vandergraff had gone to the golf and might
be back in one hour, maybe two, perhaps three, if the *Señor
Policia* wished to wait.

Roan wished, but decided against it. He'd find a hotel

instead, take a quick shower and get a bite to eat. Then he'd be back.

Before he started his car again, he looked back at the house. The place was like a palace. In it, Tory was a real princess, wrapped around with silk and diamonds and all the traditional snobbery of those who had never known want or imagined it. It was her rightful place. The only one she needed, ever.

And abruptly Roan knew that he had dreamed. He knew that somewhere in his mind he'd thought that maybe, just maybe, Tory would want to leave Sanibel and her rich life for the down-home comfort of Dog Trot. That she might do it for him and Jake, Pop and Beau, and all the other Benedicts who would welcome and surround her and make her one of them.

Stupid. So stupid and egotistical a dream. Yes, and proof of his incredible ignorance of the high pinnacle she'd been standing on when she'd first dared to look down on his town and his people.

Dumb backcountry sheriff that he might be, undoubtedly was, he could see, now, that it was impossible she would ever leave it.

18

Tory heard voices coming from the living room as she let herself into the house on her return from Fort Myers. She glanced back at the parking apron half hidden among the trees for some clue as to her stepfather's guest. No vehicle was visible. Frowning a little, she closed the door. The voices stopped. After a second, Paul Vandergraff appeared in the doorway with a glass of malt scotch in his hand.

"Tory, my dear, here you are at last," he said as if she were merely late to dinner instead of returning after being kidnapped. "Come in and join us for a drink."

She hesitated, surveying him from what felt like a new perspective. Slender, tanned to a perfect toast brown that set off his close-cropped silver hair, he had a dapper appearance that he cultivated with white Polo shirts in summer and cashmere sweaters and ascots in the winter. Where once she'd considered him the epitome of East Coast sophistication and polish, he now seemed merely superficial. He hadn't changed, which meant that she had, drastically. As he swung back into the room, she put her keys and handbag on the foyer table and followed him with the heels of her Italian leather shoes clicking on the marble floor.

Her ex-fiancé got to his feet as she entered. "Darling, what a surprise. I thought you were settled in Louisiana."

"Harrell. How lovely," she said with a twist of her lips for the obviousness of the charade. Moving to the drink table, she poured cold mineral water into a glass. Over her shoulder, she said, "But you thought wrong. Naturally, I returned to Florida. It's where my business interests are located, after all. But I can't say I'm surprised to see you here with Paul, thick as thieves, after our last meeting."

"Please, darling, let's don't start that again." Harrell glanced at Paul Vandergraff as if to say, *What did I tell you?*

"Why not? Your threats aren't something I'm likely to forget. Believe me." She turned to face them armored in her gray designer suit worn with a silk blouse, her mother's gray-pink pearls, and with her hair in a smooth French twist. She could do the lady of wealth and breeding as well as any debutante when it was required. This was one of those times.

"Personally, I'd prefer not to be reminded that you ran away with a couple of beach bums. However, your little crime spree in Louisiana with them may be more difficult to wipe from the record than previous escapades."

"There was no crime spree," she declared, including Paul in the cold glance she leveled at Harrell. "Rather, I escaped being murdered by the grace of God and the quick action of Sheriff Roan Benedict."

"A man you quickly fell in love with—or at least you fell into his bed."

"I did not—" She stopped, took a deep breath. "Were you ever attracted to me at all, Harrell, or was it always about the money? Does it bother you, being a fortune hunter, or do you think it makes you look smart to dance circles around a woman because a lucky accident made her rich?''

He shook his head. ''Please don't say such things. I love you, of course, as I've always loved you. I know I said terrible things the other night, but I was hurt and angry.''

''Speaking of which,'' she drawled, ''how is your arm? No sign of rabies, I hope?''

''It's all right,'' he said, his face darkening. ''No thanks to you and your Casanova with a badge.''

She smiled at the description before she said gently, ''I'm also healing well, thank you both for asking.''

Paul had the grace to look embarrassed as he said, ''That's good news indeed.''

Harrell gave her a pained look. ''You think I haven't been worried? Your welfare has never been out of my mind.''

''I'm sure.''

''We really need to talk, darling. Let's go somewhere quiet, where we can sit down and—''

''Quiet and deserted? You must think I'm an idiot.''

''Really, Victoria, you need to cut Harrell some slack,'' Paul said before lifting his drink to take a swallow.

''Why?'' she asked as she swung her head to stare at him. ''I'm not interested in making it easier for him to kill me.''

''There's no question of that.'' Irritation was strong in his voice.

''You weren't there, so how can you know? I don't understand why you're taking Harrell's side. Unless it's because you'd as soon I disappeared so you could mismanage my estate in peace?''

He stood still, staring at her with his glass forgotten in his hand. ''Mismanage? That would be funny if it weren't so unbelievable.''

"It's neither one, according to my lawyers. You've seriously depleted my assets while increasing your own. You have, apparently, mishandled investments, manipulated stock portfolios, and transferred cash holdings in ways that look extremely suspicious. The only good thing I can say for you is that you haven't, at least so far as I know, taken a leaf from Harrell's book and forged my signature to fraudulent documents."

The color drained away from Paul's face, leaving it gray and skull-like. He opened his mouth, but no words came out. He transferred his gaze to the glass in his hand, staring into the melting ice of his drink.

Tory knew then, though the possibility had lurked somewhere in her mind for days, even weeks. She took a deep breath before she went on. "But you did, didn't you? Someone had to authorize access to my accounts after I came of age. You must have become quite good at copying my signature. You're the one who signed the documents that guaranteed Harrell's participation in the gaming scheme. How convenient, especially when I wasn't around to complain."

"I never meant for you to be hurt."

No doubt he'd closed his mind to the probability, she thought, just as he'd managed not to think of her mother's distress at being shut away all those years ago. But at least his cooperation in the deal accounted for why there had been no report, no furor, over her disappearance, even after all this time.

"Why?" she asked because she couldn't help herself. "You couldn't need the money."

"You think not?" His smile was grim. "But it's always been there for you, hasn't it? Accumulating more holds no attraction. With me, it's otherwise."

"You get a kick out of increasing your wealth? Even

when it's by stealing millions from my mother? And from
me?''

"It was just lying there, tons of it for which you'd done
nothing. Why shouldn't I?''

The affront in his tone was almost plausible. It was as if
he saw no contradiction in what he'd just said, had no understanding that the fraudulent use of someone else's
wealth to increase his own net worth was unacceptable, as
if he were exempt from the laws that applied to lesser
thieves. It made her wonder just how much of his industrial
empire was a sham, perhaps a cover for less savory forms
of making money.

"You fool!'' Harrell glared at Paul Vandergraff with
contempt curling his lips. "Now we'll have to get rid of
her, and it won't be easy after this other mess.''

"This other mess was your brilliant solution, if you'll
remember,'' her stepfather snapped back. "Anyway, we
can still put her away. Find the right doctor and pay him
enough, and nobody will listen to a word she says.''

"We can't take that chance. The people we're dealing
with don't like loose ends.''

Tory laughed, she couldn't help it, though the noise had
a winded sound. The threat Paul had just made had hovered
for years, unspoken, over their relationship. Fear of it was
what had left her so unsettled, she thought, so unable to
concentrate on where she was going with her life. It was
almost a relief to have it out in the open.

At the same time, she knew she'd made a mistake in
revealing all her suspicions. The lawyers she'd been clos-
eted with for the past several hours had warned her to leave
the house at once, then discuss the situation only in the
presence of legal representatives. She'd have been glad to
comply, given the chance. Confronted by the two men,
she'd more or less depended on her stepfather to behave in

a civilized manner about her discoveries and Harrell to control his more vicious impulses in Paul's presence. Now that she'd begun, however, she could see no way to stop. And it was good to find out the truth, at last.

Fear thrummed along her veins, but not in the same way that it might once have. Her stepfather had always seemed such a powerful man. Now he appeared effete and almost pathetic. She'd grown used to seeing the Benedict men around her, she thought, so her frame of reference had stretched to a larger scale. She had learned to measure men like Harrell and Paul against it and discovered that they came up lacking.

"Is that what Zits and Big Ears were, 'loose ends?'" she inquired in pensive curiosity.

Harrell gave a dismissive shrug. "They bungled everything, then had the nerve to put the bite on me to keep quiet about it."

"So you killed them."

"It's what they deserved."

The lack of emotion in his voice was chilling. She would not let it affect her more than she could help. "You'll excuse me, I hope, but I may be something more than a loose end. I did mention that I'd had a conference with my lawyers this afternoon?"

She had their abrupt and total attention. Paul recovered first. A frown gathered between his brows as he asked, "What have you done?"

"Something I should have seen to a long time ago. I'm now in charge of my affairs, financial and otherwise. The first order of business will be a complete audit. When the extent of the damage done under your stewardship has been established, I will abolish the elaborate structure of family trusts you put in place and assume control. Naturally, you will be expected to cooperate fully with the transfer of authority.''

Paul laughed. ''Your lawyers? If you mean the family firm, I've been playing golf with those men for decades. They're friends of mine. Hell, half of them have bought Aspen condos and fleets of Mercedes off my business. All I have to do is explain how things stand and the problem will disappear.''

''I don't think so. The present head of the firm was a friend of my mother's, a good friend. His father went to Yale with my grandfather. They understand perfectly that I am ready to see after my own interests.''

''I'm sure your mental instability will be a factor in just who—''

''We also discussed the viability of a suit for libel. They expressed themselves as happy to pursue the matter on my behalf should you attempt to bring up such an issue. In the meantime, an independent accounting firm has been retained for the audit. You will deliver all books, records and documents pertaining to my inheritance from my mother to their office within forty-eight hours.''

''That's impossible and you know it!'' Paul sputtered. ''It will take the accountants at least a week to prepare the documents.''

''Preparation isn't necessary,'' she responded. ''Nor are adjustments. You will turn everything over as is, both for our sake and yours.''

His hand shook so the ice in his glass tinkled as he raised the scotch to his lips. It was, she thought, a positive sign that he needed time to doctor the books to cover up the misuse of trust accounts. Remembering her mother's last days, it didn't exactly hurt Tory to see it.

When it seemed he would make no reply, she went on again. ''In the meantime, there will be no transfer of assets unless I sign off on them with my legal representative as a witness. A sworn statement is now on record of my refusal to participate in any way in Harrell's—excuse me, yours and Harrell's—gambling venture or any other to which either of you are a party." She looked at Harrell. "As for you, the gaming commission for the state of Louisiana has been contacted concerning your fraudulent application. You will be receiving a demand for the immediate return of all copies of documents that contain signatures forged with my name."

"You bitch," Harrell said, though the words were blank with shock.

"I did warn you, if you'll remember," Tory said, her gaze direct. "You have twenty-four hours."

"You're very big on time constraints, aren't you?" Paul sneered.

She gave him a brief glance. "Some things are better done quickly. I should also tell you, I think, that I made a will. If anything happens to me, bequests will be made to various charities, but the bulk of my estate will go to a young man in Louisiana named Jake Benedict."

Harrell swore again, though the words were little more than a whisper.

"You can't do that," Paul protested.

"I believe I can. In fact, it's done. If you don't intend to comply with the requests, you are free to retain your own lawyer to draft a response."

"That damn hick sheriff," Harrell said. "This is his doing."

"Not at all."

He snorted. "You'd never have had the nerve if not for him."

That much was true, she knew, though not in the way Harrell meant. She didn't expect Roan to back her up on

this play, but his steadfast example of doing what he
thought was right, regardless of the consequences, had
given her the courage to stand up to her fears and fight
back. No matter what happened, she would always be grateful for that.

"This is incredible," Paul said. "I can't believe you'd
do this to me."

"What's incredible is that you think I wouldn't after
what you did to my mother," she said.

"I've been a father to you, given you everything..."

"You tolerated me for the sake of the money. Barely."

"I managed your fortune, yes. It was natural that I take
charge."

"And unnatural to leave it in trust, then allow me to
handle it myself when I came of age? You would think that
way, wouldn't you? It's so convenient."

Paul's face mirrored his disgust. "It's more than unnatural, it's obscene for people like you and your mother to
have so much. What were you going to do with it? Give it
away, as you're handing it over to this young yokel?"

"What's obscene is piling it up for show or to make
some meaningless list of millionaires. What's obscene is
having me abducted with the idea of putting a permanent
end to my ability to interfere in your financial fun. As for
giving away what I own, that will happen only if—" She
stopped, since the answer to that line of reasoning was far
too obvious.

"If you die," Harrell said with grim anticipation in his
face. He put a hand under the linen jacket that he wore,
and took a snub-nosed pistol from the hollow of his back.
The bore was ugly, snoutlike, as it centered on her mid-
section.

"There's no benefit in killing me," she said with trenchant reason, even as she felt her abdomen muscles clench and her lips turn cold.

"Nothing except making sure that you don't talk to anyone who matters."

"Roan knows already. If anything happens to me, he'll be looking for you. As will my lawyers."

"Maybe, though your lawman is in Louisiana and may not care to chase after a dead woman." Harrell gave a doleful shake of his head even as he waved his pistol toward the door, then crowded her, heading her in that direction. "Besides, there's not much any of them can do if you take your own life, now is there? And I think you just may. You've been unstable for years, and Paul will vouch for it. Now there's this strange behavior of running off with two weirdos on a crime spree, getting yourself shot, pretending amnesia—oh, yes, and getting involved with the lawman who shot you. You've been ripe to tip over the edge for a long time, no doubt about it. It won't be a big surprise if you take a long swim out into the gulf and don't come back."

"*I'm* headed for the edge?" she asked in grim sarcasm. "You're the crazy one, especially if you think I'm going swimming any time soon." She eased away from him as she stepped through the door into the foyer, but there was no way to make a break for it.

"Oh, I didn't say you were going alone. It will be my pleasure to join you, then make sure that you go out with the tide. It's in, you know, and it's high." He indicated the hallway that led off at a right angle. "Come along, darling. Let's get this over."

He really was insane; there was no other word for it.

She thought of refusing, of making him drag her kicking and fighting from the house. Dignity wouldn't allow it.

More than that, it seemed foolish to waste energy that she might need for better things.

Appealing to her stepfather for intervention seemed worse than useless. He'd raised no objection to Harrell's plans to this point, and there was no reason to think he would, or that Harrell would listen if he did. All she could do for now was move ahead of her former fiancé while keeping her eyes open for a chance, any chance, to get away from him.

It seemed so unreal that she might die. In spite of what she'd gone through in Turn-Coupe, her mind rejected the possibility. She felt invincible inside herself, full of life and hope and promise. That it could all end, that one person could remove the surge and flow of life from another human being, was an outrage and a tragedy. It should not be physically possible.

The hall they were in led to an exercise room and sauna on one side and a courtyard on the other. The courtyard was a secluded oasis of greenery and silence, with palms that cast moving shadows on the walls and a wrought iron gate for beach access.

The live-in housekeeper was nowhere in sight. She was either preparing dinner in the kitchen wing of the house, or else had retreated to her own quarters. Harrell seemed alert to her possible presence since he kept checking behind them and paused before stepping past open doors. Only when they reached the courtyard, moving along the winding path that led to the beach gate, did he appear to relax his guard somewhat.

Sanibel was an island with few public beaches. Gulf or bay frontage was private, a privilege included in the astronomical cost of beachfront real estate. The stretch that went with the Vandergraff place was larger than most, a wide swath of deserted beige-white sand. It was washed this evening by the thunderous waves of an offshore storm combined with high tide. The wave action had left a black lace border along the sand's edge of broken shells and plant debris. The wind off the water was strong enough to take the tops off the surf and carry the salt spray all the way to the courtyard. It rustled the sea grapes and waved the palms overhead so they clattered with a sound like rain. Gulls dipped and soared overhead, their sharp cries piercing and mournful yet wild.

The evening light still lingered out over the water, but the beach was almost dark. Few lights shone from the houses set back amid their tangles of greenery. Most were winter homes, open only during the high season from Christmas to Easter. Their occupants had rolled down the hurricane shutters over the windows and retreated from the fierce heat, monsoon rains and tropical storms of summer to cooler climates. A few houses belonged to true islanders, but they had sense enough to stay in, avoiding the beach during a storm tide.

Harrell laughed, a hard and satisfied sound, as he saw the deserted sand. He motioned her away from the house, then fell into step beside her as she walked toward the water line with her high heels sinking into the sand.

She couldn't just march calmly to her death. She had to say something, do something, to gain time. She had to get past the sense of disbelief so her mind would work enough to find some way to stop him. But how? How?

"This...really is a lunatic idea," she said, her voice not quite steady as she lifted it above the wind and waves. "I'd advise you to rethink it."

"Would you?" His tone was patronizing, too full of assurance to be curious.

"Police have all kinds of ways to tell what happened to a murder victim now. According to what I've been reading lately, they can tell whether a person drowned or was choked or suffocated, whether skin damage came before or after death. You can't touch me without leaving a mark of some kind, and if you think I'm going to walk in and drown for your convenience, you need your head examined.''

''Oh, I think you will. You've been shot once. I'd be surprised if you risked it again.''

Her scalp tightened at the idea, but she ignored it. ''That's not much of a choice. But maybe I'll take the one that's most likely to get you death by lethal injection.''

He gave her a narrow look. ''That what you're doing?''

She shook her head so quickly that the wind tore soft strands from her French twist. ''I'm only suggesting that you may have a problem.''

''The problem's yours, darling,'' he said with emphasis, ''though you do have a point. If it wasn't for leaving those marks you're talking about, I'd like nothing better than to give you exactly what you deserve.'' He continued for several more sentences with a graphic description of what that might be.

''You're a sick man,'' she said, looking away from him at the endlessly rolling breakers. Cars were passing in the distance on the San-Cap Highway, the main island artery. The sound came and went with the wind gusts, making it sound as if they were slowing near the driveway of the house before speeding up again. People were going about their safe, ordinary lives neither knowing nor caring what was happening here on the beach.

''But a rich one,'' he answered, ''or I'm going to be.''

''I give you less than six months,'' she said in contempt. ''Then you'll do something so stupid and arrogant that either the police or your own new business partners will take you out.'' It might not be the wisest thing in the world to goad him, but she felt reckless and defiant, and he could only kill her once.

"You wish." He laughed. "Truth is, I'm going to make a mint. Then I'll buy the fanciest beach house on Sanibel and rub my money in the faces of all the Ivy League idiots who smiled behind their hands and looked down on me because I wasn't born in a dollar-lined diaper."

She turned to search his face in the dim light. "That's what's behind this," she said in sudden recognition. "You really hate me."

"I didn't, not until you decided you couldn't lower yourself to my level. Then I despised you as an idle, whining, poor-little-me rich bitch."

"Breaking our engagement had nothing to do with your birth or how you made your living!"

"Oh, come on! I saw the way you looked at me, at how I dressed, my car, my apartment and my friends. You thought you were above me in taste and culture and stupid-ass breeding—as if that kind of thing matters a shit when push comes to shove. I was so far beneath you, you couldn't even bring yourself to crawl into my bed, much less fall in love with me."

She didn't want to feel sorry for him, and she wouldn't. She wouldn't. Standing toe-to-toe with him, she said, "You've got that backward, don't you think? Or maybe not, given your mentality. So you had me kidnapped to pay me back as much as to keep me from screwing up your deal, is that it? You thought I deserved to be hauled off by the two creeps you hired. You thought whatever they might do to me would be just fine. Before they killed me, of course."

He snorted, before a snide grin curled one corner of his mouth. "I paid them to haul your pretty little ass to Louisiana. When they got there, they were supposed to save it for me, since I was scheduled to check out the gaming boat site. Afterward, the alligators could have what was left.''

She'd cheated the death he'd planned for her in Louisiana. She'd escaped it, and found something else that she'd needed all her life. She'd found a place where money and social position were neither a source of conceit nor a goal worth killing for, and a man who stood for home and family and everything else that was right and good. She'd found love. She'd found Roan.

She'd found him, and she didn't want to die without ever telling him how she felt, without knowing if there was some hope that he might care about her, at least a little. She didn't intend to give up and let things happen to her without protest, as her mother had done. She would not be cheated out of life. She would not let all hope of love and joy go without fighting back.

Rage, blood-tinted and life-giving, surged up inside her from some internal reservoir she didn't know existed. She didn't think, never once considered the consequences. She just doubled her fist as she'd been taught in her self-defense class and hit Harrell in the nose with every ounce of her strength behind it.

He staggered back with a yell, then tripped in the wet sand and went sprawling. Tory didn't hesitate, and took off at a dead run.

Behind her, she heard him cursing. She snatched a backward glance in time to see him roll over and get to his feet. She expected any second to feel the impact of a bullet between her shoulder blades. She didn't care. The salt wind was in her face, plastering the silk of her suit against her. The surf hissed around her feet as a single wave reached farther up the wet sand. She had done this a thousand times, running every morning for years.

He was coming after her. She could hear his treads pounding on the sand.

He didn't want to shoot her, that was it. He was going to run her down. He still meant to drown her. Fine. Let him try. She'd been swimming in the gulf most of her life. He might find it harder than he thought.

But would it be hard enough?

Her mind was clear, moving at warp speed under the impact of adrenaline. Escape, she had to escape. She could hit the water, since it would make her a harder target. But she couldn't move as fast against its drag, and it was where he wanted her. She wouldn't do that, wouldn't make this easier for him. Run, she had to run.

Her breath was coming in gasps. She wasn't as strong as she had been. The days of forced inactivity had taken their toll. Her shoulder ached. Her heels caught in the sand. She could go faster if she kicked them off, but there was no time for that. She could hear Harrell's thudding footfalls closer behind her. He was gaining.

Run, run. She was running away. Running again, as always, in spite of everything.

Only this time she was going to get caught.

19

Harrell grabbed the back of her jacket, dragged her to a halt. Pain ripped through her shoulder as he slung her around. She jerked free for a second, staggering backward with her own momentum. His face was twisted, his eyes murderous as he lunged after her. She snatched her wrist from his grasping fingers and danced away with her eyes narrowed against the wind. A wave washed around her ankles so she almost tripped in waterlogged sand. He splashed after her, grabbed a handful of her blouse front, and snaked an arm around her waist. She gave a choked cry as she was dragged against him and lifted off her feet. He laughed, a raw sound of triumph as he began to wade deeper into the surf.

She couldn't breathe for the arm that clamped her to him. Agony throbbed in her chest and shoulder. Her shoes were sucked off her feet by the water. Roaring like a gunned engine sounded in her ears, one that that seemed to grow louder with every step Harrell took. She tried to kick, tried to bring her knee up between his thighs, but the waves rising around them absorbed and deflected her efforts. She scrabbled for purchase with her toes, but could find none. Desperately, she clawed at his back in an obscene parody of a passionate embrace. Her nails only found cloth. Darkness crowded into her brain. The roaring of wind and waves was so loud now that it drowned out thought and hope, leaving only terror.

Then she touched metal. Harrell's pistol that he'd shoved into his belt against his spine again, the better to grab her. She curled her fingers around the butt, jerked the pistol free. She rammed its snub-nosed barrel into his armpit.

He jolted to a halt. His curse had a strangled sound.

Then a huge wave hit them, as if some monster had plunged from the darkness to strike the water behind them. Harrell was knocked sprawling. Tory was torn away from his grasp. The pistol was plucked from her hand. Tossed like a rag doll, she rolled in the water. Waves thundered around her, over her, gurgled in her ears. Her lungs ached. Her throat and nose burned. She hit sand, scrubbed against the sea floor with her face. Shoving against it with her good arm and hand, she tried to find her feet, began to struggle upright.

Abruptly, she was caught again. Long arms wrapped around her like steel hawsers. Blind from stinging salt water and sand, she struck out in a wild punch.

Her arm was captured, held in a loose grip even as she was gathered close and was rocked side to side. The man who held her rested his cheek against the top of her head as he crooned above the sound of wind and waves and crying gulls.

"It's all right, Tory. Don't, don't. It's me, it's only me."

Roan.

He was here.

She didn't know how or why and didn't care. She flung herself against him, holding tight, absorbing his strength and the security of his arms for the space of a deep, half-strangled breath. Then panic surged inside her again. She wrenched backward as she said, "Harrell! He's—"

"He's over there."

Roan swung her gently to where she could see the beach. Harrell lay there on his belly like a beached shark, as if he'd been thrown down while Roan went to her aid. He was cursing in a vicious monotone, spitting sand and salt water with every word, while the surf washed back and forth around his legs. His hands were cuffed behind his back and a second pair of cuffs decorated his ankles.

"I don't think he's going to be a problem any longer," Roan said, his voice even.

Nor did she. Still, her attention didn't linger on her ex-fiancé. She stared past his prone figure toward the dark-purple bulk that sat up to its windows in the water.

"The Super Bird," she said in wonder and distress. "How did—"

"I was here at the house earlier, but you were out. Vandergraff answered the door when I returned just now. He said you'd gone again, had maybe driven down to some beach at the other end of the island where you liked to walk. That didn't quite add up to me since the Bird was still on the drive, parked facing the gulf. I walked over and climbed in to check it out. You'd left the keys in the ignition. I had my hand on them when I saw Melanka dragging you out in the water." Roan lifted a shoulder. "Running him down with the Bird seemed as good a way as any to get his attention."

The torn-up sand that stretched from the beach to the house told the tale plainly. Roan had driven the Bird, his pride and joy, straight into the corrosive salt water of the gulf. She'd heard the engine's roar without recognizing it.

"It got his attention all right," she said in tight acknowledgement as she recalled the great wave that had torn her away from Harrell. It had also saved her ex-fiancé's life, she thought. Another second, and she'd have pulled the trigger on the pistol. At least, she thought she would have, was almost sure of it.

"My stepfather was a part of...of everything," she said. "He was going to let Harrell..."

"I know." Roan's arm tightened a fraction as he cut across what she was saying. "Don't think about it. I spoke to the authorities here. Seems they've had their eye on Vandergraff for some time. This should do it for him. He and Melanka will be picked up as soon as I give them a call."

"Good," she said quietly. "Good." It was over, really over. She closed her eyes and leaned her head on Roan's shoulder. With her right hand, she held on to the strong wrist of his arm, which circled her waist. She could feel his pulse, steady and firm, beneath her fingers. He was so alive, so alive. And so was she.

"We'd better go in," he said, easing away, then urging her toward dry land. "I can make that call from the unit."

"Hey! Hey, what about me?" Harrell yelled from where he lay on the sand, twisting his head around to watch them over his shoulder.

The sheriff of Tunica Parish barely glanced in his direction. "You'll keep. The tide will turn before long."

Tory didn't want to go. She'd much rather have stayed where she was, away from the problems that must come, the explanations and the endless, endless questions. Or rather she longed to run away again, back to Dog Trot with Roan where things were simple and no one dared interfere with the man who was The Law in Turn-Coupe.

She couldn't do it. There were things that had to be done, and only she could do them.

"Yes," she said on a long sigh.

"Lean on me," he said.

She didn't need his support now, could have walked by herself. Still, she waded at his side, in the strong circle of his arm, as they left the boiling waves and went up the beach toward the big, faceless house among the trees.

Roan made his call. They had five minutes, perhaps ten, to wait until the police could arrive. The two of them stood in the tree shadows, watching the house. There was no movement, no sign that Paul Vandergraff was aware of the change in his circumstances.

Roan was restless. He paced, alert and impatient. It galled him, Tory thought, that he had no authority to go in and make the arrest that would end the fiasco once and for all. He wasn't used to standing back and allowing someone else to do a job he was more than capable of handling.

In an effort to distract him, she said from where she leaned against a casuarina tree, "I haven't thanked you for what you did just now, have I? I really am grateful that you came, more grateful than I can say."

"No need," he answered, though his gaze remained on the house. "You must have known I would."

"Not really. Oh, I know I left without telling you...."

"You escaped." The words were flat.

"Did I? I mean technically speaking, since no charges had been filed? You could have let me go, could have written me off. But even if you only came to get me, I'm still amazed."

"Is that what you think, that I came to take you back?"

"Unless it was to retrieve the Super Bird. It occurred to me that you might, just not so quickly. I'll have any damage repaired, I promise. They know all about saltwater problems down here."

He lifted a dismissive shoulder, as if he'd barely heard her. After a moment, he raked his fingers through his hair and turned to face her. "I'm sorry I didn't believe you when you first told me what happened to you, more sorry than I can say. If I had just listened..." He stopped, compressed his lips.

She couldn't read his face in the dim glow from a mercury vapor security light half-hidden among the tree branches. Since she had no clue to what he was thinking, what he was feeling, she could only do her best to be honest. Moistening her lips, she said, "I didn't exactly make it easy, I know. I wasn't used to...to trusting anyone. I'd run away before, a lot of times, when I was younger. No matter what I told the police, they always sent me back to my stepfather."

"So you thought I'd do the same."

"I was afraid you'd send word to him, and that he'd turn the responsibility for bringing me back to Sanibel over to Harrell. Since that could have been a death sentence, it wasn't a chance I wanted to take."

"Smart move," Roan said succinctly. "Even if it did get you shut up at Dog Trot."

"I didn't mind. After a while."

He was silent, staring at her through the darkness. When she thought he wasn't going to speak again, he asked, "What happened once you got here? Where did you take off to so fast that you were gone before I could catch up with you? And how did Melanka persuade Vandergraff that drowning you on his property was worth the risk?"

She told him, leaving out nothing of her visit with the lawyers or of her confrontation with Paul and Harrell later. It was a relief to be perfectly open with Roan about it all, to know that the secrets she'd kept for weeks no longer lay between them.

He whistled when she finished, a low sound of amazement followed by an admiring shake of his head. "You have nerve, lady. I'll hand you that."

"It would have been much smarter to wait and let my lawyers handle it," she answered in wry disagreement. "But I suppose I'd been holding everything in too long. It just all came out."

"I'd loved to have seen you stand up to them."

She grimaced. "It was no big deal. They just made me mad."

"Remind me never to do that." Humor laced the edges of his voice.

"You think I overreacted?" she inquired in quiet tones. In the distance, she could hear the sound of sirens. The police were coming, drawing nearer with every minute.

"Could be, I suppose," Roan drawled, tilting his head to one side. "I mean, why should you be so hacked off when all they wanted was to take your money and put you away?"

He was teasing her in his own dry fashion. It was her turn to look out to where Harrell still lay on the sand as she said, "It's over now."

"Is it? When you'll always carry the scars. Particularly the scar of my bullet?"

"You didn't know I was innocent when I tumbled out of that van." She didn't like the sound of self-blame she heard in his voice, though not long ago it might have been balm to her wounded ego. Her impulse now was to excuse it, to urge him to forget it.

"Doesn't matter. I just keep thinking—what if I'd killed you?"

"It didn't happen."

"It could have, nothing easier."

She took a step toward him, lifted her hand to put it on his arm. Whether she meant to absolve him or only to comfort him, she didn't know. She did neither, however, for he turned away at that moment, toward where the screaming police units were turning in at the drive. Headlights swept through the trees and pinned them where they stood. The flashing blue lights of a black and white illuminated the grim lines of Roan's face, caught the desolation in his eyes. Tory's heart hurt in her chest, but there was nothing she could do. It was time to step out where they could be seen.

The next few hours passed in a blur. Harrell was hauled up from the beach and taken away. Paul Vandergraff, confronted in his study where he'd taken refuge, shouted and protested and demanded a lawyer, but was finally hustled out of the house and into a police unit. The housekeeper, Maria, was questioned but had seen nothing, heard nothing, because of the action movie she'd been watching. Tory was allowed time to shower and change from her wet, salt-encrusted clothes, then was driven to the police station for a statement.

The recital of the events over the last few weeks was long and detailed and seemed to take an eternity. Roan was there, using both his comprehensive knowledge of the law and strong right arm to ensure that she received respectful treatment and room to breathe. Without pushing himself into the picture, he not only shielded her but advised and guided her on the finer points of her story. Early in the proceedings, he asked for the name of her lawyers and went away to call them. A team of three soon appeared, and protecting her interests became a collaboration between these legal representatives and Roan.

Finally, it was done. Roan drove her back to the house on the beach. He pulled onto the parking apron and cut the engine. Tory sat for a long moment, making no effort to get out. She was suddenly so tired, too tired to do anything except stare out through the trees at the beach and the endless waves that shimmered in the moonlight. In her mind's eye, she could see Harrell forcing her closer to the water, see the cold calculation in his face.

"Don't," Roan said, his voice rough as he turned in his seat to face her. "Don't think about it."

She closed her eyes and drew a deep breath, then let it out with a sigh. Leaning her head back against the seat's headrest, she said, "No. No, I won't."

"It's done. Now you can rest."

"It's hard to realize that someone really wants you dead," she said. She opened her eyes, faced him in the dark. "It must have happened to you before. How do you get past it? How do you get over something like that?"

"You let it go and get on with your life. You push it aside, into an unused corner of your mind, and shut the door on it. One morning, sooner or later, you wake up and you're all right. Or else, you think of what happened less and less often until the night comes when you lie in bed and realize it's been months since it crossed your mind, much less interfered with your sleep. It's nature's way. Nothing lasts forever, not doubt, not pain, not terror or grief. You just...live over it."

"And until then?"

"You do the best you can."

She looked away from him, back out over the water. "I don't know what I'm going to do. There's so much that will have to be taken care of, so many business decisions to be made about Paul's holdings and investments. I suspect there may be other irregularities he's been involved in that will come to light. Longtime business rivals, and even friends, may try to take advantage of this crisis within his company."

Roan didn't even hesitate. "You can handle it."

"I'm not sure I want to do that."

"There's no one else. Besides, it was all built, apparently, from your mother's estate. That makes it yours. No one else has the right to say what happens to it.''

That was undoubtedly true, but it wasn't what she had expected. What had she wanted from him? An offer to help her with the problems, to see her through the morass of legal and financial details that lay ahead of her? But to what end? He had no use for the pretentious life-style her stepfather had lived.

Roan belonged in Turn-Coupe where life was placid and good, and evil, when it existed, was of a plain and outright kind. He had a job to do there, duties to perform, people who depended on him. That came first. Of course it did.

She turned her head, staring at him in the moonlit dimness. His features were so firm and sure, his shoulders so straight even as he sat behind the wheel. More than any man she'd ever known, he was certain of who and what he was and made no excuses for it, no allowances for straying from it. He was what had once been known as a good man, upright, honest, scorning to be anything other than the way he was born and shaped by the family who had brought him up and the land where he lived.

He was everything she loved, and always would, even if he never heard her say it. She'd known it before, when she'd thought she was going to die. It was even stronger now, when she was sure she was going to live.

She spoke without thinking, without plan or any real purpose beyond the deep, instinctive need. ''Stay with me tonight.''

''If that's what you want.'' The words were even, with no hint of anything behind them other than the courteous agreement to a lady's request.

''I mean...''

''You need to know that somebody is around besides the housekeeper,'' he said in interruption. ''Don't worry, I won't misunderstand. I won't take advantage of the situation.''

It wasn't what she'd needed at all. To say so was impossible, however; his remote attitude made it clear that he had no desire to take advantage, even if the chance were offered.

''What about tomorrow?'' she asked. ''Do I need to go with you to Louisiana to take care of the paperwork on whatever might be pending there?''

''There's no reason for you to be inconvenienced any further. I'll take care of it.''

''Thank you,'' she said, the words toneless. So much for that excuse.

She had the sudden feeling that she was going to cry. She didn't want him to see it; the last thing she needed was his pity. Reaching for the car door, she stepped out. He climbed out as well, and walked around to shut the door and take her arm. The housekeeper must have seen them drive up and been waiting for them to come inside, for she opened the door and held it while they walked into the foyer.

''Thank you, Maria, that will be all. No, wait,'' she said, turning to Roan. ''Would you like something to eat, or maybe a drink? It's been a long evening.''

He shook his head. ''I'm fine. If you'll just point me to the spare bed.''

That was certainly putting it plainly. ''Yes. Fine. Maria will show you the way. I'll just…say good night, then.''

''Good night,'' he answered, his voice quiet and deep.

She turned from him, moving blindly toward her bedroom. When she had taken three or four steps, he called behind her.

''Tory?''

She turned back, her gaze not quite focused. ''Yes?''

He said no more while long seconds ticked past and Maria waited to escort him to the opposite wing of the house. Finally, he answered, "Nothing."

She forced a smile. "Sleep as late as you like in the morning. Maria will have breakfast for you whenever you're ready."

"Thank you," he replied, his voice gravely polite and nothing more.

She didn't answer, but walked away with her head held high.

It was a long time before she fell asleep. She only managed it, at last, because she made a decision. She did not intend to allow a stubborn backcountry sheriff to dictate what she would and would not do. With daylight, she intended to come to an understanding with Roan Benedict.

But when she'd dressed next morning and run lightly down the stairs, the breakfast room was empty. The guest room bed had not been slept in, and there was no Tunica Parish police unit sitting on the drive.

Roan was gone.

20

The evening was velvet soft. Roan stood with his shoulder against one of the thick white columns that supported the back gallery of Kane's place, The Haven. Cigar smoke wafted around him from the Cuban Cohiba Panatelas Kane had finally passed out in honor of his daughter's birth. This after-dinner visit was the first time they'd had a chance to get together in more than a month. Kane had been sticking close to his wife and baby, with little time to spare for male company. Not that Roan blamed him. Little Courtney Morgan Benedict was a beautiful mite, with the most amazing cap of fiery red curls anyone in Turn-Coupe had ever seen.

Behind him, the voices of Luke, Kane, Clay and Pop blended in a deep bass rumbling punctuated now and then by Jake's unreliable falsetto. They'd been talking about how the plan to have a gaming boat on Horseshoe Lake had fallen through and now had about as much chance of being revived as the old drive-in theater. When they segued into fishing tales, Roan stopped listening. He had other things on his mind.

"Hey, Roan, you heard anything from Tory?"

It was Clay who asked. Roan glanced over his shoulder

at his cousin with a frown between his brows before he answered, ''Not since I got back.''

''Well, hell, Roan. Have you called her?''

' He looked back at the lake glinting through the trees. ''I've been busy, catching up. And so has she.''

''Right.'' The word was dry. ''For a whole month. Or is it six weeks?''

''It's too damn long,'' Roan's dad complained. ''Lord, I miss that girl.''

Roan felt a squeezing around his heart, a sensation that had become so common since he got back from Florida that he was almost used to it. He missed her, too. Memories of Tory were everywhere he looked at Dog Trot. The house seemed darker, dustier and emptier since she'd gone. Beau sometimes howled at the time in the evening when Tory used to walk with him, putting his head back and letting his long wail of misery and longing echo from the woods around the house. Roan wished he could do the same.

''Saw her a couple of days ago,'' Pop said, his voice contemplative.

Roan swung around. ''You what? Where?''

''Saw her on CNN. They did a report about Vandergraff and Melanka and how they were mixed up in a money-laundering operation involving three states and a half-dozen islands and countries—allegedly, of course. They showed Tory leaving the courthouse after the arraignment of the creeps, and ran back over all the stuff about her kidnapping in connection with the case. The news folks tried to get a statement from her, but our Tory just walked through the whole kit and caboodle like they weren't there, head up and proud and every inch a princess.''

''I didn't see anything about it.'' Roan's voice was sharper than he'd intended.

''You ought to be retired, like me,'' his dad replied with

an expansive smile. "You'd get to watch all the soap operas and round-the-clock news. Anyway, it was a one-hour sensation, shoved off the air by some earthquake overseas."

It crossed Roan's mind to wonder if his dad was making the whole thing up just to see how he'd react. If so, he must be mighty pleased with himself.

A lot of people around town had made veiled remarks about Tory, as if they thought there must have been something lasting between the two them. They didn't understand the huge gulf between someone like her and a man like him. He hadn't understood entirely himself, until he'd seen Sanibel and the standard set by the houses there. For all the size of the Vandergraff place, it had been no more than a vacation cottage to Tory's stepfather. No telling what the places looked like where she spent the rest of her time.

He'd rather not think about it. It hurt less that way.

"I guess that means the hassle's still not over for Tory, huh?" Jake asked.

Roan shook his head. "The trial could go on for years, counting the appeals. But I expect she's cleared away a lot of the paperwork by now."

"Maybe she'll come see us."

"Don't get your hopes up," he told his son. "Her memories of this place probably aren't the happiest in her life."

"I bet she'd come if you asked her."

Roan made no reply.

"The boy's got a point," Pop said.

"So he does," Luke agreed.

Kane, watching him with a certain sympathy in his eyes, added, "Never know until you try."

"Forget it," Roan said. "It's not happening."

"Well, why the tarnation not?"

That was Pop, but he was talking to Roan's back. The

sheriff of Tunica Parish stepped off the gallery and walked toward where his patrol unit was parked.

For some things, there were just no answers.

The back porch light was off at Dog Trot when he pulled up in the drive. Jake must not have remembered to turn it on before he and Pop left. Beau didn't come to greet him, either. The dog had been moping around a lot lately. Roan had thought he was just missing the extra attention he'd gotten from Tory, but maybe he was coming down with distemper or heartworm or something. He'd better have Clay take a look at him.

The house was quiet and had a dank, closed-in smell, as if it needed a good airing after the long summer of being shut up tighter than a drum against the heat, or else the air-conditioning filter needed cleaning. He'd have to see to that, too, the first time he had the chance.

It was quite a while since Roan had been alone in the house; usually Pop and Jake were around when he found time to stay home. Of course, he'd been tied down with work these last few weeks. It was amazing how many people had things backed up that they'd wanted him to do while he was occupied with Tory. Sometimes he wondered if they weren't manufacturing errands and requests to keep him busy, as if the whole town were trying to help him forget.

He didn't want to forget. He wanted to remember every detail of how she looked, the way she smiled and the taste and feel of her in his arms. He sometimes thought he could still see her sitting at the kitchen table or on the upper gallery, or else playing with Beau out on the patio with the sunlight on her hair and the warmth of the summer in her eyes. Flashing images of her pain that he'd caused, of their arguments and strained silences, made him ache with re-

gret. How he wished that things had been different. Better
use could have been made of their time together.

Strange, but he hadn't realized, while she was there, just
how much Tory had taken over the house with her presence, or what a huge hole she would leave in his life when
she left. Caught between duty and the high voltage of the
sexual attraction between them, he hadn't noticed the natural and sweet way she had settled into his life.

He hadn't known how much he loved her.

Not that it would have done him any good if he had
realized. They were miles and worlds apart. She wasn't for
him. If he told himself that often enough, one day his stupid
heart would get the message and stop hurting.

Upstairs, light from the lamp on his bedside table cast a
soft glow into the hall. He stopped in the doorway for a
second while he went over his movements before he'd left
early that morning, the last time he was in the room. He
hadn't turned off the lamp that he remembered, but then he
didn't remember turning it on, either. He was losing it, or
else he needed to have a serious talk with Jake and Pop
about the electric bill.

One other possibility existed. Someone else had been
there. Or was hiding in the room.

Still, how likely was that? There was precious little
worth stealing at Dog Trot. Besides, any burglar with an
ounce of sense would know better than to try to rip off the
house of the one man in town who was not only armed at
all times, but sure to put the whole weight of his office
behind apprehending the guilty party. That didn't take his
enemies into account, of course—and he'd had a few lowlifes vow revenge. But how likely was it that they'd leave
the light on for him when they came to get him? Or that
Beau, who was lying in front of the bathroom door, thump-

ing his tail on the floor in sleepy welcome, would let them stick around?

Overactive imagination, that was his problem. Like the idea that he could still recall, still almost smell, the lingering scent of the perfume that had clung to the white silk jogging outfit Tory had been wearing the night he shot her.

Roan shook his head with a sigh as he moved on into the bedroom. He spoke a quiet greeting to Beau as removed his badge and stepped over to toss it onto the polished top of the dresser. His radio and the collection of equipment from his belt followed it, as did his wristwatch. He unbuttoned his short-sleeved shirt and pulled it from the waistband of his pants by rote, his thoughts light-years away from what hc was doing. Leaving his shirt hanging open, he levered his boots off, one after the other, and set them neatly beside the dresser, next to a nearby chair. Then he shrugged the shirt from his shoulders and tossed it in the general direction of the chair back before turning toward the bathroom.

"Keep going. I like what I've seen so far, but it's just getting intcresting."

"Tory." That single word sounded every bit as stunned as he felt, Roan was sure. He stared at her as she moved to lean in the bathroom doorway. She was wearing a T-shirt and jeans and her hair was pulled back in a long ponytail. In her hand was the pistol from his nightstand. He looked from its black bore to her clear, hazel gaze.

"What are you doing here?"

"I came to bring your Super Bird home, all shiny and running like new, since it appeared you weren't coming after it." she answered. "But as long as I was here, I decided you need to find out what it's like to be at someone else's mercy for a change. Come on, take off the rest. Strip for me."

"Or what? You're going to shoot me?"

"I just may. You can find out what that's like, too."

He gave a slow shake of his head. "What is this? What's it all about?"

"Call it vengeance. That's as good a reason as any."

"Because I kept you here as a prisoner?"

"And for that damned, stupid monitor. I hated that thing, and you knew it."

She was right, though he thought he'd explained his reasons perfectly well at the time. He shook his head again. "I just can't believe you're actually here."

"You were maybe expecting somebody else?" she inquired, her voice as cool as the look in her eyes.

"God, no. I just never thought..."

"Obviously. I'm the last person you ever thought, or wanted, to see again."

"I wouldn't say that." His voice was husky, but he didn't care.

She tilted her head. "Wouldn't you? After the way you ran out on me down on Sanibel? But you aren't going to leave this time, not until we get a few things straight."

"And that's why you want me naked."

She gave him back stare for stare. "Why else?"

Why indeed? It was amazing, how disappointed he felt. In the meantime, the pistol was leveled directly at his belly button. He'd like to think that she wouldn't use it. He'd also like to believe that he could disarm her if he wanted, but this wasn't the movies where the hero could walk up to the girl holding a gun and calmly take it out of her hand. Any idiot who tried that in real life could wind up severely disabled, if not downright dead.

On the other hand, he had no intention of walking out on what had all the earmarks of a promising scenario. If Tory wanted to see more of him, he was willing to oblige her. He put his hands on his belt buckle, manipulating it without taking his gaze from hers as he asked, "What needs straightening out? I thought we were even."

"Did you now?" Her smile was no more than a slight upturn at one corner of her mouth. "You almost kill me, and to make it right you save my life? Is that what you mean by even? I don't think so. I was kept shut up here for weeks with all sorts of possibilities and promises dangled in front of me. Then you found out who I was and suddenly the future vanished. And so did you. Why was that?"

"Everything was different," he said as he slid the belt from his pants, then reached for the waistband button. "You were different."

Her gaze flickered down to what he was doing, then away again. "How? I had a real name and past, but I was the same. It was you. You're the one who changed."

"Did I really? You lied to me and everyone else in Turn-Coupe. You hid behind that lie while you made fools of us. Then when the time came, you took off without a thought for what we might think or how we might feel."

"That's not true!"

"I think it is." He wrenched open the pants button, then jerked the zipper down but left his pants hanging, barely, on his hipbones. "You didn't want or need our help. You preferred the advice of your lawyers and accountants and all the other support people that make up your life. Fine. Understood. Just don't expect us to hang around waiting for you to notice we exist."

She stared at him a long moment. Then she said, "You used the word *we* but you mean *you*, don't you? You think I don't need you."

"I know you don't. I saw how you live."

"Did you? Did you see how lonely I was, or how lost?

Did you notice that there's not a single person in my life that I can love or who will love me back without complications and, most likely, applications of money to keep the relationship running smoothly?''

"So you'll meet a man who has as much money as you do, as well as the same friends, background and ideas. If you're lucky, maybe he'll even have a title."

"Do you think any of that matters to me?'' she cried. "What I want is a family. I want people around who relate to me because of who I am inside, not who my grandfather was or what I own! I want someone to belong to and who belongs to me. I want…''

She stopped abruptly, and Roan hated that. The feeling that he was about to hear something important was so strong that he asked softly, "You want what? Or should I say who?''

She lifted her chin. "As you said, I want you naked.''

"You've heard the old saying, 'Be careful what you wish for?''' He shucked his pants and briefs without taking his gaze from her eyes, without regard for the color that rose in her face.

"I'm tired of being careful,'' she said. "I've been careful all my life, and what did it get me? A fiancé interested only in my money, kidnapped, shot, held prisoner, slobbered over by a big dumb dog, tricked, cheated, half drowned, and then dumped in the hands of the Florida police—oh, and enough lawyers to row an ocean liner from here to China. I'm sick of it. And I'm through with it.''

"So,'' he said as he straightened and threw the pants on the end of the bed, then held his arms wide in an expansive gesture. "Now that you've got me naked, just what was it you wanted to get straight?''

She narrowed her eyes as she stared at him, keeping her

attention strictly above the belt line. "You're enjoying this, aren't you? You think it's funny."

"I think," he said carefully, "that I've been in worse spots."

"More dangerous ones, you mean." The words were tight with offense.

"Less enjoyable ones," he corrected.

She lifted her gaze toward the ceiling, then gave him a glare that was hot with accusation. "I knew it! You think I won't shoot. You aren't afraid of me at all."

"I'm terrified," he said softly as he moved toward her with slow care. "I'm terrified that you won't stay here with me after we stop talking."

"That's dumb. I don't intend to leave here ever again."

"I'm afraid that you won't get naked with me," he suggested with a smile in his voice.

"Dumber. I never intended anything else."

The next was more important. "Afraid that you'll never be happy in my backwater."

"I've had enough waves in my life, thank you very much."

"Afraid that you'll never love me enough to put up with a ready-made family that includes a hormone-crazed teenager, a know-it-all old man, and the whole nosy, interfering Benedict clan who will be forever, eternally, breathing down our necks."

"Truly stupid. I can't think of anything I'd like better than sharing your family. And I love you, too. If you must know."

"I'm beginning to get the idea."

She looked away from him with compressed lips, then flung the pistol onto the bed. "This thing wasn't loaded anyway."

"I know," he said apologetically.

"You did." The words were resigned.

"It's a revolver. I could see that the chambers were empty."

"It was a stupid thing to do, anyway, holding it on you."

"No, it wasn't. At least, not if what you wanted was to get my attention." He was close enough to reach out, to touch her lovely, sweet face, to make her look at him again. "You certainly did that."

"I was mad, too," she muttered, shielding her gaze with her lashes.

"I know, and I'm sorry for whatever I did that was so wrong."

She looked at him then. "You don't know? You really don't have any idea?"

It was his turn to scowl. "I thought you just gave me a pretty full list, beginning with shooting you and ending with running out on you after Melanka was arrested."

"You also," she said distinctly, "failed to sleep with me in Florida, you gallantly refused to take me back here with you to stand trial for my crimes, *and* you didn't kiss me goodbye."

"So much to make up for," he said with a remorseful shake of his head as he drew her close against his heart and rocked her gently back and forth. "I don't know where I'm going to start."

"I do." The words were muffled against the column of his neck, and ended with a small, butterfly kiss that thrilled him to his bare toes.

"Where?"

"By telling me, finally, just what you wanted with me when you brought me to Dog Trot."

"What?"

"You said you would, when I was well enough to hear it."

He groaned, holding her closer and brushing his lips against her hair. "Me and my big mouth. It was this, only this. Always this."

Her arms tightened. "You could also tell me that you love me."

"More than life itself, though I have to say, before we go any further, that I'm really not sorry for making you wear that monitor."

"I know," she answered.

He leaned back a little so he could look into her face. "You do?"

"You like to keep up with the people you love. You need to know where to find them every second so you can reach them instantly if they are in trouble."

"You do," he said, and breathed a sigh of relief.

"But I'm still not going to wear the thing after we're married. Unless…"

"What?" he asked, his voice not quite steady for the gladness rising inside him.

"Unless you wear one, too." She raised on tiptoe to press a quick kiss to his chin.

"Not a chance!"

"You're sure?" She kissed the corner of his mouth.

"Positive."

"How positive?" she murmured just before she settled the tantalizing sweetness of her lips over his.

He'd think about it. Later.

Author Note

Heroes come in many varieties, and I readily admit to being a sucker for them all. I like the strong, silent type, the dashing, piratical blade who skates close to the moral edge, the devil-may-care gentleman who operates with style and wit, and many others. A real favorite, however, is the knight-errant, the authority figure with rigid principles and a deep need to be useful to those around him, particularly to women. In *Roan,* I wanted to put this knight-errant in a situation where he is responsible for harming the very person he should have saved, then see what he would do. This was the springboard for the story. How well I succeeded with it I don't know; the writer is often the person least qualified to say whether a story works. At least you know where I was headed when I began the book.

The stories about Turn-Coupe, Louisiana, were planned originally as a trilogy. However, my fascination with my fictional place and its people continues to generate book ideas. The series has been well received also, with Book 2, *Luke,* appearing on the *New York Times* Extended, *USA Today* Top 100 and Waldenbooks bestseller lists. The Turn-Coupe trilogy will continue then, becoming the Louisiana Gentlemen series. The story of nature photographer and devastatingly handsome "wild thing" Clay Benedict will be next. I'm excited about this turn of events, and look forward to exploring the lives of more of my gentlemen heroes for your entertainment.

Since it's become my practice to include Louisiana recipes in these books, the offerings for *Roan* are below. The first is the gumbo mentioned by Kane, one that Regina and April were thinking of making to take to Roan's house before they were discouraged from the gesture. The other is the dessert that Tory prepared for Pop's homecoming, Blackberry Cobbler. I hope you enjoy them both.

Chicken and Sausage Gumbo

6 chicken breast halves
2 bouillon cubes, chicken flavored
1 pound smoked sausage
²/₃ cup plain flour
³/₄ cup cooking oil seasoned with 2 tbsp bacon drippings
2 large onions, chopped
3 cloves garlic, minced
1 bunch shallots, chopped
2 stalks celery, chopped
1 bell pepper, chopped
¹/₂ cup fresh parsley, minced
2 bay leaves
¹/₄ tsp thyme
salt and pepper to taste
Red pepper to taste

Cover chicken with water and simmer with ¹/₂ onion, chopped, 1 garlic clove and bouillon cubes until tender. Reserve the liquid. Remove bones, etc., and cut meat into bite-size pieces. Set aside. Cut sausage into bite-size pieces and set aside.

Make a roux by browning flour in oil over medium heat, stirring often with flat-edged spatula. When the roux has browned to the shade of well-tanned English leather, immediately add the remaining onion and garlic, other vegetables and parsley to the hot mixture. Sauté over medium heat, stirring constantly, until onions and shallots are wilted. (The mixture will be extremely thick; take care not to burn it.) When vegetables are done, add hot, reserved chicken stock and stir well, breaking up any lumps with the back of the spatula. Adjust liquid by adding water until you have 3 to 4 quarts of gumbo, total, of a souplike consistency. Add chicken meat and sausage. Adjust salt and pepper to taste. Add bay leaves, thyme and red pepper. Simmer 1 to 2 hours to blend flavors. Remove bay leaves. Serve over rice. Serves 8-10. Freezes well.

Blackberry Cobbler

4 cups blackberries
1 cup sugar
1 cup flour
1/8 tsp salt
1 tsp baking powder
2 tbsp butter
1/4 cup milk
1/4 tsp cinnamon

Place blackberries in a casserole dish and sprinkle with sugar, reserving 2 tablespoons. Sift dry ingredients. Cut butter into the flour mixture until coarsely mixed. Add milk, and stir until just mixed. Turn out onto a floured surface. Knead dough lightly, then roll out to 1/4-inch thickness. Cut into strips. Crisscross the strips of dough over the sugared berries. Add cinnamon to remaining 2 tablespoons of sugar. Sprinkle over the dough strips. Bake at 425° F for 30 minutes.

Bon appétit!

Warmest regards,

www.jenniferblake.com